# Galena, IL

N
W
E
S

Turner Hall
Bench St.
Main St.
Commerce St.
305 North
Galena River
DeSoto House
Grant Park
Depot Park
Belevedere Mansion

Bike Trail
Stairs and Footbridge
Road

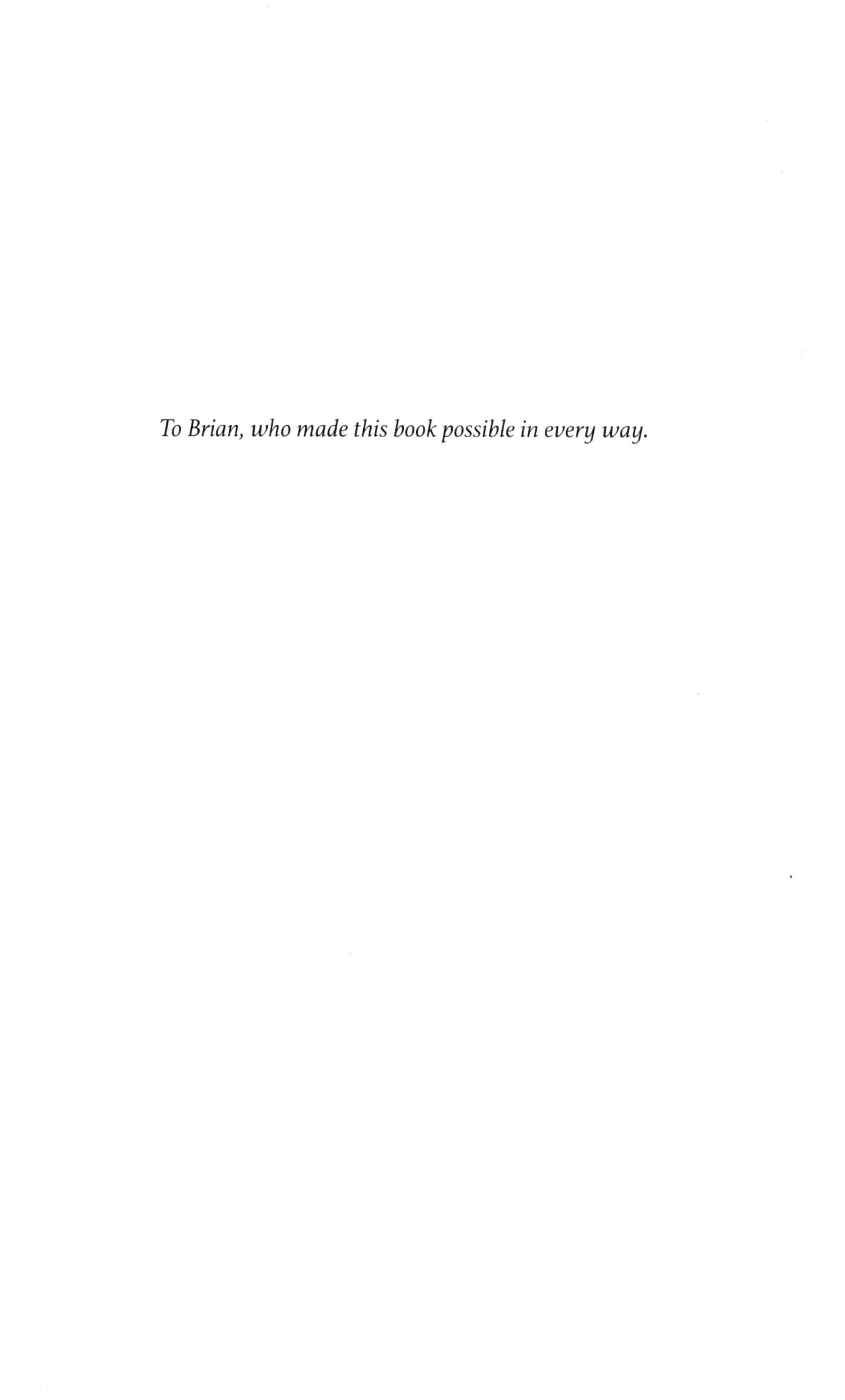

*To Brian, who made this book possible in every way.*

# OLD WORLD WAR

---

MELISSA F. OLSON

Old World War

Melissa F. Olson


MelissaFOlson.com
Cover by Clarissa Yeo.

## ALSO BY MELISSA F. OLSON

The Old World Series

Dead Spots

Trail of Dead

Hunter's Trail

Boundary Crossed

Boundary Lines

Boundary Born

Midnight Curse

Blood Gamble

Shadow Hunt

Bloodsick

Boundary Broken

Boundary Haunted

Companion Pieces: Tales From the Old World and Beyond

Born Magic: the Diary of Scarlett Bernard

Spell Bond: More Tales From the Old World

The Nightshades Trilogy

Nightshades

Switchback

Outbreak

The Big Keep

# PART I

# 1

## SCARLETT

Los Angeles, CA

On a Tuesday morning near the end of July, I huffed along my second-to-last mile of the Ballona Creek trail with a bargest loping happily at my side. The bikers and other runners, most of whom were passing us at a speed that felt personally insulting, often did a double-take when they saw Shadow, but most of them were moving too fast to really get a proper look.

For the last four months, the two of us had been running some portion of the Ballona Creek Bike Path nearly every day. Once upon a time, Ballona Creek was supposedly a vast length of connected lagoons and salt marshes, but after a shitload of LA development it had degenerated into yet another mostly empty, concrete-lined channel without much reason to exist. (Insert joke about shallow LA residents here.) Eventually, the local conservation authority stepped in to "revitalize" the creek bed. Now there was a path running along the edge of the concrete channel, going from Marina del Rey all the way to Culver City, and to other trails beyond that.

I was hoping to run all thirteen miles of the larger interconnected trail at some point, but for now, I contented myself with sucking at Ballona Creek. Every morning, Shadow and I went in the Fiji Way gate and ran northeast on the trail for three miles to Slauson Avenue, where we stopped for water and turned around. After months of this, I could run most of the way back, but I had to start walking a mile from home.

I tried to run early now that we were deep into summer, but I'd had a work call last night, and Shadow and I hadn't gotten going this morning until ten, when it was already eighty-seven degrees outside. I worried about her running in the July heat, but if the gigantic black dog-monster was bothered by the temperature, she wasn't letting on. Shadow was the picture of graceful athleticism—in other words, the complete opposite of me. I was a wheezing, red-faced mess in the morning heat, dripping with so much sweat that I had to reach up and right my sunglasses about every five steps.

I longed to stop and sit for awhile, but on my left was a hot metal fence and a drop down to the disgusting creek, and on my right was another concrete embankment going *up,* to Culver Drive. It was like running along the interior bowl of a volcano. So I forced myself to barrel along, trying not to think about how badly I wanted to be doing anything else. I would never bother with running if I hadn't accidentally created a career path where my life often depends on my ability to escape very quickly.

Jesse, on the other hand, claimed he *loves* running—he and Cliff took Annie in the jogging stroller most afternoons, with a somehow-still-energized Shadow—but to me, it's a boring, jarring grind that feels both pointless and impossible. Jesse and Cliff always ran south toward the beach, steering clear of the

Ballona trail. He said it has too many bikes, but I suspected his avoidance has more to do with the Ballona Creek trail looking so much like the wide concrete channel of the LA River, where we fought the Wild Hunt two years ago.

Jesse didn't like to talk about that night, or the ley lines underneath the river, or how close we came to losing everything. But that was exactly *why* I chose this path every day. It was a reminder of why I had to be there.

As I slogged my way toward the overpass at Centinela Avenue, where there would at least be some shade, Shadow did one of her over-the-shoulder checks on me. Her tongue hung sideways out of her mouth in a happy grin, and she occasionally glanced over her shoulder at me with a certain look of benign tolerance, as if to say, *See how nice and slow I'm going for you?*

I would have said something sarcastic in response, but I didn't have the breath. Instead I gave her a pointed little wave, which caused the ring on my left finger to glint in the sun and practically blind me through the sunglasses.

I made a noise that came out like, "Yuarg!" and Shadow smugly turned to face the front again.

The engagement ring. It had been months since Jesse's proposal, but the ring still surprised me when I caught sight of it. The romantic bastard had tracked down a ring that was, before it came into my radius, thoroughly cursed. I made fun of him for his obsession with the symbolism—something about me taking bad things and making them safe again, blah blah blah—but I loved it: the ring, the proposal, the whole thing. Just...not enough to set a date yet.

Molly said I was stalling my own happiness for ridiculous Scarletty reasons, but I chose to ignore her. The truth was, I wasn't sure why I was reluctant to wedding plan. I loved Jesse, I wanted to marry him, but something in me couldn't go there. Not yet.

When I was about ten steps away from the nice shady area, my phone buzzed in the zippered pocket of my running shorts. No one called me in the mornings, which made it a perfect excuse to slow down to a walk. Shadow felt the movements in her long canvas leash and slowed too, tossing me an annoyed glare over her shoulder.

"Not...my fault," I panted, tugging the phone out of the pocket of my leggings and lifting it out to show her the screen. It was a FaceTime call from Corry. "See? Real call."

The bargest made a little snorting sound, but I ignored her and hit the answer button. "Hey..." I took off my sunglasses and squinted at the screen. The sun was painfully bright, turning the phone into one massive glare. I kept moving toward the shade of the overpass. "What's...up?"

My attention was pulled for a few seconds by the runner zooming by me on the left, and I missed Corry's response. "What?" I said, hitting a button on the side of my phone to turn up the volume.

There was a garble of something breathy, and Shadow's huge muzzle swung around, her ears perking up with attention.

"Corry?" I slowed down even more, trying to catch my breath. Even with the phone a few inches from my face, I could only make out the outline of her face and hair. "You okay?"

"*No.*"

It came through as a broken cry, but I forced my face to stay even and calm. Corry struggled with anxiety, and sometimes she just needed to cry and vent.

I finally reached the shade, blinking rapidly while my vision adjusted. "Where are you? What happened?"

"S-Scarlett...I don't..." Her voice was ragged, like she was struggling to catch her breath. I could finally see her face, and it was blotchy and swollen from crying. Her image was also moving jerkily as though she were running, so it took me a second to register the smears of red on one of her cheeks. I knew fresh blood when I saw it.

"Corry, hang on one second." I looked around me for witnesses out of habit, but not many people used this trail at eleven am on a hot weekday. Just to be safe, I ducked under the fence on my left, stepping off the path onto the downward slope of concrete. I leaned against the fence to brace myself so I wouldn't tumble and fall into the gross-looking water. When I dropped the leash, Shadow did that ducking doggie-limbo thing to follow me under the fence without being asked.

I raised the phone again, but before I could speak, the high-pitched whine of police sirens exploded nearby. I looked around me wildly for a moment before I realized they were coming from Corry's side of the call. "What happened?" I shouted over the noise.

Corry was still moving, but she raised her voice, too. "Louisa is dead!"

My stomach did a little flip over itself. Louisa was a vampire, one of the four young women Corry was looking after at Berkeley. Corry must have taken her out in the daylight for something. "They shot her!" Corry shouted in a broken sob. "I think they were aiming at me!"

My insides went cold. "Take deep breaths for me, honey," I said, with all the firmness I could pull together. "Are you hurt?"

"No..."

"Okay. Listen to me. I'm hanging up, and I want you to call me back after you get somewhere safe and quiet."

"I don't know where," she wailed. Tears streaked down her face, smudging the smear of fresh blood. She wasn't looking at the phone, her head whipping around wildly instead.

"*Yes you do*. Are you on campus?"

"Yeah."

When I was dating Eli, he'd once spent a whole weekend reinforcing the doors and windows of Corry's apartment at Berkeley. I'd spent that time scouting the security on the route to and from her classes. "You need people and cameras and a quiet corner to talk. A library or cafeteria."

"I can't," she mumbled, the picture swaying around with her distraction. She was in shock, or very near it.

"Corry!" I turned it into a bark, and her face jerked down to look at me. "Do it *right fucking now*."

"Okay!"

I hung up the phone. I needed to call Jesse, of course, but I decided to give Corry a couple of minutes to call back first. I found myself looking around in a daze of my own, one hand still steadying myself with the metal fence. There were no runners on the path, though I could hear the traffic whizzing by on Centinela just over my head. The sluggish creek water reminded me again of the river, the attack from the Luparii.

No. I wasn't going to think about that now.

Doubling over, I slipped back through the bars of the fence, and Shadow ducked her massive bulk under the bottom rung to join me. She watched intently as it took me several tries to pick up the end of the leash. My hands were trembling.

"Someone shot at Corry in broad daylight," I mumbled to her, even though the bargest would have heard the call much better than I could. I didn't know what to do. Jump in the car and head for Berkeley? Should I try to fly? Dashiell was going to be furious about the shooting, and he had a private plane he'd probably let me use. But it was half a day until sundown. Should I wake him up? That was a DEFCON 1 move, and the only other time I'd done that, it had *not* turned out well. I considered a threat to Corry's life to be more than serious enough to wake Dashiell–but would he agree?

"Who would shoot at Corry?" I wondered aloud. She was a null, like me, and that would always have value...but she wasn't a particularly strong one. And she wasn't a player in Old World politics. More importantly, she was under the protection of both the cardinal vampire of San Francisco *and* Dashiell. Hurting her would mean taking a hell of a risk. Why do that for someone with so little power?

I didn't want to be all "everything's about me," but hurting Corry would be a great way to stab me right through the fucking heart. Could someone have shot at her to hurt me?

"But things have been quiet," I mumbled to myself. I was cleaning up the same old messes I always did, of course, but it wasn't like when we'd faced enemies in LA in the past. The only thing going on was Dashiell and Maven setting up their new government body, but I wasn't involved in that, not really. I just got the updates at our monthly meetings. And even if someone was pissed at Dashiell for trying to govern, I couldn't see how killing Corry could be part of their revenge.

A strange new thought popped into my head. Could it have been...random? A mistake, or a human shooter? That would be a hell of a coincidence, but maybe it was possible?

Shadow tugged at the leash. "I agree, we can't wait any longer," I said to her. Corry might not have reached a safe place yet—it took a few minutes to walk anywhere on campus—but at least I could be on my way to do something.

Starting with talking to Jesse, who would know a hell of a lot more than I did about human crimes. I would call him to come pick me up. Just ahead on my right, there was a trail switchback to the bike path exit on Centinela, which opened into a short dead-end road, Milton Street. I could have Jesse bring the car and pick us up there so we'd get home faster.

"Right." I felt better for having a plan. I lingered in the shady area just long enough to hit Jesse's number on my phone, then strode forward into the sun while it rang. I headed for the switchback with Shadow pulling me forward like a sled dog.

I never called during a run, and Jesse answered on the second ring. "Scar, are you okay?"

"It's Corry; something's hap—" But the phone was flying out of my hand as something dark plowed me to the ground. In the heat and shock of it I almost missed the familiar *crack* of a rifle right above us.

# 2

## SCARLETT

It wasn't a bullet that knocked me down. It was a bargest.

Shadow must have seen something—the metal glint of the rifle, maybe, or the car window going down. Whatever it was, she had reared up and half-spun in the air, putting her paws against my chest so the sniper's bullet hit her back instead of my chest. I caught the fastest, blink-and-you'll-miss-it image: an SUV up on Milton Street, metal barrel in the open window. Then Shadow's push knocked me completely flat on my back, and my skull cracked against on the concrete path. My phone skittered down the embankment toward the water, miles out of reach.

Shadow herself landed ungracefully on my chest, whooshing the air from my lungs. We fell so awkwardly that her heavy jaw struck my nose, which seemed to explode water balloon.

Shadow's unmoving form pinned my legs down, and there was a terrible, endless moment where I automatically tried to scream, despite the air knocked out of me. My mouth was full of warm, coppery blood.

I turned my upper body sideways to spit out the blood... which meant that the sniper's second bullet missed me by about ten inches, driving into the concrete instead of the back of my head.

Suddenly my head was clear. Ignoring the pulse of blood from my nose and my ringing head, I wriggled my legs free and grabbed Shadow's front paws, getting my legs under me so I could heave us both backward toward the shade from the overpass. She let out a terrifying whimper of pain when I moved her, but I paid no attention, throwing my weight back again, and then a third time, until we were safely under the overpass.

Putting my back against the embankment, I crouched with one hand on Shadow's chest, feeling it move as I tried to think defensively. My eyes jumped around, scanning the path. This was a perfect ambush spot. I couldn't get up the switchback without full exposure, but there was nothing to prevent the shooter from running in the Centinela gate and dropping onto the pavement in front of us. I wasn't sure why they weren't already here.

I moved my hand away from Shadow and reached for my right ankle. Even when things had been quiet in my job, I always ran with two throwing knives tucked into a compression stocking, one of them tipped with silver. I got one in my hand now, pushing out my radius to see what I was up against.

I strained myself, concentrating, but I felt...nothing. Whoever was after me had to be human. A human sniper, probably with at least one lookout.

That meant only one thing: skinners. Humans who hunted the supernatural for sport or money. Not so long ago in Las Vegas, skinners had killed my friend, Annie's biological father, Jameson, and had nearly killed me.

Until that second, I hadn't been afraid, not really—there was too much adrenaline, too much shock. But now I felt fear wrap itself around my spine and squeeze. In the years since I'd met her, I had never wished so strongly or desperately for Allison Luther. Shadow was a hunter, and I was more of a walking party trick, but Lex was a strategic thinker. "What would she do?" I mumbled out loud.

I couldn't see my phone; it must have slid all the way down to the water, or so close it wouldn't matter. Jesse would be on his way, but I had no idea how long it would take him, or even how long it had been since I dropped the phone.

This wasn't helpful. *Breathe, Scarlett, you idiot, and think.* Okay, the shooters had picked a perfect ambush spot, which meant they'd done their research. They'd tried to avoid a face-to-face confrontation, probably because Shadow was deadly as hell. I may not have had supernatural powers, but I could still hit a moving tennis ball with a throwing knife at fifteen paces.

For the first time, I looked properly at Shadow. She was sprawled out on her side, breathing in short shallow pants, her eyes unfocused and staring. I swallowed hard. The Luparii spell had made bargest skin permanently bulletproof, but we hadn't exactly tested it since I'd altered the spell during the Wild Hunt battle—and certainly never with a high-powered rifle.

I crouched over her so I could get a closer look. All the blood on the ground seemed to have come from my nose and a few scrapes on my hands, so she wasn't shot. Reaching over her, I felt along the pebbled, hairless skin of her back until my fingers ran over something *wrong*—a kind of dent in the bones of her back, caving inward. My breath caught, and Shadow whimpered at the touch, a sound that twisted my heart.

There were questions here, about the bargests' skeletons and bone density and magic, but I shoved them aside for later. "Shadow, can you get up?" I asked. "I think we need to move."

She gave me a dubious look, her meaning as clear as day. *Where?*

Fair question. If the skinners hadn't come down the path yet, they probably wouldn't try now that we'd had a moment to collect ourselves. Which meant they were probably moving in another direction, like farther down Milton Street to get a better angle under the overpass. We couldn't stay here.

I started to move, then froze. What if they didn't go down Milton—what if they went to the top of the overpass itself and each took a position on Centinela? There had to be at least two skinners—I'd seen the rifle barrel in the passenger window, so there was likely a driver. If Shadow and I ran out either side of the path under the overpass, we would be the world's easiest targets to someone overhead.

In other words, we couldn't stay put and wait for Jesse, but we couldn't leave the overpass either. Great. I looked around for a second, my eyes landing on the massive concrete wall at the bottom of the channel, before the creek. It was sturdy enough to hold up a busy city street, which meant it could stop an awful lot of bullets. "We'll hide behind the bridge support until Jesse gets here," I told Shadow quietly.

The support was parallel to the path and as wide as the overpass it supported...which meant we were going to have to get under the fence, scrabble down the concrete decline, and duck out from under cover for a second to get around it. If we could move fast enough, they wouldn't be ready for it.

I stood up. "Come on, Shadow, we're doing something dumb," I said, trying to lift her onto her feet.

Shadow's eyes rolled up at me, and her clubbed tail thumped once on the ground in frustration. "No. I won't leave you here," I said firmly. "Come on." Shadow struggled for a second, trying to roll to her feet, but then she fell back onto her side, panting, eyes on me.

Seconds were ticking by, the pain in my head all but screaming at me. I made myself say the only thing that might move her. "Shadow, I'm staying with you—so if you don't get up I'm going to die."

It worked. She began struggling upright, and I went around to her back, sliding my fingers carefully under her pelt to heave her to her feet. It took longer than expected—something in her spine had definitely been affected—and the whole time I felt exposed. How long had it been since the second gunshot? Two minutes? Less? What were they doing?

Once Shadow was on her feet, I snaked my hands under her belly to help support her weight. Then I sort of duck-walked us toward the fence, where she had to lower her bulk down again to squeeze under, a process that had her whimpering in pain and me cursing myself for the plan. What if the shooter was long gone, and I was doing permanent damage to her spine by making Shadow go through this?

But I didn't stop. Clumsily, I wormed my body through the middle bars of the fence and landed on the other side so I could help Shadow duck under the lowest bar. We were on the other side and half-sliding down to the support beam when the second attack began.

It wasn't a gunshot this time—it was two large metal boxes, dropped off either side of the overpass. I caught the movement of one out of the corner of my eye and spun to see the other one drop with a thud. Each box was about the size of a filing cabinet drawer, and when they hit the ground the boxes' insides sort of popped out of their casings. They were filled with what looked like a hundred round metal softballs clustered together, emitting a high-pitched ringing.

Inside me there was some sort of chemical reaction between my half-assed survival instincts and every movie I've seen in the last twenty years. Without really understanding what I was doing, I dove down lengthwise next to Shadow, wrapped one arm around her, and pulled hard, log-rolling us down the short embankment, at the very edge of the concrete support. I couldn't turn and get us around it in time, so I made an instant decision and kept throwing our collective weight farther down, rolling us toward the water.

Just before we hit the surface, I caught a glimpse of the first orange and green bursts of explosion, and then everything went black.

# 3

## LEX

Boulder, Colorado
An hour earlier

When my cell phone started ringing on the bedroom floor, I was in the middle of another dream about Atlanta.

It had been four months since I'd returned, but there were moments from that trip that had earned regular places in my nightmare lineup. Especially those last moments with Becca, when I struggled to roll or crawl over to her.

I often woke up thrashing.

It was disorienting to wake up partway through that particular dream, and it took me a second to recognize my own ringtone. I lifted my head to squint at the alarm clock on the dresser. 10:30 am. Shit. No one I knew called before early afternoon, even my (very human) family, who believed I worked second-shift security for a powerful businesswoman.

If my phone rang before noon, I generally assumed

someone was bleeding or on fire. Unfortunately, I've often been right.

The ringtone stopped, then started up again. Ignoring Pongo's attempts to lick my arm, I leaned out of bed and felt around on the floor until I found yesterday's jeans. When I pulled the cell phone out of the pocket, Sashi Brighton's picture was on the screen, and suddenly I felt alert. Sashi was a good friend and a powerful healing witch, not to mention a member of my tiny, ragtag witch clan. If she was calling at 10:30 on a Tuesday, it was important.

I hit the talk button. "Hey, Sashi."

"Sorry to wake you," she said hurriedly, "but Will and I need to talk to you right away. We're out front."

"In front of my house?" I said stupidly.

To her credit, she didn't say, "duh, Lex." "I know the dogs go mental when the doorbell rings, so I thought I'd call. Can we come in?"

"I'll put them outside and be right there." I hung up the phone and swung my legs onto the floor, disrupting Chip and Cody, who gave me reproachful faces just before their tails started wagging. Labs don't hold a grudge.

"Come on, fellas," I said, patting my leg. "Outside."

Dopey, who'd been sleeping under the bed with the cats, wriggled out to follow us, and I led the whole parade of canines through the house to the back door to let them into the fenced-in backyard.

It was a warm summer morning, but as I padded back toward the front door I stopped to grab a lightweight robe from my bedroom, pulling it on over my knee-length sleep shirt. The shirt, a gift from my six-year-old niece, had a drawing of cartoon wolves, their muzzles pointed skyward. The caption read, "Howl of a Night." If it had just been Sashi I wouldn't care what I was wearing, but I didn't know her new husband well—

certainly not well enough for him to see me in cartoon pajamas.

I also grabbed my birth mother's bloodstone necklace from the table next to the bedroom window, where it had been "charging" in the moonlight. I looped the cord over my head and tucked the stone under the pajama shirt. Just in case.

At the front door, I'd barely twisted the knob before Sashi rushed into the house, dragging Will behind her. "Whoa. Hi." I closed the door.

"Sorry, sorry." Sashi was in casual clothes, for her—expensive cropped jeans and a blousy silk T-shirt—but she looked disheveled and panicked. Will, on the other hand, was giving me a slightly apologetic face. "Kitchen?" Sashi asked. "I didn't think to bring coffee, but I can make some."

I waved them on. "Sure. You know where everything is." Sashi had been over for a lot of cups of coffee with Katia and me. It was how we conducted our "clan meetings."

She was already moving past me, which was a surprise. My friends Simon and Lily routinely raided my snack cupboard and put their feet on my furniture, but Sashi and I didn't have the same level of familiarity. She would probably say she was too British.

In the kitchen, Sashi began bustling around, slamming cupboard doors and sloshing water around the coffee pot. "Sorry, I'm a bit frantic," she said over her shoulder.

That was obvious, and worrying, since the Old World didn't usually have emergencies at ten-thirty on a weekday. At the same time, though, neither of them seemed hurt, so I sat down on a kitchen stool, pointing Will toward the other one. While Sashi's back was turned, I raised my eyebrows at him. He gave a little shrug, as if to say, *better ask her*.

"Can one of you tell me what's going on?" I looked back and

forth between them. “Sash, forget the coffee for a minute. Come sit down.”

My friend didn’t turn around to look at me. Instead, she went still, leaning her hands against the counter like it might be the only thing supporting her. I started to stand up, but Will raised a hand and gave me a tiny head shake.

“Sashi?” I asked. In my belly I felt the first stirrings of real fear. “What happened?”

“We don’t know that *anything* has happened.” This was Will, but he was clearly talking to Sashi’s back, trying to reassure his wife. “It could be nothing.”

Now Sashi whirled around. “It’s not nothing, and you *bloody* well know it,” she spat at him. She turned to me. “Will is missing time. About six hours, we think, from three days ago when I was at work. And it started twenty minutes after sunset.”

I’d spent enough years living with a vampire to know what she meant. “You think he’s been pressed?” Per capita, Boulder has a much larger than average vampire population, thanks to the presence of my boss, Maven, the cardinal vampire of all of Colorado. And when those vampires feed on humans, they press their victims’ minds to forget the transaction entirely.

“I’m sure he has.” She launched into a longer explanation of how they’d figured it out—something about comparing text times after realizing he didn’t remember a conversation.

I held up my hand to stop her. “Sash, I believe you. But Will is human.” I glanced over to include him. No one likes to be talked about like they’re not there. “And you work nights, in a human bar. It sounds like maybe one of the local vampires fed on—”

“Lex, wait.” Sashi pushed out a breath. “This is more than a coincidence. It’s about who he is. Or rather, who he used to be.”

Will took her hand, and the two of them looked at each

other intently for a moment, having one of those unspoken couples debates. *Do you want to tell her, or should I?*

I didn't feel awake enough to get in the middle of it, so I stood up and went around the counter to start the coffee. It gave me a chance to think, too.

It didn't surprise me that Will had a secret, of course—both of them had always been cagey about where Will had been for the last twenty years. I always figured Sashi would tell me if she thought I needed to know, but that didn't stop me from wondering. I was sure he'd never been in the military, and I was skeptical about prison time—the guy practically exuded good citizenship out of his pores. My best guess was either witness protection or some type of government work.

What hadn't occurred to me, though, was that the secret might involve the Old World in some way. Now I had to wonder just how much Will might be keeping from me.

When the coffee was ready, I set a mug in front of each of them and returned to my stool. Sashi had to unclench her hands from the counter to pick up her coffee. She gave Will a tiny nod, as if to say, *go ahead, you do it*. He twisted his stool to face me properly.

"I appreciate how respectful you've been of my privacy," he began. "You've never tried to pry into my history, which means I haven't had to lie to you. I'm really grateful for that."

I blinked. "Um…no problem."

"The reason Sashi and I have never explained my past has nothing to do with her trust in you. It's because, despite how much it's affected my life, it's not my secret to tell. It's Scarlett's."

"Scarlett Bernard? The null in LA?" I glanced at Sashi, who wasn't meeting my eyes.

Scarlett Bernard had made the worst possible first impression on me, years earlier, but since then we'd helped each other out a few times. Now her boss and my boss were working on a big long-term plan to form an Old World government, so we were in some of the same Zoom meetings.

"Scarlett isn't an ordinary null, Lex," Sashi said.

I held up a hand. "Stop. I'm worried about Will getting pressed too, but if Scarlett Bernard has some dark secret she doesn't want me to know, we need her permission to discuss it."

Sashi gave a brief smile. "You're absolutely right. Which is why I spoke to her about this four months ago."

"You did?" I looked back and forth between them, confused. Four months ago was about the time I'd been in Atlanta, where I tangled with some Civil War-era ghosts and a few absolutely wretched teen witches. I'd been a wreck afterward. How had the topic of Scarlett come up in all that?

"Yes. It was just after we moved here, and you were starting the witch clan. Scarlett said she trusted my judgment, that if I thought it might be life-or-death to go ahead." The smile returned, a little amused now. "She trusts you, too. I think she rather admires you."

That surprised me, but I tried to stay on task. "Okay, then just spit it out, either of you. What's the big secret?"

Now it was Will's turn to take a deep breath. "I used to be a werewolf," he began.

By the time Will finished his explanation, we had drunk the whole pot of coffee and were brewing a second. While it percolated, I tried to get my thoughts in order. "Okay, so, you used to be Will Carling, the alpha werewolf of Los Angeles, and then you lost your arm and Scarlett permanently cured you. Do I have that right?"

Will winced. "I don't love that term, especially since a lot of vampires or even werewolves would rather die than become human again. But yes, that's the gist."

"Huh." I drummed my fingers against the countertop, thinking. It was annoying to discover yet another thing about the Old World that I hadn't known about...but at the same time it didn't seem like that much of a leap. Witches had a complex spell that could bind magic. It made sense for powerful nulls to be able to do their own version. Well...to the extent that anything in the world of magic made sense.

Had Maven and Quinn known about this? I'd barely talked to my boss over the last couple of months. For a while she'd been training me to be an operative for when her parliament was finally assembled, but lately she'd been so busy talking to different parties across the country that I barely saw her. Quinn and I still ran her security, but it wasn't that hard when she mostly hung out in her coffee shop having video calls.

Sashi refilled my mug with the fresh coffee, and I murmured my thanks, still lost in thought. Quinn had taken over a lot of the day-to-day running of the state, so I didn't see him much either. But surely he would have mentioned that turning permanently human again was possible for him.

Wait. I froze with my coffee mug in the air.

Quinn could be human again.

That's when the full implications of removing magic from someone finally sank in. All the werewolves who hated their lives and would do anything—literally—to be human again. All the vampires who would be terrified of losing their power, or decide they wanted to forgo it for a human life. Nulls were already a volatile commodity in the Old World—as Charlie's aunt, I knew that better than anyone. If what they could do was permanent...it would complicate everything.

"Holy shit," I muttered. Will and Sashi both nodded sympathetically, as if they'd just been waiting for me to reach this obvious conclusion.

"Yeah, okay, I can see why she doesn't tell people. But why do you think this is related to someone pressing Will?"

"It practically has to be," Sashi replied, squeezing her husband's arm. "Will is living proof that this is possible. A vampire must have suspected her abilities and come looking for him. It might even have been someone he knows."

Oh, I really didn't like *that.* Either one of Maven's people had figured out Will's identity and pressed him for information, or, more likely, an unknown vampire had come into Maven's territory and pressed a human without Quinn or I knowing. "But you think this is about Scarlett, not one of the other LA leaders?"

He nodded. "A year ago, I might have had some juicy information about Dashiell's security or long-term plans, but everything will have been changed by now. I'm done with anything having to do with magic—well, other than being married to Sashi, but she's not political."

That was true. Thaumaturge witches like Sashi were useful for healing humans, but they weren't exactly major players in the supernatural world.

"Besides," Will added, "If someone wanted information about the Las Vegas underworld, or blackmail material on someone she healed, the smartest move would be to threaten me in front of her. It doesn't make sense to mess with my memory when they could use me to ask her directly."

He said this frankly and without any kind of concern, as calmly as if he were explaining the plot of a movie. It gave me pause, because for the first time, I could see him as an alpha—not the tough-and-gruff kind, like Dunn had been, but someone more charismatic and caring. The kind older brother trying to keep you on the right path.

Interesting. I was going to need to reconsider a lot of what I'd thought I understood about Will, not to mention Scarlett.

(And *Quinn could become human again*, a voice in the back of my brain insisted.) But all that had to wait.

"Okay. This is going to take some time to process, but let's try to stay focused on the immediate issue," I said. "If you're right, and someone used Will to find out that Scarlett Bernard can—" I almost said "cure" again, but changed it at the last second—"reverse magical transformations, what does that mean?"

"We'll need to warn Scarlett," Will said immediately. "I texted her on the way here and asked her to call, but there hasn't been a response yet."

I glanced at the clock on my living room wall. It was 11:35, which made it just after ten-thirty in LA. Surely Scarlett's baby would have them up by now.

"Can you try her again now?"

"Let me," Sashi said, pulling her phone from a pocket. "Will, you try Jesse."

Jesse Cruz, Scarlett's fiancé, was a friend. He would know about Will too. Damn, I was some security expert. I'd missed this whole secret conspiracy right under my nose.

Sashi and Will began calling. I waited, getting a little tenser with each second that passed. If someone had found out that Scarlett had this volatile ability, they might have gone after her immediately. She could be under attack right now.

"Maybe not just Scarlett," I said distractedly, my thoughts in a whirlwind. Will lowered his phone with a little head shake. "Jesse's not answering, and neither is Kirsten. Something is happening there."

"Stop for a second," I insisted, focused on Will. "The magic removal thing, can all nulls do that?"

His eyes widened. "Not that I've ever heard of—Scarlett is really powerful."

I hadn't even known there was a scale of power for nulls.

"But would everyone know that?" I demanded. "Or would someone who finds out about Scarlett curing you just assume..." My voice trailed off as the penny dropped.

Sashi took in a sharp breath, meeting my eyes. Hers were full of horror. "Charlie," she whispered.

# 4

## LEX

I bolted out of my seat, hurrying down the hallway to the bedroom for my phone.

It was a Tuesday, which meant John would be working from home. Charlie would be with him. I had to squeeze the cell phone hard to make sure my fingers didn't shake, but I got the number to connect.

"Good morning, Lex," John said, using the "at work" voice he'd probably been stuck in all morning. I felt my heart decompress, suddenly giddy with relief. "You're up early."

"John, Charlie's nap time is over," I said firmly, making my way back to the kitchen.

There was a pause, but only a short one. "Are you sure?" John asked, all the confidence leached from his tone.

"Yes. Right fucking now. Just like practice." I hung up the phone before he could argue.

Sashi and Will were looking at me. "I take it Charlie doesn't nap anymore?" Sashi said mildly.

I shook my head. "Not for almost three years."

"What will happen?" Will asked, looking concerned.

I gave him a long, flat look. I liked Will just fine, but he'd kept a pretty incendiary secret about his past, and there was an outside chance that Charlie could be in danger because of it.

When he realized I wasn't going to answer, Will had the grace to flush. "I'm sorry. Of course you have an emergency plan."

He was right: John was rushing Charlie down to their basement, where Clara, her vampire bodyguard, spent most of her daytime hours. Charlie would "wake up" the vampire, and John would hustle the three of them into a next-door neighbor's old minivan, which sat unused in his garage while the guy waited for his fourteen-year-old to get her license. John had a key to the van, and a lot of goodwill built up with the neighbor.

Sashi looked back and forth between Will and me for a second, putting it together. When she looked at me, her expression was offended. "You can't possibly think Will would be involved in an attack on a child!"

"Sash—" Will started to say, but I interrupted. I could speak for myself.

"This isn't about Will or trust or friendship, Sashi. It's Charlie."

She held my eyes for a long, hard moment. My friend might come off as a kindly, slightly detached do-gooder, but I knew that when push came to shove, she was made of steel. I still didn't back down, though.

Finally, her shoulders sagged and she nodded. "You're right. I would be the same way if it was Grace."

All of a sudden, Will burst out laughing. He had a deep, joyous laugh, but the sound was so shocking in that moment that I might have reached for a weapon if I'd had one. I looked questioningly at Sashi, but she seemed as surprised at me.

"I'm sorry," Will said, recovering. He pointed at my chest. "I just saw it."

I looked down at myself. When I'd run for my cell phone, my robe had fallen open, exposing the silly wolf graphic on my nightgown. Sashi saw it too and clapped a hand over her mouth to stifle a giggle. She shook her head apologetically at me. "Howl of a Night," she said behind her fingers.

"You're telling me," I muttered, already heading for the bedroom. "I'll get dressed."

I went back into my room and threw on clothes from the night before, jeans and a T-shirt. As I was walking back to the kitchen, my cell phone buzzed in my hand.

"Is it Scarlett?" Sashi asked.

"No," I said, frowning down at the screen. I hit Talk. "John, you were supposed to get rid of this—"

"Phone, yeah, I know!" he shouted.

I went still. "What happened?"

"They were waiting for us!" In the background, I heard an unmistakable *pop-pop* that made adrenaline flood every inch of my bloodstream. He swore loudly, and there was a bit of fumbling static noise.

"John! *John*!"

He didn't answer, just more fumbling. Will and Sashi were looking at me, but I just shook my head, pacing a tight circle in the kitchen as I waited. I felt so helpless I wanted to scream. I was gripping my mother's bloodstone necklace, and felt its warmth in my hand. *Easy, there*, came my dead twin sister's voice in my head. As always, Sam picked the best moments to jump in with commentary. "Thanks a lot, spirit guide," I muttered.

Then a new voice came on the phone line. "Lex. It's Clara. Charlotte is okay. John must drive now."

I remembered how to exhale. "What happened?"

"After your call we went out the back door to go to the neighbor, like at practice," she reported. "While running across the lawn we saw a man and a woman with instrument cases in front of John's garage door."

There was a certain *tone* in her voice, and I understood that she was trying not to scare Charlie. And that there had been weapons in those instrument cases. "Was there shooting?"

"Yes, mistress. As John pulled away, they shot again at the vehicle. I returned fire, but no hits. They hit me in the thigh muscle as I was getting into the van."

Her tone was still as calm as if she was describing a pimple, but I didn't buy it. Years of living with Charlie and John had softened the edges of the former Viking's speech patterns, and I'd finally gotten her to call me "Lex" consistently. If she was slipping up and using "mistress" again, she was more stressed than she was letting on in front of Charlie.

"Is that the only injury?"

"Yes. Charlie is on the van floor now, hands over ears. She is unhurt."

"Okay. Good job, Clara. Do you remember what the couple looked like?"

"Woman had gold-blonde hair, short with muscles like a gymnast. Pale eyebrows. The man was farther away, but perhaps John's height, dark beard."

There was a pause, and I could hear John's low voice saying something in the background. "Yes, okay," Clara said to him, and then she came back on the line. "John has suggested I draw you a sketch. I took figure drawing spring semester."

I had to smile. Clara got bored when there was no one actively trying to kill her charges, and she'd been taking night classes at CU for the last couple of years. I often wondered if she chose the classes at random. "That would be great," I said. "You'll probably also need to cover up the bullet holes on the van. Have John run in somewhere and buy some bumper stickers."

"Yes, Lex."

With everyone's safety assured, my brain finally caught up to the details. "Clara, when they shot you, how far were you from Charlie?"

"We were holding hands. To stay close during daylight hours."

*Shit, shit shit.* "And when they shot at the van just now, were they aiming for the tires?"

"No. There are bullet holes in the windows." Her voice was still just as calm. "Shall I throw phone away, follow the plan?"

"Not yet. Hold the line, I need to think." Still pacing, I rubbed my eyes with the back of my hand. I knew Sashi and Will had to be giving me alarmed looks, but I ignored it.

I'd spent actual years fearing, and preparing for, another kidnapping attempt on my niece. In addition to the neighbor's van thing, I had two other possible emergency plans: one for an attack on my parent's house, and one for an attack here at the cabin. The thing all those plans had in common was that John was supposed to trash his phone and take Charlie to a remote location that he'd found himself—one even I didn't know about. Within twenty-four hours he'd get me a message through an encrypted email, and we'd make a plan from there.

But in every situation I'd envisioned, the enemy's objective had been to *kidnap* Charlie. This attack didn't make any sense–if you were planning to steal a young null and program or torture her to do what you wanted, you needed her alive.

It would still be wise to have John get Charlie somewhere safe—but before she could do that, I would need to use my niece for something else, as much as I hated to. But my house was the first place anyone would look for Charlie next. "Clara, don't throw the phone yet. Tell John to go to location delta."

There was a brief pause. "Are you certain?"

I almost smiled. As a vampire, Clara was bound to me in a permanent sense. Only as a human could she question my direct orders. "Yes, I'm certain. Go there now and wait for us. Twenty to thirty minutes."

"Yes." The line went silent.

Looking up, I realized that Sashi and Will were both staring at me, Sashi wringing her hands with concern. "They're okay?" she asked.

"They're okay," I promised her. "Someone was waiting outside John's house, but they were counting on surprise. John got them away in time, thanks to you two."

I didn't miss the little look Sashi shot her husband, the time honored *see, I was right* face, known to couples everywhere.

"What do we do now?" Will asked me.

"Now," I said, checking my watch. "I need you two to come down to the basement and help me move a body."

SASHI AND I, with an assist from Will, spent the next fifteen minutes getting Quinn into a body bag, out to the garage, and fitted into the special lightproof compartment in Quinn's Jeep. I might have been able to drag him up myself, but I was grateful that Sashi and Will were there. Quinn and I had been together for years now, but I still didn't like seeing him in this state. Vampires don't *die* during the day in the same sense as rotting and rigor mortis, but his body was just as lifeless. Quinn, the man I loved, wasn't in there right now. It was unsettling.

But it had to be done. When John had pointed out that someone was trying to kill Charlie, rather than use her, it was obvious that this situation was officially above my pay grade. I needed to wake Quinn, who was in charge of Maven's security. He would know what to do, up to and including waking Maven to inform her about the attack. But that meant I needed a null, and I couldn't let John bring Charlie to the cabin. After the failed attempt at John's house, my place was the obvious next target.

We needed to meet somewhere the bad guys would never think to look for us. And it just happened that one of my contingency plans involved a meetup at the back of the Boulder Police Department parking lot.

I could bring Charlie and Clara into the Jeep, get Clara into the lightproof compartment to heal, and sit with Charlie and Quinn in John's car to discuss matters. Meanwhile, John would go into the station and chat with my cousin Elise, to make the whole thing look like an innocent family visit.

When we got Quinn secured, I checked my watch again. "I need to get on the road," I said, looking at Sashi. "Can you call Katia, and then probably Lily, and fill them in on what's been happening?" Katia was my aunt and a member of our tiny witch clan—not to mention Charlie's great aunt. And Lily was the Head Witch in Charge of Colorado. They both needed to know about the attacks, and that was one thing I could delegate.

"Of course."

Sashi was a bit of a touchy-feely person, like Lily, so I stepped forward and hugged her. "Thank you for this. Deeply."

She nodded when I stepped back, flushing with pride. I hated to ruin her moment, but I had to add, "The two of you should get out of town for a few days."

Sashi's eyes widened, and Will instantly stepped forward to put his arm around her. "You really think they'd come after us?" he asked me.

"I can't think of a reason they would—they got the information they wanted from you, Will, and you're not able to remember anything about who pressed you. But they already surprised us once, and I don't want to take the chance that it'll happen again."

"But isn't that exactly why I should stay close?" Sashi argued. "If you think they might surprise you again, someone could get hurt. And if they're human, I could help."

"Sashi," Will said gently, his eyes on his wife. "You should tell her."

I had been sidling toward the driver's door, my thoughts on the next steps in my plan, but that brought me up short. "Tell me what?"

My friend's face went red. "That's not—it shouldn't matter..."

I looked back and forth between them for a second, until I saw Will's eyes drop to her stomach.

A smile spread across my face. "Really?" I asked her. "How far along?"

She flushed even deeper, but it was at least partly pride this time. "Thirteen weeks. I'm forty; we're *complete* idiots, but...yes. Thought we might do it again, properly this time." She gave me a tiny smile. "Grace will be furious. Or ecstatic. I never know these days."

I threw my arms around her, which made Sashi laugh. "Two hugs in one day? Blimey, you're going soft," she said into my hair.

"Congratulations."

When I stepped back, Sashi seemed like she was torn between about six different things to say. Then she gave Will a severe look. "Pregnant women are police officers and firefighters and soldiers, you know," she said. "I shouldn't be excluded if I can help."

Will kissed her temple. "We could go back to Vegas for a few days," he suggested. "See if we can have a conversation with Grace."

It was a smart move on his part. I didn't know all the details, but Sashi and Will's daughter was barely speaking to them these days. She'd taken spring semester off college and was currently in Las Vegas, working as a nanny for a witch family. I got the sense she didn't want to be geographically close to her parents right then.

"All right," Sashi said, making a face. "Just promise me you'll call if you need me."

"I will," I lied.

As I was pulling out of the driveway, the Bluetooth dinged a text, which displayed on the console screen. It was from Jesse Cruz, and said simply, *911 call me right now.*

Frowning, I made the call.

FORTY MINUTES LATER, I reached the parking lot at the Boulder Police Department and drove up and down the parking lot rows until I found a minivan with oddly placed bumper stickers. John, Charlie, and Clara were waiting inside with the engine running to keep the air-conditioning on. Looking through the windows, I could see Charlie holding an iPad in a child case, engrossed in her eleven thousandth viewing of Moana. Something in my stomach uncoiled. She was okay.

The meet went more or less as we'd planned. John went inside to bring Elise the drive-through lunch they'd picked up. Holding Charlie's hand, Clara limped over to the Jeep and climbed in. Quinn woke up and found himself in a police parking lot in broad daylight.

Leaving Clara in the Jeep's lightproof compartment to heal, Charlie, Quinn, and I climbed back into John's neighbor's minivan, where Charlie put her headphones on so I could fill Quinn in on the morning's events—including the attack on Scarlett Bernard in Los Angeles.

I was flustered trying to explain, and the day's events came out all out of order. But of course Quinn, with his attention to the details of security, touched my knee to interrupt. "How did you figure out they were coming in time to get Charlie out?"

"Oh. Right." I glanced at my niece, who was sitting in the front seat with her brown bare feet on the van dashboard while Quinn and I had the middle row. Charlie was too little to ride shotgun, but she loved being up there when the van was stopped. She was completely absorbed in her movie.

I looked at Quinn. "Sashi and Will came to my house this morning because they realized that someone had pressed Will."

He looked completely baffled by that, and any lingering doubts I might have had about him knowing about Scarlett disappeared.

But that also meant I had to tell him. "Will knew Scarlett Bernard, in LA," I said carefully. "Specifically, he knows an important secret about something unusual she can do. The theory is that someone figured out the two of them are connected, tracked Will down here in Boulder, and pressed him to confirm it. When he did, they must have put this attack in play." I paused long enough to take a breath. "Only they didn't know that Scarlett is unique, for a null. So they hired skinners to come after *all* nulls, at the same time. So we wouldn't have a chance to react."

I knew I was starting to babble, but suddenly I couldn't look Quinn in the eyes. My gaze fell on my hands, folded in my lap.

*Stop dancing around it, babe*, came my sister's voice in my head. *Pull off the Band-Aid.*

Quinn wasn't stupid. His hand moved into my vision and rested on my balled-up fists. His skin was cool to the touch—not cold, just kind of room temperature. "Are you going to tell me?" he asked softly.

I couldn't help it; I turned my head and looked out the window. Soldier or not, boundary witch or not, in that moment I turned out to be a coward. "She can turn supernatural beings human again. Permanently."

There was a long, long silence. "You're...certain?" Quinn said at last.

"Will used to be the alpha werewolf of the Los Angeles pack."

"Oh."

The silence between us grew thick and uncomfortable. There were so many things I wanted to say in that moment, and so many things I wished Quinn would say. I wanted to tell him I would understand if he wanted to talk to Scarlett about becoming human again, so he could go to Georgia and be with his daughter. Simultaneously, I wanted him to promise he would stay a vampire forever so he could be with me, no matter what Scarlett could do. But all I could do was watch my leg jiggle up and down

Finally, Quinn shifted in his seat, and I turned to see what he would say, relieved that he was going to talk first. "We have to go wake up Maven," he said at last.

"Right. Yeah."

# 5

## SCARLETT

Los Angeles, CA

B*eep. Beep. Beep.*

Even if my body hadn't felt like a single massive bruise underneath a haze of painkillers, I would have known the sound of the damned heart monitor and the stink of disinfectant anywhere. With a great deal of effort, I cracked open my eyes and found water-stained institutional ceiling tiles.

Yup. Back in the fucking hospital.

"Oh, thank God," I heard Jesse say. It really did sound like a prayer.

Hearing him made it worth the phenomenal effort required to drag my eyelids all the way up and look for the source. Jesse was sitting in the room's visitor's chair, which he'd pulled up right next to the bed, by my head. That was a good sign—it meant I didn't have a lot of machines and wires crowded around me.

"Annie?" My voice was hoarse.

"She's right here." He stood long enough to heave something from the floor onto his hip: the handle of the baby's heavy car seat. "Cliff is in the hallway, keeping an eye on things."

I relaxed a little. Cliff was the professional bodyguard looking after Annie. His first year of help had been a gift from Maven. If he was in the hall, we were okay...or at least, we would have plenty of advance warning if we weren't.

I turned my face enough to peer in the car seat. There was some gauze on my nose, which wasn't a good sign. I'd clearly been given some top-shelf painkillers, but even the tiny movement made pain lance through the back of my head, sharp and sudden.

It was worth it, though, for a glimpse of our daughter. She was fast asleep in her green froggy pajamas, a lightweight muslin blanket draped over her legs. Her head was crooked to one side and her little lips were moving like she was narrating her dreams.

I had to blink back tears so I could look at Jesse again. No matter how much it terrified me, I had to ask the question. "Corry and Shadow?"

"Both alive," Jesse promised, putting the car seat down and taking my hand.

I squinted up at the clock on the wall. It was one-thirty in the afternoon. "Are we in the same day?"

"Yes. The doctors think you were only unconscious for about fifteen minutes, but you've been in and out since then from the meds."

"Kay." I wanted to close my eyes and drift back to sleep, but I forced myself to look at him. "What else?"

"I talked to Corry while we were in the ambulance." He reached over to brush back my hair, stroking my cheek to reassure himself. "When she hung up with you she ran to the campus security office, but they didn't take her seriously. I called and talked to the dean of students myself."

I felt a tiny, involuntary smile on my face. When he wanted to, Jesse could do authoritarian cop voice with the best of them. "I take it they took you seriously."

"Yeah. The dean got a campus security team to escort Corry to the airport. She's already at her gate, waiting to board a plane to LA."

I nodded, wincing at the pain in my head. Stop doing that, Scarlett.

"Is Shadow okay?"

"She's healing, but more slowly than before the Wild Hunt. I had Astrid pick her up and take her home to hang out with Magnus."

A haunted look came over his face, one that I recognized. It was exactly how I felt whenever I remembered how close he'd come to dying during the Luparii attack. "What happened?" I asked. "Those things that fell...?" For some reason I didn't want to be the first one to say the word.

"Bombs," he said, confirming my fear. "I was already on my way after your call, so I got to the scene before the first responders. There was all this wreckage, some of it still on fire, but no sign of you, just a few smears of blood. At first I thought they took you."

With effort, I squeezed his hand. "That must have been scary."

"Yeah. But I yelled your name, and Shadow barked. I ran down to the creek and saw you both in the water. She was keeping your face above the surface." He paused, not looking at me. "I was so scared you'd go under before I could get to you."

"But I didn't," I told him. "I'm fine."

I didn't actually know that, of course. Nothing was in a cast or in traction, but between the everywhere-pain and the layer of painkillers masking it, I couldn't tell much about my status. I looked down and held up my left hand, just enough to see that my engagement ring was still there. It was still perfect. I felt a dreamy smile on my face. Smart boy, picking a ring that could take a hit.

"Scarlett." There was forced patience in Jesse's voice, like maybe it wasn't the first time he'd said my name. I made myself find his worried face. "You're *not* fine, sweetheart. They need to run tests, but the theory is that you got two back-to-back concussions, which your doctor has never even seen before. They had to reset your nose, and you have serious bruising and several patches of road rash. There was one on your leg that needed surgical debridement; that's why you were out. They're also giving you a massive dose of antibiotics, because that water is disgusting, and you had open wounds."

"Aw man. I won't be able to drink."

He gave me a hard look. "You're also slurring your words, did you know that?"

"Am not," I said immediately. Then I amended it with, "And if I am, I'm sure it's just the drugs."

Now Jesse pointed to himself. "See how I'm wearing my go-bag clothes? That's not because of the creek. It's because you threw up on me in the ambulance. Twice. You don't remember that?"

I tried to recall an ambulance...or anything else between rolling into the water and waking up in the hospital. I could only conjure up a few confused images and sensations. The ice-cold metal scissors on my skin when they cut off my clothes. The incredible shriek of a siren when I just wanted to sleep. "No," I admitted.

He shook his head like a disappointed parent. "The doctor doesn't think you're going to have permanent brain damage, but she already said how important it's going to be for you to rest and recover."

"When can I go home?"

Jesse's face fell, all the anger gone now. "Baby, we can't go home," he said softly, taking my hand in both of his now. "Someone tried to kill you. We're going to have to hide until we figure that out."

"Oh. Right." I blinked at him for a long moment, working out how to revise my question. "But when are they going to discharge me?"

"You're staying at least overnight, but two or even three days is more likely. They need to monitor you for signs of second impact syndrome, which is potentially lethal. And I had to tell Jack, who wants to order like a dozen other tests. He's on his way."

I groaned. My brother was an emergency room doctor. He was going to turn this into a whole thing, which meant I would need to come up with a story to explain all this...wait a minute.

My brain had caught up to the conversation. "Wait, what did you mean, wreckage?" I asked Jesse. "There wasn't anything under the bridge to wreck."

"Not before the attack, no. But I ran into one of the bomb squad guys in the ER, when they were bringing you in. He said the explosions were caused by two cluster bombs."

My eyelids had been drifting down again, but I forced myself to get them back up. "The fuck is a cluster bomb?" I mumbled.

"The devices," he explained. "A cluster bomb involves two separate explosions: the first blows off a casing, exposing a whole bunch of smaller bombs. They left shrapnel behind."

I couldn't remember much about the bombs—I'd been too busy hauling Shadow down to the creek. I did recall the flares of orange and blue light, like fireworks in broad daylight. And it had been loud and confusing.

"Whoever did this dropped one device off either side of the overpass, so you'd be trapped," Jesse continued. "If you hadn't gotten in the water so fast, you would have died, and probably Shadow too."

The words fell out of my mouth without me really planning on it. "I've never heard of cluster bombs."

"They're used in war, Scarlett. Do you understand what I'm saying? *It should have worked.* You're supposed to be dead."

Ah. That explained why Jesse was so freaked out. People had tried to kill me before, but no one had ever gone to quite so much effort. It would have been a little flattering if it wasn't completely terrifying.

"But I'm not," I told him. "Shadow saved me. I know I'm hurt, Jesse, but I'm *going to be* fine."

He shook his head again, resisting the comfort. It reminded me of Annie when she's starving but doesn't want to eat pureed vegetables. I felt like I should say something else to make him feel better, but my thoughts were so hazy, and I just wanted to stare at the ceiling and drift.

I might have done that for a while, I think, but then Jesse cleared his throat, drawing my attention back. He was wearing what I thought of as his Cop Thinking Face. "Can you walk me through what you remember?"

Slowly, I told him about the sniper shooting Shadow, and my decision to hide behind the bridge support. "It was just luck that we were almost there when the bomb went off."

Jesse picked up my hand and kissed it. "That wasn't luck," he told me. "Your instincts were dead on, and because of that you and Shadow are both alive. You are a fucking badass."

I felt a lump form in the back of my throat. "Goddammit, Jesse, what's the one rule?"

He smiled. "Don't be too nice to Scarlett during a crisis." He went to retrieve a box of tissues from the wheelie table on the other side of the bed, handing me a wad. I blew my nose noisily, ignoring the pain from the scrapes on my arms as they bent. I was going to have to ignore a lot of pain. We absolutely needed to know who had made a run at Corry and me. "The thing is," I said out loud, "I haven't really pissed anyone off lately."

Jesse gave me a look. "Really? You?"

"I know, right? But things have been pretty business-as-usual."

He looked troubled, but all he said was, "The police are going to want to talk to you as soon as you're well enough. Those devices were way too professional for you to pass it off as a mugging gone wrong."

"Ugh."

"But," he added, a hint of reluctance bleeding through his voice, "We can put them off until at least tomorrow."

I knew what he was really saying: *we can put them off until Dashiell can put pressure on his police network*. Jesse may have more or less accepted the way the Old World worked by now, but there were still things he didn't want to admit out loud.

"Okay." I tried to make my brain think. He was right, this had been a serious attempt to kill Corry and me. I was going to need to talk to the other Old World leaders. "I should start making calls," I mumbled to Jesse. "Gotta tell everyone." Corry could come to the hospital as soon as she got off the plane. As long as she and I were both safe, we could afford a little time to come up with a plan. "I need a phone."

Jesse didn't answer, but his face went very flat and still. I knew this expression well: he had bad news. "There's something else," he said.

"Tell me."

"Someone also took a run at Allison Luther's niece today," he said, but he was smart enough to add, "She's okay!" before I could even open my mouth. "I called Lex to tell her what happened, and she was in the middle of her own crisis. Charlie is safe now, but Lex is pretty freaked out."

I tried to imagine what that would even look like. I'd seen Allison Luther angry before—the first time we met, for example, when she'd hit me in the face—but I couldn't picture her panicking.

"You, Corry, and Charlie were all attacked on the same day," Jesse said patiently, "at nearly the same moment. I think Lex is worried because they weren't trying to use or manipulate any of you. They tried to *kill* you."

I stared at him for probably several minutes, while the importance of those words worked its way through the drugs.

Oh. That was really bad.

I had thought it was bad before, of course, but the scale had gotten so much bigger. It wasn't that someone was trying to kill me and Corry out of revenge for something I'd done, or to get to Dashiell, or any of the other LA-based scenarios I'd been imagining.

Someone was going after *all* nulls. At least the nulls in the—

"Wait," I blurted. "I need my phone."

Jesse winced. "Uh..."

Right, right, it must have gotten trashed. Poor Abigail Haynes was going to have to hook me up with a new cell *again*. "Yours, then. Quick."

Jesse raised an eyebrow, but he unlocked his phone and handed it over.

Then we realized that between the IV and my shaking fingers, that wasn't the best plan, so I recited the number while he dialed. It was one of the few numbers I knew by heart, even with the extra country codes.

Jesse pushed the Talk button, putting the call on speaker.

Rhys's phone rang for a long time, long enough that I was mentally organizing my voicemail message. But I didn't get the usual recording, where the jovial Scottish null invited me to "feckin' send a text instead."

Instead, after seven rings a tearful woman's voice answered in a similar accent. "This is Rhys's phone, Maura speaking."

I blinked. Maura was Rhys's wife, but she'd never answered his cell before. "Oh. Hi. I'm looking for Rhys."

"He's dead," she said shortly. "He was killed two days ago."

My stomach lurched. Jesse met my eyes, looking as horrified as I felt. "What- How—" I sputtered, then took a breath. "Sorry, let me start over. My name is Scarlett Bernard—"

"Aye, and this is your partner Jesse Cruz's phone. We do have caller ID here in Scotland," she said bitterly. "I know who you are. You're the one that's like him."

Her voice was filled with so much hostility that Jesse raised his eyebrows and pointed to himself, asking if I wanted him to take over. He was about a million times more personable than me on my best day. But I gave a little head shake. I felt dazed and punch-drunk, but I didn't want to risk annoying the woman if Jesse's charm offensive didn't work. "Please, could you tell me what happened?" I asked.

"He were shot in cold blood, out in front of our home," she snapped. "I assume it was something to do with your world."

My world? Rhys had barely been *in* my world. He'd always claimed he must be the weakest null alive. The Old World leaders in his area had known about him, but they mostly left him alone. He'd once told Jack he had a misspent youth, but now he was a carpenter who lived a normal life—other than an occasional errand for the local vampires.

He had kids.

"I'm so sorry," I said to his wife now. "Do the police have any—"

"Stop talking," she snarled. "You were not part of his life, understand? I was. His children were. Now he's taken from us, for *nuthin'*. I never want to hear or see your name *ever* again."

She hung up.

A horrible new feeling hit me, and the phone slipped from my fingers. Luckily, Jesse took the hint and grabbed a ring of plastic from the wheelie table beside him, snapping it open into a vomit bag.

There wasn't anything in my stomach to come up, but my body tried to expel the contents anyway, until there was an inch of yellow bile in the bottom of the bag.

When it was finally over, Jesse took the bag to the trash, and I laid back on my pillow, panting and sweaty, my thoughts racing despite the pain and drugs. I'd never believed I knew all of the nulls who currently exist—I was working off Olivia's old contacts. But every living null I was aware of had just been attacked at roughly the same time. "We have to start calling everyone," I mumbled.

"It's okay, Scarlett, the cardinals are on it." Jesse's voice was soothing, and it took me a minute to process his next words. "Maven called a meeting. They're coming to LA tonight to talk to Dashiell. It's being handled."

I stared at him again. "Wait, what? There's a meeting?"

"Tonight at ten. They said they would set up a video chat for us, if you can stay awake that long."

I wanted to shake my head but remembered the pain just in time. There was no way in hell I was missing that meeting, though.

I took a few breaths, staring at the ceiling. Annie shifted in her car seat, making the little whimper sound that meant she would wake up soon.

"Jesse," I began, as calmly as I could. "I need you to call Wyatt. He's out until sunset but you can leave a message. He still actually listens to voicemails."

Jesse glared at me. "Scarlett Kaylie Bernard, you are absolutely not checking yourself out of the hospital for a meeting."

"Of *course* not," I said weakly. "I would never just walk out against doctor's advice. I'm a mother now, Jesse, Jesus."

He relaxed a little. "Okay. So why do you want me to call Wyatt?"

I gave him the most angelic smile I could muster. "I just want him to come convince the hospital staff that I need to go on a *very* quick field trip."

# 6

## LEX

Boulder, Colorado

"Waking up Maven" wasn't as easy as it sounds, but we had set it up that way by design. Only Quinn, as the head of her security, knew where she spent each night. As Maven's daytime security person, I could get Charlie to wake Quinn, who could then get Maven.

We'd just never actually had to *use* the system before.

That day she was in the vacant basement apartment of one of the buildings she owned, this one in Lafayette. We walked into the complex with John holding one of Charlie's hands and Quinn holding the other, while I trailed behind the three of them, making sure we weren't followed.

When we got to the apartment itself, the interior was completely bare of decorations or furniture—this wasn't a home, just a hiding spot. *At least*, I thought, *she didn't spend the day in another fucking septic tank.*

Maven was in the back bedroom, so John, Charlie and I

leaned against the adjoining wall while Quinn went in first, speaking to our boss in low voices. Charlie still had her iPad and headphones, although she'd moved on to watching *Bluey*.

When Maven and Quinn came out a few minutes later, I felt a jolt of shock. Maven wore a simple T-shirt dress with her neon green hair in a pragmatic ponytail, no makeup or accessories. Usually when I saw Maven, she practically radiated power. When she was human, though, I was reminded of how short she was, how young she looked. And Maven without costume jewelry was like a general without stars. Without the jewelry and fake glasses, it was also impossible not to notice her remarkable beauty. Helen of Troy had nothing on my boss.

"Hello, Lex," she said as pleasantly as if I'd arrived at Magic Beans for a latte. Then she looked straight at John. "Mr. Wheaton, I'm so sorry for what happened this morning. Please be assured that I'll pay for any damages to your home and replace your neighbor's vehicle."

"And what about keeping my daughter safe?" John asked. His voice was mild, but I still had to give him credit. Most people wouldn't challenge the world's most powerful vampire like that.

John probably sensed this, because he added, "My understanding was that she was under your protection. That she would be safe because of your, um, unique standing."

He glanced at me to see if he'd put his foot too far in his mouth, but I just gave him a tiny smile. *That's my man,* came my sister's proud voice in my head. She was right—John had a point, and he'd made it with more respect than many parents could have mustered in his place.

I was still a little surprised when Maven laid a hand on his shoulder and looked directly into his eyes. "Mr. Wheaton, I could stand here and try to convince you that the system worked, that Charlie is still alive because of the training and experience I've given my people. But I think we both know that luck played a part this morning. Luck, and some quick thinking by Ms. Brighton."

John flushed a little at Sashi's name, but he nodded. "There are also the California attacks to consider," Maven continued. "My dominion is Colorado. I've never promised to be infallible here, but the Old World is territorial, and *this* is my territory." She shook her head a little, a very human gesture. "What happened today, it's bigger than this state. It's bigger than what a single person, no matter how strong, can anticipate."

She looked at me, making sure I was included in what she said next. "The skinners should never have gotten this close to success—but it's a blind spot in how the Old World currently works. Skinners can cross state lines, a single vampire can sneak in and out quickly, and there's no system of government to monitor or stop them. It's exactly why I've been trying to build a parliament."

"No offense," John said, "but you sound like a politician."

Maven gave him a grave look. "Mr. Wheaton, that is the meanest thing anyone's ever said to me."

She got John to smile. "No it's not," he said.

"No, it's not," she agreed. "But I apologize. I didn't mean to sound glib, or like I was turning this attack into an opportunity. What I really want you to know is that it has hardened my resolve." She lifted her chin. "I *will* set up a governing body that can serve as a deterrent. And I'll create a system where I can protect people in my state from threats outside my state. I just need to ask you for a little time."

John looked at her for a long moment, then turned to me. "Should I trust her?" he asked directly.

I smiled, especially when I caught Maven's look of surprise in my peripheral vision. "I can't tell you what to do, brother. But I have absolute conviction that Maven is our best chance at keeping Charlie safe until she's old enough to find her own place in the Old World. It's why I work for her."

John nodded to himself, pulling a pair of headphones out of his pants pocket. "Okay. Then I'll join Charlie and leave you all to your plotting."

As soon as John was settled on the floor next to his daughter, Maven looked at me. "Are Mr. And Ms. Brighton safe?"

I needed a second to realize she meant Sashi and Will. "Yes. Did you...you knew about Will?"

Maven nodded gravely. "Of course. Dashiell and I are allies. That's why he sent Will to me."

So Maven had known what Scarlett could do. I wasn't offended—I was used to reporting to people who had a hell of a lot more intel than I did. But, not for the first time, I felt a wave of helplessness at the amount of crap out there I didn't even know about yet. How was I supposed to keep Charlie safe with so many secrets around?

(And Quinn could become human again.)

*Don't spin out right now, babe. You're needed here.*

I took a breath. "Where would you like to start?" I asked my boss.

"We have to meet with Dashiell, in person," she replied, her face revealing nothing. "Since the three nulls who were attacked in the US were under Dashiell's and my protection, we'll start there. I would like to assemble the whole parliament, but it's just not enough warning to get everyone there in time."

"You want to go to LA?" I asked.

She nodded. "If Scarlett Bernard is in the hospital and her apprentice is traveling, Dashiell won't learn of the attacks until sunset. It makes sense for us to go to them."

"When?" Quinn asked her.

Maven pulled a cell phone out of her dress pocket and glanced at the clock on the screen. "Tonight. As soon as we can make all the arrangements." She touched her stomach with one hand, looking around the empty apartment. "But let's get some food delivered while we plan," she added.

TRAVEL ARRANGEMENTS TOOK ALL AFTERNOON, especially since Quinn and Maven had to stick close to Charlie...including when my niece needed to stretch her legs or pee. Seeing two powerful vampires leaning against the closed bathroom door in the empty apartment was a little funny. It was less funny, though, when my aunt Katia pulled up in a massive van containing two empty coffins.

"Did you have any trouble leaving work?" I asked Katia.

She shrugged. Katia worked in the shipping department at Luther Shoes, my father's company. I had no idea how she managed to wrangle time off whenever we had an emergency, but I also wasn't sure I wanted to know.

Charlie had to stay within range while Quinn and Maven climbed inside the coffins, but John was careful to angle her away from them as she watched her show. When the coffins were sealed, John led Charlie toward the Jeep, and Katia and I traded keys.

"I should drive them to the airport?" Katia asked me. I felt a knot in my throat and could only nod at her. For now, John was going to take Charlie to get a rental car at the airport. They would wake Clara, and the three of them would hole up in a hotel somewhere until at least after the meeting, when we'd have better intel. Maven had already given John a package she'd had delivered from Magic Beans, which contained an untraceable credit card and perfect passports for him, Charlie, and Clara. The photos weren't recent, and I realized Maven must have had them made ages ago.

She had been making plans to keep Charlie safe.

Katia shifted her weight, looking from me to the Jeep. "You want to say goodbye to them?"

I shook my head. "They know," I said quietly. "I'll wave while you pull away."

I'd approved every step of this plan, but smiling and waving while Katia drove John and Charlie away from me nearly broke me. I forced myself to focus on getting the coffins to the private plane before I began sobbing.

I SPENT the first half of the flight looking quietly out the window, lost in a swirl of thoughts—about Charlie and Scarlett, but mostly Maven's parliament. Early on, Maven had explained the plan: Once the parliament was up and running, Quinn would temporarily take over many of the day-to-day operations in Colorado so Maven could focus on parliament business. I would become a sort of operative, responsible for carrying out the parliament's communications and solving problems.

Eventually Quinn would join me as the parliament's investigator, and Maven could either return to running the state or find another successor. Quinn had no interest in becoming a full-time cardinal vampire, even if he had been old and powerful enough to hold the position.

That conversation had been ages ago, though, and I really hadn't been keeping up with developments. Instead, I'd come home from Atlanta and sort of gone on autopilot, helping at Maven's coffee shop, doing security patrols, holding casual witch clan meetings, working out. In my defense, Maven had been constantly on the phone or doing video calls, and I'd been relieved not to have any ghost bombs or witch attacks to deal with.

Now, though, I had to wonder if Maven had gotten so distracted with her big plan that she'd left vulnerabilities at home. Either one of Colorado's vampires had turned traitor and pressed Will, or someone from outside the state had managed to sneak in and question him. Either way, if we'd missed that, what else might we have missed?

Maven and Quinn woke up when we were an hour from our destination, the Burbank airport. I heard them rustling around back there, but I stayed put, giving them a chance to recalibrate for the night and drink from the thermos of blood I knew Quinn had brought for the occasion.

"Lex?" Maven came out first, heading straight for the plush leather seat across from mine. She was in full Maven getup now, wearing a shapeless khaki dress and piles of costume necklaces, her neon hair in a messy bun. "You seem quiet, even for you. What's worrying you?"

"I appreciate what you said to John today," I said. "And I know you've been very busy working on the parliament. But, with respect, maybe that's how a vampire was able to get into your territory and pressed someone you were protecting."

"Lex—" Quinn began, but Maven held up her hand.

"You're right," she said. "I grew careless. I've been focused on building my parliament. You and Quinn have had to take on a lot."

"Mostly Quinn," I admitted. "I've been...out of sorts...since Atlanta. I haven't been on my game."

Maven's face softened. "Lex, this attack wasn't your fault."

"No," I agreed, "but if I'd been more vigilant, maybe I could have stopped it."

"Remember what I told John. This is bigger than Colorado. An attempt to kidnap Charlie, I could understand that. But trying to kill all nulls..." She shook her head. "It doesn't make sense. That worries me."

Great. The most powerful vampire alive was concerned

about her ability to protect my niece. "Okay, how *is* the parliament coming?" I asked.

"Dashiell and I are hoping for nine leaders, similar to the American Supreme Court," she explained. "With Beau's help we have recruited an important witch leader in Savannah, and there is a powerful alpha werewolf from Maine who has agreed to serve. I am still waiting on several werewolves to respond to my calls." She gave me a faint smile that showed just a hint of teeth. "For some reason they don't seem to trust me."

"For some reason," I echoed. Maven had once masterminded the death of a psychotic alpha werewolf in Colorado.

"When there are nine, or even seven of us," Maven continued, "we'll start spreading the word that we are available to resolve conflicts and hear grievances. We'll become a sort of mobile court, investigating corruption and violence in different territories." She paused, then added, "I expect it will take a few demonstrations of power before the various enclaves begin to rely on our leadership."

I nodded. It wasn't a perfect system, but it could be flexible and impartial. And it would fill a great need. A parliament like that could have helped us several times in the last few years, including when Simon and Lily's sister was terrorizing us from across state lines.

In theory, Maven's parliament would be able to prevent wars...but only if it could get off the ground. And all that depended on Maven, on her ability to lead and to keep herself and the rest of the court safe.

"It's not just about protecting Charlie anymore," I blurted. "I believe in what you're doing, with the parliament."

She blinked a few times, the only sign of emotion on her face. "I'm not sure I knew that," she said simply.

"At the same time though," I continued, "if the tide turns for you, if you don't think you have the juice to protect her anymore, I need you to tell me. Please."

My boss tilted her head, her face hard, and for just a second a little video played in my head, of the night she'd reached into a vampire's ribcage and yanked out his heart like I would pick an apple. She could kill me in maybe a second and a half, faster than I would be able to react.

But I sat and looked at her, holding my ground.

After maybe thirty seconds, Maven's expression softened. "We're not there yet," she said quietly.

# 7

## LEX

Pasadena, California

From the Burbank airport, Quinn drove the rental SUV to Pasadena. Maven rode in the front seat next to him, while I sat in the back wearing a baseball cap pulled low over my eyes. It was after sunset now, and like every city everywhere, Los Angeles had more than its share of ghosts. For the moment it was easier not to look.

When we reached Dashiell's house, it was immediately clear that the cardinal vampire of Los Angeles had to be almost absurdly rich. If it wasn't obvious from the gate—twelve-foot wrought iron spikes tipped with what looked like silver—or the imported Spanish tiles on the driveway, it was certainly clear from the actual...okay, "house" didn't feel like the right word. John lived in a house. My parents lived in a really *nice* house. As we left the gilded foyer and entered what I was told was the "east wing," I suspected that Dashiell might live in a supervillain lair trying to pass itself off as a mansion.

The fancy gate and fancier driveway had me expecting a butler, but Dashiell met us at the door himself, a blandly handsome man who appeared to be in his mid- to late-30s, though Scarlett had once told me he'd been turned in his late twenties, during the early nineteen century. I didn't know if he'd led a hard life as a human or if skincare just hadn't been what it was, but I'd never dream of asking.

"Good evening, Maven, Lex, Quinn," the vampire said now, nodding at each of us in turn. A beautiful woman with glossy black hair stepped up beside him, and Dashiell introduced her to all of us as his wife, Beatrice. "We're meeting in the east wing," Dashiell announced. "The other Los Angeles leaders are joining us there, along with Scarlett Bernard and Jesse Cruz."

"Please, this way," Beatrice said. She was perfectly balanced on five-inch stilettos, somehow moving soundlessly down the long hallway.

I tuned out the conversation on the way through the mansion—it was mostly polite small talk about antiques and home decor style, two topics I couldn't even pretend to enjoy.

I did take an interest when we paused at the door to the security center, a windowless, secure room filled with sophisticated electronics and monitors. The main control area was just inside the door, but farther into the room, equipment tables had been pushed to the walls, and chairs had been arranged to face a blank white wall. Jesse and Kirsten Harms, along with a man I didn't know, were sitting in a group in the back of the room.

I was a little shocked to see Scarlett was there as well. When Jesse and I had talked on the phone that afternoon, he'd made it sound like she wouldn't be able to make the meeting in person. She must have talked her way out of the hospital, but she looked terrible. She wore cutoff sweatpants and a baggy T-shirt, her hair in a matted-looking bun. She had two fresh black eyes, angry scrapes on her arms, and a hospital-grade wet bandage covering one lower leg.

Before we made it across the room to them, an African-American woman in a wheelchair came into the room, pausing just inside the doorway. "You're all here, right? Can I start, please?" She looked impatient, openly annoyed by how long it was taking the cardinal vampires to mosey into the room. I liked her immediately.

Beatrice smiled. "Maven, this is Abigail Hayne. She runs all of our electronic security."

"Yes, Abigail, we'll start." Dashiell looked at his wife, who pecked his cheek.

"I'll leave you all to it," she said, turning to glide back down the corridor.

As our group came into the room, the LA people stood, except for Scarlett, who gave a little wave and a weak smile. There were a few minutes of introductions and pleasantries, like at the beginning of any briefing. The one man I didn't know yet turned out to be Eli, the alpha werewolf of LA. I remembered that the power structure worked differently here. Theoretically, Kirsten, Eli, Dashiell, and Scarlett were all equal partners, though I suspected Dashiell was somehow a majority voice. Maven said he was one of the more modern and forward-thinking cardinal vampires, but I figured there was still a difference between sharing power and sharing power *equally*.

There were more available seats in the second row, so I took the empty chair next to Jesse, and Quinn sat on my left with Maven on his other side. Jesse reached out and gave me a fist bump. I smiled at him, then leaned forward to see Scarlett on his right. "Are you okay?" I whispered.

She winked at me. "I am fucking glorious."

Jesse made a face. "She's on a lot of painkillers, and she has terrible vertigo from the concussion. She is *not* okay."

Scarlett raised a flat hand to conceal her mouth, like a villain in a silent movie. "Don't listen to Jesse," she stage-whispered. "He's jealous because the world doesn't spin just for him."

Great. I exchanged a glance with Jesse, who shrugged helplessly. "The good stuff should wear off in an hour or so."

At the front of the room, Dashiell cleared his throat. "Normally, I conduct meetings out in the atrium," he began, "but tonight I thought it important to give a more visual explanation of events. Thank you for joining me here in the security center."

I happened to glance at Abigail Hayne, who was openly scowling from the closest workstation, where she had set up a laptop next to a black device I didn't recognize. I thought I understood her expression—I wouldn't want a bunch of strangers in my professional nerve center either, allies or not. I also assumed Dashiell's mansion was normally warded with magic, and those spells would need to be redone when the null left. That was exactly why my own house had security cameras instead of wards.

"Of course, I was unaware of this situation until after sunset," Dashiell went on, frowning. "However, Kirsten and Eli were informed of the attack on Scarlett within minutes, and were able to redirect Abigail, my technology specialist, to dig into what happened before sunset. I have since worked with my...connections...within the police department for additional information."

Out of the corner of my eye I saw Jesse shifting restlessly in his seat. Of course—he was former LAPD. He wouldn't like Dashiell putting the fix in.

"What do the police think happened?" Scarlett asked.

"They believe some teenagers dumped fireworks and

garbage off both sides of the overpass to scare random joggers," Dashiell told her. "It's handled."

Dashiell gestured to Abigail, who pressed a button on the black device and typed a few commands into her computer. The overhead lights dimmed, and a massive screen appeared on the blank white wall behind Dashiell. The small black machine was a projector.

"Abby was able to obtain traffic camera footage from Boulder and LA, and then cross-reference it with vehicle registrations and the sketch provided by the Colorado team," Dashiell began, pointing at the image on the left. It was the drawing that Clara had sent me of her attacker. It was surprisingly good—not the same as a police sketch or anything, but she'd gotten the eyes and nose perfect. I knew that because the right side of the screen showed a photo of a woman who practically *had* to be the shooter.

"As you can see, Abby was able to identify her." Dashiell stepped to the side to give us a better look, and I studied the picture. The woman had dark blonde hair and blue eyes. She was pleasantly pretty in that blank-canvas way, where the right makeup and clothes could make you look like different people. I leaned forward with interest.

"Her name is Adelaide Preston," Abigail said from her workstation." Thirty-nine, no family, based out of Chicago." She pressed a button to change the image, and I felt a little jolt of shock. The photo was a posed group shot of a Marine unit. I had several army photos just like it in a box somewhere. Adelaide Preston was in the front row, looking smug.

"When the Pentagon opened access to elite training to women in 2016," Abigail went on, "Preston was one of the first to earn a green beret—or she would have been, if she hadn't failed the psychological evaluations."

I winced. I'd been through similar training, and I remembered the psych evals. I wondered which wire Adelaide Preston had tripped that made her own government afraid to use her.

"Instead, she spent the next three years as a private mercenary overseas. Today..." Abigail pushed a button, and the wall projector cycled through half a dozen surveillance photographs, all collected from different locations. Each photo showed Preston either entering or exiting a building, always wearing a baseball cap and sunglasses. She often carried one of those long, colorful bags made for yoga mats, which could hold any number of weapons. "Preston runs her own mercenary company in Chicago. She and her people specialize in a certain type of short-term assignments around the US."

"Skinners," Scarlett muttered darkly. "She's a skinner."

My stomach dropped. I'd heard of skinners—mercenary groups, usually human, who hunted people from the Old World, for money or sport. A similar mercenary group had attacked my friends Lily and Simon and their witch clan. But I'd never gone toe-to-toe with them personally—and I had never expected them to come after Charlie.

Abigail nodded. "Precisely. The traffic cam footage wasn't good enough to identify the rest of the attackers from this morning, but their general descriptions correlate with Preston's known employees."

The werewolf lifted his hand for attention. "Are we sure she's human?"

Abigail looked like she'd been expecting the question. "As far as we know. I found surveillance of her on full moon nights, and obviously she was seen during the day this morning. Witchblood is a possibility, but it's unlikely given her romantic connection."

"Sorry, what?" Scarlett blurted.

Abigail hit the button again, showing a grainy picture of a busy city street, possibly taken from a traffic camera. Abigail zoomed in to two figures on the side of the image: Adelaide Preston, looking over her shoulder to check the road, holding the hand of a man who was turned toward the camera. He appeared to be in his mid-forties, handsome and stone faced. Abigail pointed at the image. "This guy. For almost a decade now, Preston has had a romantic relationship with a vampire. His name is Orvil Grant."

"Why is that name familiar?" Maven asked.

Abigail pressed the button again, showing a black and white photo of an adult family, posed on the lawn in front of a low porch. The youngest man, in the top left, was clearly Orvil. I found that my eyes were drawn toward an older man, posed in a chair just below him. He was staring off into the distance, his eyes faraway. I knew that face from somewhere.

Scarlett Bernard yelped. "Holy shit! That's Ulysses S. Grant!"

We all looked at her, and Scarlett gave a self-conscious shrug. "My father taught American history," she said. "Even with the goodest of drugs, I know the presidents."

At the front of the room Abigail's face had soured a little, like Scarlett had stolen her punchline. "Yes. Orvil Grant was the younger brother of Ulysses. He had a messed-up life, even by nineteenth century standards. After committing a bunch of war crimes, Orvil was tried for corruption." She looked down at a notebook in her lap, reviewing her notes. "He spent time in at least one mental hospital, in New Jersey, disappeared for awhile, and died in 1881 at age forty-six...only he didn't, because he became a vampire."

"I've heard of Orvil Grant," Maven said thoughtfully, and I could tell she meant she'd heard of him as a vampire. "He's allied with some powerful vampires, including in a few in New York. Is he cardinal somewhere?"

Dashiell responded first. "No. I have made a few discreet

inquiries among my contacts this evening. Orvil splits his time between the Midwest and the northern East Coast. Much of his time is spent in Chicago now, with Adelaide Preston."

Huh. The split residency thing was interesting in itself—Vampires had to relocate now and then to change identities, but I didn't think I'd heard of any who kept multiple homes at the same time.

"Is Orvil the one going after nulls?" I asked, directing my question to the room in general.

Maven was frowning. "I never got the impression that he was violent, or even particularly interested in power. He's more interested in..." she tilted her head, searching for a word.

"Glory," Dashiell finished for her. "You're right. Orvil seems to have spent both his human and vampire lives as a borderline con artist who trades on his brother's reputation and burns through money as fast as he can get it."

"The skinners who attacked in California and Colorado definitely work for Adelaide," Abigail added, "not Orvil. Most of them are connected to her from way before she started seeing him."

"So who hired her?" This was Jesse.

"Ah." Abigail's smile was a little smug, like she'd been hoping for just this opening. "That's what I've spent today figuring out."

She clicked her mouse, and the projected image became a new screen, which filled with a collage of documents. "As soon as I started digging through Preston's most recent invoices and payments, I hit a massive knot of shell companies and routing codes," she said. "I had to untangle everything to find out who paid Preston for her most recent jobs."

She said this with well-earned pride, clicking the button again. Another photograph filled the wall, a wide shot of a man in a dark coat on a busy city street at night.

I didn't recognize him, but most of the group reacted—Eli, the werewolf, let out a small growling noise, and both Quinn and Maven went rigid, forgetting to pretend to be human. Scarlett muttered something that sounded like, "fuckity fuck."

"I was able to confirm that Adelaide Preston's primary employer is Malcolm," Abigail announced. "The cardinal vampire of New York."

# 8

## LEX

A number of people started talking at once. While Dashiell was settling them down again, Quinn and I exchanged a glance. We were thinking the same thing, but I let Quinn be the one to lift his hand and speak up.

"I tried to trace financial records back to Malcolm last year," he said to Abigail, "but my experts in Denver couldn't find any evidence."

"Your experts aren't me and my family," she said simply. "This is what the Haynes do."

He blinked for a moment before nodding, and I thought I understood what she meant. I'd heard of human families were were inextricably linked to a vampire, over many generations. If the Haynes took care of Dashiell's money, of course Abigail would have insight into how to trace another vampire's finances.

Maven was looking thoughtfully at the projection of Malcolm. "I did hear that Orvil Grant is close to him," she said almost to herself.

"If Malcolm wanted to send a team to kill nulls, but didn't want anyone to be able to trace it to him, asking Orvil to put him in touch with Adelaide is a good plan," Dashiell added. He looked at Abigail Hayne, who was unceremoniously closing her laptop. The wall projection went to blue. Clearly the presentation part of the meeting was over.

"Thank you, Abby. I'd be grateful if you could stick around for a little while in case we have more questions. Alejandro can get you something to eat in the kitchen."

"Yeah, I figured." Abigail turned and wheeled out of the room without another word. Dashiell resumed his stance at the front of the room.

After she'd left, no one spoke for a long moment. My thoughts were racing, and I jumped in my seat when Quinn touched my hand. I looked over, and he mouthed, "Are you okay?"

Shit. My pulse must have picked up. Which meant every vampire in the room knew that I was fucking terrified. And the werewolf, although he looked pretty irate himself.

"Malcolm tried to *kill* Charlie," I said, enunciating every word, not caring that everyone else would hear.

"Yeah." Quinn squeezed my hand.

Of course it had crossed my mind that Malcolm might one day want to replace his pet null with my niece. But I'd always assumed he would try to take her and keep her alive and healthy, which would give me a chance to bring her back or die trying. I'd never once, even in my nightmares, expected him to try to kill her.

"Sam?" Quinn murmured. He knew me so well.

I shook my head. This was a bombshell, but my sister/spirit guide was silent. That meant either she didn't have anything to contribute, or she was planning to talk to me later in my dreams. Or it might mean nothing at all. Sam's presence in my thoughts didn't exactly come with an instruction manual.

"We should have done something about him *years* ago," The werewolf, Eli, spat the words. He looked at Scarlett. "Corry almost died, too."

"I know," she said quietly, and some kind of current passed between them that I didn't really understand.

There was a gentle buzz, and Dashiell took a cell phone from his pocket, checked the screen, and returned the phone.

"You know, I understand trying to kill me," Scarlett said. "I mean, I'm an acquired taste. And I could see Malcom deciding I corrupted Jameson, or whatever, and wanting revenge. But why kill a little kid?"

I glanced sideways at Maven. "Perhaps now would be a good time to share what we've discovered," she said clearly. Then, unfortunately, she nodded at me.

Crud. I looked at Dashiell, raising my voice. "We believe the person who hired the skinners—Malcolm—found out that Scarlett can turn vampires permanently human."

Pretty much everyone had a reaction to that, but I was watching Scarlett. She looked so bruised and shrunken, leaning against Jesse's shoulder. It took a moment for her to process my words, but then she blinked. The penny dropped. "Oh fuck," she said conversationally.

"Yeah." As briefly as I could, I told them about Sashi and Will's visit early that morning. There were some glances I didn't really understand, especially from Kirsten and Eli, but I kept my focus on Jesse, who looked pale, and Scarlett, whose lower lip trembled.

When I was finished, Dashiell sighed. "So Malcolm knows she can take away magic, but he doesn't have any details about how it works. He must think all nulls are capable of it."

"And he wouldn't want the parliament to have access to that

power," Maven put in. "Imagine if we could just strip magic away from any werewolf or vampire who crossed us."

"That's not how it works," Eli said, sounding annoyed. "It affects Scarlett. She has seizures, her radius shorts out, that kind of thing."

There was a very brief, very uncomfortable pause, which probably had to do with just how much Eli seemed to know about this.

Then Maven picked up the conversation. "But Malcolm doesn't know that part," she said. "Or he doesn't care—in his mind, Scarlett's physical health would be a small price to pay for that kind of power. He can't let us hold that kind of leverage over him."

I expected Scarlett to jump in and complain about everyone talking about her as though she wasn't there, but the null was silent. She looked especially pale, which made the bruises under her eyes stand out.

Jesse must have also been surprised by her silence, because her turned in his seat to focus completely on her. "Scar? Are you okay?"

She swayed in her seat for a moment, then seemed to rally herself. "Can we fucking kill the shit out of this fucker already?" she blurted.

Quinn, of all people, let out a sharp burst of laughter, which he tried and failed to disguise as a cough. Everyone looked at him, and he held up a hand apologetically. "Sorry. That's, um, not how we usually phrase things."

"But it's certainly one way to put it," Maven replied. "More to the point, I'm not sure I disagree with the sentiment."

"Same," I said. Jesse looked at me questioningly, wanting an explanation. "It's not just about wanting Charlie safe," I explained, both to him and the rest of the room "With or without evidence, *I'm* convinced that Malcolm was behind the attack on Colorado's witches, which resulted in the death of the state's leader."

"He and I had run-ins in New York when I was first changed," This was Eli again. He had to be close enough to Scarlett to be in her radius, but even as a human his voice was filled with rage, and his hands were now bunched into fists in his lap. "Last summer he sent a vampire here to destabilize the pack."

"And he killed Jameson, and almost certainly Rhys," Scarlett said, her voice surprisingly strong. She was sitting up again, her bruised face hard. "I know none of you care about nulls outside your territory, but I do. It matters." She was clenching her fists, and beside me, Quinn and Maven both gasped, clutching their chests. I knew this particular reaction—they were human again.

Right. Nulls expand their circle of non magic when they get upset. I'd known that, but I hadn't seen it since Charlie's last temper tantrum at my house.

"Sorry," Scarlett covered her mouth as though she'd just belched in public. "I was holding it in, but I'm having a hard time."

"I think I'd prefer to simply stay human than risk a number of rapid changes," Maven said, not unkindly. "Please do relax."

The null nodded gratefully and sank back in her seat.

Dashiell said, "So we're in agreement then."

Maven nodded. "If the Old World has one rule, besides the need for secrecy, it's that we don't kill each other. Malcolm has murdered many times over, and not just his rivals—anyone who he perceives as a threat. The time has come to end his reign."

There were murmurs of agreement throughout the room. "Wait, so you're going to just *assassinate* him?" Jesse Cruz broke in. The whole group turned to him. "Look, I want to stop

Malcolm as much as anyone—he very nearly killed people I love today, including my fiancé."

Something flashed in his face, an anger I hadn't seen before. Malcolm did seem to bring out a certain side of people. "But if we just murder him like it's nothing," Jesse continued, "how are we any better? How are we obeying the Old World's one rule?" He turned to speak directly to Maven. "And, with respect, ma'am, what kind of government can you build on that?"

She didn't answer right away, just looked at him with renewed interest. There was a moment of silence, which I used to take stock of everyone's reactions. Quinn, Dashiell, and Eli all had similar, condescending expressions. They obviously thought Jesse was being naive but wanted to let a beat go by to acknowledge him before shooting him down. Scarlett and Kirsten were thoughtful. And Maven…even now, when she was human, I couldn't quite read her.

It was Dashiell's meeting, but his eyes were on my boss. We all waited while Maven considered Jesse's question. A long, long minute ticked by on the wall clock over the computer bank.

"You're right," she said finally. "I'm tempted to say, 'from the mouth of babes,' but of course you're not a child, Detective Cruz. And not a detective anymore, either," she added, seeing him opened his mouth to correct her. "I'm aware. But that has been your role here, yes? You support your asset and help solve the puzzles. Just like Quinn does in Boulder." She turned pointedly toward Dashiell. "Puzzles that seem quite small at first, but bely a much larger potential crisis."

Dashiell's jaw clenched, and I saw what she was doing. Jesse wasn't Scarlett's plus one, and whether it was an unconscious or a political choice, Maven wasn't going to let the LA vampire get away with acting like he was. Reminding him of Jesse's skill set also forced Dashiell to consider the ex-cop's words more carefully.

I really liked my boss.

After a moment, Dashiell nodded stiffly, and Maven continued. "At the moment, though, *how* we hold Malcolm accountable for his actions isn't even the issue."

She paused to take a breath, and Eli, of all people, finished the thought for her. "It's New York."

"Yes. Malcolm has held that city in thrall for generations now. He's killed or exiled everyone who's ever crossed him, including all werewolves"—Maven tilted her head to acknowledge Eli—"and anyone who dared to leave his service." She looked at Scarlett. The null had her head down, and I saw tears falling onto her lap. Jesse put his arm around her.

"Dashiell and I, and probably many others before us, have looked at possible ways to attack Malcolm in his stronghold," Maven went on. "We've both concluded that there's no way to do so without so many casualties that we'd risk exposure to the human world. That's how well-defended he is."

"Then the only solution," drawled a voice from the doorway, "is to draw him out of his city."

Everyone turned sideways to see the newcomer. I heard myself let out an involuntary sigh as he grinned at me. "Hi, Beau," I said tiredly.

"Everyone, this is Abner Beaumont Calhoun," Dashiell announced, "the cardinal vampire of Atlanta."

Beau grinned at me, his large handlebar mustache sticking out like broom bristles. "Good evening, Miss Lex," he said as he strolled through the room toward us. He was a short man who always dressed like he was about to jump on a dressage horse. Tonight he wore a spotless white linen dress shirt, black riding pants, and tall boots. "Fancy seeing you here."

"Nice timing, Beau," I said, not bothering to keep the skepticism from my voice.

Scarlett let out a snort. "Not really. He's been outside the door for like five minutes waiting for a good entrance line."

Ah. Dashiell's text had probably been about the Georgian vampire's arrival. As much as I knew Beau enjoyed a dramatic entrance, I suspected the delay had less to do with him waiting for a good line and more to do with him not wanting the rest of us to see him react to a null.

Now Beau raised an eyebrow at Scarlett, and for a moment I wondered if his famous temper was about to flare. But he gave her his charming Southern gentleman smile. "You've caught me out, my dear. I daresay you must be Scarlett Bernard."

She looked at him blearily. "I hope so, I'm wearing her underwear."

There was a muffled snort, and when I glanced around Eli, Jesse, and even Quinn seemed to be suppressing smiles. I'd probably missed another pop culture reference. "I like your boots," Scarlett added to Beau. "Frye?"

"Lucchese."

"Nice."

Dashiell cleared his throat, and Beau turned toward him. "It's good to meet you in person, Dashiell. I appreciate the invitation. And I apologize for my late arrival—Maya, my assistant, couldn't reach me until after sunset, of course, and then I had to get to the airport. At least the time zones worked in our favor."

I couldn't help myself. "Not to be rude, but why *are* you here, Beau?" I almost asked who was watching Atlanta for him except I already knew the answer. It would be Milburn or Vick, his closest surviving friends. Or maybe both of them.

He winked at me. "My insider knowledge, I suspect. I met many of General Grant's boys at Kennesaw Mountain. I don't know Orvil personally, but I know a few of his acquaintances, and I'm quite familiar with the Galena area." He looked at Maven and gave a small bow. "And I do believe I owe this lady a favor."

Maven smiled pleasantly, but said, "It's Lex who's owed the favor. And you might want to show her you can be useful before you offer to return it."

Her tone was gentle, but I didn't miss the subtle reminder: get to the point.

Beau gave her a courtly nod, not missing it either. "Of course, madam. Where was I?"

"You suggested getting Malcolm out of New York." This was Eli, who looked frustrated. "But from everything I've heard, he hasn't left the five boroughs in decades. He's like a spider who never leaves the web."

"That's true," Beau allowed. "There's no reason to, when he has already killed everyone who objected to him."

"I don't understand that," Quinn said next to me. "Why has this guy been allowed to run his city like this?"

"There was never anyone to stop him," Maven said matter-of-factly. "Not since the Concillium fell."

I winced. The world's only boundary magic conduit, Lysander, had been the one to kill off the last Old World governing body. He also happened to be my birth father, though I tried not to think about that.

Eli grumbled something about werewolves being exiled from the city under his breath.

"What about the vampires who work for him?" Kirsten asked, looking around the room. "I know they're bound by oaths, but surely if they'd wanted to, they could have found a way to turn against Malcolm."

"That's true." Beau turned to her. "And I suspect they would have done just that—except he's never left strong evidence of his actions."

Next to me, Quinn was nodding. "Most people suspect he's done these things, but without hard evidence, Malcolm and his supporters could always explain it away." We'd seen that ourselves—when we tried to prove Malcolm's involvement with Morgan Pellar, we could only ever find rumors.

Beau pointed at him, smiling broadly. "Ah, you must Lex's young man."

Quinn raised an eyebrow at me, as if to say *young man?* I just shrugged. Quinn had only been turned in the nineties. To a Civil War-era vampire, he probably did seem pretty young.

"Yes," Beau continued, "you're correct. I believe Malcolm *enjoys* having the whole country know what he's done, with no real way to prove it. It lets him keep the waters muddy and his supporters in New York happy." He turned to Dashiell. "But for the first time in my *very* long memory, he's made a mistake. Two mistakes, really."

"Letting witnesses live, so we could identify Adelaide Preston and follow her trail back to him, that's one," Dashiell said, frowning. I tried not to think about how "witnesses" referred to my niece and her protectors. "What's the second?"

"Not a what, but a who," Beau answered. "I believe you already mentioned Orvil Grant, Miss Preston's romantic partner?"

Almost idly, Dashiell reached over and opened Abigail's laptop, pressing a few keys until the projection turned on again. The wall filled with the photo of Adelaide and Orvil on the street. "Yes."

"Ah, of course." Beau sauntered over to the wall and reached up so he could tap on the image of Orvil, his shadow making it look like an assault. "Malcolm's second mistake was getting Orvil involved."

He clearly wanted someone to ask, so I did. "Why's that, Beau?"

Beau turned to look at his audience, his big *ta-da* moment. "Orvil is, so far as I can tell, the only vampire Malcolm has ever turned himself. My sources say Malcolm considers him his true son and heir."

All around me, people reacted, sucking in air and shifting in their chairs. Even Quinn.

"That's not common knowledge," Dashiell said thoughtfully. I took that to be vampire politics-speak for "I didn't know that."

"No it's not," Maven said. Even she looked surprised. "Everyone senses that the two are allied in some way, but the contacts I've spoken to think they are friendly because Orvil has no interest in being a cardinal vampire. I'm sure Orvil and Malcolm cultivate that rumor, or something similar." She looked at Beau. "Truly, this is information worth knowing, Mr. Calhoun. Thank you."

Beau sort of scuffed his boots on the floor, looking pleased —and was he even blushing a little? I'd never seen Beau human before, but he seemed almost in awe of Maven. "Please do call me Beau, my lady."

"Okay, wait," said Eli, holding up his hands like a traffic cop. "Even if Orvil is Malcolm's pseudo son, how does that help us draw Malcolm out of New York?" He paused just long enough to blink. "You want us to kill Orvil?"

Now Maven smiled, and although she was currently human, it was all flashing teeth and the promise of violence. "Much more than that," she said. "I want us to do exactly the thing that Dashiell and I have been planning all this time."

She stood up and went to the keyboard by Dashiell, hitting the arrow keys until the wall screen showed all the bank account information again. "With this evidence, and testimony

# 9

## SCARLETT

By the time my excessively moral boyfriend was objecting to assassinating the world's most evil vampire, I was already half in love with Lex's boss, Maven.

I'd met the cardinal vampire of Colorado only once before, when Molly and I had driven to Colorado a few hours after I learned I was pregnant. Within the space of that day, I had met Lex's niece, spoken to the most powerful vampire I'd ever heard of, and been called back to LA to save Jesse before the Luparii could kill him with magic. It wasn't that Maven hadn't made an impression, but I'd been so overwhelmed that the whole experience felt like a blur of panic and questions.

An hour into our big Old World meeting, though, I had decided I wanted to have, like, a thousand of Maven's babies. It may or may not have something to do with my severe head trauma, but I chose to believe Maven was just really fair and good. And pretty! She was very pretty.

Gently, Jesse nudged me out of this, my hundredth

daydream, and I sat up straight. I was still woozy from the really good drugs at the hospital, but I thought they were starting to wear off. Also: had Maven just said something about a trial?

"Like the Vampire Trials?" I blurted. "Because that didn't go so well last time."

Maven looked blank, and Dashiell murmured something to her in a low voice, probably along the lines of "remember that thing I told you about."

"Ah, yes," she said, nodding. "The Los Angelean custom of raising inter-species concerns in front of a tribunal. Somewhat like that, but using the parliament of Old World players. This can be our..." she waved a hand, looking at Lex. "What do you call it? Like restaurant openings?"

Lex gave her boss one slow blink, then said, "Soft opening."

"Yes." Maven turned back to the rest of us. "We can gather the members we've assembled so far and bring the trial to Orvil as a soft opening for the new parliament. We'll do it publicly, which will ensure that word gets back to Malcolm."

"Interesting idea." Dashiell was nodding slowly. "Malcolm objects to the parliament; that's his main grievance with us. He'll *have* to intervene, or he'll look like he's afraid to face us."

"How do you know he'll come himself, though?" Eli asked. Dashiell had pressed the button to return the wall-screen to the image of Malcolm, and Eli kept glancing at it. He was practically vibrating with the desire to kill the New York vampire. "Won't he just send more skinners?"

"Our evidence is strong," Dashiell said. He was using his *I'm plotting against someone* voice, all low and growly. As someone who's been on the wrong end of Dashiell's plotting, I almost felt sorry for Malcolm.

Not really, though.

"Malcolm will come," Maven said, picking up his line of thought, "because Orvil Grant and Adelaide Preston will be made to testify." She gave Eli a toothy smile. "And they know where all the bodies are buried."

It took me a second, but I caught up: Lex could press vampires, and the vampires could press humans. They were going to put Orvil and Adelaide on the stand and make them tell the truth.

Oooh, Malcolm *really* wasn't going to like that.

"Maven, I love you," I told her earnestly. Whoops. I'd said that out loud. I wanted to sleep so bad.

I felt Jesse tense in the seat next to me, but Maven's smile just softened into something good-natured. "Oh, to be young, human, and on drugs," she said mildly.

To the rest of the group, she went on, "We need to secure the nulls and confront Orvil and Adelaide as quickly as possible. I don't want to give them time to organize another strike. This one was too close."

Next to me, Jesse made a little grunt of serious agreement.

Lex's boyfriend, the Daniel Craig lookalike with the world's smallest collection of facial expressions, broke in. "If Orvil and Adelaide moves around so much, how will we find them quickly?"

The Southern vampire with the great boots was still at the front of the room, and now he broke out into a broad smile. "I can assist with that. While I don't know where Orvil is at this moment, I can tell you that in four days he will be in Galena, Illinois."

"How could you know that?" she asked.

"Because every year on the Saturday in July, vampires in the Midwestern cities gather just outside Galena for Rendezvous," he said promptly.

"What is that?" I asked.

Maven was the one to answer. "When the county was being settled by the French and British, a rendezvous was an annual celebration and market for traders and settlers to exchange goods. In the Midwest, vampires have continued the tradition."

"The local cardinal vampire hosts an annual Rendezvous," Beau explained. "An underground night market, in the middle of nowhere." He glanced at Lex, then added, "It's a popular place to buy and sell historical artifacts, including many from our nation's wars. I have attended many times in the past. Orvil never misses it."

"How can you be sure?" Quinn asked. "If he is working for Malcolm against us, won't he go to ground somewhere?"

"Just the opposite—he'll wish to appear as if everything is normal." The broad smile turned wry. "Besides, I don't think he could stay away if he wanted to. Orvil spent much of his life enjoying Ulysses's fame and glory by proxy. Now there's no one to contradict Orvil's stories. He's far too narcissistic to pass up a weekend of unfettered adoration."

Lex was frowning at him, although I could probably count on one hand the times I'd seen her *not* frowning. "Hang on a minute," she said. "I understand not wanting to go to New York to go after Malcolm. But if we lure him to some little town in Illinois, how do we know it'll be any better?" She looked at her boss. "It's still not our territory, and Orvil will have insider knowledge of the town."

"It is still dangerous," Maven conceded, "but I can't imagine a scenario where Malcolm will set foot in Colorado or LA, even with Orvil at risk. This isn't perfect, but we're not going to get a better chance at him."

"Getting the consent of the local cardinal vampire is going to be imperative," Dashiell said, in one of his bossy voices. He had a whole collection.

"Who is the cardinal vampire?" I asked. Yay me, participating in the conversation. I knew from experience that the Old World was a territorial place. It was one thing to go on an off-duty, short vacation somewhere with the humans in your life. But if you're going to mess around with vampires, you need permission. I'd had to do the same thing on a weekend trip to Las Vegas.

Maven was strong enough to do pretty much whatever she wanted, but this was her attempt at starting a government. It made sense that she wanted to do things by the book... even if the book was more of a handful of unwritten rule.

Several people started to answer, but Beau who got there first. "Julien Dubuque," he said. "He first came to the territory in the 1700s as a trader. I don't know him well, but he's always struck me as a man willing to make a bargain."

Lex nodded, her face unreadable. "So we get the permission, grab Orvil, and get everyone to Galena for the trial. Then hopefully Malcolm shows up and we...what?"

"Ideally," Maven replied, "we put him on trial as well. But that's assuming he would consent to that." She turned to Dashiell. "You and I should talk about how to handle Malcolm and his security, but that might be a longer conversation."

Lex's hot boyfriend waited for his boss to stop talking, then lifted an index finger for attention. "This is going to be very complicated logistically," he said. "Four days isn't very long to get everyone in the parliament to Galena. Plus, we need to find a location in that area where we can hold the trial," Quinn went on. "We're not going to be able to keep all that travel secret, especially with so many other vampires in Galena at the same time. What's to stop Orvil from skipping town the moment he gets wind of our arrival?"

"Lex," Maven replied.

Out of the corner of my eye, I saw the Colorado witch give a little start. "Me?"

Maven turned to her. In my radius, she looked like someone I might hire to babysit Annie, but she addressed the ex-soldier like a general. "Quinn is right, it will take a few nights to organize travel for the whole parliament—but you can get to Galena much more quickly. You can speak to the cardinal vampire in charge of the area, and press Orvil not to leave town," she said.

"We can send a vampire along as well," Dashiell added, "to press Adelaide and start making some of the lodging arrangements."

The vampire with the Colonel Sanders mustache touched the brim of an imaginary hat. "I believe that's my cue. I do so hate owing favors."

"Don't you like, run a town?" I blurted. "How can you be away from Atlanta for so long?"

He raised a smug eyebrow at me. "I have my own trusted companions, Miss Bernard."

"Call me Scarlett," I told him, not caring that my voice came out all crabby. "Miss Bernard is my bargest."

Lex ignored this exchange, but she still looked uneasy. "I don't know about this. I've pressed pretty strong vampires before, but never to last several days like that."

"I have every confidence in you," Maven told her.

My head drifted down to Jesse's shoulder again. The good drugs were starting to wear off, replaced by a screaming headache that pressed down on my skull like an anvil.

I raised my hand for Dashiell's attention, mostly because I was too tired to shout. He nodded at me. "How soon do the rest of us leave?" I asked.

Dashiell's eyes slid to Jesse, which annoyed me more than I had words to express. "I think you should take Annie and go to the safe house," Jesse said, speaking to me, but loudly enough for the whole room to hear. "I can help the team in Illinois."

I stared at him for a long moment, ignoring the murmurs and shifting bodies around us. "I understand why you had to try," I told Jesse, forgiving him. "But Malcolm isn't going to stop coming until I'm dead, along with Corry and Charlie. We have to take our best run at him, and that means having a null along. They'll need one for the trial anyway, if it's going to work like the Vampire Trials here in LA."

I turned to face the rest of the room, since they were all listening anyway. "Rhys is dead, Charlie is a little girl, and Corry just watched her friend die in front of her eyes. Anyway, she's not a fighter."

"Are you?" Beau asked, raising one eyebrow.

Jesse shifted nervously in his seat. Ignoring him, I pushed away thoughts of my aching everything and looked at Dashiell first. He did the next best thing to rolling his eyes, but he nodded.

Quick as a flash, I had my emergency throwing knife out of the boot sheath and into the air. It sailed through the air into the light from the projector and *chonked* into the drywall—right in the middle of Malcolm's forehead.

None of the LA people reacted, having seen me practice, but I thought Lex and her boss looked a little impressed.

"Okay, some of them are going home," Jesse muttered under his breath. I shot him a sideways grin. God, I loved him.

Beau was staring at the wall with his eyebrows about as high as they could go. "I see," he said.

"No, I'm not a great fighter," I told him. "But I have a handful of tricks that I'm great at. Even hurt, I'm the best option."

"She's right," Dashiell said in a low voice. Next to him, Maven was watching us quietly, not missing a thing, but not interfering. We weren't her people to command, but she was interested in how Dashiell operated.

I looked at Dashiell. "But I want protection for my brother and his family," I told him. "I'm not going unless I know they'll be safe." Jesse's parents were on vacation in Australia, thank goodness, and his brother Noah was shooting on location in Vancouver.

The cardinal vampire nodded, and I could tell he'd been expecting this. "I will make sure."

The cardinal vampire checked his watch, which probably cost more than my van. "Before we iron out the details of this trip, why don't we all adjourn to the patio for a short break? I'll have Alejandro serve some refreshments."

There were agreeable noises from the vampires. Its always funny to see powerful, ancient magical beings get excited to eat Oreos because they're near me.

Tentatively, I pushed my radius out, expanding it to include most of the building. It didn't seem to affect my headache in any way, so I did my best to leave it there. This was like trying to force a song to keep playing in your head when you were distracted by other sounds, but I tried.

Everyone had started filing out of the room, but I waited to go last, and kept my eyes fixed on the floor. I didn't want to deal with Kirsten's worried look, or whatever passive-aggressive facial expression from Eli. I also didn't want anyone watching me try to walk.

Jesse had argued hard for a wheelchair, but I'd insisted that my legs worked fine, and I wasn't going to let a bit of vertigo and some bruising prevent me from moving on my own power. This meant, however, that I had to walk leaning on Jesse's arm like one of those Victorian women trying not to pass out from corsets.

Everyone else went through the house and out to the courtyard in the center of the property, but I directed Jesse to veer down the hallway to one of the first-floor bedroom suites. I wanted to visit the mansion's *other* guests.

Part of me had hoped Annie might be awake for some weird

baby reason, but the door hadn't even swung all the way open before I saw her sprawled out on the king-size four-poster bed, snoring gently. I grinned. At seven months, Annie often slept in starfish position, which made it look like my tiny daughter was trying to take up as much room as possible. Good for her.

"Scarlett." Corry, who'd been leaning against the headboard, closed the iPad she'd borrowed to watch movies. She set it down and swung her legs to the floor, looking at me worriedly. Jesse had picked her up from the airport that afternoon without any luggage, so she was wearing a pair of my pre-baby jeans and one of my T-shirts, her hair bound in a tight French braid.

I just stood there for a second, looking at her. She'd showered at our house—there had been some of Louisa's blood in her hair—and as she stood up and stretched I caught a whiff of baby shampoo and my laundry detergent. I'd come so close to losing her. I felt sorry for Louisa, and for Molly, who had learned about her friend's death at sunset and was already on her way up to Berkeley to keep an eye on the other three baby vampires.

"How did it go?" Corry asked now.

"It's still going, I think, but there's a plan. The beginning of a plan. But we're taking a break for food," I said. "Are you hungry? I could stay with Annie if you want to grab something."

"No—Jesse got us In 'N Out on the way from the airport... remember?" I saw Corry's eyes slide over to my partner.

"Of course I remember," I lied. Maybe I did have sort of a fuzzy recollection of a drive-through, but I wasn't going to let Jesse see that I was struggling to recall it. "But you're a college student. Your kind is always hungry."

Corry rolled her eyes and dropped back onto the edge of the bed, scooting close to Annie so there was enough room for me to sit near the head of the bed. "Here, sit. What can you tell me?"

Carefully, I lowered myself to the bed, leaned against the headboard, and let myself relax. I still didn't look at Jesse. I couldn't deal with his worry face right now. "I'm not going to go into detail, but we think we know the guy behind everything, and there's a plan to go after him."

I expected relief, but Corry's face hardened. "What can I do?"

"You can stay safe," Jesse said quietly. He was standing with his back to the wall, not too far from the closed bedroom door, like he planned to get the jump on anyone who burst in. Dashiell's place had to be the safest building in LA County, but I appreciated the sentiment.

"They killed Louisa," Corry said through clenched teeth. "I don't want to stay safe. I want in."

I try to treat Corry like an adult, but this time I couldn't help myself. I lifted my hand to her cheek. "That's not you, sweetheart."

Corry flinched from my hand. "I wasn't—I can help!"

"You *can* help," I promised. "I need you more than anyone. I want you to get somewhere safe with Jesse and Annie while I go get this guy. You're the only other person who can keep her magic contained."

Both of them started to argue at the same time. I heard Corry's opening statement "I can be more than a babysitter," but then Jesse's voice caught my attention. As usual.

"There's no way in hell you're going there without me," he said. The sentence didn't surprise me, but his face did. He was wearing the flat, emotionless mask I always associated with his police work. I couldn't remember when I'd last seen it applied to me.

"I need you with our daughter." As the words left my mouth

I was distracted by my radius. On the other side of the door, two people were approaching, a witch and a vampire.

"Our daughter," Jesse said, pushing off the wall, "needs her mother. And her mother is hurt. I swear to God, Scarlett, I will handcuff you to a bed before I stay behind on this one. I'm not fucking around."

I sighed, feeling exhausted and dizzy. He had really good cop handcuffs, too. Raising my voice, I replied, "You want to open the door so Lex and Quinn can join this conversation?"

# 10

## SCARLETT

Jesse blinked at the interruption to his rant, but he went over and opened the door.

Lex was standing in the doorway with her back straight and her boyfriend at her shoulder. "Hey," she said, and sort of soft-punched Jesse on the arm, a brotherly hello gesture. Then she looked at the baby on the bed and made a soft, very non-Lex noise.

"This is Annie," I said. "Don't worry, she can sleep through anything. It's her baby superpower....well, along with her actual superpowers."

"She's beautiful."

I followed her gaze, and for just a moment, allowed myself to drink in the sight of my daughter. She had Jameson's long limbs and natural hair, which I was learning how to care for as it got longer. She loved to babble and clap and was just starting to laboriously creep along the floor after Shadow. She'd only started solid foods a month ago, but already preferred it to nursing so much that my milk had dried up. I wasn't sorry to be done feeling like a cow, but I did miss the cuddling.

"Thank you," I said to Lex.

"How did you know it was us at the door?" Quinn asked me.

I waved a hand. "I recognized the...well, 'signature' isn't the right word, but something along those lines. And there aren't a lot of vampire-witch pairs running around." I didn't mention that Lex's boundary magic had a darkness to it, like black licorice flavor. If she didn't already know, I sure as hell wasn't going to be the one to tell her.

"Is the meeting back on?" Jesse asked them.

"Informally," Quinn said. "Dashiell and Maven are plotting and eating Oreos together."

Lex actually gave a tiny smile. "At one point Dashiell started setting out cookies to represent all the different players, and then Eli ate two of them, and now it's a whole thing."

"That sounds entertaining." If I wasn't so tired and hurt, I'd get some popcorn and go watch.

Lex looked at Corry, who was still sitting on the bed, looking awkward now. "Hi. I'm Lex."

"Oh." I said, feeling dumb. "Shit, right. Corry, this is Lex, the boundary witch from Colorado. Lex, this is Annie's godmother, Corry. She's a null too."

The two women shook hands. Corry looked a little intimidated.

"Anyway." Lex cleared her throat. "There are a lot of details to go through, but it sounds like they're putting us into two teams to go to Galena." Was I imagining things, or did her face pucker a little with dissatisfaction? "I'm going to fly out tomorrow with the first group."

That surprised me a little. "Tomorrow? I know Dashiell's in a hurry, but that seems fast."

She shrugged. "We need to get clearance from the local

cardinal vampire, and I need to start laying some of the city's ghosts if I'm going to be able to operate there at all."

Quinn glanced at Lex. It might have been the drugs talking, but I thought there was a wave of tension in the air between them. "Beau and his assistant Maya are also going with the first team," Quinn reported, "so they can start getting everyone lodging and dealing with logistics."

Right. Vampire travel is complicated. They can get around on airplanes by traveling in private, sun-tight jets or riding commercial in coffins, but hotels are another matter. You need somewhere dark and secure, but you also need secrecy about it.

"What about you?" Jesse asked Quinn. He had probably sensed the same awkwardness I had; he was good at that kind of thing.

"I have to stay with Maven," Quinn said evenly. "She hasn't left Colorado in years, and she doesn't have partners or surrogates the way the other cardinals do. We need to keep it quiet until the last minute."

"When is the trial actually going to happen?" Jesse asked.

"Hopefully Friday, since the Rendezvous is on Saturday," he replied. "Either way, Maven and Dashiell will fly in at sunset the night of the trial."

Despite all the Zoom meetings we'd both been in, that had to be the most words I had ever heard Quinn string together.

"But that's only three nights from now," Lex said to him. "I don't think we'll be ready."

He reached for her hand, squeezed it, and let go again. "Then we'll do it Saturday night, well away from Rendezvous, while all the other vampires are distracted." To us, he added, "Beau says most vampires arrive at sunset Saturday night, and are gone by dawn, either out of town or in hiding. They all love Rendevous, but they don't trust each other. Orvil is the exception, because he likes to strut around town for a few days."

"When do you leave?" I asked Lex.

She grimaced. "Early tomorrow morning. I'm part of the first team, along with Beau, Maya, and Laurel Knox."

I blinked. Laurel was a witch in Las Vegas. I considered her an ally, but she wasn't exactly inner circle. "Laurel's coming?"

"And some of her sisters, yes. They're going as contractors, basically, to help clear people out of the town. It's tourist season there, and we don't want collateral damage."

I opened my mouth to ask what that had to do with Laurel, but Jesse, who'd been studying his phone for the last couple of minutes, looked up. "Galena is prone to floods," he reported, holding up the phone.

"Ah." I closed my eyes for a moment, leaning back against the headboard. If there was going to be any kind of fight between vampire groups, getting as many bystanders out of town as possible was a great idea.

"Wait, that's it?" Corry looked back and forth between all of us, like she was waiting for a punchline. "Two small teams? That's not many people. Why aren't we sending *everyone*, like when you went against the Wild Hunt?"

Lex started to answer, but I overrode her. "First, because three cardinal vampires is already a hell of a lot of firepower, and second, because we can't leave Colorado and LA that vulnerable. That's why Dashiell and Maven aren't coming until the last minute."

"There's also an optics issue," Lex added. "If we have to send an army to deal with two people, the parliament looks weak before it even gets started."

"But Malcolm—"

"Is a third person, yes," Lex said gently. "But we can't make it look like we're expecting Malcolm."

Corry looked disappointed and scared, but she fell silent. Jesse came over and put his arm around me where I sat. I found myself leaning into him. He tilted his head down to murmur into my ear. "We need to get you back to the hospital."

"I don't—"

"You promised me," he said, loud enough for everyone to hear. "You swore you would go back until the doctor signs off on your release. Wyatt's going to press the staff to get you back in."

"The meeting isn't over." I was whining. I could hear it.

"Actually…" We all looked at Lex, who seemed strangely hesitant. "Scarlett, there's something I wanted to talk to you about before you go." She eyed the men for a second, and I realized just how crowded the bedroom felt. I reached up and patted Jesse's hand where it sat on my shoulder. "Jesse, could you and Quinn give us a minute?"

Quinn did the thing where he checked in with Lex using secret couple eye contact, but Jesse shrugged and said, "You want to see Dashiell's cars?"

I had never cared about Dashiell's collection of sports cars, but Jesse and Hayne talked about them sometimes. Quinn was so interested that he actually made a facial expression. The two men headed toward the door.

Corry stood up to follow them out, but I caught her wrist. "Hang on, kid. You're staying for this talk."

Corry looked at me with wide eyes. But I had a feeling I knew what Lex was going to say, and it would make more sense for Corry to be present.

I waited for the door to close behind the men, then waved at the bed. "Do you want to sit?" I asked Lex.

"I'm fine here." The boundary witch glanced at Corry.

Oh. It was going to be *that* kind of talk. "Anything you can say to me, etc," I said tiredly.

Lex nodded, pushed out a breath. "I assume you have a safe place for Annie," she began. "With protection."

"Yeah, you could say that." Jesse and I had come up with a number of emergency plans over the years, but Malcolm trying to kill nulls was probably the most dangerous scenario I could imagine. I was going right to my very best option, which I'd been saving for, basically, the apocalypse. "I own a small property under a made-up identity," I told Lex, choosing my words carefully. "Abby helped me set it up a couple years ago, and she got rid of the paper trail. Then she consented to being pressed to forget the details."

Lex nodded. "Do you visit often?"

She wanted to know if someone could have observed me going back and forth. "Nope. I've never even been there in person. Even Jesse doesn't know the exact address." We had learned a few things from our encounter with the Luparii.

Lex nodded, looking relieved. "I want to know if Charlie and John can go with Annie," she said simply. "Maven gave John some ID and a clean credit card to get through tonight, but I need to give him a destination later when he checks in, and just in general, John could use some help staying hidden." She paused, then added, "I could use some help."

Oof, that had to cost her.

Heroically not saying that out loud, I looked at Corry. "You wanted to be more than a babysitter? There's a six-year-old null who could use your protection."

She gave me a very *teenager* look. "That's still babysitting. You can't keep sidelining me during every fight, especially when these people killed my friend." She pointed to her chest. "*My* friend. Who died to save me. You barely even knew her."

I sighed. I was so tired. "That's true. And I'm sorry I didn't know her better. But I did know her well enough to suspect she wouldn't want her death to turn you into something you're not."

Corry scoffed. "You're just trying to protect me, like I'm still a little kid."

Lex started to speak, but I overrode her, trying to keep my patience. "When you *were* a kid, yes, of course I wanted you out of danger. But now, it's not about protecting you. It's about giving everyone the job they're best at." I pointed at Lex. "She fights. Jesse fights. *I* even the playing field...and every now and then I make super mean remarks."

Lex studied her fingernails, murmuring something that sounded suspiciously like, "Sarcasm is really underrated in battle."

Corry still looked sullen. "So, what, my best skill is figuring out what to binge-watch with the B-team?"

The Tylenol wasn't nearly as helpful as the good drugs. I was hurting and cranky and, god help me, starting to look forward to the hospital bed. I snapped. "Goddammit, Corry! Stop acting like you have to be holding a weapon to be in the fight."

Corry opened her mouth to respond, but Lex broke in, surprising me. "Scarlett's right. Being on the front lines doesn't mean anything without another company backing you up. Scarlett and I can't do our jobs without someone protecting our assets."

"And our asses," I muttered, but I was kind of touched. I didn't think Lex had ever suggested I was right about anything.

For her part, Corry looked at Annie for a long moment, then nodded at me. "Okay. Fine. I'll look after my goddaughter and Lex's niece."

"And Shadow," I said. "I know she'd love to eat some bad guys, but she's hurt, and she needs to heal." I thought about it for a second, then added, "I'll send Cliff and Wyatt with you too. Daytime and nighttime coverage." I looked at Lex. "I won't be offended if you want to send your own security for Charlie. I get it."

"Thank you." She looked a little relieved. "Charlie has a

vampire bodyguard who is bound to me—Clara. And Katia can go with them as well."

"Lex's aunt," I said to Corry. "She's a boundary witch, too." To Lex, I added, "It's only a three bedroom; they might need to use that magic credit card for some air mattresses or something. But there's a—" I stopped myself from revealing any details, and finished, "A place where vampires can be safe."

Corry tried and failed to hide a smile. "Wait, if I'm counting right, that's two vampires, two kids, a bargest, a human, a null, and a boundary witch?"

"I know, right? It's like supernatural *Big Brother*. We should set up hidden cameras and sell it to Pay Per View." I smiled at the thought, but my eyes were drifting shut. My head had never hurt quite so much. It was actually drowning out the pain from my leg wound.

Lex took the hint and stood, moving toward the door. "Thank you, Scarlett. I'll see you in Galena."

"Do you want me to go get Jesse?" Corry asked me, her eyes narrowing with concern, "so he can take you back to the hospital?"

My eyes dropped to Annie, who'd managed to roll sideways and flop all the way over onto her stomach, still fast asleep. Her hair was sticking out in all directions, her perfect bow lips turned down in concentration. "Yeah…but look for him really slowly, okay?"

"You got it."

As Corry padded out of the room, I stretched out on the bed next to Annie, carefully cuddling in so I could lay on my side without putting pressure on any of my injuries. I rubbed her back gently, and Annie sighed in her sleep, content. I felt my heart swell up with Big Mommy Feelings.

I wished, not for the first time, that Jameson could see how we'd made a beautiful and perfect daughter. He and I had only had one day together, really, and Jameson had been killed right afterwards. He'd never even known I was pregnant.

Now that Scarlett seemed like a different person, and I wondered, as I often did, how fatherhood might have changed Jameson, too.

When I had first returned to LA from Las Vegas, I'd tortured myself, wondering if Jameson and I might have truly fallen in love, if he had lived. I knew better now, though—part of me had been in love with Jesse Cruz since our first case together, and despite both of our best efforts over the years, nothing had ever really broken that.

Now I knew nothing ever could. Jesse was my person.

But Jameson had been my friend, and one of the very few people on the planet who understood what it was to be a null. If he had lived, and had been able to settle safely in LA, he would have been a great dad to Annie. I liked to think we would have stayed friends, and he and Jesse would eventually become friends, too. There would have been some awkwardness and arguments, but we could have made it work as co-parents.

"Hey," came Jesse's voice from the doorway.

I started. I wasn't used to anyone sneaking up on me at Dashiell's house, since most of the people who came here were Old World. "Where's Corry?"

"I sent her to the kitchen to get some food." Jesse came into the room and perched on the edge of the bed next to where Annie and I lay. "You've got that look again."

"What look? There's no look."

"Scarlett." He reached for a piece of my hair, played with it in his fingers. "You were thinking about Jameson, weren't you?"

I was too tired, too hurt, to come up with something glib. "Yeah. I was just thinking we could have worked as co-parents, the three of us. If he'd gotten a chance." I felt a fresh, and familiar, wave of guilt.

"We've talked about this before," Jesse said gently. "His death wasn't your fault."

I shook my head, but instantly regretted it. "Ow. Yes. I know. I'm not Lex, dude. I don't blame myself for every death in my orbit. Malcolm killed Jameson, not me."

Jesse made a *I'm not buying the bravado* face. "But."

"*But*," I acknowledged, "I didn't save him either. I wasn't fast enough, or clever enough, and I missed his killer by about thirty seconds."

Jesse, to his credit, didn't say "that's ridiculous." We both knew that my feeling responsible for Jameson wasn't logical or fair, because we'd already had this conversation many times. Jesse had told me a lot about survivor's guilt and some of the feelings he'd struggled with over the years, first as a cop, and then as the human who kept surviving one disaster after another in the Old World. It had brought us closer, those talks, but they didn't change how I felt.

Instead of saying anything, Jesse kicked off his shoes and crawled onto the bed so he was behind me. He wrapped one arm around my waist, and I caught his familiar smell: Armani cologne and oranges.

Annie shifted in her sleep, tossing her head and wriggling her legs. "It's not fair," I whispered, knowing it wouldn't change anything. "It's not fair that I get to see this and he doesn't."

"Mmm." Jesse shifted a little and kissed my hair. He wasn't as tall as Jameson, which meant we fit a lot better as spoons. "You're right," he murmured. "I can't give you fair. But if we get Malcolm, we maybe get a chance at justice. Would that be enough?"

I thought about my trip to New York, years ago. Malcolm and Dashiell had been playing nice back then, but even then, I always had the impression that if I crossed Malcolm, he'd do more than just kill me. He would take the time to break me first.

And now we were going after his son—basically, a declaration of war.

Carefully, so I wouldn't move my head around too quickly, I leaned over and kissed Annie's head, squeezing Jesse's arm at the same time. My family. "Let's find out," I said.

# PART II

# 11

## LEX

"Gods above and below, Lex, this town is like vampire Disney World."

I opened my eyes and turned to look at Simon, which caused a tiny squeak from the leather airplane seat. We were flying first class, which may have been Maven's way of quietly acknowledging my claustrophobia...or she might just not realize there was any other way to fly. Money doesn't mean anything to most vampires.

"What do you mean?" I asked, trying to sound more awake than I felt. Unlike me, Simon was practically bouncing in his seat with enthusiasm. He always did love a new research project.

Simon tapped excitedly on a paragraph in his book. It was a big, glossy paperback volume about the history of the Galena area. It wasn't the kind of book you bought at airport stores, and I had no idea how he'd gotten ahold of it overnight. "In 1828, Galena—well, it wasn't called Galena yet, but the town—had its first major flood, complete with steamboats floating down Main Street. Then there were fires, like a lot of cities in the 1840s. Anyway, city officials got tired of rebuilding and started requiring new buildings to be made of brick and stone."

"Okay..." I picked up my Nalgene water bottle, which I'd refilled at the airport, and took a sip.

"Then, in 1965, they put in all these requirements about historical preservation," he went on, "way earlier than most American cities. Today more than *eighty-five percent* of buildings in Galena are on the historic registry."

I rubbed my eyes. In the last twelve hours I'd attended a major Old World summit, flown back to Denver, driven home, scrambled to make arrangements for my house and rescue animals, picked up Simon, and returned back to the Denver airport to fly to Illinois. Somewhere in there I'd grabbed about three hours of sleep, but it wasn't enough. I'd let Simon talk me into taking half an anxiety pill for the flight. It was helping with the claustrophobia, but it also made me even more tired. "I still don't get how that makes it vampire DisneyWorld."

"Because," he said patiently, "plenty of vampires today were around in the mid-nineteenth century. For them, going to Galena has to be like an immigrant visiting their home 'country' at Epcot. It's not the *same*, exactly, but comfortingly familiar."

I couldn't help smiling. Despite my exhaustion, I appreciated Simon's eagerness. It made me feel a little guilty that I'd resisted bringing him on this trip.

The night before, I'd left Scarlett in the bedroom at Dashiell's and found my way back to the outdoor patio space, which was nearly as big as my backyard. Dashiell, Maven, Kirsten, and Beau were sitting at one end of a massive oval table, working through a large platter of snacks. Eli paced next to the long oval table, his movements so fluid and unconscious that I guessed it was his regular spot. They all nodded when I came in and sat down, but they didn't pause their conversation.

"Which is why," Dashiell was saying, "we're going to need another witch along, someone who's good with wards and shielding."

"I'll go," Kirsten said immediately. To Maven, she added, "I do all the wards here."

"And she did that spell at my cabin, when the draugr was a threat," I said.

Dashiell shook his head. "I need Kirsten here. This will be the first time I've left my official post, as it were, in decades. I want you and Eli in Los Angeles, maintaining your leadership to our community."

In my peripheral vision, I saw Quinn slip out on the patio. He nodded respectfully at Maven and took the chair next to mine.

"But—" Kirsten started.

"Furthermore," Dashiell continued, with a little warning glance at her. He may have been willing to share power, but he wasn't about to share the floor. "This will be a complex delegation, with many moving parts. We need an operator."

Kirsten's mouth closed, and she seemed to consider this for the space of a few blinks. Clearly the phrase meant something to her. "All right," she said at last. "I can do that."

Dashiell nodded. "Good." To the rest of us, he explained, "Communications on this operation are a concern. I know that Malcom has access to at least one computer security specialist; we can't rule out the possibility that he has his own version of Abigail." That was a terrifying thought. "I have a supply of burner phones ready, but Abigail tells me there's not enough time to get devices that are truly impossible to breach. If you're all in contact with each other and someone's phone is stolen, or one of you is taken, the enemy may be able to track the rest of you."

He paused, and the room fell silent, everyone exchanging looks. "To prevent this," Dashiell went on, "you'll communicate with each other through our operator, Kirsten. She can connect calls between you and keep vampires updated about daytime activities." He looked at those of us who'd be going. "I'll make sure each of you gets a burner phone with the operator's number pre-programmed. Do *not* call any other numbers."

Beside me, Quinn gave me an uneasy look. I felt the same. There had always been times when we weren't able to communicate, of course—he was unavailable whenever the sun was up. But this would be multiple days, in a dangerous situation, and right after finding out about what Scarlett could do.

I reached over and squeezed his hand, hoping to reassure him.

Eli, the werewolf, stopped his pacing to glare at Dashiell. "What about me? I *have* to go with you. There's no way I'm going to miss taking a run at Malcolm."

Dashiell gave him a speculative look. "You and I can discuss that later," he said, not unkindly.

"We still need a trades witch," Maven mused.

"I have a contact who excels at warding," Beau offered. At that moment he was dunking an Oreo in a mug of milk. "I could see—"

"Wait, you can't be talking about Tallulah Finch," I broke in. I tried to sound calm, but I felt Quinn put a supportive hand on my lower back.

"You and she may have had your differences, but she was able to keep working for me after Odessa's betrayal," Beau said to me. "She's excellent at her job, and her rates are very reasonable."

"Fuck the money." My voice had risen. "I don't trust her."

"Trust is paramount on this little adventure, wouldn't you say?" Maven said to Dashiell, as though making a comment on the weather.

"Yes, I agree."

Beau shrugged, unoffended.

"Why not Lily Pellar?" I said. "She's a strong witch, and we can trust her."

"True." Maven had twisted apart an Oreo and was licking the frosting with a pensive expression. "But Lily is an essential clan leader in Colorado, and her magical strengths are more offensive," she said. "Simon is better with wards and shields."

I fought the reflex to look sideways at Quinn. Only a few months ago, Simon told me he was in love with me. I'd never really discussed it with Quinn, but he had to be aware of Simon's feelings.

"Lily's motivated to stop Malcolm, and she's stronger than ever—" I began, but I fell silent as Quinn reached over and took my hand bringing it to his lips for a brief kiss. It was barely more than platonic, but it still surprised me. We didn't do public displays of affection.

"Maven is right," he said, returning my hand to the table. He was human at the moment, like everyone else, but I still couldn't decipher his expression. "It has to be Simon. He's better at wards, and he'll watch your back when I need to stick with Maven, not to mention during the day."

"Quinn..." I began, but what could I say in front of all these people?

He smiled, but there was sadness in his eyes. "It's all right."

"Quinn..." He got like this sometimes, but I hated the martyr bullshit. And I couldn't call him out in front of these people. "Don't do that," I tried.

"We're going after the most powerful vampire in North America, present company excluded," he replied, looking into my eyes. For a moment, it felt like the two of us were alone out there, in the cool California air. Pasadena was closer to the mountains than the ocean, but it still felt tropical to me after living in Boulder for so long. "The most important thing is to use every asset we've got."

I wanted to argue more, but I could see that the more I protested, the bigger a deal it would become. I looked at Dashiell and Maven. "Okay, I'll call Simon. I'm sure he'll be happy to go after the guy who killed his mother and sister."

AND OF COURSE, he was. It was summer break at CU, and Simon had agreed to the trip with a zealousness that scared me a little. He'd been practically humming with energy all day. I might have even tried to sleep on the flight, except he'd spent the first hour regaling me with tidbits of information from the Galena book.

Now, though, Simon closed the cover and set it on the tray table in front of him. "Okay, Lex, what's going on with you?"

I blinked, forcing myself to focus on him. "Sorry?"

He leaned his head on the backrest so we were eye to eye. "Charlie wasn't hurt, was she? You didn't leave anything out of the story?"

I shook my head. "I talked to John and Clara both late last night, on an encrypted line." I'd had to pass the phone to Scarlett all too quickly, though, so she could get John the information about her "hideout." Her word. "Charlie is fine, and Clara's completely healed. They're going to be safe while we handle this."

"Then what's going on with you? You're even...." He paused, looking for the right word, and settled on, "*grimmer* than usual."

I couldn't help smiling a little at that one. "Nothing. I'm fine, Si."

"Come on, Lex," he said softly. "It's your old pal Simon here." He gave a little start, as though he'd just cracked a code. "Is that it? You don't want it to be me on this trip with you, because of...the weirdness?"

A little butterfly flock stirred in my stomach for a moment, but I ignored it. "No. Maybe a tiny bit, but no."

"Is it Quinn?" Simon wasn't stupid, and I'd had to tell him about Scarlett's ability to undo magic. "You're worried he's going to ask to become human when all this is over?"

"No. Maybe. It's not about that." Jeez. I thought of Lily as the Pellar sibling who was always in my business, inserting herself into my emotional status with her trademark filterless gusto. But Simon, in his quietly persistent way, was just as bad.

I *had* tried to talk to Quinn the previous night, while I was packing, but he'd been wildly focused on logistics, his eyes perpetually glued to his phone or computer. "I know there's been this bombshell revelation, but I can't think about it right now," he'd said, his eyes practically pleading with me to accept the lie. I knew him well enough to know that at least part of his brain couldn't think about anything else.

And he probably knew me well enough to know I didn't really want to talk about it either. So I'd let him get away with it.

Now I shifted in my seat, making the leather squeak again. "I'm trying to keep my eyes on the prize here. Malcolm is trying to kill Charlie. We've taken precautions, but how long do you think we realistically have before he finds the right pressure point and figures out where they are?" I heard the shake in my voice, hated it.

"Even if he does, they're not helpless," he said kindly. "She's got Clara and Katia, and all of Scarlett's people. You know they're going to be preparing this whole time."

"Yeah, but I'm not *there*. I'm not protecting Charlie; I'm running around pressing powerful vampires like it's my circus trick." I sighed. "Last night Scarlett talked about giving everyone the job they're best at."

"And you're best at protecting Charlie," he said, finishing my thought.

"I thought so, but maybe I was being naive. It seems like what everyone else thinks I'm best at is...you know. Death."

Very, very carefully, Simon rested his hand on mine where I was clutching the armrest. The heat and roughness of his skin surprised me for a moment—I was used to Quinn's vampire coolness. "They don't have to be mutually exclusive," he said softly. "People are complicated, and magic is even more so. It doesn't have to be a bad thing to be skilled with death magic *and* use that to protect your niece."

I shook my head. Scarlett had something similar to her protege, and I'd backed her up. But now I felt silly and helpless, and pathetically grateful for Simon's touch.

A quiet moment ticked by, and then Simon recognized its passing and returned his hand to his lap. "What happens when we get to Dubuque?" he asked me with a little smile. "I'm assuming you have a plan."

We were landing at three pm, and would have nearly five hours until sunset. "Beau and his assistant, Maya, are flying to Dubuque after sunset, but the two of them are going to run around Galena tonight and set up rooms at three or four different locations, all in Beau's name."

"Why in Beau's name?"

I gave him a thin smile. "For the cover story. The idea is to keep Maven and Dashiell's presence quiet until the trial starts. We're going to make it look like Beau is coming to town for the Rendezvous, just like he used to."

"Ah."

"Meanwhile, I have to go see the local authority," I continued. "Galena is too small in population to have much of a supernatural presence, but it's within the territory of the cardinal vampire of the upper Mississippi. His name is Julien, and he's based in Dubuque, Iowa, where we're landing. I'm going to go see him tonight to get permission to operate in Galena."

I'd asked Beau if he would come meet Julien Dubuque with me, but he'd advised against it. "Julian and I have a more complicated history that you'll want at this meeting," were his exact words. But Beau's assistant Maya had been able to set up the meeting through Julien's daytime person.

"Julien has agreed to meet me," I told Simon now, "although he won't give me a meetup location until after sunset."

Simon rolled his eyes, picking up his bottle of Perrier water and unscrewing the lid. "Oh good, Midwest vampires like power trips too."

I shrugged. "Apparently this guy is a particularly big deal in Dubuque. He founded the town or something."

Simon had been in the middle of swallowing the Perrier, and for a second it looked like he was going to do an actual spit-take, like a cartoon character. Instead his face turned beet-red and he began sputtering and coughing.

"Simon?"

"Bubbles," he croaked, still struggling to catch his breath. Glancing up, I saw the first-class flight attendant taking a few concerned steps in our direction, but I waved her off.

"Sorry," he said when he recovered. "Julien fucking Dubuque is a vampire? Seriously?"

"He's a big deal?"

"Um, in the history of late eighteenth-century French-Indian fur trading? *Hell* yes."

"Simon." I tried to sound more patient than I felt. "Why would you possibly know that?"

He shrugged, looking a little defensive. "There was a new biography of Dubuque just last year, by a university press. And I have too much free time."

"Can you give me the highlights?"

He closed his eyes, like there were bullet points on the inside of his eyelids. "Dubuque came to the Midwest when he was still in his early twenties. He started in the fur trade, which was a big industry at the time. Then he turned to mining."

"Okay..."

"Sometime in the 1780s, I think, Dubuque made a deal with the Fox Indians to mine for ore downriver. He set up his own outpost and went to the annual Rendezvous." Simon opened his eyes, frowning a little. "From what I remember, Dubuque was a skilled trader who worked mainly with Indian tribes. He supposedly used a lot of dirty tricks, like convincing the Indians he knew how to use magic...wait a minute."

I shook my head. "He couldn't have been an active witch, not if he was turned into a vampire."

He shrugged. "True. Anyway, there's a story that he told a local tribe their river itself would burn if he didn't get what he wanted. Then he put gasoline in the river and lit it."

I made a face. "Charming."

"Yeah." Simon picked up the bottle of Perrier, thought better of it, and set it back down. "We should be careful. There's surprisingly little information out there about Dubuque, for a guy who founded a city. But even when he was alive, Dubuque was considered very slippery, and very influential."

"Hmm. I'd love to know about any relationship between Orvil and Julien, but that wouldn't be in any history books." Maven hadn't had enough time to reach out to all of her contacts for gossip or rumors, so we didn't know how the two vampires felt about each other.

"No, but Julien did warrant a mention in my Galena book, see?" Simon handed me the volume, and I skimmed a few paragraphs.

"So he's cagey, he wants us at his beck and call, and he's a cardinal vampire," I mused. "Which means he's arrogant."

I handed the book back to Simon, grinning.

"What?" he asked.

I pointed to the page I'd left open, tapping on a photo. "I know where he's going to want to meet tonight."

Simon read the caption, a smile spreading across his face. "Ah. I see." He glanced sideways at me. "Are you going to be, um, armed?"

The only people nearby wore massive headphones, but I automatically lowered my voice anyway. "I brought my Glock in my checked luggage, since Iowa honors concealed-carry permits from other states. Since they're flying private, Maya and Beau are going to bring more firearms," I said. "We'll meet them after the Julien meeting. But I also brought...you know. My knitting." I reached for the backpack I'd carried on the plane, unzipping the side pocket to show him the two shredder stakes I'd packed. They were actually size-50 knitting needles that I purchased in bulk and sent to a witch in Denver, who then added the magic that created a small explosion when they were embedded in living tissue.

Regular wood through the heart could kill a vampire (or just about anything else), but it required a great deal of power to pierce the bones of the rib cage, or a very specific angle to go underneath and through the organs. Most vampires assumed a woman with human strength wouldn't be able to achieve that kind of thing, and they underestimated the stakes. No pun intended.

"There's a dozen more in my checked bag, along with the sheaths and a few other goodies."

Simon nodded. "That's good. And I'm going with you to see Julien tonight."

"You don't have—"

"Shut up, Lex," Simon said conversationally.

So I did.

# 12

## LEX

Dubuque, Iowa

Twenty minutes after sunset, Simon and I sat on a split-rail fence at the top of a small cliff within the Mines of Spain park, watching the sky turn colors over the Mississippi.

The sun had dipped below the tree line only moments earlier, so the sky was painted in shades of orange and yellow. At this elevation, we could see how the water zigzagged around small islands and tendril-like peninsulas, but we weren't quite high enough to trace where they began and ended. The effect was like looking at ribbons of land and water that had been braided together.

"This view is amazing," Simon marveled. "I'd never seen the Mississippi before. I keep thinking of all the books and songs."

I nodded absently, adjusting the bracer-style leather sheaths on my forearms. Simon and Lily had bought them for me years earlier, at some kind of fandom convention. They were designed for cosplayers to hold wands, but they happened to perfectly fit a shredder stake.

Now, though, the underside of each one was slippery with sweat. More sweat was pooled in my sports bra, under the bloodstone necklace from my mother. Iowa in July was *hot.* I hadn't sweat this much since I'd spent a summer in Baghdad.

I'd looked up the temperature before we'd left, of course, and I'd thought I packed accordingly—lightweight trail pants and tank tops, with a couple of blousy linen shirts to hide weapons or the griffin tattoos that circled my forearms from the heels of my hand to my elbows. What I hadn't expected, though, was just how much the humidity would affect me. I was used to high elevations and mountain dryness, so from the moment we first stepped out of the artificially cooled airport, I felt as though I was wading through a massive hot sponge.

Simon glanced over and saw me adjusting the buckle of one of the sheaths. "Are you sure you want to wear stakes to the meeting?" he murmured. "Won't it be considered...aggressive?"

"It sends a message, yeah, but I'm hoping the message is that I'm not trying to hide anything." I shrugged. "Besides, they didn't tell us *not* to bring weapons. They'll be expecting me to have *something*."

"Well, we wouldn't want to disappoint," Simon said good-naturedly, turning his head back to the view.

I forced myself to look in the same direction, and not at what lay at our backs: a monument and then a sidewalk that snaked through woods, leading back to the parking lot and our rental car. There were so many places for the enemy to lay in wait, especially as it got darker. I tried to look casual while ignoring the itching between my shoulder blades.

"How long do you think he'll make us wait?" Simon asked,

checking his watch. I'd been checking mine every few minutes, too. It was after nine pm.

"It depends on how desperate he is to convince us he's powerful," I said, just as a test.

"What a rude thing to say," said a dry voice about three feet behind us.

Simon jumped, half-falling off the fence. He had to put his feet down and stand up, steading himself on the top railing. I'd been expecting something like this, though, and turned my body around on the railing so I could face the shadowy form materializing out of the woods.

"Good evening, sir," I said to the cardinal vampire of the Upper Mississippi.

Dubuque did an annoyed, throat-clearing noise, but he stepped forward into the light: a short, slender man with suspicious eyes. Simon had told me there were no actual photographs of Julien Dubuque, but in life, he had been nicknamed "the Little Night," and it fit. He had dark hair and eyes against pale skin, and his whole frame seemed coiled with contained energy, like at any second he might pull out a violin and dance around as he played, tempting the devil to a contest.

Dubuque scowled at me. "You must be Maven's new errand boy. So to speak."

"Yes sir," I said easily. "I'm Allison Luther, but everyone calls me Lex. This is my friend Simon."

Simon gave a little wave. He'd positioned himself to my side and a step behind, making it clear that I spoke for both of us. "Pleased to meet you."

Dubuque frowned at me—but he kept his eyes fixed on my forehead near the hairline, never looking straight into my eyes.

Ah. So he'd heard of me. As long as his head was aimed in my general direction, I could have channeled enough boundary magic to pull his gaze toward me...but there was no need for him to know that.

"How did you know where to find me tonight?" he asked, his voice hard. "Did one of my people speak to you?"

I'd expected this question. "No one told us anything about your location. I took a guess." I gestured at the structure behind him.

This particular section of the Mines of Spain park was organized around a massive monument to Dubuque. It also happened to be his burial spot, though it wasn't like any grave I'd ever seen. The burial chamber was in the center of a single brick turret, which looked like one tower from a medieval castle had been transplanted to a cliff overlooking the Mississippi.

"We had plenty of time between arriving in the city and sunset," I said, choosing my words carefully. Vampires could usually tell when you lied to them. "I hoped this might be the meeting place you had in mind, but I also figured a view like this was worth seeing either way."

"And you were right," Simon offered. To Dubuque, he said, "It's a beautiful spot, sir."

I fought not to smile. High school Simon must have made a great impression with his girlfriends' parents.

Julien glanced at Simon for the barest second, then stared at me, probably listening to my pulse and scenting changes in my pheromones. I kept my perch on the fence, waiting. His eyes fell on the stakes strapped to my forearms, the tattoos underneath. "That's not very civilized of you," he noted.

Without hurrying, I let my feet and butt slide off the fence until I was leaning against it in a slouch, so I wouldn't be looking down at Dubuque. "Would you say civilization is an important quality in an errand boy?"

"An errand boy, yes—but not in an enforcer. Or a hired gun."

I opened my mouth to respond to that, but the vampire overrode me. "Let me ask you a question, Miss Luther. If you suspected that my memorial would also be my preferred meeting place, and you're determined to demonstrate careful respect, why not wait for my call to summon you?"

I didn't see him give a signal, but in the woods behind the memorial, I heard a twig snap. Then another, perhaps twenty or thirty feet to one side, and several more. Vampires didn't make that kind of noise unless they wanted to. Dubuque wanted us to know he had us surrounded at the edge of the cliff.

On my right, I could practically feel Simon pulling in magic, preparing a shield. But I didn't reach for boundary magic, because with vampires that was more or less the nuclear option.

"I'm short on time, and not fond of posturing," I told Julien calmly. "I *do* want to show you respect, as a guest in your territory. At the same time, though..." I stood to my full height, two inches taller than Julien Dubuque, and stared right into his eyes. "You do not get to *summon* me."

There was a long, terrible pause, and the woods went so quiet that I could hear Simon's breathing.

Then Julien took a tiny step back, relaxing a little. "Let's move this along. I have much to do tonight. Why are you here, Miss Luther?"

"Orvil Grant."

I didn't add anything else, not knowing the relationship between the two vampires. To my surprise, though, Julien let out a short bark of laughter. "That's what all this is about? *Him*?"

"My understanding is that he'll be in Galena this week for your Rendezvous."

Julien paused, as if considering whether to confirm this or

not, but after only a moment he gave a little shrug. "He comes to every Rendezvous. As far as I know this year is no different. Why?"

Simon and I had had the whole day to get ready for this meeting. I'd had time to plan my words. "A couple of days ago, Orvil orchestrated an attack on someone who is under Maven's protection. I'm here to hold him accountable. We want permission to be in your territory for the duration of that...process."

"Process," he echoed, his expression unreadable.

"Unless, of course, there's a reason why you want to protect Orvil. Are the two of you close?"

Now his eyes narrowed. "He is no friend of mine, and I didn't get this far by fighting other people's battles." He held up a finger. "But when you speak of staying in my territory, you're not just talking about you and Mr. Pellar here, are you?"

I hadn't mentioned Simon's last name. Julien had done his research, and he wanted me to know it. "Our party is bigger than just the two of us, yes."

"How big?"

I smiled and shook my head.

He bared his teeth for a second, not liking that. "What *exactly* are you asking from me?"

"Two things," I replied. "First, tell me where Orvil stays when he's in the area."

He didn't react. "And the second?"

"Turn a blind eye to Galena for the next week."

Julien bounced on the balls of his feet for a moment, thinking that over. I'd never seen a cardinal vampire do something so close to fidgeting.

Finally, he turned away, moving around the side of his monument. "Why don't we finish this conversation on the way back to your car, Miss Luther."

Without waiting for a response, he began walking quickly

toward the sidewalk leading to the parking area. Vampires loved this move.

Simon gave me a sideways look, but I just shrugged and followed Julien. If he wanted to personally escort me through the vampire-infested woods, I would take the protection. And if he decided to attack us on the walk, I thought Simon and I together could take him out first, which would likely demoralize his followers. We'd need to be close to him for that, though.

The sun was completely gone now, which turned everything that bleached blue-gray that happened in between twilight and complete darkness. I saw three separate remnants in the woods, all of them too old to be much more than a wispy human-shaped haze.

"Do you know why this park is called Mines of Spain?" Julien asked.

I was certain Simon would, but I just shook my head.

"When I arrived here in 1788, this whole area was populated by the Mesquakie Indians. I knew I would need their trade to survive the winters here, and their labor to work my mines. So I made myself very useful to them."

According to Simon's book, he'd manipulated and lied to them. But all I said was, "That must have been a very different time."

"In some ways."

We reached the beginning of the narrow sidewalk and started through the trees. Julien and I walked next to each other, which left Simon trailing a few feet behind, literally watching my back.

"When the Europeans first arrived, Spain had claimed this area, but the nearest Spaniard was in St. Louis, days away. As I expanded and my mines prospered, though, I caught the attention of the Spanish governor."

I wanted to reach up and wipe the perspiration off my face. Sun or no sun, the humidity was brutal, and just the short walk had me sweating.

"So I asked for an official government grant," Dubuque went on. "In my petition I called the area the Mines of Spain, to honor that government."

"You hedged your bets," I said.

"If you like."

My stomach churned, sudden and sickening, and I nearly stumbled on the sidewalk. The feeling had come out of nowhere, but I told myself I was just nervous about the unknown number of combatants in the dark woods. Ahead of us, the path opened into the parking lot, where there were at least streetlights.

"It worked, though," the vampire continued. "My claim to the mine was verified by the Spanish governor. When the land sold to France, and finally to the United States, the treaties guaranteed my right to keep it." We crossed onto the parking lot asphalt, and Dubuque stopped, turning to look at me. "Can you guess what happened next?"

My stomach had quieted, but something still felt *wrong*. Without understanding why, I drifted a few steps to my right. "They took it away, didn't they?"

"Indeed." Julien's voice had darkened. "To keep my territory, I had to 'die' and become a vampire. I moved my control into the shadows, and I built this city."

I wasn't listening. The thing—the thing that was wrong—was definitely ahead and to my right. But if I could pinpoint that, it meant it *was* a real thing. Or maybe a feeling?

"I know who you work for, and the control she is trying to inflict on territories that are not hers. I am not interested in yet another government showing up to take what's mine."

"She hasn't—" I began, but he overrode me.

"I want you and your *party* out of my territory. I have a Rendezvous to run. Orvil will move again in a week or two. Go after him somewhere else."

The sensation of being pulled toward something got even stronger. I *knew* this feeling; it was like a magnet in my brain. I couldn't ignore it another second.

Just for a moment, I tuned the conversation out completely. I didn't quite drop into my mindset, but I sort of reached out, with the same imaginary sensors I used to do magic.

And I felt the gleaming.

Understanding finally washed over me, as I heard Nellie's voice in my memory. *The dead. They'll begin to call to you.*

I hadn't responded to Julien's last remark, and Simon had jumped in while I was distracted. Julien turned to look at him as Simon began to say, "We mean no harm—"

Neither of them saw me drop sideways and kick in the back of both Julien's knees, forcing him to topple the ground.

He recovered quickly, rolling sideways to spring to his feet, but I had already pulled a shredder from my forearm and buried it into his left quadricep.

There was a wet, gruesome-sounding *splugh*, and a chunk of Julien's leg the size of a softball simply *disappeared* from Julien's leg. The vampire collapsed, bellowing something in French. "Lex!" Simon looked shocked.

Then, all around us, there was a rustling of pine needles and branches as vampires ran forward through the trees.

# 13

## LEX

The first time the recently dead cried out for me, I was in Chautauqua Park, running with a couple of my dogs. That body had been a complete stranger—a retired professor who'd collapsed of a heart attack. But his... whatever you want to call it, his soul or life force or whatever, had still hovered over him, a sickly yellow cloud that had begged for my attention. Even then, I'd had the impression that it wanted something from me, something hard to put into words: justice, peace, rest.

It *wanted* to be found.

The second time the dead had called me, it was someone I knew, at least a little: Becca, the security expert that Beau had hired to keep tabs on his niece, Odessa. Odessa had poisoned both of us, but because of my boundary magic blood, the poison hadn't killed me. Instead, I'd watched Becca die, both of us paralyzed and helpless, and then I'd passed out. I woke up to find Becca's wispy yellow ghost waiting.

Both times, though, I had felt the body's pull long before I'd been able to see it, like magnetic attraction. With Becca it had felt familiar, like a voice I recognized on the phone. Now I recognized it again, and I felt a fury so strong it was like being possessed.

The vampires in the woods began to rush us. "Simon, the shield!" I yelled, but my friend was already dropping into a crouch. His fingers touched the circle of black chalk we'd drawn on the parking lot hours earlier, activating the spell. A transparent half-dome shield shimmered to life around us.

The previous spring, in a cemetery in Atlanta, Simon had used magic to make a protective barrier strong enough to stop bullets. A spontaneous shield of that quality required a great deal of channeled power, and he could only keep it up for about seven minutes before it would exhaust him. But if you gave him a couple of hours of preparation time and a chalk circle to control the magic?

He could hold it for hours.

Almost the same second it went up, there was a *thud* on the shield, and then another, and soon a mob of vampires had materialized all around us, pounding on Simon's barrier and snarling expletives.

When he saw them looking, Julien immediately tried to roll to his feet, but I used one foot to press on his injured leg, just enough to hold him in place. He howled in pain and rage, and I snapped my fingers, pulling his surprised eyes to my face. Probably nobody had ever snapped their fingers at him before.

When I had his attention, I drew the other shredder stake from my left forearm and showed it to him. "Your leg will heal," I told him. "But there are things that won't."

Julien shut his mouth, glaring at me murderously. I could have pressed him then, but I was too angry for the focus required. It didn't help that at least ten vampires, all men, were still hammering at the barrier.

I raised my voice to be heard over the racket. "Simon, I need the full audio/visual!"

"I have to feed it more power." Simon crouched on the pavement next to the chalk line and mumbled something that sounded like vegan swear words. A second later the sound stopped. I glanced up to see the transparent shield had turned a rosy, opaque color that somehow emitted light. Damn. Simon had been practicing.

With the extra light from the barrier, I could now see into Julien's wound. The shredder seemed to have cauterized the crater of flesh, which made it easy to see a thick white line with a two-inch gap. It took me a second to realize I was looking at a missing piece of femur.

Huh.

"Um, Lex?" Now that the barrier spell was in place, Simon sort of skidded across the asphalt to my side. "What just happened?"

"There's a dead body twenty feet northeast of us, in the woods," I said over my shoulder.

"*What*?"

Ignoring him, I crouched down, planting one knee on Julien's chest and holding the shredder against his shirt, just over his heart. As soon as it punched through the fabric, it would explode. "Tell me that's not who I think it is."

He smiled at me, proud and defiant, and I felt myself leaning onto the shredder just a little. "Lex!" Simon touched my shoulder, keeping it very light."Are you planning to kill him?"

I was so furious that part of me had stepped back from it, surveying the moment with perfect calm behind a wall of rage. I forced my hand to relax, but said, "I haven't decided."

"Who's the body?" Simon asked quietly.

"She feels...familiar," I said grimly. I hadn't looked away from Julien, and I didn't plan to. "I think it's Maya Elkins, Beau's human assistant. He must have had her snatched from the airport. This *just* happened." I didn't say it, but I could *feel* the freshness of her death. She had only recently crossed the boundary, probably while we were talking to Julien at the damned tower.

Dubuque sniggered. "A human woman traveling from Atlanta *was* killed in a feeding accident this evening," he said loftily. "Unfortunate, but these things do happen."

I leaned my knee down a little harder on his chest, and my words were forced out through clenched teeth. "Not very *civilized* of you."

"Why would he kill her?" Simon asked me.

"To send a message, I'm guessing. Prove this territory is more trouble than it's worth."

Julien bared his teeth, and I figured I was close enough. "This human woman wasn't one of Maven's people," he said. "And you work for Maven. By your own rules, you can't touch me for this."

The body was still gleaming at me, pulling my focus, crying out for...something. God help me, I wanted *so* badly to push the shredder right through his shirt and into his skin. I wanted to hear the squelch of his—

*Allie, get a grip right fucking now.*

"Lex," Simon's gentle voice came at the same time as my sister's. I felt a warm hand on my shoulder. "You control the boundary magic, remember? It's not the other way around."

I breathed out, easing up on the stake again.

"You're right," I said. "It's mine." I pressed the edge of my griffin tattoo into Julien Dubuque's neck and dropped straight down into his brain.

Pressing vampires usually requires more preparation, or at least a few seconds to concentrate, but I'd already been drawing in boundary magic without really knowing it, and my mother's bloodstone was practically pulsing with it. Julien was mine the instant I decided to take him.

"Tell me where Orvil Grant stays when he comes to your territory," I ordered.

Julien's face was slack and open. "He chooses a new place each year. He doesn't tell anyone where he's staying."

Shit. All this could *not* be for nothing. I would not allow that. "Tell me where Orvil spends his time in Galena," I tried instead.

Julien blinked, in a way I recognized as confusion. I hadn't phrased the command properly. "I don't know," he said. "I only see Orvil at Rendezvous. It's in the abandoned mines on Saturday night."

I tried the question a few other ways, but couldn't get anything else on Orvil, so I changed tack. "Why kill Maya?"

The confused face again. "Tell me why there's a dead human near us," I tried instead.

"My people brought it here to show me."

I clenched my jaw, frustrated. That could mean he'd ordered them to go get her, or they'd killed her by accident. "Tell me who killed her," I demanded.

He stared. "I don't know."

Right—he wouldn't know which of his vampires had caused the moment of death, or possibly even the cause. Most vampires used a blade to cut humans, but Maya might have died from the wound, from shock, or something else entirely.

It had been a while since I'd pressed a vampire, and I was being too clumsy about it. The combination of my anger and the incessant gleaming from Maya's body were making me feel like I might lose my grip on him at any moment.

"Lex," Simon said softly beside me, "They're all still out there, and I can't hold the full shield forever."

Despite the gleaming, *that* got my attention. I couldn't save

Maya, but I could still protect Simon. Blinking hard, I broke eye contact, releasing Julien from the press.

The vampire flinched and sat up with supernatural speed. "What was that?" he demanded.

I stood and took a step back, crossing my arms over my chest. "You just told me everything you know...which is basically nothing."

Julien bared his fangs and flipped up to his feet—or he would have, but he'd forgotten about the wound in his quadricep, which hadn't had time to heal all the way. He flopped down on his ass, where he called me a few names that were almost impressively filthy.

"Damn, vampires *really* don't like it when you press them," Simon observed.

I flashed him a smile, grateful for the break in tension. "Kind of ironic, huh?"

With more care, Julien turned sideways and rolled gracefully to his feet, putting all his weight on his good leg.

"Monstrous bitch," he hissed at me.

"Shut up," I snapped, holding up my other shredder. The vampire went very still, and I made myself take a breath.

"You've got two options now." I tried to sound calm. Tried to *be* calm, despite the continuous call of the dead in my mind. "If you want a fight, we can fight." I gave a little shrug. "Then again, boundary witches are notoriously hard to kill, I'm armed to the teeth, and unlike Maya, I *am* under Maven's protection. Even if you succeed in killing me, the strongest vampire on the planet will devote her eternity to killing you."

"That would make it pretty hard to stay in Dubuque and run this territory," Simon mused. "But I'm sure you've delegated a really good second-in-command who'll protect it after your death, right?"

I had to suppress a smile.

Dubuque glared at me. "And the second choice?" he spat.

"Simon will drop his shield, and you and I will put on a show. We'll smile and hug, and you'll tell your men it was all a prank, and we're great friends. Tell them any story you want. You can even cover that leg—I doubt they got a great look at the injury with all the chaos."

He started to answer, but I held up a finger. "Then, tomorrow," I continued, "my people will do whatever we want, for as long as we want, in Galena."

"You're taking the city?" Julien cried.

God, and I thought Beau was overly dramatic. "For the last time, I don't *want* your goddamned town. I just need you and your people to stay the hell out of it for, let's say, two weeks. And you won't let any of this get back to Orvil." Before he could answer, I added, "Keep in mind that I could have simply pressed you to get all of this. But I'm trying to give you a chance here. I've heard you know your way around a deal."

"That isn't much of a deal."

Simon's arm actually twitched toward me, like he thought he'd have to hold me back. But I had control now. "It's a lot better than what Maya got," I snarled. "Which reminds me—No matter what happens tonight, you'll be answering for her."

"You can't—"

"Oh, it won't be me," I interrupted. "Or Maven. You're right about that; Maya didn't work for us, so I have no right to seek justice on Maven's behalf. But Maya *did* work for the cardinal vampire of Atlanta. That right belongs to him." Beau had cared about Maya, that had been obvious since the moment I'd met him. He would be coming after Julien.

The Mississippi River vampire sort of rolled his eyes, like he'd never consider Beau a threat. He might have been older than Beau, but I knew where I'd put my money. "Fine. I'll do it."

I held up a finger. “One last thing: we’re taking her body, tonight. She deserves a proper burial.”

He flicked a hand carelessly, as though Maya’s body was a speck of lint on his shirt. “Whatever.”

I gave Simon a nod.

“What’s to stop him from telling his people to tear us apart with I drop the shield?” he asked.

I shrugged. “I suppose he could. But then you’ll put your shield back up, and I’ll explode his fucking heart while he’s only got one working leg. And there’s the Maven thing. Oh, and I expect that if he hurts, you he’s going to have to deal with Lily.”

“Good point.” Simon looked at Julien. “You don’t want that, trust me. She can be really annoying.”

The vampire glowered, and for just a second, I thought he was going to lunge at us on his one good leg. My arms were still crossed, but with my right hand, I squeezed the shredder stake in its other sheath.

“Fine,” Julien snarled. “Give me a moment to collect myself, and we’ll put on your little show. I’ll do the talking,” he added, which was just fine with me. In the best of circumstances, I couldn’t lie well enough to fool vampires. Standing there pretending to smile while Maya called to me was already asking a lot.

But that’s what I did. Simon dropped the shield, and Julien made a big fuss about how we were old friends and it was a ruse, or whatever. I glued a smile to my face and didn’t bother listening until he ordered his people to depart. Then Julien himself tossed one more furious look at me, and the Little Night disappeared into the darkness.

When all the vampires had left, Simon and I climbed into the rented Forester, with Simon behind the wheel. We waited in silence for several long minutes, until finally I dropped into my boundary magic mindset and scanned the area. There was only darkness, and a few small glowing lights representing animals. Plus, of course, the gleaming of Maya's body.

"They're gone," I told Simon. I blinked hard a few times to release the mindset. All the tension went out of me, and I felt my shoulders slump forward. I reached into the backseat for the cheap denim jacket I'd worn on the plane. Then I pushed open the car door.

"Are you okay?"

"Stay here," I said tiredly. "Call Kirsten and give the update."

Without waiting for his response, I got out of the Forester and trudged across the parking lot.

I was being summoned.

## 14

### LEX

On the far side of the parking lot there was a short gravel area for cars to turn around, and beyond it, a slope down to a ravine. This area was beyond the reach of the street lamps, but I could make out a lump just at the top of the slope, like someone had discarded it from the back of a car without bothering to throw it all the way down the ravine. It was the size and shape of a human in the fetal position.

They hadn't even bothered to cover her.

A yellow, glowing figure was sitting in the center of the body, watching me come toward her.

I'd only known Maya on the phone and through emails, but I'd seen a photo of her, and this figure matched: a white woman in her late forties, her face lined and her glamorously graying hair in a sharp bob. Her face was patient and expectant, but not really *there.*

Like Becca, I thought. But Becca had died in mid-afternoon, long before sunset. Would Maya be different—more sentient, or maybe able to talk to me? I didn't know anything about this type of ghost: the very new dead. I didn't even know the word for them.

*Tyros*, came Sam's soft voice in my head. *They're called tyros.*

When I reached the body, I dropped down and sat cross-legged a foot away, ignoring the sticks and pine needles underneath me. "Hello, Maya," I said softly. "I know we haven't met face-to-face, but I'm Lex. Um, Allison Luther."

She stared at me blankly for a second, and I was reminded that the newly dead don't blink. There was no cognizance in her expression, though, and I knew it wasn't going to be that easy.

There's no manual for boundary magic. I've learned some things from Nellie, the ghost of a boundary witch in Denver, and a little more from my aunt Katia. Nellie doesn't give anything away for free, though, and Katia isn't as strong as I am. Most of the boundary magic I've done has been sort of made up as I go along, and this was going to be one of those times.

I thought about my options for a moment and then looked down at my hands. It always came down to the same damned thing, didn't it?

There were a few sharp gravel rocks on the ground nearby. I picked one up and quickly, without giving myself time to think about it, drew it across my right forearm with a grimace. It took three tries, but I got a couple of drops of dark blood to well up. Then I had to scoot close to the corpse's head and brush the bloodied hair away from her face. Pulling boundary magic into myself through the tattoos, I forced myself to dip my index finger in my own blood and spread it across Maya's lips. "Talk to me," I whispered.

"Miss Luther."

I started, but it was the glowing figure who spoke, not the actual body. Small favors.

She had turned her head to look at my face, and now there was an awareness in her eyes. She wasn't all there, but something of her was.

"That's right," I said. "Lex."

"I don't understand where I am."

I winced. I'd had to explain to Becca that she was dead, which allowed her to move on. As much as it pained me, I needed to ask questions before I helped Maya go. "Do you remember traveling to Illinois?"

"The plane is early," Maya said, her voice a monotone. It was like I'd rewound a taped report. "We are waiting on the tarmac. The pilot is Beau's trusted servant. He suggests I go ahead to Galena and he will send Beau when he awakens. There is a car waiting."

Okay, so it was like a memory in real time. "What happens next?"

"I must find Beau's lodgings first. I visit potential places from a list of seven options we made last night."

I'd done a brief search on Galena's hotel options myself, and I had noticed that the town was mostly set up with bed-and-breakfast places, each with only a handful of rooms. "I thought everywhere was booked. How would you find a place without a vampire along to press employees?" I asked.

Maya paused without blinking, her face full of effort, like it was an enormous undertaking to derail her thoughts from their current course. "What is your plan, Maya?" I tried instead.

"I will assess the security and location myself, then make my recommendation to Beau," she says in a flat, empty voice. "When he arrives, he will press management and the other guests, and I will make the financial arrangements."

I knew about that part. The cover story was that Beau had decided at the last minute to attend the Rendezvous this year.

He'd make three reservations: one for the LA team, one for the Colorado team, and one for himself.

"Did you go to all seven locations?" I asked.

"No. The third inn is perfect for Beau's tastes. I tour it myself, then go out to the street to call his secure voicemail line–" Her voice abruptly cut off.

"What happened next, Maya?" I asked gently.

"There is pushing. The side of my head hurts. Where is the blood coming from?" Her voice is still in a monotone, but the words are coming in stops and starts now, so quiet I'm having trouble making out the words. It's spooky, like someone reading a transmission from space.

"Can you see who hurt you, Maya?"

"No. There is a hood on my face. I am woozy. We are moving, in a vehicle. I vomit in the hood."

Shit. Tears welled in my eyes, but I ignored them. "Did you hear their voices?"

"They are talking about me. They say I am dead. They are worried." Her voice is less clear now, though I don't know if it's because she's less certain about the information, or if maybe her ghost is beginning to fade. Or something else entirely.

"What are they worried about?"

"About what to do with me. One wants to bring me to Julien, while the other wants to put me well."

I didn't understand that phrasing. "Put you well?"

"Yes."

Maybe an old-fashioned vampire term? "How many were there? Men or women?"

"Two male voices. We stop moving. I can't breathe. Time is moving strangely. Then it stops. The pain and the car and time."

For the first time, the blank look faded from her face, and

her eyes focused on me, brow furrowed. “What happened? Where am I?”

I couldn’t bear it. Maybe I could squeeze more information out of Maya and maybe not, but I wouldn’t prolong this for another second. I just couldn’t. “I’m so sorry, Maya, but you died,” I said, as gently as I could.

“Died?” She looked down at herself then, at the slightly translucent yellow hands, the dark form beneath her.

“Yes. Those men killed you.”

Her gaze lingered on her body for another minute, then she looked up at me again. “Beau will be furious.”

“Probably,” I agreed. “He won’t blame you, though.”

“Who will help him now?” Her voice was beginning to get agitated. A knot formed in my throat.

“He’s going to be okay, Maya,” I assured her. “I will make sure he finds your body. He’ll put you to rest.”

“No one will come to my grave,” she said matter-of-factly. “I have no family left, no other friends.”

“I’ll come,” I promised. “You will be honored, and you will be missed. But you can rest now. It’s okay.”

Maya stared at me with that clear recognition for another few seconds, then it slowly faded away, her eyes going distant. Her face relaxed, the severe lines smoothing away into...well, not a smile, but a look of peace. “All right. I’m ready. Goodbye, Miss Luther.”

“Goodbye, Maya.” Somehow I understood that I wasn’t supposed to watch this part. It was private, between Maya and whatever came next for her. I bowed my head for a long moment. My mother’s bloodstone was hot on my chest, and I had a dim understanding that I’d just channeled a lot of magic in order to have that conversation.

When I lifted my head again, she was gone, and I was alone in the darkness.

I stood up and draped my jacket over her still form, covering her head and face. Then I stumbled back the way I came, hot tears blurring my vision. The heat was still oppressive, and sweat soaked my hair and clothes. At the edge of the gravel, my foot landed on a loose stick and rolled, and I started to go down. I put my arms out to cushion the fall, but I never hit the ground.

Simon's arms caught me, my nose filling with the smell of his lavender detergent. He guided us awkwardly to the ground.

"We have to call Beau," I told him unsteadily. "He has to come get her. I promised."

"He's already on his way," Simon told me, smoothing sweat-dampened hair back from my face. "I talked to him, through Kirsten, and I already took down the privacy ward around this area."

"I made a mistake, letting Julien go. We should find him again; I want to kill him myself."

The words fell out of my mouth without thought, but Simon didn't blink. "It's late, Lex, and you haven't slept. We've both burned through a lot of magic tonight. Let's find a hotel and grab some sleep. We can always kill him tomorrow."

A tiny snort escaped me, though it was dangerously close to a sob. Even I had seen *The Princess Bride*.

Simon started to stand up, and my body naturally followed. He took a step toward the car, but I stumbled away, feeling off-balance and dizzy. "No!"

"Lex? What's the matter?"

"I don't know. I feel weird." I thought I was speaking calmly, but it came out as a near-sob. "Maya…"

Way in the back of my mind, I remembered feeling like this the first time I felt a body: queasy, emotional, and sort of torn, like part of me had crossed into death with Maya. "We can't leave her alone, Simon," I said, helpless to explain myself. I was crying again, goddammit.

"Okay." Simon's arm was at the small of my back, supporting me. I was surprised at how solid it felt. Like the safety bar that goes across your lap at a roller coaster. "Okay, we won't. We'll wait. But you need to sit down before you fall over. Come on."

There were benches along the outside of the parking lot, and he helped me over to the closest one. Simon put his arm around my shoulders and dropped a kiss on top of my head. It should have been awkward or even uncomfortable, but it was the kind of simple gesture he would show Lily, and I relaxed into him, letting myself lean against his side. "Tell me something about you," I said in a small voice. "Something that has nothing to do with any of this." I gestured at the scene around us.

There was a moment of quiet. I could hear some kind of insects in the trees, different from the kind back home.

"I'm so bored," Simon admitted finally. "You and Quinn are off creating a whole government. Lily's busy all the time now, and I've pulled back from the clan a bit so no one thinks I'm influencing her leadership. All my friends from school have settled down and are having kids, but I'm not there yet." There was real longing in his voice.

He let a moment go by, then added in a near-whisper, "I'm in love with my best friend's girl, and I can't get her out of my head."

I cringed.

Not long after Simon and I first met, he'd died helping me track Charlie's kidnapper. The kidnapper was injured at the same time, and I'd stolen his life-essence and pushed it into Simon.

It had only barely worked, buying him enough time to get

to the hospital, and I couldn't regret it. But in the years since, I'd wondered if I'd done something else to Simon at the same time. Had I pulled his attention toward me? Did I cause the unhappiness that seemed to have plagued his life since then? Was this why he thought he loved me?

"Simon..."

"I know. I don't want you to say anything. You and Quinn are the perfect couple. But I just feel like I'm drifting. I used to just work all the time so I wouldn't have to think. But lately it doesn't get me excited anymore."

My heart ached for him. "I'm sorry," I said, turning my head to look at him. "That all sounds really lonely."

He looked down into my eyes, and I realized my mistake. Our faces were inches apart. His arm was still around me, and suddenly my skin prickled wherever it was touching his. Heat surged between us that had nothing to do with humidity.

I looked away, my whole body going rigid. Simon retracted his arm and scooted away from me on the bench, looking embarrassed. "I'm so sorry," he said, "I shouldn't have—"

"No, you didn't do anything," I said quickly. I took a breath. "I should let you talk more. You're always there for me, and I've been..."

"You've been avoiding me." The words were quiet and without blame, but they still felt like a punch to the stomach. He held up his hand. "It's okay. I get it."

We sat there for a moment, waiting out the awkwardness. The night was just beginning to cool now. If we hadn't put on bug spray before meeting Julien, I was pretty sure we'd both look like giant slices of Swiss cheese by now. But we were alive.

"Can you tell me what happened with Maya?" Simon asked eventually. When I didn't answer right away, he added, "For science?"

I choked on a laugh. "Oh, well, if it's for science."

So I did my best to explain the gleaming, the conversation with Maya, the way it all affected me. Magic that felt like a surge of emotion I couldn't escape.

"How do you feel now?" he asked when I'd finished.

I had to think about that. "Sam used to get migraines, like a headache that got worse until she puked," I said finally. "For a couple of hours afterwards, she was…fragile, I guess would be the word. She called it the exposed time. That's how I feel."

Simon gave a wry chuckle, and I could practically hear the unspoken words. *Yeah, me too.*

After that, we sat in silence.

Beau arrived at the Mines of Spain parking lot ten minutes later, on foot. One minute the lot was empty, and the next he was stalking toward us from the shadows. Simon and I had both stood as he approached. I could tell Beau had already fed that night, but there was a different kind of hunger to his expression. It reminded me of how he'd been in Georgia after losing one of his Horsemen. He practically radiated tension and rage.

"Hello, Beau," I said. "I'm so sorry about Maya."

I'd gotten used to loquacious speech patterns from the southern vampire, but this time he just looked at me and said bluntly, "Do we know who killed her?"

I straightened up, instinctively responding to the command in his voice. "We suspect Julien Dubuque ordered it, but it's unconfirmed until I have another chance to talk to him or his people." I felt myself redden. "I did press him briefly, but I lost my cool before I got a straight answer."

"It wasn't your fault," Simon began, but I elbowed him to shut up. That wasn't how responsibility to the dead worked.

Beau ignored us and went over to Maya's body, turning his

back and crouching down. Gently, he pulled back the denim jacket, exposing Maya's crumpled figure. He reached out and slowly rotated the body onto its back, his own shoulders slumping.

It was too dark for Simon and me to see any details with our human eyes, but I recognized the limp way Maya's limbs flopped. She wasn't even in rigor mortis yet. It made me wonder how much earlier I would have needed to find her in order to save her life. Five minutes? Twenty? If I had given her my blood, I could have delayed her death. I'd done it before.

*You can't do that to yourself, Allie. This death is not on you.*

The hell it isn't, I thought. I hadn't kept an eye on my team. If I had checked in with Maya, or even left her a message to call me as soon as she landed, she might still be alive now.

When he finally stood and walked over to us, Beau looked at Simon first. "I do hope you'll pardon my manners," he said formally, inclining his head. "I am Abner Beaumont Calhoun, but please call me Beau."

"Sorry," I said, shaking myself. "I should have...Beau, this is Dr. Simon Pellar, the witch friend I was telling you about."

"Doctor?" Beau raised his eyebrows.

"A PhD," Simon hurried to say. "I'm an evolutionary biologist. It's an honor to meet you, sir. I wish it was under better circumstances."

"A male witch and a doctor," Beau said. "How remarkable." He turned to me. "Miss Lex. I can see that Maya hasn't left a spirit behind. Was it here when you arrived?"

Right. I had forgotten that Beau could see ghosts too. Before he'd become a vampire, he'd been a nonmagical member of a boundary witch family.

So once again, I described my conversation with Maya, adding, "I don't think she was conscious at the end."

Beau nodded, clearly not consoled by this.

"Do you know her precise cause of death?" This was Simon, ever the scientist. He hadn't wanted to disturb the body before Beau arrived, but he'd still be curious.

"The head wound clearly came first," Beau told him. "There's a great deal of blood in her hair and scalp. There are also, however, sharp cuts at her brachial veins. Exsanguination was the cause of death."

With all the advances in forensic medicine, most vampires used blades, rather than teeth, to draw blood from their victims. But they always cut at a vein, for the faster bloodletting.

"So humans hit her on the head and brought her here to the Mines of Spain, where Julien's vampires drained her," I concluded, shaking my head. "I'm sorry, Beau."

"But why kill her at all?" Beau's face was tight. "I don't understand it."

"Well, Julien is against the parliament, and seemed half-convinced Maven is making a play for his territory," Simon mused.

"Maya was moving around Galena to look at different lodgings," I added. "One of Julien's humans must have spotted her and made the connection." I frowned. "Wait. How would Julien know Maya was connected to Maven?"

"She used Maven's name when she called to set up your appointment," Beau said grimly. "Julien and I have a complicated history; that's why I instructed Maya to say she was calling on Maven's behalf." He grimaced. "I suppose it's possible that he killed her out of animosity toward me."

"I'm sure that wasn't it," Simon said instantly. "He didn't even mention your name."

I tried to phrase the question as delicately as I could. "Beau, I'm sorry, but I need to know how Maya's death will affect our plans. Do you need to leave the mission?"

"No." Beau put his hands in the pocket of his riding pants, his head bowed. "I'm on this trip to return a favor. You saved my life and my territory, and having Shoemaker has brought me more joy these last months than I can say." He shook his head. "No, it would not do to divert from my original obligation in service of another. I will go on to Galena tonight and set up lodgings, as Maya and I had planned. My response to Julien shall wait until Maven's business is concluded."

I let out the breath I'd been holding. I had to admire him. Beau had joined this mission practically on a lark, to repay a vague sense of obligation. Now he'd lost his trusted human aide, but he was still going to stick around and serve Maven, doing the kind of logistical work that most vampires considered beneath them. "We can help," I said. "We can come to Galena right now."

Beau smiled. "I have no doubt of that fact, but I suspect the two of you will have more daytime responsibilities tomorrow, without Maya. I suggest getting some sleep while you can. Whatever I don't finish tonight, you can work on in the morning."

It seemed as good a plan as any, so I agreed. Beau turned to go, but I called after him before he could disappear into the darkness. "Beau?"

He turned. "When all this is over, let me know about the service for Maya, okay? I want to be there."

Emotions flickered over his face—sorrow, gratitude, grief. "Thank you, Lex. I will."

# 15

## SCARLETT

Los Angeles, California

I woke up Thursday morning because the bed was swaying.

A well-trained subconscious part of my brain thought, *uh-oh, earthquake*. I opened my eyes to go get Annie and yell for Jesse to meet us under the kitchen table.

Except I wasn't at home, and Annie wasn't here, and there was no earthquake. And we were moving.

"Sorry," Jesse called over his shoulder. "Bumpy road."

I yawned and stretched, feeling the soreness in my body and the low-grade headache in the back of my head. My various bruises and road rash scrapes ached, especially the scrape on my leg that had required surgery. It was probably time to change the bandage. I just didn't want to stand up.

It still kind of blew my mind that I would have to stand and take several steps just to reach the kitchen in the Winnebago we had rented from one of Kirsten's witches.

"It's fine," I said to Jesse, feeling awkward. He and I had a nice moment right after the big Old World meeting Tuesday night, but then we had a big fight in the car. Jesse knew better than to try to convince me to stay in LA, but he thought I should spend the rest of the week resting in a hotel room somewhere before flying to Illinois at the very last minute before the trial. I'd pointed out that we didn't have that kind of time—Orvil Grant would likely leave Galena after the Rendezvous on Saturday. We had argued the whole drive back to the hospital.

Well, *he* had argued, at full power, while I sort of drunkenly lashed out in a weak whisper voice. What I lacked in volume, though, I made up for in stubbornness.

By the time we reached the hospital parking garage, we had settled on the Winnebago plan, and we were both a little pissed with each other.

Now I was on a cross-country road trip with my fiancé and our work colleague, on our way to start a supernatural revolution. I had never been inside a camper in my life; I wasn't even sure of the terminology (was it a camper or an RV? Did we still say left and right, or was this a port/starboard situation?), but hey, life is funny.

We had brought Theodore Hayne (almost everyone called him Hayne, including his sister Abigail) along as an extra driver, since I wasn't allowed to drive yet and we were on a time crunch. In Galena, Jesse and I would rent a car to get around, and Hayne could take as long as he needed to drive back to LA.

At the moment, Hayne was sleeping in the bedroom (!) in the back of the camper. I'd set up my own nest on the full-sized couch in the front part of the camper, which we called the cabin. I wasn't allowed to read or look at screens with a concussion, and it had taken about five minutes and three refrigerator stab wounds for Jesse and Hayne to forbid me from throwing knives in the RV. It was really shaping up to be a boring road trip.

Now, I slowly worked my way over to the counter for the new hydrocolloid bandage and the wound cleaning supplies. I brought everything back to my nest to change the bandage.

"How is it looking?" Jesse called back to me.

I peeled back the old bandage. "Still very gross, but not any grosser than last night. Have you heard from Lex?"

In the rearview mirror I could see his face go sober. I felt my stomach lurch. "I'll come up there," I said.

With the new bandage applied, I made my way to the seat next to the driver's, and Jesse gave me the update: Beau's aide, Maya, had been killed by local vampires. Most of us hadn't even arrived in town, and there had already been a casualty. "Jesus."

"Yeah." Jesse looked troubled.

"What's bothering you, besides the obvious?" I asked.

"Malcolm." He glanced at me, then back to the road. "From everything you've all said about the guy, I'm worried we're moving too fast. Maybe we *should* be sending an army."

I snorted. "That's not really a thing, at least not in another person's territory. In a modern world it's pretty much impossible to do something that big without the humans finding out about us."

Jesse gave me a startled look. "What?" I asked again.

"Nothing, you just...you said 'us.' You never talk about yourself as an 'us' in the Old World."

I shrugged, not really interested in arguing the point. I did think of myself as part of the Old World, but part of the human world, too. And at the same time, not really part of either. That's what it meant to be a null.

Jesse's thoughts were on a whole different track, though, because after another half mile of road he said quietly, "Is that why you don't want to set the date? Because I'm human?"

"What? Jesse—" I sputtered, thrown by the change in subject and the wild leap of logic. "No, of course not!" I sort of waved my hand. "Everyone is human to me, remember?"

"If you're not sure about getting married—"

"*Jesse.*" I reached over to squeeze his leg. "I love you. I know we had a fight Tuesday night, but I am like, stupid in love with you. It's disgusting." I gave him a suspicious look. "Wait, are you just sitting up here staring at the road and stewing about the wedding? Because it seems like we have bigger fish right now."

"Scarlett." He wasn't going to be deterred. "You almost died two days ago, so yes, I've been thinking about our future. And every time I talk about the wedding, you look at Annie and change the subject."

My instinct was, of course, to snap at him, or make a joke to change the subject. But Jesse deserved better than that, so I tried to find a way to put it into words. "I feel like I have...unfinished business."

He glanced sideways at me again. "Jameson."

I sighed. "Not like *that*." My head was aching again. "It's only ever been you, you dumbass."

"But you won't pick a date. Or just jump in the car and go to City Hall with me. You say you want to marry me, but you can't tell me why you keep pushing it off."

"This is hardly the time—"

"Why, because you're hurt, or because we're on our way to confront the vampire who tried to kill you?" He shook his head, getting angry. "Come on, Scar, we've talked about this. Scary things aren't going to stop so we can do normal-people things. We just gotta push forward. This is the life we made." He reached over to touch my left hand, the one with the engagement ring. "For better or worse, right?"

That made tears well in my eyes, but I swallowed hard and

shook my head. "I feel a little carsick," I said quietly. "I'm going to go lay down."

"Fine." Jesse's voice was tight.

I went back to my nest to do my own stewing.

AFTER I RETURNED to the hospital Tuesday night, I'd tried to be the perfect patient, letting myself be tested and examined by a small battalion of doctors for most of Wednesday. Jesse had gone home—with Hayne, our friend Owen, and a couple of Hayne's daytime people keeping watch—to pack clothes for us, as well as all the various baby gear for Annie. She and Corry had spent the day at the hellhest ranch, meeting up with the rest of "Team Safe House."

With Jesse occupied, my brother Jack had taken off work to hang around the hospital during my tests, holding my hand through bouts of vertigo and asking my doctors a million questions. By late afternoon, even Jack concluded that I could probably go home, although I suspect he was mostly trying to spare the nurses and doctors he liked from having to have further contact with me.

Jack drove me to his house, where we met up with Jesse. The two of them started discussing my aftercare summary, but I bailed on that to spend a little time playing Legos with my sister-in-law's older kids, Logan and Riley, and cuddling my new nephew, baby Liam.

Then, after an early pizza supper, I got to have a very difficult conversation with Jack about why bodyguards would be keeping an eye on him and his family for the next couple of weeks.

"Jesus, Scarbo, what are you into now?" He bent and scrubbed feverishly at a spot of red sauce on the counter, while I sat in a kitchen chair because I was not allowed to help. Juliet was feeding the baby and watching television with the older kids in the master bedroom, and Jesse was in the hallway, talking on the phone. This left the two Bernard siblings alone in the kitchen to reenact the same fight we'd been having regularly for the last few years.

"You know I can't tell you that." Jack only knew that I worked for Dashiell, and that some of Dashiell's businesses weren't legal.

He made a little grunt of frustration. Jack looked more like our dad every day, and for a second I was back in high school, dodging my father's disappointed lectures. "But I don't know *why*," Jack argued. "If my family is going to be in danger, shouldn't I at least understand the reason behind it?"

I sighed, fighting the urge to rub the back of my aching head. I knew from experience that this would only make it hurt more, like poking a bruise. "Jack, the less you know about my job, the better off you are. I realize that sounds like a line from a really shitty action movie, but in this case it's also true."

He scrubbed the counter harder, glowering down at it. "Oh, bullcrap. You're so full of it, Scarbo. Like that *prank* you described today, where someone set off fireworks and you fell and hit your head in the front *and* the back?"

Admittedly, this was not the best story I'd ever come up with, but you try explaining away a cluster bomb.

He gestured at my injuries. "I'm not an idiot. I know this is from your job...a job so sketchy that it puts my children in danger." He glared at me. "What am I supposed to do with that?"

I was cranky and irritable, but I also hurt too much to snap at him. "You have to do your best to trust me," I said tiredly. "Trust that what I'm doing matters."

He turned on the faucet to rinse the sponge, but I could hear his sigh over the water. "Oh, I'm convinced that *you* believe in what you're doing, Scarlett. But I hate seeing you get your butt kicked. Not to mention displacing my family every time you say so, without any kind of warning or control."

"Then move out of my town," I wanted to say. I *hated* this. Jesse had convinced me that we could still keep our human families in our lives, and ninety percent of the time, I agreed with him. This was one of the ten percent times.

But I loved my brother and his family, and I didn't really want to lose them. "I'm sorry," I said lamely. "I would understand if you want to go back to just not being in contact."

"Argh!" To my complete shock, Jack spun around and threw the sponge, which hit one of the kitchen cupboards with a slurping sound and flopped onto the counter. "That's not what I want, and you know it!"

At that moment a fresh wave of vertigo struck, and I folded my arms and rested my head on them for a moment, suddenly reeling. These bouts had been a lot more frequent earlier in the day, but they still weren't any fun when they arrived.

Jack was instantly by my side, in doctor mode, resting a hand on my back to steady me. "Keep breathing, Scarlett. It will pass in a few seconds. You're all right, just breathe, come on..."

He was right—it did eventually pass, leaving me disoriented and weak. "Come on, let's get you to the couch," he said, putting his arm around me.

When I was laying on the couch in the living room, he crouched in front of me to see my face. "You really should have stayed another night, you know."

"I don't sleep well in hospital beds," I mumbled.

Jack sighed, softening. "Yeah, me neither."

I decided I was not above taking advantage of the moment. "Jack, listen. About Annie's biological father..."

His eyebrows went up, just like our dad's used to. I had never made a secret of the fact that Jesse wasn't Annie's birth father—it was obvious from her skin tone—but I had never talked about Jameson with Jack. "You said it was a one-night thing during the bachelorette party weekend," he said cautiously.

"It was. And then he died. The next day."

"Oh my God." Jack lowered himself to the floor and folded his long legs to sit where our faces were more or less level. "You never mentioned that part."

I paused for a second, choosing my words carefully. "I knew him, Jack. We met years ago when I was in New York. We kept in touch in a friendly way, and then we sort of ran into each other again in Vegas."

Jack's green eyes, identical to mine and Annie's, widened, but he didn't say anything, just waited for me to continue. "The next day, he was shot and killed. They never caught the people who did it."

"Oh, Scarbo." Very gently, Jack took my hand in both of his, squeezing gently. I was surprised to find that my eyes were filling with tears. "Why didn't you tell me?"

"It was complicated." But I knew that wasn't good enough, so I blew out a breath and tried again. "I was told, years ago, that I would never be able to get pregnant. So we weren't...careful." This was an awkward thing to say to your brother, but at least Jack was a doctor. I was sure he'd heard worse. "Then he died. And Jesse and I finally got our timing right, and Annie came along. I'm happy...but I never forgot about my friend." How could I, when Annie already reminded me so much of Jameson?

"Of course not," Jack said. He leaned sideways to tug a tissue from a box on the coffee table and handed it to me.

Wiping the tears off my cheeks, I met Jack's eyes. "The people who killed Annie's father? They're the ones who are after me now."

I knew he'd probably assume Malcolm was trying to kill me because of my connection to Jameson, like I was a mob moll in some crime movie. But at least my words were true. It felt really good to tell my brother the truth.

"Can't you go to the police?" Jack asked. "Jesse must know—"

"Jack, I really can't tell you more than that right now," I interrupted. "But Jesse and I are sending Annie somewhere safe, and then we are going out of town to try to get the evidence we need to stop these guys." Okay, skirting the edges of the truth here, but still not all the way in lying territory. Go, me. "I want justice for Annie's birth father, and I want to make sure they can never come after us again," I concluded. "I know you don't understand my job, but can you try to understand that much?"

Jack closed his eyes for a moment, his hands flat on the table. Then he opened his eyes and wrinkled his face at me, like I'd orchestrated a tragic backstory just to manipulate him. Then his face relaxed. "Okay. What exactly do you need us to do?"

# 16

## LEX

Dubuque, Iowa

I went to bed that night worried about nightmares, but it was Sam who visited my dreams.

I saw my twin sister as I always did, in the room we'd shared for most of our childhood. She was sitting on her twin bed across from mine, her legs crisscrossed, wearing the blousy maternity top and leggings I'd last seen her in.

"Sammy. Is Charlie okay?"

My sister hesitated for a second, her head tilted to one side like she was listening. Then she gave me her warmest smile. "Yes," she said. "I can't tell you details, but...yes."

I thought about asking after the others—Scarlett's daughter, Katia, and all the rest—but decided not to press my luck. There were limits to how much Sam was allowed to tell me in this space, and besides, if Charlie and John were fine, the others pretty much had to be as well. "Why am I seeing you?" I asked instead.

Her smile turned wistful. "I didn't call you, babe. You called me."

"Oh." I felt a little embarrassed, like I'd been caught crying for my mom at sleep away camp. "I probably just missed you," I said lamely.

Sam made a perfect arch with one eyebrow. When we were teenagers I had been so jealous of that ability.

When I didn't say anything, she added a fake cough into her hand, only the sound came out as the word "bullshit."

"Sam..."

"Babe," she said seriously, "You called me because you're struggling, whether you know it or not."

"I'm fine, Sammy."

"Like hell. You almost fell apart last night. You could have killed that vampire, or gotten yourself killed by being reckless. You've gotta stop trashing your psyche."

I let out a choked little laugh. "Excuse me?"

"The dead people thing," Sam said vaguely. She waved her hand around, as though that one gesture could encompass dozens of complex ideas. "I mean, have you considered *not* stumbling upon fresh bodies?"

"Samantha."

She sighed. "Yeah, I know. It comes with the job. But look—remember when you first met Sashi? The scar tissue?"

It took me a moment, because so much had happened. Normally witches can't do magic on other witches, much less anyone else from the Old World. But Sashi had gotten a massive power boost from some of Boulder's ley lines, and for a short time, she was able to circumvent that particular rule. She'd done something to my mind, erasing a sort of psychological scar tissue I'd built up after all my...experiences. "You're saying I'm making brain scar tissue again?" I asked. "Couldn't that be a good thing, though? I mean, before Sashi healed it, I wasn't seeing ghosts." I could do with a few less ghosts.

But Sam shook her head. "It doesn't work like that. You built that wall in your head when we were teenagers, while you were still growing in body and mind. Everyone kind of hardens as they get older, but your gorgeous brain really took the job seriously. "

"Okay..." I still didn't see the problem.

"You can't remake that wall, Lex," she said gently. "Haven't you noticed how much things get to you, since Sashi healed you? I mean, after you met Lysander and Jasper, you were so..." She paused. "I'm really trying to avoid the word 'haunted' here."

"Sam—"

"Affected. And then you had to fight that *thing* that raped our birth mother." She said this in practically a snarl. But then again, Sam knew our birth mother, Valerya, a lot better than I did. "And it damn near broke you. Then it was the wraiths in the tunnel, and you *raised the fucking dead,* and corpses started talking to you, and the spirit bombs in Atlanta—"

"You don't have to give me the highlight reel, Sammy," I interrupted, irritated. "I was there."

"But you keep taking these hits, and they are *affecting you*," she insisted. "I know you're great at denial, babe, but you can't keep fucking around with this stuff. You mind needs time to heal."

"That's all I've been doing since I got back from Georgia!" I protested. "I've been sitting on my ass while Quinn and Maven work on this parliament. It didn't help. And now I'm needed."

"Yeah, yeah, you're the key to the whole thing, I heard that," Sam said, rolling her eyes. "Do you have any idea how fragile you are, how dangerous it is to push yourself so hard?"

"Look, when we get Malcolm, I promise I'll take a break," I

offered. "I'll let Lily do her Reiki or go lay on a beach, whatever you want."

"You hate the beach."

"The beach is fine. It's lying around doing nothing that drives me nuts."

"Maybe you should take that hot Simon dude along, then," she suggested. "I can think of a few things you two could do."

Now it was my turn to roll my eyes. "You were in California too long, *dude*."

She pretended to throw a pillow at me, and I pretended to duck. "You know what I mean," she said. "You're taking psychic damage *and* bottling too many feelings. Like the ones you have for Simon."

"As you already know," I said pointedly, "Simon and I are just friends. I love Quinn."

"You love Simon, too."

I refused to take the bait. "Sure I do," I agreed. "Just like I love Lily, and John, and Tobias."

"You know there's more to it than that," she insisted.

I sighed. "Sammy, why are we even talking about this? A cardinal vampire who's terrorizing half the country tried to *kill* Charlie. She—"

"Needs you right now, yes. And I know you'll always be there for her. But you're not just protecting her anymore. You've organized your whole life so she's the center."

"What's wrong with that?" I said stubbornly.

"Oh, shut up, Allie." There was a little bit of genuine anger in her tone now, which surprised me. It had always been rare for Sam to get really sincere about her feelings, even with me. "I see you, Allison Alexandra Luther. You decided a long time ago that your purpose in life was to serve. Now you've traded the army for my baby."

I opened my mouth to object, thought better of it, and shrugged. "I can't think of a better purpose."

Sam pointed an index finger at me. "And that's my point. I'm glad you've got Charlie's back. But your whole existence cannot be training for danger or facing danger, never having your own life or dealing with your own feelings. If you keep this up, you are going to live a very, very long life in a goddamned psychic coma."

"Sammy—"

"No! Don't 'Sammy' me; *listen* to me." Her face softened. "It's all connected, babe, can't you see that? And even if you manage to keep going like this without completely trashing your brain, you're missing out on your own life. I don't want to be the reason for that."

I blinked. So much had happened in the last five years; I'd almost forgotten that Sam's death really had been the catalyst for all of this. John and Charlie moving back to Boulder, meeting Jesse and Scarlett, finding out Charlie was vulnerable, taking the job with Maven.

It would be easy to wonder what our lives would have been like if Sam hadn't died...which is exactly why I tried never to think about it. "It's more complicated than that, Sammy."

She waved a hand. "I know it is. But your boss has sworn to protect Charlie whether you're working for her or not. You don't have to do this shit you hate, dead people screaming in your brain and chicken sacrifice and fighting armies of ghosts. Take a break. Have some magic babies with the hot science witch."

Something rose up in me then, a complicated knot of love and worry, power and panic. It threatened to overwhelm me, and I found myself hugging my arms around my stomach.

"One," I said very quietly to my dead sister, "I love Quinn. Two, I don't want kids. Three, my life is just fine the way it is."

She sighed and shook her head. "Okay, babe, have it your way. But the cost of loving Charlie doesn't have to be your life, or even your sanity. Try to remember that."

THE NEXT THING I KNEW, I was opening my eyes to a generic hotel room ceiling.

I hated how Sam always got the last word.

I rolled over and checked the digital clock on the bedside table: nine am. Simon and I had checked into the Holiday Inn just outside Dubuque a little after midnight. We'd been able to get adjoining rooms on a high floor, and Simon had suggested we leave the doors between the rooms cracked all night "just in case."

I knew it was his way of worrying about me without embarrassing me. Simon and I had once (platonically) shared a hotel room, and he was one of the people who knew about the nightmares that had plagued me since I'd left the Army. *The nightmares that keep getting worse with every shitty adventure,* came Sam's voice in my head.

"Stop it, Samantha," I said firmly, and her voice went quiet.

"Lex?" Simon's voice called from the other room. "Did you say something?"

Whoops. "Just wondering if you're up," I lied.

"Yeah." His voice was morning-scratchy but alert. "Just reading the news on my phone."

That reminded me that I needed to call Kirsten and get an update. I felt a stab of guilt—I hadn't talked to Quinn yet about what had been going on, and now it was after sunrise.

My stomach grumbled, though, reminding me that we'd skipped dinner the day before. Neither of us felt like eating after seeing Maya's corpse. "Continental breakfast?" I called. We'd seen a sign in the lobby, right next to the remnant of a dead frontiersman. Or at least, a ghost who'd been wearing furs when he died.

"Twenty minutes?"

"Sure."

I'd showered before bed, so I just had to brush my teeth and get dressed, although that took a lot longer than usual. I started with a pair of cargo pants and a workout tank that had a built-in bra. Then I added my mother's bloodstone, which I'd recharged on the hotel room balcony overnight, and strapped on the reloaded shredder sheaths. I fitted my pancake holster into the small of my back and secured my Glock 21 inside it, courtesy of Iowa's ridiculously lax gun control laws.

When I had the Glock secured, I stared into my suitcase for a long few minutes, considering the Kevlar vest and other protective gear inside. The safest move would be to wear the vest 24/7, but it would be awfully conspicuous, especially in this climate. It made rustling noises when I moved, and it would make me sweaty and stiff. If Adelaide was the soldier I thought she was, she'd realize I had Kevlar on and go for a head shot. Frankly, she was likely to do that anyway. At the same time, though, not wearing the gear felt foolhardy.

I compromised by stuffing the vest and a couple of other items into my carry-on backpack, shoved everything else into the suitcase, and checked the hotel mirror. I had to smile a little at my ridiculous reflection. With the shredders strapped to my tattooed forearms, I looked like a deranged militant knitter.

I'd left the lightweight denim jacket with Maya's body, so I went back to my suitcase and grabbed a men's linen dress shirt to go over my tank top. Then I pushed a key card, headphones, and my phone into my pants pockets and headed for the elevator.

Downstairs, I found the breakfast set out in a small room just off the lobby, with square Formica tables and a TV blasting local news. Simon was just sitting down with a tray of yogurt and fruit, so I went to get my own breakfast before dropping into the chair across from him.

"Hey. How'd you sleep?" he asked, sounding suspiciously casual.

"It took me awhile to drop off, but then it was okay," I replied, then added without thinking, "I had a Sam dream."

"Oh?" Simon was always fascinated by my conversations with my twin, for obvious science reasons. "What did she want to talk about?"

I paused with a spoonful of oatmeal half-raised to my mouth. There was no way I was going to tell Simon about the psychic damage warning, much less...the other stuff. "Oh, you know. Charlie."

We ate in silence for a few minutes, until Simon swallowed a bite of toast and said, "So what's the plan for today?"

"Oh, right." I dug in my pocket for the new burner phone and earbuds, handing one to Simon. "Let's call Kirsten."

With Simon and I each wearing an earbud, I called the only number in my phone's contacts.

It was just seven thirty am in LA, but she answered almost instantly. "Operator." Her voice was crisp and confident.

"Um, hi. It's Lex, and Simon Pellar's on the line too. Any word from Beau?"

"Good morning," she said warmly. "Yes, I spoke to him shortly before sunrise, and then to Maven and Dashiell before they retired for the day."

"Okay..."

"Beau made a lot of arrangements in Galena overnight," Kirsten went on. "He reserved a place called Turner Hall for the trial. He also secured three residences for the full group. Do you have a pen?"

Simon was already pushing a cheap hotel pen into my

hand. As Kirsten recited addresses, I scribbled out the details on a paper napkin. "All of the reservations are in Beau's name," she added. "Each place believes Beau is staying there with his aides. The idea is to keep the true identities of the guests secret as long as possible."

I found myself nodding. Beau had been to the Rendezvous before, so any vampires in the area who heard about his people staying over wouldn't think twice about it.

"What's left for Simon and me to do today?" I asked Kirsten.

She cleared her throat. "Dashiell and Maven would like you to find Orvil Grant and Adelaide Preston this evening and inform them of their trial. It's set for Friday night at eleven fifty-nine pm."

Simon and I looked at each other in surprise. Friday? "That's *tomorrow*," I blurted.

"I know. We don't want to give them too much time to flee or rally support, and Maven would like to be out of the area before the Rendezvous starts."

That meant the trial was going to happen in just over thirty hours. I understood the importance of speed, but that didn't seem like much prep time for us.

"Okay," I said, because there wasn't much I could do about it. "Anything else?"

"The water witches are already on site and at work," she said. "Scarlett and Jesse are on their way; they decided to drive an RV. They should be arriving in Galena tonight around seven, Central Standard time."

"Got it."

"One last thing, Lex," Kirsten added, her voice taking on an extra layer of seriousness. "I have a message from Beau; he asked me to repeat it to you word for word."

"Go ahead."

She began to read. "Miss Lex: I know you were expecting

ghosts in Galena, but their numbers are greater than expected. There are Unsettled here."

Shit.

I found myself avoiding Simon's eyes. He knew about the Unsettled in Atlanta; he'd been at that fight.

Kirsten had stopped talking. "That's the whole message?" I asked in disbelief.

"That's it, sorry."

Vampires and their dramatics. I genuinely liked Beau, especially after everything we'd been through, but sometimes he made it hard.

"Thanks, Kirsten. I'll check in after we find Orvil and Adelaide."

I hung up the phone and made myself meet Simon's eyes. My friend gave me a sad, sympathetic smile.

People became ghosts after a violent or traumatic death, but there were still plenty of different kinds of ghost. The Unsettled was a name for the ghosts left behind after a battle. As I understood it, this happened when a number of people died for the same cause, over a short period of time and in the same place. Usually they hadn't been laid to rest properly, and as a result, they wandered until they found each other, pooling together like gravity. They were drawn to each other and to the relics of their former lives: weapons, uniforms, tools—

"The buildings," Simon said, following my train of thought. "Eighty-five percent of the town's on the historical register."

"Yeah. Shit."

"So we're laying ghosts tonight?"

"Not until I talk to Beau," I said reluctantly. Beau believed that the Unsettled were an important reminder of soldiers' sacrifices, and therefore shouldn't be laid by boundary witches. The only reason I'd put the Unsettled in Marietta to rest was because Odessa had destroyed their corpses. "I need to find out where they Unsettled are located and how much he's going to fight me on sending them through the door. It's going to be a whole thing. Besides, we need to focus on finding Adelaide. She's the key to getting Orvil."

"Okay..." Simon squirmed in his seat, looking pensive.

"What?"

"You hate pressing vampires," he said bluntly. "There's... ethical considerations."

I tried not to think about how much I'd enjoyed pressing Julien Dubuque, making him do what I wanted. "I don't like taking anyone's free will away, no. But Orvil is part of the group that tried to kill Charlie. There are no ethical considerations."

Simon opened his mouth, closed it, tried again. "Okay," he said finally. "What's the plan?"

I took another bite of the yogurt, thinking it through. "Going against Adelaide and Orvil together would be like going up against Quinn and me," I mused. "Guns and fangs are a pretty formidable threat."

He nodded, following my train of thought. "So we split them up."

"Yes. We'll try to find Adelaide today, before sundown. Maybe even before the rain starts, if we're lucky." But that meant we'd have to hang onto Adelaide all day. I put my spoon down and looked at Simon. "Do you have a way to hold her until Beau wakes up?" Beau would be able to press Adelaide into compliance.

Simon made a face. "I don't like it, but yes. We could get her to our hotel, or even in a car, and I can put the same type of shield over her that we used last night. Only reversed, to keep something in instead of out."

"How long can you hold it?"

"Humans are easier to hold than vampires, for obvious

reasons, but I probably wouldn't risk it on my own for more than six hours. Eight at the outside."

"Okay, that's plenty of time."

"But we have to find her first," Simon pointed out. "Where do we start?"

"Hmm." I chewed on an apple slice. Orvil had lived in Galena as a human, and Adelaide came to town every year for this Rendezvous thing. They probably knew Galena almost as well as I knew Boulder. I thought about how they must have found Maya, and a plan began to form.

I looked at Simon with a small, mean smile on my face. "We start by making some noise."

# 17

## LEX

Galena, Illinois

An hour after leaving the hotel, Simon drove our rental car through a set of massive floodgates, and we finally got our first glimpse of downtown Galena.

We spent the first half hour driving back and forth across the main streets with the car's windows open, getting a sense of the geography. There were three main streets, which ran diagonally from southwest to northeast, curving gently around what used to be the wide Galena River. Now the river was more of a large creek, but with green fields on either side, so you could see its former width. Two massive earth levees framed the valley, and sidewalks had been built along the top of them. Despite the heat, pedestrians were out walking dogs and pushing strollers along the sidewalk.

On the drive from Dubuque, Simon had summarized the town's history for me. Apparently Galena was founded and built on the mining industry—galena was actually a mineral that contained lead sulfate. By the late 1820's steamboat traffic from the Mississippi was detouring over to Galena to pick up millions of pounds of lead, and the town's population skyrocketed.

But mining required foundries, and the foundries ran on furnaces. As the town grew and the demand for lead increased, the locals chopped down Galena's trees to fuel the forges and create farmland to grow food. They didn't realize how this would damage the river.

The resulting erosion caused the river to silt up, until eventually the steamboats couldn't pass through. "I could give this story to the English Department for when they introduce freshmen to the concept of irony," Simon told me, sounding almost awed.

The siltation, which Simon promised me was an actual word, lead to increased flooding, and made it harder, and then impossible, for the steamboats to come in. After the Civil War ended, the demand for lead began to decline as well.

Galena could have folded up at that point, becoming like the many ghost towns in Colorado, abandoned after a local mine closed. But the town hung on, and eventually its leaders committed themselves to historical tourism.

I had expected a town of beautiful old brick buildings with a touristy atmosphere, kind of like Pearl Street in Boulder, and that was all here. Like downtown Boulder, the businesses in downtown Galena were mostly dedicated to shopping and eating, rather than functions for the local citizens. We saw tour trolleys and street barkers, storefronts and signs advertising wine tasting, magic shows (Simon snorted), and blacksmith demonstrations. Ulysses S. Grant was a common theme, with various signs boasting the places where he'd lived, went to church, or made important announcements.

It should have felt like a cheap money grab, but despite all the emphasis on tourism and commerce, there was something about Galena that felt grounded by the weight of everything it had seen.

"It feels...real," I said. "Not the Disney World version, like we were saying, or even the painted-over version like I saw a lot in Atlanta. It feels like things really happened here, and the city still has the scars to prove it."

Simon nodded. "History-wise, it's the perfect storm: the longevity of these buildings, the commitment to historical accuracy, and the unusual layout."

Another thing I hadn't expected was the town's shifting altitude: most of the Illinois we'd driven through had been flat terrain, but Galena's downtown began at the foot of one levee and extended back to the foot of the hills beyond. As the city's population had expanded, more streets had been added going up into the hills.

"It looks like the lower streets are businesses, and the higher streets are more residential," I pointed out. "I've seen that in mountain towns, too."

We were at a stoplight just then and Simon leaned over the steering wheel to point in between buildings. "See the stairs?"

Sure enough, there was a massive staircase going from the downtown streets up to the crest of the hill. At the top, just to the left of the stairs, there was a huge red brick building rising above the skyline. "That's the old high school," Simon explained. "It's luxury apartments now, but for decades students would have to climb those stairs every day to get to class."

"Good cardio." I squinted up at the sky. When we'd left the hotel, the summer sun was just starting to disappear behind clouds. Now dark, heavy rainclouds had appeared overhead.

It reminded me that I needed to check in with the witches.

"There are actually two sets of stairs connecting the downtown to the higher areas," Simon was saying, as I got out the burner phone. "There are a hundred and ninety steps to the old school, but the other staircase has even more—two hundred and forty, I think."

I raised an eyebrow at him. "Did you *memorize* that book?"

Simon smiled, a little sheepish. "Just trying to be of service, boss."

Before I could say anything to that, the light changed and he drove the car forward again.

I texted Kirsten to contact the water witch, Laurel, and we made plans to meet up late that afternoon. As I put the phone away, Simon pointed at a rare treasure we hadn't seen yet: an empty parking spot. Galena's downtown wasn't a very car-friendly district, having been built before anyone needed to worry about parallel parking or passing lanes.

I unbuckled my seatbelt. "Let's go see this town."

For the next few hours, Simon and I played, as he put it, a game of Very Conspicuous Tourist. We wandered up and down the streets, weaving through crowds, visiting local businesses. Simon even bought a few souvenirs, not to mention some board game stuff from a toy store with the unfortunate name of Poopsies.

We quickly fell into a rhythm: at each store, Simon would start chatting with a friendly shopkeeper, while I focused on the exits and people, watching for Adelaide. To make sure my hands were free, I didn't buy anything, although I did marvel at the number of stores that seemed to sell weapons, from hammers turned into hatchets at the blacksmith shop to folding knives with inlaid handles at a place selling T-shirts. There was even a shoe store with a whole cache of swords. Many of them were replicas from movies, but several looked pretty sharp.

"Did you see the tactical pens?" Simon whispered as we walked out of an outdoor supply store.

"*Pens*?" What the hell was a tactical pen? "I must have missed that. I saw the knife that fits in a corset, though. And the punch dagger with the skull on the sheath."

"Who knew there was so much need for stabby things in the Galena economy." Simon grinned.

"Right?" The weapons stuff seemed odd because this was a tourist destination, but I'd seen similar products in plenty of stores in Colorado, especially once you got outside Boulder. "I bet the LA people will be flummoxed."

"Great word. Vocab high-five?" Simon held his hand up, and I slapped it.

We played tourist well into the afternoon. We tried to get in front of every security camera we could find, and we made a point to check out any store that might have Old World relevancy: an apothecary, a rare books store, a high-end antiques shop, and even a so-called witch shop, where Simon was impressed with the herb selection but not much else.

Every hour or so we bought iced coffee or ice cream and sat with it on wrought-iron benches, keeping an eye on the other visitors and overhearing snatches of the walking tours. "Of course, Galena is known for the nine Civil War generals who hailed from here," said a middle-aged main in full Union Army getup, swaggering in front of a cluster of tourists. They were all fanning themselves with brochures, except the red-faced guide. Maybe brochure fans weren't period-accurate. "But you ladies might be interested to know this was also the birthplace of one of the first girls to join the Navy's Nurse Corps, Katherine Eddows Sutcliff, in World War I. Katherine was even rumored to be up for a Navy Cross medal, until she got herself in some kind of scandal with the Nurse Corps Superintendent—who was *also* a girl." He winked elaborately at a lesbian couple in their sixties. They did not seem amused. "Come on now, ladies," he said, walking backward and motioning for everyone to follow. "All in good fun." The tour group moved on.

Simon cut his eyes at me. "His costume looks *very* hot," I said, taking a sip of my iced coffee. "What a shame."

This public jaunt around town was stressful—I was never great in crowded tourist areas, and now I also had to be on constant high alert. But to my surprise, I also kind of had fun. It helped that Simon was relaxed and chatty, making friends with practically every clerk we met. This was a side of him I didn't get to see much, where our lives weren't in obvious danger and Lily wasn't around for him to banter with.

As the day went on, the storm clouds overhead got darker and heavier, like a weapon charging up for use.

By mid-afternoon, I was starting to get discouraged. There was still no sign of Adelaide Preston or anyone who might work for her. You can never be one hundred percent certain, but I was pretty sure we hadn't been followed, and none of the locals we'd encountered had seemed suspicious or even paid particular attention to either of us. I'd either overestimated Adelaide's knowledge of what was going on in this town, or I'd underestimated her caution when it came to approaching me in broad daylight.

I was exhausted from being on high alert, not to mention feeling a little foolish and stressed. So much of Maven's grand plan depended on me being able to clear this first hurdle. It was time to admit that Simon and I needed to regroup and get a new plan.

Simon suggested we go check in to the bed and breakfast Beau had secured for the Colorado people: a converted residence called 305 North, after its street address. It was on Main Street at the northeast end of the commercial section, and Beau had managed to rent out all seven suites. This must have displaced a lot of innocent tourists, but I had too many other things on my mind to feel guilty about it.

The hotel didn't have a lobby so much as a converted living room with a counter in one corner. There was an elderly man behind the counter, working on a crossword puzzle. The half-glasses perched on the tip of his nose looked like they might fall off at any second.

When Simon and I came in with our bags, he looked up with a huge smile. "You must be Mr. Abner's party. I'm Dave, and I'm so pleased to have you," he said. "You're checking in for the whole group, right?"

When I nodded, he reached for something under the counter, coming out with a fistful of actual, physical keys. "Mr. Abner said I should give you all seven keys when you arrived." He deposited them on the counter.

"Thank you," I said, scooping up the keys and putting them in the front pocket of my backpack. Maven, Quinn, Simon, and myself would all be staying here, but Beau must have decided it was safest to just clear the whole building.

"This is a beautiful place," Simon said gazing up at the brick walls.

Dave smiled at him. "Thank you. The wife and I put a lot of work into it...which is why we're looking forward to having the weekend off. There are extra towels here under the counter. Mr. Abner said you wouldn't need anything else."

Ah. Beau had made sure this man wouldn't be around to get hurt. Smart. "I'm sure we'll be fine," I told Dave.

He stood up from his stool, holding onto the wall for support. I thought he'd say goodbye, but instead he reached for a plain white box on a shelf behind him. "Almost forgot," he said. "Package arrived for you 'bout twenty minutes ago. From one of the local stores."

He handed me the package, one of those flat shirt boxes

that my mother used to give sweaters at Christmas. There was a shop business card taped to one corner.

I felt my whole body tense. Even after all these years, an unexpected package still had the ability to bring me back to driving a Humvee across the Iraqi desert.

Simon picked up on my tension and filled the silence. "Um. Do the stores around here usually deliver?"

Dave grinned, displaying crooked yellowed teeth that were probably all his own. "Nope. Your friend must have charmed someone."

Right. Beau was the only one who knew where we were staying. He must have gotten to one of the store owners before dawn and set this up. "I'll open it later," I said.

Dave looked slightly disappointed, but he just reached for the edge of the counter and pulled himself to his feet."Would you like me to show you to your suites?"

We assured Dave that we could find our own way, and he gave us a little wave and departed through a back hall, where we could see another exit.

When the door had closed behind him, I reached for the box and flipped off the lid. There was tissue paper inside, and I brushed it aside, exposing a new jacket made of a soft, stretchy denim.

"Nice," Simon commented, reaching out to touch the fabric. "Beau has good taste."

I checked the label. Based on the brand, this one probably cost four or five times what I'd paid for the jacket I'd left with Maya's body the night before. "It's too extravagant. I get my clothes at secondhand stores or at Christmas."

"Keep it," he advised. "It's Beau's way of saying thanks, for Maya. And you know how vampires are about money."

I knew what he meant. Vampires had spent centuries perfecting their own elaborate financial systems, which was a lot easier when you had mind control capabilities. And if they ever ran out of money, they could press some poor bank manager to get more.

"Yeah. Okay." I picked up the jacket and draped it over my duffel bag. "Let's go find our rooms."

I'm not sure what I was expecting the rest of the odd little building to look like, but the farther in we went, the less it resembled anything like a hotel. The interior layout was winding and strange, with a lower-level library and narrow hallways that required a lot of doubling back to find the common areas.

The vampires would need to stay on the lower level, so I went to the basement to pick the room I'd share with Quinn. Simon opted to go upstairs to check out the rooms.

I was sweaty from the sweltering day, so I got my stuff into the room and took a quick shower, dressing in a clean pair of cargo pants and another athletic tank. This time I put on the Kevlar vest, followed by a second, loose tank layered over it. It was still sweltering outside, but I decided to add the new denim jacket anyway. I unbuttoned the cuffs to reach the bottom of each shredder and checked the mirror. Beau had bought a size bigger than what I usually wore, and now I realized this had been intentional. The jacket was big enough to hide weapons and the Kevlar vest without looking too bulky. It even had a vent in the lower back, so I could reach my sidearm. I practiced drawing the Glock a few times until I was sure I could do it smoothly.

Simon was right—Beau *did* have good taste.

At five o'clock I slung on the backpack and left the room, locking the door behind me. My first stop was the hotel library, to check in with Simon.

He was sitting in an easy chair, rummaging through a messenger bag in his lap. I recognized the bag he reserved for witch materials. "I need to get started on the wards," he explained, closing the bag's flap and buckling the straps to secure it. "I can see why Beau wanted three separate residences, but it's going to take me a while to get everything protected in this rain."

Hotels don't build up the hearth-and-home magic that protects private homes from vampire attack, so Simon would need to ward the hotels used by our group. He had to create a circle that could withstand rain and allow our people to come in and out freely—all while working around the tourists and locals. It was a job that I did not envy.

"Well, you don't have to worry about the LA team's building," I pointed out. Scarlett and her colleagues were staying at a different downtown hotel, the DeSoto. It was a very old, somewhat famous hotel where a number of historical figures had once stayed—sort of the equivalent of the Boulderado in my hometown. "Scarlett Bernard is going to be in and out of there, so wards aren't really going to work."

Simon made a face. "Good point. Will Dashiell be okay with that? He's supposed to be at the DeSoto."

I shrugged. "The other vampires aren't coming until sunset tomorrow night, and they'll mostly be at the trial. I'm guessing they'll be with Scarlett the next day. If not, we can put Dashiell in one of the extra suites here. There's plenty of room."

He nodded. "Okay, so two buildings. I'd still like to get as much done before sunset as I can...which means I won't be able to meet the water witch with you."

He looked so disappointed, I had to pat him on the back. "Maybe you can talk to her when it's all over," I said cheerfully. "Assuming we don't die."

Simon gave me a wry smile, and I pretended not to feel anything from it. "Assuming."

Before I left, I wanted to say something else, something

about being careful or calling me if there was any sign of Adelaide. But Simon already knew all of that. He was smart and powerful, in his way, and if I didn't respect his abilities I had no business bringing him on this trip. So I just said I'd see him later and turned toward the stairs for the main floor.

"Hey, Lex?" he called after me.

I glanced over my shoulder, expecting him to spout one of his own be-safe platitudes, or maybe a blessing of some kind. Instead, he shifted his weight back and forth awkwardly and said, "The jacket looks really good."

"I—um. Thank you."

I turned and jogged up the stairs the hotel's front door. Outside, the first fat drops of rain began to splash down.

# 18

## SCARLETT

After my argument with Jesse, I slept in my nest for a few hours, and then I spent another hour icing and re-dressing the various deep bruises and scrapes from when I was attacked. By eleven-thirty, I'd realized my mistake in fighting with my fiancé at seven am during a road trip when I wasn't allowed to read or look at screens.

I stared out the window a lot, looking at the flat, endless landscape and feeling irrationally annoyed with Jesse—not about the fight, but about the boredom. If this was three years ago, I would have said fuck the concussion orders and done whatever I wanted.

Back then, I put my life at risk pretty regularly, and never thought much about it. It's not like I didn't have people who cared about me, even then—there was Jack and Molly and even Shadow—but fundamentally, my death never seemed like that big of a tragedy, so I didn't worry too much about it.

Now, though, I had Jesse and Annie, my own little nontraditional traditional family. If I died, it would mess them up for a long time. That made a difference.

I sulked about it through our gas and lunch stop and the rest of Jesse's driving shift, counting down the minutes until I could get out of the damned RV. We'd already been on the road for twenty hours, so we were supposed to arrive in Galena a little before sunset. At that point I would need to be rested and as ready as possible to do actual things…which meant Jesse and I would need to be on the same page.

Sighing, I got to my feet. Hayne met my eyes in the rearview mirror. He'd been listening to an audiobook, but he pulled an ear bud out of one ear and raised his eyebrows slightly. "I'm going to go talk to Jesse." I told him.

He nodded and said something that sounded suspiciously like "about damned time." Apparently the tension in the RV had not been subtle.

The little bedroom at the back of the Winnebago was tiny, of course, and almost completely taken up by a double bed. I opened the door quietly in case Jesse was asleep, but I found him lying on his back, staring up at the ceiling.

"How are you feeling?" I asked him.

"Shouldn't I be asking you that?"

I shrugged. "You're the one who has to do all the tedious driving. I'm just sitting around brooding like an emo high schooler."

That got me a smile. Without saying anything, Jesse shifted over to one side of the bed, and I laboriously crawled onto the bed next to him, ignoring the soreness in my body. The Tylenol helped, but only so much.

For a long moment we just laid there, side by side. The ceiling was plain beige and very boring. Finally, I couldn't stand the silence any longer. "We should probably just have sex, right?"

That got me an actual laugh. "Yup, just like I've always dreamed. In a moving vehicle, with Hayne twelve feet away and you barely able to stay awake."

"Wow, I've heard of some fetishes in my day, but that is *specific.*"

He reached over and took my hand. "I'm stupid in love with you too."

"But you also have this traditional streak," I continued for him. "Deep down in your heart. And you want the whole wedding...spectacle."

He raised my hand to his lips and kissed it. "When I got married before, we just went to City Hall," he said. "And yeah, part of me wants to stand up in front of God and everyone we care about and say the vows. It's a whole fantasy I have, where we don't have to keep all the parts of our lives separate, just for one day. Our families and our friends, Old World and modern world. Hell, I'd even invite a few old friends from the force and a couple of people from the studio. All in one place."

Jesse's day job was consulting with Hollywood types about the LAPD. "But I recognize that it's probably going to stay a fantasy," he went on. "And I can live with that. What I really want is the marriage."

"You know that making it official doesn't guarantee happily-ever-after or anything, right?" I asked him. "We already live together; we already have a kid. Our work lives aren't going to change. When we get married, nothing really changes for us."

He was quiet for a long moment. "That's the thing about having a traditional streak, Scar," he said quietly. "I think something changes for me."

Well...shit. "Because it's official? In front of God and everyone?"

He sighed, and I regretted my words. "Scarlett. We have this makeshift life with patchwork jobs and a casual housing arrangement with your vampire best friend landlady. This spring our magic baby blew away our house and we had to replace it. Our whole lives are just this patchwork jumble that we're throwing together every day from the seat of our pants."

"I like to think of us as more of a ragtag team," I said, but Jesse didn't answer.

Right. Maximum effort, Scarlett. "Patchwork doesn't necessarily mean temporary," I said softly.

"That's true." He shifted on the bed, still holding onto my hand. "I guess I just want this one thing that's not thrown together. One thing that's—yes—old-fashioned and traditional and legally binding."

"And I've said yes." But I felt something churning in my stomach. Not uncertainty. Not cold feet. Just...unease.

"And every time I bring up setting the date, you're suddenly very distracted by something," Jesse said.

I lay there, thinking about that. "It's not distraction," I said finally. "It's more like...guilt."

I turned onto my side to face him. Luckily the really bad scrape was on my right side, so I was only putting pressure on bruises and regular scrapes.

"That isn't like you, to hold grudges and let your conscience weigh you down. What happened to the girl I met in that puddle of blood, the one who only cared about getting the next job done?" he teased.

Maybe it was the drugs, or the pain, or the endless monotony of the road trip, but I told Jesse the truth. "You. You happened to me."

He reached over to brush my hair away from my face, his warm fingers stroking my cheek. "And I always *had* a conscience; I just let it sleep for a little while," I added. "A lot has changed, but sometimes it's still my job to pick the least bad thing, and I won't apologize for that."

"I know, sweetheart."

I took a breath and made myself try again. "I never thought I'd get to have this. And Jameson...he doesn't. Malcolm dominated his life while he was alive, and when Jameson finally got away, he killed him. And we all just moved on with our lives."

"So your plan is to not move on? Refuse to be happy?"

I sighed. It was obvious that I wasn't going to be able to make him understand—hell, *I* barely understood. I wasn't exactly known far and wide for my excellent grasp of feelings-talk.

"I'll make you a deal," I said instead. "After this trip, when we get back to LA, that night we'll sit down with the calendar and pick the day. "

"Really?"

"I promise. You have my word."

He leaned over to kiss my forehead. Then he gave a suspicious look. "Wait, are you expecting us to die, and figure that will get you out of marrying me?"

"Dammit! I hate when you catch onto my schemes."

Jesse shook his head, smiling, but there was worry in it. He settled back down on the bed. "Tell me more about Malcolm," he said. "From your trip to New York."

"Ugh. Do I have to?"

"Yes."

I usually tried not to think about that trip. After I found out that my ex-mentor, Olivia, had been turned into a vampire, Dashiell had sent me to New York to stay with Jameson for a few weeks. At the time he'd made it seem like he was trying to keep me safe and promote null outreach, or whatever. Later, though, I realized that at least part of the point was for me to witness the twisted, cruel dynamic between Malcolm and Jameson.

By that point Malcolm had already spent nearly a decade

abusing Jameson, physically and psychologically. Dashiell was impatient with my attitude and general belligerence, and I think he wanted me to see how much worse it could be.

I hadn't spent much time in Malcolm's actual presence, though, and I'd never been alone in a room with him. "There's not much to tell," I told Jesse now.

"Scar, come on. How old is he? I know you get a sense of that."

I leaned back in my seat and closed my eyes, thinking. I had gotten a lot more awareness of my radius in the years since that trip, but I could sort of remember how Malcolm had felt. "Older than Dashiell," I said. "But not by much." Dashiell had been turned in 1821.

I opened my eyes and looked at Jesse. "Looking back, I think he's like Dashiell—one of those vampires who was strong the moment they were turned." A thought popped in my head. "Beau's like that too, now that I think about it. He's a little stronger than a Civil War-era vampire should be."

My partner considered that for a moment. "Most of them get stronger as they age, right, over time?"

"Right. Molly's a good example: she's exactly the right, ummm, power level for her age. Now and then, though, someone is 'born' weaker or stronger than usual. Wyatt is weaker than he should be, which is probably why no one ever considered him a threat back in Las Vegas." It was probably also why Wyatt and his wife had been allowed to have close ties to humans.

"Is age something you feel in your radius?" Jesse asked, glancing over with interest.

I held up a flat hand and tilted it back and forth. "I mean, it's not like I have Terminator vision, and little stats pop up every time I see a vampire."

"Though we can agree that would be cool."

"Obviously. It's more like, if I really focus on a vampire in my radius, I can get a general sense of their age and power. Sometimes the two don't quite match. Like when you see someone walking around LA who's clearly had a shitload of plastic surgery and Botox. They *look* young, but it doesn't...fit."

Jesse nodded. "Okay, I get that. What else do you know about Malcolm? Anything, Scar, even if it doesn't seem relevant."

I shrugged. "You've seen the photos. He's short with bristly black hair, and kind of swarthy-looking, like a pirate. But he always looks immaculate. I remember thinking he must spend a lot of money on facials and manicures and other stuff." Vampires had a natural glow, but Malcolm had also had a personal null who could take him to do those things as a human.

Jesse raised his eyebrows. "The cardinal vampire of New York is a metrosexual?"

"First, I don't think we say metrosexual anymore, and second...that's not quite right. It's more like...remember Capone in *The Untouchables*? Getting a personal shave and a manicure and fancy suits to hide that he was really a thug?"

Jesse's eyes lit up. My man liked himself a movie reference. "Okay, got it. What else?"

"I don't know, Jesse!" I threw up my hands, and immediately regretted the sudden movement. "We had like four conversations, all of which were surface-level small talk about New York or the value of nulls. He didn't exactly give me his life story."

"What did Jameson say about him, then?" Jesse persisted. "You two must have talked about Malcolm, at least a little."

I was already shaking my head. "I've told you this before—Jameson was super close-mouthed about Malcolm. He literally never said a bad word about the guy, not one mean remark.

Even in Vegas, when I really pushed him, it was just sort of these insinuations."

"Okay, don't focus on the bad things," Jesse offered. "Try to think of *anything* Jamison may have said about Malcolm, even just random details. Did he like women? Men? A certain kind of food? Did he have hobbies or follow sports teams?"

That gave me pause for a moment. I was getting a little annoyed that Jesse was doing his cop interview thing on me, but he had a point, too. In all the time since Jameson died, when I'd been wracking my brain to find a way to get to Malcolm, I'd never really considered these questions. But Jesse had a point. "He liked the horse track," I said slowly. "Jameson would take him during the day, and he said Malcolm *never* interfered with a race. It would be easy for a rich vampire to mess with the race results, one way or another, but he never did. Malcolm told Jameson it wouldn't be any fun that way."

"That's good," Jesse said. "What else?"

I closed my eyes, trying to focus. It had been so long ago. So many versions of Scarlett ago. "He's obsessed with New York City, you already know that. He's had to be a bit of a politician to hold a city that big, with that many vampires. Jameson said he throws donation money around sometimes, makes a fuss about helping people for the good publicity."

"Helping the other vampires?"

"No, like, when the New York witch clans need a little help or plan a big event, he kicks in money. And he funds a lot of blood banks and homeless shelters...because it helps his vampires get food."

I wished, not for the first time, that I'd been able to get in touch with some of Jameson's family. He had an aunt who was a powerful witch, which I only knew because Jesse had paid a PI in New York to track her down. I'd tried calling her a few times, leaving voicemails with my first name and mentioning Jameson, but she'd never answered or called back. Malcolm had the witches of New York on a very tight leash, so maybe she was afraid to talk to me.

"What did Malcolm think about you being there?" Jesse asked.

"He agreed to it, obviously, but he didn't like it. It was as though he was...jealous isn't the right word, but he acted like he was the only cardinal vampire who should get to have a null. And he clearly didn't believe me when I said Dashiell shares power with the local witches and werewolves. I don't think he could wrap his head around the idea of voluntarily sharing power at all."

"Hmm."

I turned my head so I could face Jesse. "You know what? I think the guy just honestly doesn't like *change*. He would get a little huffy about Dashiell's newfangled—emphasis on the fang—way of doing things. He didn't like conversations about technology or politics the way the world was moving. It's like he always just wanted everything to stay exactly as it was, and Malcolm himself would only do the minimum amount of adaptation required to keep his power."

"Hmm. I can see why a guy like that wouldn't want Maven's parliament. What about personal security? Did he have henchmen?"

"I think you mean henchpersons," I corrected, but I knew what he meant. Having bodyguards was always a loaded subject for cardinal vampires. If they had too many, they looked weak, like they couldn't hold territory without hiding behind a wall of muscle. But if they didn't have *any*, they were much more vulnerable to attack. No one could watch their own back every second of every night, and even a very powerful vampire could be killed in an ambush by four or five other vampires.

Most cardinal vampires I'd encountered either had a small,

trusted entourage, like Beau, or they conducted most of their business from secure strongholds, like Maven and Dashiell.

"Jameson was his main bodyguard, for obvious reasons," I said. "There was a human woman who barely spoke…Kendall? Kendra? She was in charge of getting humans for Malcolm to eat. Then there were two male vampires who went around with him." What were their names?

I suddenly had the strangest impulse to text Jameson, like "hey, what was the name of that guy who sneezed in the middle of a meeting that time?" That was how our relationship had been during the years between my visit to New York and our reunion in Las Vegas. But Jameson was dead.

"I think one of them was named Creedon," I said. "And Mikey. I remember those two, because they were weird vampire names. But that was a lot of years ago. He probably restructured some things when Jameson left."

My eyelids were getting heavy again, lying there on the bed. Jesse must have seen it, because he pulled me close. "Time for sex?" I mumbled into his neck.

He chuckled. "Sleep now, okay?" He kissed my hair. "You're going to have work to do."

# 19

## LEX

Laurel and the other witches were working their water magic ten miles upriver, so it made the most sense for us to meet up at a sandwich shop on the eastern end of downtown—which also happened to be next door to my hotel.

I had a rain jacket and umbrella in the backpack, but I didn't bother taking them out as I ducked from one doorway to the next. The rain was already picking up, though, and I managed to get wet going just a few feet.

Like every other building I'd seen in Galena, the inside of the sandwich shop had been overhauled and renovated a few times in order to serve modern purposes. The door opened to a sort of foyer, which led into an open-air dining room broken up by brick supports and various raised platforms. There were far too many big plate-glass windows for my taste, but at least with the rain starting to pour down outside, I didn't have to worry about Adelaide Preston and a sniper rifle.

I asked for a booth in the back of the building, on a raised platform against the windowless support wall. I couldn't see the bar area, but at least I could keep an eye on the entrance.

Laurel Knox arrived a moment later, a slender woman with a long red braid and a gauzy, pistachio-colored dress, shaking out an umbrella in the foyer. She scanned the room as she closed the umbrella, and waved enthusiastically the moment her eyes landed on me. Weaving through the tables, she stepped up onto the raised platform to sit down opposite me in the booth. "Grace showed me a picture of you," she explained without preamble. "And she said you'd have your back to a wall."

I blinked. "Grace Brighton? *Oh.*" Sashi had told me Grace's summer employer was a witch, but I hadn't put it together. "*You're* the Vegas witch she's been working for?"

Laurel had pulled the chair out across from me and sat down. "She's my nanny, yes. And I'm teaching her as much about magic as I can, within our very different disciplines."

The server, a twenty-something woman with painful-looking braces, came over with her notepad, and I asked for a hummus wrap. Laurel began chatting with the young woman about sandwich ingredients, which gave me a moment to process the new information.

Grace was practically my surrogate niece: Sashi and John had dated for a few years before Will had reentered her life. Even after they split up, Grace was considered an extension of the Luther family. She had babysat Charlie, looked after my herd of animals when I had to leave town, and been present at every Luther family gathering over the last few years.

Then she'd needed to run away from her life in Boulder—and this was the woman she'd run to.

I was tempted to put our situation on hold and ask all about Grace: how she was doing, whether she was going to come back, if she seemed happy. But Laurel had said she couldn't leave the other witches for very long, and time was short. An update would have to wait.

When the server had left again, Laurel looked at me expectantly. Up close, I could see that her red hair was frizzing around her face in the heat, and she had that exhausted-but-exhilarated look people get after pulling a successful all-nighter.

"How is it going?" I said, feeling awkwardly. "Your, um, water stuff."

In answer, Laurel smiled and cocked her head, pantomiming listening. Even over the noise of the sandwich place and the traffic outside, rain was pounding down on the ceiling.

"Yeah," I said. "Your clan does good work."

"I like to think so, but we've never had a request like this," she admitted. "Flood a town that's prone to floods—but only enough to evacuate the people, not to do any real harm. It's a serious undertaking. We're using magic that no one has even attempted since my grandmother was my age."

That explained her look of exhausted excitement. It hadn't occurred to me, but it made sense that creating a partial natural disaster might be more difficult than a full one. Dashiell and Maven wanted to keep structural damage to a minimum—not because cardinal vampires were particularly concerned about preserving buildings, but because the worse the disaster looked on the news, the more attention it would get. Our objective was for every event in Galena to be cancelled and for the tourists to stay away. The last thing we wanted was for the Red Cross and National Guard to swarm the town.

Later that night, Beau would try to help things along by whispering in the ears of town leaders, encouraging them to evacuate the city itself. The local vampire population would probably figure out by then that something was up, but we only needed to keep things quiet tonight and for the first part of tomorrow night.

"How does the water magic work?" I asked, feeling the inadequacy of the question.

Laurel blew out a breath, causing the loose hair around her face to dance upward. "Like any other kind of magic, really—we pull it into ourselves and channel it out to do things. In this case, though, we're pushing around molecules of water." She gave a little shrug. "Any trades witch can work with the elements, but it requires a *lot* more training, which means your clan has to have communal knowledge. Mine does."

She paused long enough for the server to deposit our drinks and depart again. "Anyway, calling the rain isn't difficult, especially in a humid climate where summer showers are common." She took a sip of her water. "The hard part is making the rain look completely natural."

"What do you mean? Isn't rain...rain?"

She smiled. "Sure, but it can't come out of nowhere—it has to gather, to be predictable for the next few days. That's why it just started now—we needed yesterday and most of today to make it look normal. That's the only way to make sure human meteorologists get the word out that Galena won't be a fun place to visit this weekend."

"Sounds like a lot of work."

I was trying to keep up the conversation, but at the same time I was very aware of the increased dinnertime activity in the room. People were crowding in the foyer dripping, laughing as they looked down at their soaked clothes. More people hurried past the big arched windows facing the street, jogging to get through the rain quickly. All the fast movements had me on edge.

"Even in a family that's used to water magic," Laurel was saying, "we don't usually mess around with the weather. It requires *so* much power, and in a continual flow—no pun intended—for several days. My sisters and I are working in shifts, but we could never keep this up indefinitely."

I noticed she never mentioned how many witches were with her, or any of their names, or even if they were her biological sisters or other members of her clan. Laurel may have looked like a hippie college professor, but she was operating the same way I would in her shoes. "So you don't do this kind of thing often."

She snorted. "Hell no. I live in the desert. My clan has spent the last century trying to pull water out of the ground, not the sky. This is..." she paused, looking for a word. "It's really fun," she admitted.

I smiled. Simon and Lily got like this when they got to play with new magic.

The server approached again to deliver our plates. We talked through the loose schedule for the next few days as we ate. Laurel's team wouldn't be involved in anything in Galena, other than monitoring the rain, but I figured it was worth giving the broad strokes of the plan in case something went wrong and either of us needed an assist. It wasn't like me to divulge information, but hearing that Grace was living with this woman had changed things a little. I'd reclassified Laurel from "paid ally of an ally" to someone who could be trusted.

As we finished eating and began gathering up trash, a woman with glasses and jet-black hair cut in a bob strolled past the window, glanced in briefly, and continued on, ignoring the pounding rain that was soaking her.

She'd behaved like anyone else trying to decide where to eat, but an alarm in the very back of my head pinged. She had been wearing wet jeans and a men's XXL maroon...but the glasses and the hood of the sweatshirt had been completely dry.

No umbrella, no purse. I hadn't gotten a close look at her face, but she'd been the right age and build.

Shit. Of all the times for my plan to actually work.

"Laurel," I said, sliding to the edge of the booth, "I need you to go to the bathroom now."

"Um..."

"I'm about to be attacked, I think, and I don't want you to be seen with me." I would have told her to just leave, but if that was Adelaide, she might have friends at the exits. "Go to the bathroom; hide there 'til I call. If you see a fire alarm on the way, pull it."

To her credit, Laurel didn't say another word. She picked up her purse and slid out the booth, turning a sharp corner to the hall with the bathroom.

I eased the Glock out of the pancake holster at my back, holding it against my left thigh, out of sight. A shrill, undulating siren exploded through the room, accompanied by strobe lights. The other diners looked around themselves in surprise. Laurel had found the fire alarm.

A harried-looking manager in a white shirt and bolo tie hurried out of the back area by the bar. He clapped his hands to get attention over the loud noise. "Everyone! I apologize for the disturbance!" he yelled. "There is *no* fire, but state law requires us to leave the building in the event of an alarm! Please head outside now!"

In between the siren's screams there were a lot of groans and scraping chairs. It took a few minutes for the manager to finish hustling everyone else through the foyer, but eventually he turned for a last look and spotted me. He took a few purposeful steps back into the room, looking exasperated. "Miss, come on, I need you to..." His voice trailed off as he took in the look on my face and my hand hidden under the table.

"You should go outside and check on your customers," I called over the noise. The manager turned and fled.

I put the Glock down just long enough to text Simon that Adelaide might be here, knowing that he'd figure out a way to help. When that was done I just sat and waited, perched at the edge of the booth with the Glock in my left hand just below the table, ignoring the piercing wail of the fire alarm and the fluttering in my stomach. I hadn't done anything like this since Atlanta. I didn't know if I was ready...but no one was going to wait for me to be sure.

A moment later, Adelaide Preston strolled through the front door like she was part of the dinner rush.

She was still wearing the dark wig and XXL hoodie, but she'd taken off the glasses and was frowning at me with a hint of amusement in her face. I kept my eyes on her hands, which were jammed in the hoodie pockets.

She came right over to my booth and sat down, ignoring the screaming alarm and the flashing strobe lights. "The glasses were too much, weren't they?" she called.

I shrugged, still holding the Glock by my left thigh. "Not so much the glasses themselves," I yelled back, "but the fact that they were still dry. Your hoodie, too. Like you put them on one second before walking past the window."

"Damn." She sounded almost impressed. "I'm not sure I would've caught that."

I shrugged again. Adelaide was clearly expecting some witty back-and-forth, a testing of each other, but I wasn't interested in playing her game. "I assume you have a sidearm in that pocket?"

"And I assume you have one in your dominant left hand," she said sweetly. "And in case you get any other ideas..." She took one hand out of her pocket and tugged the hoodie's zipper down a few inches, exposing not one, but two tiny burlap bags on a silk cord. It took me a second, because it had been awhile since I'd seen a witch bag.

Adelaide was protected against witch magic. Probably vampire magic too. If the original plan to hold her until sunset was going to work, I'd need to get those bags off her.

It had been stupid of us not to anticipate a witch bag, but then, we rarely went up against humans...and apparently I hadn't learned anything at all from going up against Odessa.

Then I realized what she'd meant by "other ideas." "You thought I was going to, what, pull the life force out of you?"

She just gave me a look that said, *duh*.

It hadn't even occurred to me. I knew boundary witches could draw life from anything nonmagical, but I'd only intentionally done it with plants. The idea of trying to pull magic out of a human until they died...it was too much. Too dangerous.

"*Anyway*," Adelaide sounded impatient with my pause. "I got your *message* about being in town. Not exactly subtle."

"It wasn't supposed to be subtle."

"Where's your hot friend now?" she called, looking around curiously. "Sniper nest across the street?"

I almost snorted at the idea of Simon as a sniper. He wasn't great with guns at ten feet away. "He's around," I yelled back. "Is Orvil?"

Adelaide's eyes narrowed a fraction, but all she said was, "You know, I was pretty disappointed we didn't run into each other in Boulder." She looked me over, like she was inspecting a prize calf at the fair. "I went there instead of LA specifically because of you. I thought you might be fun to play with."

"Oh, I'm no fun at all. Ask anyone."

The fire alarm stopped blaring as abruptly as it had started. Even with the background noise from the rain and the people outside, the room suddenly felt shockingly quiet.

We didn't have a lot of time. "Where's Orvil, Adelaide?"

She snorted. "You can't possibly expect me to answer that."

She was right—of course she wouldn't tell me his daytime location. "Fair enough. We need to meet tonight. I have a message for him."

"Give me the message," she said promptly. "I'll pass it along."

I shook my head. "It has to be in person. Orders, you know."

"That's right." She leaned back in the booth's bench, her lips curving in a predatory smile. "You traded one master for another, didn't you, Sergeant Luther? What's it like being a vampire's lackey?"

I wasn't about to take the bait. "I prefer the term 'henchperson.' And I still need to talk to Orvil."

Adelaide turned her lips up in a smirk. "Why would I bring a vampire to see you? I know what you are." Her voice was disdainful, but at least she didn't bring out "abomination" again. I got that one a lot.

I sighed, letting her see it. "Did you think there wouldn't be repercussions?" I asked. I was genuinely kind of curious about the answer. "That you could kill four nulls, three of them under serious protection, and no one would care?"

Adelaide's expression flickered, just for a second. I'd surprised her, but I wasn't sure how. I took advantage of her momentary quiet. "Lucky for Orvil, you're shit at your job," I said. "Our people are fine. But Maven wants to talk. You and Orvil have to answer for the attempt." This wasn't exactly a lie, though it wasn't the full truth. At least Adelaide wouldn't be able to tell the difference.

"That's the message?" she said skeptically.

I shook my head. "I need to talk to him, Adelaide. If you won't bring me to him, we're going to have to do this the hard way."

She studied me for a second, all playfulness gone. In my

peripheral vision, I saw two firefighters peering into the windows. They'd probably tried the door already, but there had been too much noise in the room to hear. Simon must have figured out a way to shield the building.

Slowly, Adelaide stood up from the booth, keeping her body turned toward me. "You know," she said. "The whole 'can't die' thing, that just fascinates me. I mean, what about through the brain?"

I eased my finger inside the Glock's trigger guard. I really didn't want to kill her—that would blow Maven's plan to hold a trial, and I might never find Orvil. "Head shots are tough. Especially shooting from gut level," I said.

"Good point. Maybe the heart then."

I opened my mouth to reply, but a tiny hole appeared in her sweatshirt pocket, at roughly the same second I heard her gun fire. Pain exploded in my chest.

# 20

## LEX

She shot me twice with a small caliber sidearm—probably a nine-millimeter. I raised the Glock and returned fire on instinct, almost before realizing that I couldn't see. One of Adelaide's shots had traveled through the water glass in front of me, exploding a foot away from my face. Shrapnel and water flew at me, blurring my vision, and for the first few seconds, I wasn't sure what had hit eyes and what had hit skin. By the time I blinked away the water and realized the glass was only in my cheeks, the Glock was being wrenched from my hand.

"Don't fucking move," she said, stepping backward to set the Glock on a table behind her. She made a little motion with the gun. "Hands."

I lifted my hands, still blinking hard.

"I can't believe I was excited about you," Adelaide said scornfully. "This is the great boundary witch, the scourge of every vampire? You barely got a shot off. No wonder you wear a vest."

She had a point, frankly. I could survive most fatal hits, but I'd gotten complacent about regular human enemies.

Or I was just slipping. It was a terrible moment to realize Sam might have been right about me.

And now, without a way to get the witch bag off Adelaide, what did I really have?

Behind Adelaide, something moved. For a moment I thought there was still water in my eyes, but no, it was the water on the floor, in the puddles left near the foyer and tracked into the dining room. It was moving. I had to fight a smile as I made myself focus on Adelaide.

"That's me," I said cheerfully. "Such a letdown."

She frowned. She even took a very quick glance over her shoulder to see if someone had gotten past Simon's shield and into the room with us, but she wasn't watching the floor. Then she turned back, scornful, and took a step toward me. "Whatever. We asked around about boundary witches. A couple of head shots should do the trick...especially if Orvil drinks you dry afterwards. I hear you're like a special vintage."

Behind her, a ball of water the size of a volleyball had collected in midair. I had to fight not to stare at it. I may not have known much about witch bags, but I did know that they weren't the same as shields. I couldn't suck the life out of Adelaide, but physics still applied to her. I just needed to keep her talking for a few more seconds.

"You know, Adelaide, you're a huge disappointment for me too," I said conversationally. "You're supposed to be this badass mercenary, and you spend all your time following a guy around? All that training, all those missions, and you're going to finish your life as a fucking human servant?"

Adelaide's eyes narrowed. "That's not going to work," she spat, but then she added, "And you don't know anything about me, or my training, or my missions." She took a single step forward, so we were only four feet apart. The shimmering ball of water had to adjust, starting to circle around her head to the front. I couldn't see Laurel from where I sat, but she must have been around the corner, peeking out at us. Or maybe she had a mirror.

Adelaide's attention was still fixed on me. "You know the difference between us? The Army threw you out because you were too weird and creepy." She raised her sidearm so the barrel pointed between my eyes. "They threw me out for being too good at my job."

I smiled. "Is *that* what you call failing all the psych evaluations? I think of it more as being crazy. For example, look over your left shoulder."

"What—" Adelaide swung her head around, already lifting the gun, but there was no one there to shoot. Instead, the ball of water dipped down slightly and then drove straight up toward her face.

More specifically, straight up her nose.

Anyone who went swimming as a little kid knows the body's involuntary reaction to flooded sinuses. It doesn't happen as often to adults, who know how to avoid getting water up the nose, but Adelaide hadn't been prepared for the equivalent of a bucket of water splashed up her face. Her sidearm lowered as she began coughing and spitting, eyes streaming from involuntary tears. She didn't drop the gun, but she had to lift her free hand to clear her eyes before she could fire at me, and by then I was on top of her.

I tackled Adelaide around the waist, driving her flat onto her back on the wooden floor. By a stroke of luck, her right arm crashed into the legs of the nearest table, and her gun fell out of her hand, skittering a few feet away. I glanced away to see where it landed, and Adelaide got her hands up, flailing wildly with her fists. She got me in the cheekbone, and we grappled for a few eternal seconds until Adelaide managed to knee me in the chin, snapping my head back. By the time I righted myself Adelaide had wriggled out of my grip and was already staggering to her feet, still coughing furiously. She looked toward the dropped gun, but she'd have to go through me to reach it. Instead, she spun on her heel and fled for the back exit.

I lunged for the Glock and went after her. She was about to disappear around the corner when I squeezed off a single shot, aiming low. I was rewarded with a loud curse. I had clipped her, but not enough to stop her from running.

I grabbed my backpack and followed her, still holding the Glock. The restaurant's back door opened onto a rainy downtown street. I stopped at the door and peeked out, half-expecting Adelaide to be waiting in an ambush. She'd lost one sidearm, but she could easily have more.

The rain made it hard to see more than fifteen feet in front of me, but I caught a glimpse of her hoodie disappearing around the far corner to my left.

I put the Glock back into the pancake holster at my spine and put on my backpack. I couldn't shoot Adelaide, not if I needed her to lead me to Orvil, and I wasn't going to run through town in pouring rain with a live firearm in hand.

"Laurel!" I yelled, in the direction of the bar. I was pretty sure that was her hiding spot. "Call Kirsten and tell her I'm going after Adelaide!"

Without waiting for a response from the water witch, I ran out into the rain.

I was fast, but between the slippery streets and the poor visibility, it was all I could do to keep Adelaide's black hoodie in sight as she sprinted along Main Street, veering left onto Franklin. Everything I was wearing was soaked through to my skin in seconds, and the rain seemed to be driving straight into my eyes. I held up a hand to shield them so I could get a look at

Adelaide as I ran. She had the slightest limp, but it didn't really slow her down—she'd have adrenaline on her side.

I knew the streets a bit by now, and expected her to turn onto Commerce, a busy street where she could lose me in a crowd. Instead, though, she kept going on Franklin as it turned into Water Street. The road went to the right along the levee, but Adelaide turned off onto a set of concrete stairs that lead to the top of the big floodbank, running in a straight line along the top. I remembered the sidewalk Simon and I had seen during our drive.

As I reached the bottom of the staircase, she paused to glance over her shoulder at the top, checking to see if I was following. I made a quick decision to turn right instead of going up. Water Street ran parallel to the levee, and soon I was sprinting along the bottom of the levee while Adelaide ran along the top. The sound of the pounding rain hid any trace of our footsteps. It was like running inside a very slippery white noise machine.

After a couple of minutes Adelaide looked over her shoulder again at the sidewalk behind her. When she didn't see anyone following, her stride changed, relaxing into a jog. She hadn't spotted me down in the shadows.

Then she slowed down further, and I realized where she was headed: the footbridge that went across the Galena River to Grant Park. From there, she could lose me by turning in any number of directions, or even catch a ride—that side of the river was a lot more car-friendly than the downtown district.

Sure enough, Adelaide made a sudden left, turning onto the bridge. I swerved to run up the levee after her. The wet grass was slick, the ground waterlogged, and my feet kept slipping on the incline. I started grabbing fistfuls of grass to pull myself forward, but then a chunk of dirt pulled away in my hand and I fell, sliding a few inches down and face-planting on the hill.

I spit dirt and jumped back up, climbing like a monkey, but by the time I reached the top of the levee and looked across the bridge, Adelaide was just getting off the other side.

I started across, trying to keep Adelaide in sight and keep my footing at the same time. The bridge seemed to stretch on endlessly, and because of the drop on either end, I couldn't see which direction Adelaide had taken when she'd climbed off it.

By the time I made it across the footbridge, Adelaide had reached Park Avenue and wheeled right, straight toward where the road crossed the highway. She pelted through the intersection between cars and disappeared.

I tried to follow, but there were three semis in a row bearing down on me, and I knew I couldn't make it. I skidded to a stop.

When the road was clear, I let myself walk across, my lungs burning. This neighborhood was full of massive nineteenth century mansions, which loomed against the darkening sky. Adelaide had vanished. The street was silent except for the pounding rain.

"*Shit.*" I walked in a circle with my hands on my hips to cool down, but I really wanted to punch something. I'd let Adelaide slip through my fingers.

The burner phone buzzed in my pocket. I pulled it out and glowered down at the screen, which read Operator.

I hit the glowing green talk button. "Yeah."

"Lex?" Kirsten sounded concerned. "Are you all right?"

"I'm unhurt, but I lost Adelaide," I said through my teeth. It hurt to say it out loud. "You talked to Simon and Laurel?"

"They're both fine. The first responders are leaving the sandwich shop. They think it was an elaborate prank."

I rubbed my forehead, which was kind of pointless considering the rain. "Okay."

"Where are you?"

Good question. There was a sign right in front of me, and

behind it stood a particularly elaborate red-brick mansion that looked like something out of *Gone With the Wind*. I wiped rain out of my eyes so I could read the sign. "The Belvedere Mansion," I told her. "On Park Street."

"Okay. I'll have them come get you."

The "they" threw me. Laurel should have gone back to the other water witches by now. "Laurel and Simon?"

"No," Kirsten said patiently. "Scarlett and Jesse. They just got to Galena."

# 21

## SCARLETT

Galena, Illinois

As soon as we reached Galena, it was clear that I did not actually understand rain.

Desert or not, LA *does* get rain. There's usually a week in February where it drizzles every day, and we all get to find out just how unprepared we are for an attack of sky moisture. The buildings, the streets, our clothes—nothing is made for rain. It's too much of an anomaly, this freak event that derails your day for a few hours and reminds you how much you prefer the sunshine.

But the rain in Galena was different. It wasn't just that it was relentless, or how it pounded violently onto the pavement like it had fallen all the way from space. It was...well, the word that Jesse used, which I couldn't get out of my head, was "biblical." I hadn't known that rain like this existed, and I sort of preferred the ignorance.

We pulled into Galena around seven, with an hour and a

half hour before sunset. The Head Vampires in Charge were arriving the following night, which gave us just twenty-four hours to make all the preparations for the trial. I called Kirsten to see where we should meet Lex, and found myself getting the whole story of Laurel and Lex's run-in with Adelaide Preston. By the time Kirsten called Lex, called us back, and gave us the address to pick her up, we were almost to downtown—which meant we were about two minutes away from the Belvedere. Galena was *not* a large town.

We turned onto Park Street, which ended in a cul-de-sac. There were two buildings on the left, and Jesse pulled over in front of the second one, a very *Gone With the Wind*-looking mansion. I opened the RV's door to admit one extremely wet, and extremely pissed-off-looking, boundary witch. She radiated so much frustration that even I couldn't think of anything to say that I was sure wouldn't get me punched in the face.

There was a moment of awkward silence that dragged on forever. Jesse pulled away from the curb and started to turn around in the cul-de-sac, and I finally managed to come up with, "Want some dry clothes?"

Lex gave me a tight-lipped nod. My suitcase was right next to my nest, so I leaned over to dig out a pair of jeans and a T-shirt. It felt weird to lend out my underwear, but after glancing back up at her I added a pair of panties and a sports bra as well. I gave her the bundle of clothes and gestured at the RV bathroom. "Our extra driver is in the bedroom," I explained. Wordlessly, Lex marched back toward the bathroom to change.

I went up to the front cab to climb into the shotgun seat next to Jesse. "I know this is obvious, but I'm going to say it anyway," I whispered. "Remind me never to piss her off."

He shot me a sideways grin before quickly turning back to

the road. Driving in this kind of rain in what amounted to a small tank couldn't be easy. "I wouldn't want to be Adelaide Preston."

I yawned. "You know where we're going?"

"To our hotel."

THE RV PUTTERED over a bridge and into a downtown area that looked like Disneyland's Main Street, USA, only with a lot more red brick. Despite the surroundings, the word *hotel* had me picturing some generic Hilton-type arrangement, but the DeSoto House turned out to be a rectangular red brick building that I could almost mistake for a factory, if it didn't have a balcony with a bunch of those patriotic bunting flags. The streets were congested with cars, raindrops bouncing in the headlights. Jesse managed to pull into a loading zone in front.

"I'm glad we're not trying to fit this thing in a parking lot," he said, putting the behemoth RV in Park.

Lex came out of the bathroom wearing my clothes, which looked loose at the hips and bust. I tried not to take that personally. She looked a little calmer, but still distracted. "No kidding," she said. "I texted Simon to meet us here," she said. "We walked through earlier today when we were checking out the town."

We woke up Hayne and said a quick goodbye, then hurried through the pounding rain into the hotel lobby. I was first through the door, since Jesse wouldn't let me carry anything other than a small messenger bag, and I found myself stopping in my tracks just inside the door with my mouth agape. "Whoa," Jesse said, gently nudging me out of the doorway. "This is...this is a lot."

"Yeah," Lex said, carrying a plastic bag with her clothes

inside, "There may be such a thing as too much historical preservation."

The DeSoto House Hotel was, in a word, hideous. The lobby decor was done in the theme of Very Ugly Brown: intentionally splotchy brown wallpaper, brown floral carpet, brown wood everything. It looked busy and dated, like all the worst instincts of the nineteenth century had somehow merged with all the worst choices of the 1970s. "Dashiell's going to love it," I declared. Beatrice did the decorating at their Pasadena mansion, with the exception of Dashiell's unfortunately Victorian office.

Jesse went to the front desk to check in so he could hand the suitcase off to a bellhop, and then Lex led us through the lobby, which featured a massive winding staircase that would have been beautiful if it wasn't so doing such a great job showing off both the wallpaper and the carpet. Past it, we walked down a long hallway overlooking an interior courtyard below. Thankfully, the courtyard was more modern/generic and therefore didn't make my eyes want to bleed.

"Your group has reserved the whole top floor," Lex explained over her shoulder. "But *this* floor has a Quiet Room."

"Sorry, a what?"

"It's really just a lounge. I guess they don't want you to shout."

Then we arrived at a small glass-walled room off the hall, like an expensively decorated hospital waiting room, and I saw what she meant. There was a TV on one wall playing what looked like an infomercial about the hotel, but someone had kindly muted it. It had probably been the man his early thirties who sat in one off the room's easy chairs, staring at a laptop screen.

He stood up when we came in, clearly happy to see Lex, and I saw that he was great-looking in a nerdy, "I'll fix your computer while I lecture you about virus protection" kind of way. I was more or less immune to handsomeness after spending so much time around Jesse, but I still had to suppress the urge to glance over my shoulder at Lex and do a slow clap. I had a feeling it would not be appreciated.

"Hi," the guy said, coming straight to me with his hand outstretched. He wore olive pants and a soft-looking T-shirt that showed off lean muscle. A still-wet raincoat had been draped carefully over the back of his chair to dry. "You must be Scarlett Bernard. I'm so excited to meet you."

I glanced sideways to raise an eyebrow at Lex, who just shrugged. "Lower your expectations, dude," I told him, shaking his hand. "I don't know what you've heard, but I put my bra on one boob at a time just like everyone else."

"Scarlett, this is Simon Pellar, my witch friend," Lex said, in that tone that suggested she was trying very hard to be patient with me. "Simon, this is Scarlett and Jesse."

"*This* is the witch friend you brought?" Jesse asked her.

"He was expecting a woman," I explained to Simon. "He's very sexist."

Jesse protested, but Simon just smiled at me. "Lex said you're big on inappropriate jokes," he said cheerfully.

"She's not wrong."

To Jesse, he added, "Don't worry, I get that a lot. Shall we sit?"

Jesse sat in an armchair to my right, stretching his long legs out in front of him, while I lowered myself carefully into a loveseat. Lex must have been watching me, because while everyone was still getting settled she turned to me, looking contrite. "I'm sorry; I haven't asked how you're feeling."

She held up a hand to her own face to indicate my black eyes. "Those look painful."

I blew out a breath and swallowed my first response, which

was something along the lines of "I'm fine." If I tried that, Jesse would worry about just how much I was lying. "I'm sore, my headache comes and goes, and I get tired easily," I said matter-of-factly. "But it's a lot better than when we left LA. I'm probably at eighty percent."

Jesse coughed into his hand, a noise that sounded suspiciously like "Sixty." This was probably why he hadn't sat next to me on the loveseat. He was staying out of swatting distance.

When I was done glaring at him, I turned back to Lex. "What do we need to do to get ready for tomorrow night?"

Simon spoke up. "I need to finish the wards. I did Beau's hotel and ours, but I still need to set something up at Turner Hall, where we're doing the trial."

Lex drummed her fingers on her lap. "Yeah, I think Beau's planning to go to Turner Hall just after sunset; he's got the keys."

Jesse nodded. "I'd like to check out the security there."

"Why?" I asked, gesturing at Lex. "We've got security right here. She and Quinn will be on duty."

Lex blanched, which was fun, but Jesse just smiled at me. "Their job is to protect Maven," he explained. "I'm here to watch *your* back." He turned to include Simon and Lex. "I know you don't spend as much time working with a null, but Scarlett being here makes this a little like any high-stakes human event. Which means we need to look at ways in and out of the building, the security system, the locks, all that stuff."

"I can do all that," I argued, unable to help myself. Jesse was just looking out for me, but sometimes the defensiveness was like a reflex. "I know how to be safe."

Jesse opened his mouth to answer, but Lex overrode him. "You all can meet Beau at Turner Hall if you want. I still have to find Adelaide and Orvil. I need to inform them of the trial and make sure they're not going to leave town." She shook her head. "I lost Adelaide outside the park."

"I've been thinking about that," Simon broke in. "Where exactly did you last see her?"

She frowned. "On Park Street, near a big house called... Belleview? No. Belvedere. With a capital B, like a proper name."

Simon sort of shifted in his chair, looking excited. "That's what I thought Kirsten said. Look at this." He turned his laptop around, displaying a webpage that mainly consisted of a color photo of the same mansion where we'd picked up Lex. At the top it said "Belvedere Mansion and Gardens."

"This is the Belvedere Mansion," he said, adjusting his wire-rimmed glasses. "It was built for a steamboat magnate in 1857, but today it operates as a sort of eclectic museum. Lots of antiques, including some from movies, and a bunch of things that were owned by Liberace, for...reasons. But the important thing," he added, catching the impatient look on Lex's face. "Is that according to their website and voicemail, the Belvedere is closed for the next two weeks for some unscheduled maintenance." Simon looked at each of us in turn, making sure we'd caught the significance. "During the height of the summer tourist season."

"Interesting," Jesse said in his old Cop Voice.

Simon inclined his head. "To be fair, I've gone through old Facebook posts, and it's happened before that there was a sudden issue with the pipes or roof or whatever, and it had to close down for a bit. It's a really old building, lots of maintenance. But—" He set the laptop down on the coffee table and picked up a big paperback book I hadn't noticed. "The Belvedere is in this book, too. It says the walls are made of double layers of brick. Lots of small interior spaces."

"Strong construction, windowless rooms," Lex said,

nodding. "Perfect for the antebellum vampire who wants to feel like he's back in 1860."

She stood up and began walking back and forth under the television. I was used to werewolves pacing their territory, but Lex seemed more like her body *had* to move in order to think. "There were three cars parked in front of the Belvedere when I saw it," she said. "Out-of-state plates, probably rentals."

Jesse looked at his watch. "Seems a little late for construction. You think Orvil and Adelaide took over the Belvedere?"

Lex paused. "I don't know. In a way it makes sense, but Adelaide's smart, and she probably figured I was still following her. Why would she lead me right back to their base of operations?"

"You said you shot her, right?" Jesse asked. "Maybe she was wounded. Not thinking."

Lex shook her head. "I don't buy it."

"Why not?" Simon asked.

"Because it's not what I would do."

Jesse and I exchanged a glance. I hadn't exactly spent a ton of time around Lex, but I hadn't seen her quite like this—fidgety and distracted, fuming about Adelaide. Was there something bigger going on with her, or was she just worried about her niece?

I thought about bringing up Corry's group—they'd checked in with Kirsten, who said everything was fine—but Kirsten would have updated Lex on that too. And I knew I wasn't the person that Lex would want to talk to about feelings. *Any* feelings.

There was a pause, and then Lex stopped her pacing and turned on her heel like she was addressing her troops. "I'm going back to Belvedere," she declared. "I'll see if there's any sign that it's occupied by vampires. If nothing else, I'll stake out the place in case they come back."

I turned to Jesse. "You should go with her," I suggested. Maybe he'd be able to talk to Lex. The two of them were closer than Lex and I. "I'll go to Turner Hall with Simon and look at the security for tomorrow night."

Jesse opened his mouth to argue, so I added, "I'll also take a bunch of photos."

Jesse shut his mouth, swallowed, nodded. "Is that okay with you?" he asked Lex.

"Sure. We'll go on foot; it's easier to get around that way. I've got rain gear at our hotel."

Simon cleared his throat. "Um, the Belvedere's pretty old," he said to Lex. He had that look like he was tiptoeing around a dangerous predator. Funny, Jesse got that face a lot too. "There will be ghosts."

"I'll take my stuff," she told him. "If it seems like the Belvedere is going to be a hot spot in this thing, I can lay the ghosts too. Jesse can watch my back."

Simon sort of looked like he wanted to argue with that, but he just nodded and stood up. "Sounds like a plan."

Jesse looked pained. "Um, I don't have a rain jacket," he said apologetically.

Simon grinned. "You can borrow my stuff; I've got rain pants and an extra poncho at the hotel."

"Wow, you guys were prepared," I said.

Lex just shrugged. "Colorado," she said by way of explanation.

## 22

### SCARLETT

Lex and Jesse left first, since they needed to stop at the other hotel, and I looked expectantly at Simon. "Where's your car?" I asked.

He smiled. "We have a rental, but it's probably easier just to walk. This downtown wasn't exactly built for motorized vehicles."

"Right. Walking. We don't really do that where I'm from. Is it far?"

Simon shook his head. "Maybe five minutes? The hotel has umbrellas we can use," he added.

"Let's go."

We left the DeSoto House and walked, as far as I could tell, approximately north. I had studied a map of downtown Galena during the long drive from LA, but it was kind of hard to orient myself in the rain and dark, so I tried to pay attention to street names. Simon had mentioned things like going "up" and "down" to certain spots, and I quickly saw why: the whole downtown seemed to be built on a massive hill.

I had to walk fairly slowly up Green Street, which was a vertical incline, but then we turned right on Bench Street, which was much easier. Simon didn't seem to mind walking slowly for me, even though it meant our pants were soaked through below our knees before we even made the turn onto Bench. It probably helped that he was peppering me with questions the whole time: about being a null, my bargest, having a superpowered witch baby, and so on. I got the impression that if the walk had taken four hours instead of ten minutes, Simon would have been ready with four hours' worth of questions.

Normally I would find this kind of thing annoying, but today I did my best to answer graciously. It was obvious that his curiosity was just that—an honest desire to learn. At one point he mentioned his non–Old World career as an evolutionary biologist, and that made a lot of sense. I never thought about the science of the Old World, or how it worked parallel to magic. Both things simply *were*, in my mind.

To my amusement, Simon even ran a few "tests" as we walked—trying small spells now and then only to feel them zap out in my radius. Each time the spell failed, he fell silent with an excited look on his face, like he was making mental notes for a paper he planned to write.

The spells made it obvious that Simon was actually quite powerful, especially for a man—I'd only met a handful of witches who were stronger, including Lex and Kirsten. He was impressive yet earnest. I could see why Lex liked him.

As we made our way along Bench Street, we passed a tiny brick building that looked like a one-room schoolhouse, or maybe a little chapel, only with a lot of windows. Simon saw me looking at it. ""Lex and I were by here earlier. That's the restored Fire House Number 1," he explained. "It's sort of like a museum exhibit now, with the original fire wagons inside."

I started to say something like, "cool," but then I saw what was next to the old fire house and stopped short. "Whoa." It was a massive public staircase, leading straight up into the darkness. "Where does *that* go?" I asked, pointing. It didn't even occur to me that Simon wouldn't know the answer. He seemed like he could give tours of Galena at this point.

"Up to Bench Street." He explained about the town expanding up, and how early residents would have to climb up and down several times a day.

"Jesus. That's a lot of stairs."

Turner Hall, when we arrived, looked a little different from the rest of the downtown's red brick, frozen-in-time vibe. A short set of stairs went from the sidewalk to an elevated Mission-style building, made of light, rough bricks that were bigger and less colonial than the ones that made up the DeSoto. "This is the first building I've seen here that could be in Southern California," I said.

"These bricks are dolomite," Simon explained. "The Hall was made out of them back in the 1870s. When it burned down in 1926, the exterior walls were pretty much untouched."

"Damn, you're just like a hunky Wikipedia with legs, aren't you?"

Simon actually tripped on a crack in the sidewalk at that, which made me a little happy. But I did take mercy on him and change the subject. "Anyway. It sounds like this town had an awful lot of fires and floods back in the day," I said as we climbed the front steps. "Maybe that's why they rebuilt this place with a fricking fire station attached to it."

It was true. If you looked at the brick—excuse me, dolomite—structure from the street, only about two-thirds of it appeared to be Turner Hall. The third on the right was an extension, sort of like an extra wing, with *Galena Fire Department* written across the top in subtle silver letters.

The two of us walked to the front entrance of Turner Hall,

which was still locked. There was a sort of decorative balcony underscoring the big mission-style windows, and we stood underneath it to get out of the worst of the rain. "Why would the cardinal vampires want to hold a trial next to a fire department?" Simon asked.

"Because they won't be in there," called a jovial voice from, of course, the shadows. I looked around, and found that Beau had materialized from the corner of the building, by the Hall's small parking lot. He paused there, just outside my radius.

I rolled my eyes, though no one saw it under the umbrella. Vampires did this kind of thing a lot when they first met me—hovered at the edge of my normal range, so they could become familiar with my usual limits. Plenty of them never found out that I could control the size of my radius with a little effort.

"Hello, Beau." Simon's arm twitched like he was going to extend his hand, but he thought better of it.

The vampire sauntered toward us. He was wearing the fancy boots, tan riding pants that looked like they were made of some sort of coated denim, and a waxed-canvas field jacket. There was even an old-fashioned flat cap made from more waxed canvas. The full effect was "elegant country gentleman on his way to a polo match," but as he hit my radius he stumbled and made a very inelegant gurgling noise. I had to hold my hand in front of my face and fake a yawn to cover my smile.

"The rain is going to continue all through the night and tomorrow, and this town takes flooding very seriously," Beau explained after he recovered. "The emergency response teams will likely be very busy, and if not, we'll press them to go somewhere else."

The night was warm, despite the rain, but I felt a shiver hit my spine. This was real. We were setting a real trap for a killer, and he was going to respond. "What if he decides to just sneak up on us one by one and slit our throats?" Simon asked. He looked worried, and I realized he was probably used to counting on wards.

Beau looked at me and gave a little bow. "That is where this lovely lady comes in."

I straightened up and looked at Beau. "First, don't call me 'lovely lady,' and second, I assume you mean you want me to extend my radius during the trial. How far?"

"How far can you go?"

That gave me pause. How far *could* I go? I'd never really tested it, despite Molly's frequent entreating. There was part of me that didn't want to know. The farthest I'd probably gone since I learned about magic was probably the night at Erson Station when I'd covered a couple of acres, but I'd been very emotional, which made my radius extend by itself—and without my control. I shrugged at Beau. "Less than a mile. More than an acre."

"That's quite a large range of possibility," he pointed out.

"How many people can you press at the same time?" I countered. "What can you get them to do? Could you press someone to do something in a year? This is fucking *magic*, dude, not the scientific method."

Simon suddenly needed to cough into his hand, but all Beau said was, "Right, then." He reached into his pocket to pull out a set of keys on a plain ring. "Who wants a tour?"

## 23

LEX

Scarlett and Jesse's rental car hadn't been delivered to the hotel yet, so Jesse and I picked up my rental Forester and drove it across the bridge to the Belvedere. I wasn't sure we'd end up needing the car at all, given how the town was laid out, but I wanted it close in case Adelaide drove off somewhere. And it was a base where we could keep extra weapons. I had shredder stakes in there that hadn't been shorted out by being near Scarlett.

I had put on rain pants and a long, hooded rain jacket over my waterproof Merrells, and Jesse more or less fit in the rain pants and extra poncho Simon had brought. Everything we wore was either black or a green so black it wouldn't matter in the dark.

The sun had officially set a little while ago, but by the time I found a parking spot around the corner from the mansion, the sky past the city lights was an inky black that only seemed more opaque because of the quicksilver flashes of rain. As soon as I turned the vehicle off, its wiper blades stopped, and the windshield became a blur of water.

I reached over and held out the rental key fob to Jesse. "Take this," I said, gritting my teeth. "You're going to have to drive us back later."

"What? Why?" Jesse took the key fob.

"Because it's full dark," I said quietly, risking a look at him. Which was stupid. As soon as my eyes went past him and out the window beyond, I couldn't stop myself from staring.

Ghosts don't come with an on/off switch—it's not like they just blink into view for me the second the sun disappears below the horizon. Vampires wake up like that, but ghosts have their own timing: They sort of fade into existence when the night hits full darkness. Which had happened about thirty seconds ago. Now the closest remnant was practically touching the side view mirror near Jesse.

He had been a young boy, maybe twelve or thirteen, and he was coughing violently into his hand. He was emaciated and frail-looking, the coughs racking his body until he doubled over, then fell down on all fours. I leaned toward Jesse to see the boy holding his hand up in our direction, then in another, and another. He was begging for help from people walking by, but they'd all been dead for centuries.

Jesse turned his head to follow my gaze out his window, but he wasn't going to see anything but a dark, rainy street. He was smart enough to figure out what was happening to me, though.

"Ghosts?" he asked, glancing over his shoulder at me.

"Uh-huh."

"Even in all this rain?" There was a note of almost childlike wonder in his voice, and I might have smiled if I hadn't been so distracted.

"Doesn't affect them." If anything, the rain made it easier to see the glowing figures. It gave them substance.

"What do they...do?" Jesse asked.

"These are remnants, the most common type of ghost," I explained. "They're trapped on a loop, acting out the moments just before and during their death."

"Are they aware of us?"

"Remnants? No, not unless I feed them my blood."

"Are there a lot of them?"

"Um. Yes." In reality, there were maybe twenty ghosts on this block, but it felt like so many more. Partly this was because ghosts paid no attention to natural social barriers like roads or sidewalks, or even buildings; and partly because each and every one of them was dying. It was as though the street was a vast stage, and every actor stood alone, each in their own spotlight, each one pantomiming a different death. Only they weren't acting. It was an echo of something very real.

I tore my eyes away from the boy and unbuckled my seat-belt on autopilot. Before I reached for the door handle, though, I glanced out my own window. My gaze was caught by a middle-aged woman being run down in the middle of the street. Nearby, a man in a Union uniform clutched at his stomach, shock and terror on his face as he crumpled to the ground. Beyond him, a disheveled man in a waistcoat stumbled out of a building that no longer stood. He bent over to vomit, looked surprised, and clutched at his neck. Blood spilled in a curtain over his hand and chest. He flickered for a moment, then stumbled out of the imaginary building again, restarting the loop.

"Lex!" Jesse was gently shaking my shoulder. "Hey. Are you all right?"

I swallowed hard and squeezed my eyes shut. When I opened them again, I made myself look at the living person in the car with me, even though he didn't glow like the dead. "It's very...distracting."

Jesse's brow furrowed. "Okay. What do you want to do?"

That was easy: I wanted to lay the ghosts. I wanted to release all of them, these fragments that had gotten stuck on this side of the boundary between life and death.

But this mission was about the living, and Adelaide Preston had already gotten away from me once. If we didn't find her soon, she'd be able to get out of Galena and this whole plan would fall apart—leaving Charlie's fate uncertain.

This thought, terrible as it was, centered me. The world was full of ghosts. If I only tended to them, I'd lose my place among the living.

I took a deep breath, in and out, and touched the bloodstone on its cord around my neck. "If we have time, I'll come back and lay them. For now, though..." I had to think for another second. I had originally wanted to sneak around the exterior of the Belvedere and look in the windows, but there were a lot of exterior lights around the buildings. Skulking around would look really suspicious if a car passed us.

"We'll do the stakeout," I decided. "There's a group of trees across the street that will provide good cover. As long as the whole area isn't crowded with ghosts, we can watch for Adelaide and Orvil there."

Jesse's eyebrows went up. "If vampires are coming and going from that building, won't they catch our scent?"

This seemed like a stupid question until I remembered he was from Los Angeles. "The rain," I explained. "That's part of why we chose it to clear the town. It dampens air circulation, which means scents won't travel as far, and it covers a lot of noise. It's not quite the same as sneaking up on humans, but it's as close as we can get without Scarlett or Charlie."

His face cleared. "Got it. And if we do see Adelaide and Orvil?"

I explained my plan, and we spent a few minutes discussing it back and forth and checking my backpack for supplies.

When we were ready, I reached for the door handle. "Just so you know," I added, "I'm going to walk in kind of a crooked path to get down the block. Just...go with it." I got out of the car without waiting for his response.

I strode down the sidewalk with Jesse next to me. I had to make occasional detours around remnants, and he followed along with me, sort of picking his way as thought we might be avoiding a pothole together. We didn't bother trying to talk—the rain seemed louder than it had been earlier, and we'd have to shout to hear each other. Not exactly what you wanted on a stakeout.

As we walked, I tried not to stare at the deaths all around me, and I tried not to think about what Sam had said about psychic damage. When we reached the intersection where I'd lost Adelaide, Park Avenue and Decauter Street, I took Jesse's arm, slowing down a little as though we were a couple out for a stroll. The building on the corner was dark, but next to it the Belvedere was blazing with light, standing out against the rainy dark. Like so many buildings in Galena, the property was elevated off the street by a waist-high wall, probably as a defense against flooding. You had to take a short set of stairs to get up to the lawn, or rather, up to the sidewalk path that lead across the lawn to the building itself. There was a wrought-iron gate blocking the stairs, so I walked right past it, circling around a little girl in a bonnet being struck down by something much larger, probably a horse. At this end of the little cult-de-sac there was what looked like an old bike path with a Do Not Enter sign, and next to it a copse of trees and ferns that led into the woods.

Without really discussing it, Jesse and I waded into this little outcropping and dropped low. I worked my way around a tree so I could see the Belvedere and still have cover from the trunk, although the bushes were doing a lot to keep us from view. Between the darkness and the rain I couldn't even really see Jesse, but he must have done the same, because the outline of his head appeared briefly against the light from the Belvedere, and then I felt him settle down next to me on the ground.

"Why are there so many plants," he muttered, pushing leaves aside. "It's like mini Jurassic Park over here."

"There are forests in California," I pointed out.

"Pine trees that grow straight up. We don't have...whatever these are. Ferns? Bushes? I want a machete."

I smiled. Jesse might just be trying to distract me by grousing about the forest, but it was kind of working. "They're big on weapons here. We could probably find you one in the stores tomorrow."

The rain pounded down onto the street in front of the Belvedere, hitting the pavement hard enough to create a steam-like effect as it bounced off the road.

"Does it seem like the rain is more intense than it was when we got into town?" Jesse asked, as if reading my thoughts.

I nodded. "It's coming down harder than it was before."

"Do you think that's intentional?"

Huh. It was a good question. I wasn't sure if Laurel and her sisters could control it with that kind of precision, or if they were just calling the water and letting it pour down however it wanted. I gave Jesse a shrug, then remembered he couldn't see it. "I don't know. But if Orvil is in that building, I'm not worried about him hearing us through all this."

"Can you check, in case he got in another way?"

I'd told Jesse about my boundary magic mindset. "Good idea. Can you get behind me a little?"

Jesse shuffled on his butt so he was more or less at my back, and I closed my eyes, concentrating on my breathing. I reached for my boundary mindset and opened my eyes.

My brain processes visible magic sort of like I'm looking through thermal imaging goggles —only instead of a heat signature, I see a person's essence, the soul or life force or whatever you want to call it. For whatever reason this doesn't apply to remnants, who aren't really made out of essence. They're more like an echo of it.

When I opened my eyes, I still had to block out some of Jesse's blazing life force, so close to me. Then I stared in the direction of Belvedere Mansion. A vampire would have appeared as a red figure, and a human or witch as blue, but inside the mansion, there was nothing at all. I turned my head, scanning, and saw life forces moving around the building next to the Belvedere, and two more whizzing by on my left—a car going by on the next street. That was it.

I released the boundary mindset and told Jesse he could return to his position. "Nothing alive in there," I reported, "Including vampires."

"If Orvil just woke up, he may have gone out to feed," Jesse pointed out. "Or maybe Adelaide needed medical attention. You said you didn't know how bad she was hit."

"Yeah..." But I didn't like this. I didn't like any of it. "We'll just have to wait, I guess." I tried not to let my knee jiggle up and down.

A few minutes went by in silence, or as close as you can get while sitting in torrential rain. My thoughts were spinning around in a wretched circle: letting Adelaide get away, my conversation with Sam, the idea of psychic damage...Quinn.

Because of the communications ban, I hadn't been in touch with my partner in more than thirty-six hours, since before dawn the day before. Even then, we hadn't had a proper conversation. As soon as Maven, Quinn and I had arrived back in Boulder I'd had to run home to pack and make arrangements for my rescue animals. I didn't think we'd talked about anything that wasn't logistic arrangements since before Charlie was attacked.

Which meant we still hadn't had a real conversation about Scarlett Bernard's ability to turn vampires permanently human. Which left me wondering what kind of relationship I was going to come back to, if I survived all of this.

I couldn't stand that line of thought, and I couldn't fidget or walk around, so I tried to think of something I could talk about with Jesse. I considered him a friend, even if we hadn't talked for a while.

I turned my face toward his ear and kept my voice low. "I meant to tell you," I began, "congratulations on the engagement. That's really great news."

Jesse gave me a surprised look. "Oh. Um, thanks."

I'm not known for my sensitivity, but there was a note in his voice that even I couldn't miss. "Uh. Everything okay there?"

He sighed. "I proposed months ago, but we still haven't set a date."

Whoops. We were entering conversational territory where I was pretty much useless, so I tried to remember back to when Sam and John got married. "Is it that you have different ideas about the ceremony?"

He shook his head. "That's what I thought, for a long time. I have a fairly large extended family, and her parents were murdered, back before we met. Her family is just her and her brother. I thought maybe she didn't want to have the wedding without her folks."

I felt a pang of regret. I hadn't known that Scarlett's parents had been killed. We didn't really talk about our regular lives, only when there was a crisis at hand.

"I offered to make it just the two of us at City Hall, but she said no, she wants us to get to have the celebration," Jesse went on. "Then I thought it was about logistics, because most of the people we care about are Old World. She wouldn't want to get married without our friends Wyatt and Molly, you know, and maybe she was worried about having to watch her radius on the day. So I suggested having it at night." He gave a little shrug. "She just kind of demurred."

"What do you think it is?" I heard myself asking.

He sighed. "Honestly? I think she feels like she shouldn't be allowed to get married because she shouldn't get to be happy."

That made me blink for a long few seconds, not sure how to respond. I hadn't really thought of Scarlett as the kind of person who would see things that way. It wasn't that I thought she was selfish or that her life had been easy, exactly, but she'd always struck me as sort of careless and inconsiderate. In my defense, she'd cremated my twin sister's body and deprived my family of closure for the rest of their lives.

*Eh. I'm over it,* came my sister's voice in my head. She sounded dry and a little wistful, which got my attention. *Really?* I thought back at her. *Because of her, Mom and Dad didn't get to bury you.*

*You had a funeral after a year, remember? Besides, I like Scarlett. She's a dog-loving LA mom in her late 20s with a mixed-race baby and a super weird job. How could I* not *root for her?*

I felt myself smile, then realized Jesse had been talking to me. "Lex?" He had placed a hand cautiously on my forearm, like he was afraid I might deck him for it. "Are you okay?"

"What? Oh yeah, sorry. I was talking to Sam," I said without thinking.

"Sam your...um...dead sister? That Sam?"

"Right. Sorry." Jesse and I talked on the phone and texted, but we'd never spent all that much time together in person. "I know I probably space out, but the people I spend a lot of time around are just used to it by now."

"That's...huh." He sounded interested and a little unsettled, like most people who find out I talk to Sam. "What was she saying?"

I smiled again. "That she's rooting for Scarlett."

"Yeah." Jesse sighed and turned back to face the Belvedere again. "So am I."

## 24

LEX

A little after ten, a man without a raincoat came strolling toward the Belvedere.

"That's him," I said, standing up. "He's going to go in. Stay here until I take him."

"Are you s–" Jesse began, but I didn't even turn to look over my shoulder. I was moving toward the Belvedere on autopilot, running from the cover of one tree to another. I reached under my shirt and pulled my mother's bloodstone out out and over my head by its leather thong, shoving it into a pocket of my rain pants. Just ahead, I saw Orvil skip up the brick stairs, ducking under the overhanging balcony, out of the rain.

"Lex!" Jesse hissed from behind me. I motioned to him behind my back, hoping the LAPD used similar hand signals as the Army. *Stay back, take cover.* Then I began jogging toward Orvil Grant.

Under any other conditions I'd never have a chance at sneaking up on a vampire. The driving rain was so loud, though, that I got all the way to his side of the street, maybe twenty feet from the entrance to Belvedere Manor. I might have been able to get closer, but I didn't want to risk him whipping around and catching me. I slowed to a walk and wrapped my arms around my chest.

"Um, excuse me, sir?" I called, in my shallowest voice.

The vampire turned. He wasn't tall, maybe five-nine, clean-shaven, and with his wet hair slicked to one side. He was handsome, I realized. It hadn't really come through in the old photographs, but there was a light in his eyes, the dancing gleam of a con man who'd give you one hell of a ride on the way to damnation.

"Yes, my dear?" His tone was amused, almost condescending. Right. I always forgot how young I look. "Are you lost?"

Fifteen feet away. I rolled my eyes, picking up my step."Oh my *God*, yes. I walked from the hotel, and now I'm all turned around, and my girlfriend borrowed my charger, see?" I held up my cell phone, waving it around as though it was dead. Ten feet away. "Is there a phone in that..." I squinted past him, to the door of the manor. He'd just cracked it open. "Sorry, the museum or whatever?" I stopped at the bottom of the steps, five feet away. Rain or no rain, if I got much closer, he'd smell the lies on me.

Orvil's hand had drifted away from the doorknob, and now he turned to face me. A motion-sensor light over the door flicked on just behind him. Funny how it hadn't gone off when he'd practically flown up the stairs.

But at least the vampire was illuminated. His smile said he didn't entirely believe me but was willing to play it out a little. "Oh, my. No, I don't believe the landline is operational, but I do have my own cellular phone right here—" He made a show of reaching for his jacket pocket, but then there was an inhuman-fast movement, and suddenly I was hanging in the air, his iron-strong fingers wrapped around my throat.

I fought my body's automatic urge to kick my legs, forcing myself to go limp. He wasn't squeezing, but he'd lifted me in the air with his upward pressure under my jaw, something you usually only see in movies.He stepped up onto the top stair so I would dangle in the air over the other stairs. I got a noseful of some kind of cologne that smelled like cedar and bergamot and a high price tag.

Orvil just held me there for a moment, staring suspiciously, and I made my eyes big and round, playing utter shock even as he drew me closer. Our faces were inches away. "You smell like gun oil," he said.

"Second amendment," I squeaked, pulling at his fingers around my throat. He could have killed me instantly with a little pressure—well, it would have killed a human woman—but a vampire wouldn't waste blood like that.

Unhurriedly, Orvil reached up with his free hand and tugged at the cuff of my jean jacket, exposing the wooden handle of a shredder. "And wooden stakes," he observed. "Tsk tsk." He pulled the shredder out by the handle and tossed it away, into the darkness. "Toss the other one, or I *will* squeeze," he said pleasantly, his eyes on my other wrist.

I glared at him, but tugged the other shredder loose and tossed it after the first one.

Abruptly, he spun to his right, twirling me into an arc so my whole back and legs flew straight into the side of the Belvedere. We'd only turned a few feet, really, and he hadn't let my head impact, but it still felt like being swatted by a brick wall. I didn't have to fake my cry of pain, or the grimace. Nothing was broken, though.

"Who are you?" he hissed, his face inches away. With the angled spotlighting, Orvil Grant no longer looked like a handsome rogue. He looked stern and terrifying.

His eyes bored into mine, and I felt the sensation I'd been

waiting for. It was like Orvil and I were suddenly looking at each other through two cardboard paper towel rolls, or maybe those long tubes they use for gift wrap. I felt the pressure as Orvil reached out with vampire magic, trying to push into my head.

All of that probably took three seconds. Then I reached in my pocket and wrapped my hand around my mother's bloodstone so the base of my tattoo touched the cold crystal. And I pulled in magic.

I'd been so worried about subduing Orvil quickly that I overshot it, my magic slamming into him with a speed and strength I hadn't intended. Instantly, he let go of my neck and dropped to his knees, eyes bulging. His jaw actually dropped open, utterly slack.

"Close your mouth," I told him, and it snapped shut with a click that was audible over the rain. Whoops.

In my peripheral vision, I saw Jesse hurrying up the stairs toward me. He'd been waiting just out of sight. A tiny part of me that I tried not to think about was a little disappointed. Witness.

"That was fucking dangerous," Jesse muttered. "You could have been—"

"Later," I said tightly.

"Maybe we should take this inside?"

I gave a tiny headshake, fumbling in another pocket with my free hand. "Just because there's no life in there doesn't mean it's safe," I told him. "Hit the light and keep an eye out."

He grunted, and a second later there was a sharp crack and the security light disappeared. I'd been ready, though, and was already flicking a lighter, creating a single flame that illuminated our faces. I held it near my body so it wouldn't be seen from the street, but Orvil and I could see each other. He was still staring at me slackly.

Out of the corner of my eye I saw Jesse plant his feet facing away from the building, a gun held close to one leg.

Still holding Orvil with my eyes, I said to Jesse. "He doesn't know who I am. He hasn't talked to Adelaide yet."

"Got it."

"Tell me who you're meeting here," I ordered Orvil.

The words tumbled out of his mouth, like he couldn't wait to answer me. "Adelaide, my love Adelaide Preston. We meet here after I feed."

"Tell me where Adelaide is right now," I demanded.

"I don't know."

"Call her."

"I don't have my phone. Adelaide has it."

This was getting annoying. "Tell me about when you meet her."

"Nine o'clock. Every night at nine o'clock here in front of the mansion."

I risked glancing down at my watch, a Rolex I'd inherited from my sister. It was five after nine.

"I don't like this." Jesse sound calm, even cool, but he had good instincts. We didn't have a lot of time. "Do what you need to do, but hurry."

I nodded. Before I pressed Orvil to attend the trial, I had to make sure we were right, that this hadn't all been a waste of time and resources. Still looking into his eyes, I said, "Why did you try to kill the nulls?"

The vampire blinked at me, not quite getting it, and I reminded myself to get my head in the game. When I pressed vampires it had to be framed as an order. "Stand up." He did, practically flying to his feet. "You will not try to harm this man or me in any way. You will answer every one of my questions until I tell you to rest," I ordered, pushing magic into it.

Yes, Mistress," Orvil blurted. Shit. I eased up again, thankful

Simon wasn't here to see my control wobble. If it worried Jesse he didn't say anything. "Why did you and Adelaide try to kill the nulls?" I said again.

"Father asked us to. He paid Adelaide's company, but I did it for free." The night was warm, despite the rain, but Orvil's tone sent a shiver running along my pancake holster. He sounded...reverent.

"Father?" I pushed.

"Malcolm, cardinal vampire of New York City and surrounding territories." Now Orvil just sounded self-important. I didn't care, though, because I felt a rush of relief. I'd done it. We had our witness, we had proof. Even if I couldn't find Adelaide, I had what I needed right here.

"Good," I said, taking a breath. I wanted to be sure I was using the right amount of power: more than I'd ever purposefully used to press a vampire, but not so much that I fried his brain or mine. "Tomorrow night, go to Turner Hall here in Galena at eleven forty-five pm. If you understand me, repeat that back."

"Tomorrow night I will go to Turner Hall here in Galena at eleven forty-five pm," Orvil said tonelessly.

"Bring Adelaide with—"

*ALLIE DOWN NOW!*

Sam's voice exploded in my head, so loudly that I dropped to a crouch more out of reflex than because of the words themselves.

Jesse didn't have a spirit guide, but he was an ex-cop and automatically followed my lead, dropping down a half-second after me. Immediately, little puffs of red dust sparked off the brick as the bullets hit the side of the mansion, right at the height of my head. My brain caught up to what I was hearing through the rain: some kind of assault rifle being fired fired in bursts.

"Adelaide?" Jesse yelled to me. Like me, he had instinctively raised his hands to protect his face and head.

"Yes! Stay behind me!" I looked up at Orvil. Tearing away eye contact had broken my press, but it had also jarred the vampire, who stood blinking. I had maybe five seconds until he ripped out one of our throats. I wasn't supposed to kill him, so I reached for a shredder stake, thinking I'd go for his leg like with Julien Dubuque. Then I remembered the shredders were off in the bushes.

Adelaide was still shooting, so without thinking I shot to my feet, grabbing Orvil's jacket and turning him so the next cluster of bullets went straight into his back.

His eyes widened and he let out a little gurgle. I still couldn't see Adelaide in the darkness, but I heard her swearing off to my right. I let go of Orvil with a little push, so that he half-fell, half stumbled down the steps. Even vampires weren't all that graceful with three bullets in the chest.

Next to me, Jesse had pressed himself against the side of the brick protrusion and was returning fire, aiming at Adelaide's muzzle flashes. I stepped back so he could get a clear shot, reaching for the pancake holster at my back.

Orvil rose to his feet. Bullets or no bullets, I expected him to leap up the stairs and attack us. With the Glock in hand, I braced myself against the bricks, ready to push off and place myself between him and Jesse.

I was pretty shocked when the vampire just gave me a wicked grin and seemed to blur away to my right, toward Adelaide.

Then the assault rifle fire stopped. Adelaide had stopped shooting, and Jesse followed suit, tilting his head as he strained to hear.

They were running.

"Hold!" I yelled to Jesse, who lowered his weapon. Then my

legs were carrying me down the steps and after the vampire. As soon as I was out from under the overhang, I realized just how terrible the visibility had become. I could only see a couple of feet in any direction through the rain.

Swearing, I twisted around, unable to see anything, and then I remembered myself. Jesse was yelling something, but I ignored him and dropped into my boundary mindset.

Water was pouring down on my face—I'd forgotten to pull up my hood—but I squinted through it, turning in a slow circle. There was the radiant glow of Jesse's life force. There were the neighbors I'd seen before. And there—

I stopped. Two figures, rushing away. One the blue of the living, and thc other vampire red.

They were moving at roughly human speed, which meant Orvil was almost completely healed from his gunshot wounds.

I squeezed my eyes shut and shook my head, already moving forward. They'd run into the cult-de-sac and out the other side. With Jesse at my heels, I raised my Glock and crept across the cult-de-sac, dodging between two remnants. At first I thought there was nothing to see, and then I came right up on a narrow asphalt path leading into impenetrable darkness. "Let's go." I started forward, but felt Jesse grab my left arm at the bicep.

"Hey!" I spun around to face him, raking wet hair out of my face with my right hand. "Come *on*, they're getting away!"

"What's down that path?" Jesse asked me.

I shook my head. "A park, I think? I don't really know." Simon and I had driven by here earlier in the day when we were exploring the town, but the narrow entrance had a pedestrians-only sign. I had automatically thought *bike path* and forgotten about it.

Now, at night, I could see a couple of remnants along the

path, but they were so old they were little more than flickers. There was nothing else in sight.

Without really making a conscious decision, I started to drift down the path after them.

"*Lex*," Jesse said, and his tone brought me up short. It wasn't the intimacy of a lover or the politeness of a colleague. It was the tone you used when your fellow soldier was on their way off the deep end. "I know you have superpowers, but we *cannot* follow a vampire and a shooter down an unfamiliar path in the dark."

My lighter had gone out when I'd crouched down, but there was just enough ambient light from the street for me to make out Jesse's look of deep concern. Pain flared right under my jaw, and I realized it had been aching this whole time, from where Orvil had held me. My whole body was tense. I wanted so badly to race after Adelaide and Orvil that it actually scared me.

I forced myself to take a few slow, deep breaths. Then I holstered my sidearm so I could rub at my eyes, slicking away the rain and wet hair. "Okay, you're right. I don't like it, but you're right. Let's go talk to the others."

## 25

SCARLETT

When Beau said the word "tour," my inner Scarlett voice pretty much started to cry. I was already exhausted after the short walk from the hotel, and my last dose of over-the-counter painkillers had worn off, and I'd forgotten to bring the bottle with me to take more. But I'd promised Jesse I'd take photos and videos for a security breakdown, so it wasn't like I could lay down on a pile of our wet jackets and take a nap...even if that was all I could think about.

Once we started the tour, though, it actually wasn't too bad. The building wasn't all that big inside, and the design was pretty straightforward. By comparison, LA's last Vampire Trials had been held in a fancifully ornate old movie palace, filled with hidey-holes and tapestries big enough to hide several people. Turner Hall, on the other hand, was obviously designed to be simple and adaptable, so it could serve different purposes. Most of the building was taken up by the Hall itself, a massive ballroom with a raised stage and a large balcony overhead.

Everything was made of gleaming blonde wood and wrought-iron accents. Wooden chairs like the ki you'd see at a ballpark were installed in the balcony, but the main hall was a huge, empty space, apart from the stage. You could set up chairs for a concert or tables for a reception, and then clear everything to dance.

There were a handful of smaller side rooms—bathrooms, a kitchen with a big window so you could serve refreshments, a coatroom—all of them empty and utilitarian. Beau led Simon and me through every inch of it, which sounds really torturous for a crabby, concussed null. It was kind of fun, though, mostly because Simon and Beau chatted nonstop the whole time like church ladies with a scandal brewing.

The conversation was mostly about Galena's history and architecture, with Beau occasionally throwing in some Atlanta or Civil War references so we'd remember how old and badass he was. Simon and Beau got so into the discussion that they walked slowly and paused frequently, which was fantastic for me. I just trudged after them, tuning in and out of the conversation.

Because I'd promised Jesse, I took photos and videos of the exits, windows, and potential ambush/hiding places. When all that was done, and with the Galena History Podcast was still raging, I painstakingly lowered myself to the floor, leaned against a wall, and closed my eyes, feeling like a zombie.

I wondered how Jesse and Lex were doing on their stakeout. It had to be so wet and miserable to sit in the rain, but maybe they were having a great time anyway, talking about muzzle velocity and camo pants and shit. For just a second I pictured the two of them geeking out about the latest developments in Kevlar while Orvil and Adelaide strolled by unnoticed.

I felt the strongest urge to call Corry and tell her about this scenario, and just like that, I missed them all with an intensity that brought tears to my eyes. I was used to going a few days without seeing Molly or Wyatt, but it was different with Annie and Shadow and Corry. Without Annie in my arms, Shadow by my side, and Corry on FaceTime, I felt incomplete and scatter-brained, like I'd gone out into the world without shoes or a wallet.

Or maybe that was just the concussion.

I knew they were all fine—before we left, I'd made Dashiell promise he would have Kirsten call if anyone got hurt, or Shadow wasn't healing. But I felt very far away from my life and most of the people in it. It all seemed like too much to think about right then, and anyway I was dozing off.

When the burner phone buzzed in my pocket, I started awake the way you do from a nightmare, which made the pain in my head flare up. I had to fumble to get the phone out, probably because I was wiping drool from my chin with my other hand at the same time. (I'm sure the drool was just some sort of concussion-related phenomenon.)

The only number saved into the phone was Kirsten's, so I was surprised to see a string of unfamiliar numerals on the screen. I answered it anyway.

"Hey, it's me."

I relaxed. "Hi, Jesse. You're breaking the communication rules here."

"Don't care. Are you okay?"

"We're fine." As soon as I said it, I realized Beau and Simon weren't actually in my radius, so I looked around for them. The two men were standing on the other side of the hall, next to the stage, pointing up at a special side balcony (a box?) with great enthusiasm. I rolled my eyes and said into the phone, "Do you think I could secretly produce a history podcast starring a Southern gentleman vampire and a nerdy science witch without getting in trouble?"

"Hey, Scar?"

I froze. His voice was grim in a way that I recognized, and I realized it was too quiet for him to be standing in pouring rain. "Where are you?" I asked.

"Sitting in Lex's parked rental car. We've had a little development over here." I sat up straight, my stomach churning a little, and snapped my fingers loudly at Beau and Simon. Even across the vast space, Beau's head whipped around, and the two of them started toward me.

"What kind of development?" I asked Jesse. I felt, rather than saw, a vampire and a witch step into my radius. "Wait, I'm gonna put you on speaker so Beau and Simon can hear."

It took me a moment to locate the right functions on the unfamiliar phone, so Simon reached over and hit the little speaker symbol for me. "There was some action at the Belvedere," Jesse reported. "Lex was able to press Orvil, but Adelaide showed up and they got away."

"Shit." I rubbed my face with one hand. "Regroup?"

"Yeah. Lex says we should go back to the DeSoto, since they don't want you to break the wards on their hotel."

"Fair enough. See you there."

Beau locked the front door behind us, and we began the walk back to the DeSoto. After a momentary pause to acknowledge the change in plans, Simon and Beau started talking about Galena again, and what it must have been like when the mines were in operation. The sidewalk wasn't wide enough for all three of us to be side-by-side, but I was content to walk behind the two of them, half-listening.

Just past the original fire station, I caught movement out of the corner of my eye. I turned to see a woman leaning against the brick wall on the far end of the building, her big, dark eyes watching us. She wore a long black raincoat with its hood up, her skin pale against the fabric.

I stopped.

I don't know why, really. She wasn't doing anything particularly suspicious, other than standing still in a dark area during a rainstorm. But without really thinking about it, I found myself pushing out my radius again.

Vampire. Very young, a few years at most. She did the bulging eyed gasp thing that vampires always do the first time they meet a null, as their lungs remind them that breathing has become a necessity and not just a fun way to keep circulation moving.

The physical reaction was all very normal, except she didn't seem *surprised.*

I started toward her—and the woman bolted, running around the side of the firehouse toward Turner Hall again.

And I was running after her, already pulling a throwing knife from the leather belt under my shirt.

Simon and Beau had gotten a little way ahead of me, probably assuming I was right behind them since they were still human. I kept my radius pushed out as I ran, so it was a few seconds before they started after us, and by then I wasn't answering their shouted questions. I needed my breath.

The doctor who'd gone over my concussion protocol had been very clear about exercise—nothing strenuous for at least two weeks, and even then, only when I was free of any other symptoms. But by the time I remembered those words, my limbs were already moving in rhythm, my arms and legs pumping with adrenaline as if to say *we know how to do this*!

And then she veered left and started running up those goddamned stairs. And I automatically started up after her.

There were two lampposts at the bottom of the stairs, giving it that "gate up into darkness" look, but the next two lampposts were quite a ways up. And, of course, all of it was soaking wet and the rain was still coming.

The woman ahead of me was human, so she had to go fairly slowly, her feet slipping out from under her a couple of times so she had to catch herself on her hands. After five steps, I held onto the railing with one hand, but it was just as slippery as the stairs. My boots still slid out from underneath me once, twice, until I dropped the knife and clutched the railing with both hands, working my way up as fast as I could. If she got far enough to get out of my radius she'd be gone.

At twenty steps she was only another ten above me, but the distance was getting wider. At one point she turned to glance down at me, and her hood fell back, revealing a pixie haircut and an expression of disbelief She appeared to be in her mid-thirties, and a new thought popped into my head. *I know you.*

I kept plugging upward, ignoring Simon and Beau shouting below me.

At thirty steps, the stairs in front of me started to swim.

I kept trying, because of course I'm very stupid like that, but Beau and Simon caught up to me, and I could feel the vampire woman still going. "Stop...her..." I panted, and Beau ran ahead while Simon stayed with me. I ignored his questions and focused on pushing out my radius a little further...further...

Then I had to lean sideways over the railing and vomit into the dark void below.

My concentration broke, and my radius snapped to its usual size around me. I pushed it back out again, but she was gone. I heaved myself back on the stairs and dropped onto my butt, panting. My head was screaming, along with all the scrapes and bruises under my clothes. I was really hoping I hadn't pulled out the stitches on my leg, but I was too chicken to check just then. I was soaked through, so the bandage on my leg was going to need redressing.

Beau came trotting back down the stairs, shaking his head. I looked up at him, and he reached down to hand me the throwing knife he'd picked up on their stairs. I nodded my thanks.

"But who *is* she?" Simon asked, not for the first time.

I shook my head. "Don't...know."

"A vampire, certainly." Beau was frowning. "I did not recognize her. I am not acquainted with every vampire in the country, of course, but I know most of those who attend Rendezvous."

"Why were we just chasing her?" Simon sounded almost plaintive, he was so confused.

I took almost a full minute to catch my breath before I responded. "*She* knew *me*."

# 26

## SCARLETT

Beau, Simon and I were all quiet on the walk (or in my case, trudge) back to the DeSoto. I was focused on making sure no one else followed us, and the two men were busy exchanging a lot of looks that amounted to "What the hell is going on with Scarlett?"

When we walked into the lobby, I was a little surprised at the number of people bustling in and out with luggage. Wasn't it pretty late to check in or out? Simon had turned left toward the reception desk to return the borrowed umbrella. I think it took all three of us a second to realize that the two bedraggled people at the far end of the desk were Lex and Jesse. The two of them were still outfitted in the shiny rain gear, but now it was pocked with tiny tears and smears, and there were red scratches on Jesse's neck and Lex's cheek. Their hands and faces were streaked with dirt and something dark orange-red. An uncomfortable-looking bellhop was just handing over a stack of folded white towels. He handed the stack to Lex with his arms way outstretched, as though he thought whatever she had was contagious.

I saw Simon's whole body go tense when he saw the red, but I was too practiced in cleaning up blood to worry. Sure enough, Jesse looked up, saw Simon's face, and blurted, "Brick dust."

I went over to him, trying not to look like I was hurrying. "Are you okay?" I asked, though my hands were already reaching for him, pulling up the tail of his poncho and running my hands along the shirt underneath. I needed tactile confirmation that he hadn't been shot or bitten. I started to pull aside the poncho hood to get a better look at the red scratch on his neck, but Jesse caught my hand. "It's just a tiny piece of brick shrapnel," he murmured. "I'm fine, Scar."

He glanced over at Beau, who had swept past me and was lifting his hand to gently grasp Lex's chin. He tilted it up with detached concern, like he was checking a horse's shoe. There was a purple-blue bruise going most of the way around her neck right under the jaw.

"Brick shrapnel?" I looked back at Jesse. "What happened?"

Lex's eyes slid to the bellhop, who turned and practically ran down the closest hallway with a mumbled, "Have a good night, miss."

Lex turned her body so the five of us formed a tighter cluster. People were bustling in and out of the lobby, but not as many now. "We found Orvil," Lex said, keeping her voice low. "I pressed him to show up tomorrow night, but we were supposed to be hanging onto them at the other hotel. Instead, Adelaide showed up with some kind of assault rifle."

"It looked like a HK416 to me," Jesse said to her. "I knew a couple of guys with the LAPD who liked those."

Lex processed that with a quick nod. "They ran off in the dark and got away. Again," she added bitterly.

"There was a vampire following us," Simon blurted. "Scarlett kind of recognized her, but she got away too."

Jesse gave me a sharp look. I glanced around, my witness antennae activated. "Let's talk somewhere else, okay?" I remembered something and dug my slim wallet out of my jacket pocket, pulling out a small stack of room keys. I found the one at the very back and handed it to Lex. "This is for Dashiell's suite, up on the top floor. The cardinals rented them out for tonight too, out of paranoia, but at least it's got a parlor where we can talk in private. Why don't you use it to get cleaned up? Jesse and I can stop in our room for clothes and meet you up there."

Lex nodded gratefully, taking the key. As she strode off toward the elevator Simon fell into step beside her.

Beau let them get about eight feet away before he stepped up beside me and ducked his head so he could whisper in my ear.

I instinctively flinched at the movement, and Jesse's hand twitched toward his gun holster. Apparently we were all a little jumpy. But Beau just said, "Please, Miss Bernard, can you extend your influence?"

"My influ—. Oh. Sure." I concentrated, pushing my radius out and trying to kind of pin it there. Now that I've had a baby, I can confirm that manipulating the natural distance of my radius is kind of like trying to do a kegel and hold it. It's a tiny, distracting effort that no one knows about but you.

I kind of wondered if I'd feel anything else Old World as I did it, but I could only feel one vampire and two witches. I looked up at Beau. "And why am I doing this?"

"This hotel was built in 1855," he said, giving Lex's back a look I could best describe as pitying. "I've walked through here before. She could use a break from the haunting."

Before I could open my mouth to answer, he swept off to the

other side of the lobby, which opened into a modest bar. "If you'll excuse me, I believe I'll get a libation before the meeting."

Jesse and I shrugged at each other and started for our own room. I had to walk slowly after all the excitement. "Who was following you?" Jesse asked when we were alone in the long hallway.

I told him about sort-of recognizing the woman, leaving out the part where I'd run up the stairs and puked my guts out. Jesse listened quietly, but as soon as we got to the room he bolted the door and checked the bathroom and under the beds for intruders. Then he rounded on me. "Scarlett. Listen."

I had been about to drop onto the edge of the bed, but I planted my feet, crossing my arms over my chest. I was still keeping my radius extended, though luckily Dashiell's suite was just overhead and down a couple of doors. Lex wasn't that far. "Don't do this," I warned Jesse.

It brought him up short, but only for a second. "You don't even know what I'm going to say."

"You're going to try to convince me to go home," I said flatly, and didn't even feel victorious when Jesse winced with guilt. "I won't."

"Scarlett, you didn't see this woman, Adelaide. She's the Terminator, and she's the *human* in the relationship. And someone was following you around tonight— "

I shook my head stubbornly. "Come on, dude. You know better than this. It's a bullshit Eli move."

I regretted the words as soon as they were out of my mouth, but it was too late. Jesse's handsome face clouded over with anger. "Really? You're going to compare me to your ex-boyfriend now?"

"No." I forced myself to sound calmer than I felt. "I'm

comparing you a condescendingly overprotective person I am no longer with. It's very different."

His face went even redder. "You want to talk about your exes? Fine. Which do you think Jameson would prefer, you getting killed trying to avenge him, or you being alive to raise his daughter?"

I felt like I'd been slapped. I took a wobbly step backward and had to reach out a hand to support myself against the wall. Jesse, for his part, looked regretful. "Scarlett—"

"Shut up." I shook my head. Inside, I felt angry enough to scream and throw things, but my body didn't have that kind of energy. "You can think me staying is about Jameson, but it's more complicated than that. Look what happened two days ago. Three nulls, all under the protection of powerful vampires, and we almost died anyway. You said it yourself: it should have worked."

Jesse tried to respond, but I kept going, overriding him. "Rhys was a good guy, a dad, and he died for *nothing*." I could hear the tears in my voice, and I hated it. "No one is speaking for nulls, Jesse. No one is looking out for us, not really. We're too spread out and there's too few of us. But someone needs to answer."

"So you're rushing into this plan, risking your own safety, because you want to be the president of nulls?"

"No." I sat down. The anger was draining, and I just felt tired. "Somewhere along the way, I realized that Maven's special congress is important. If it had existed two years ago, I could have gotten the parliament to investigate Jameson's murder, and maybe Malcolm would have been held responsible then and there."

Understanding softened his face, but I didn't stop. "And maybe Rhys wouldn't have died, and I wouldn't have a concussion, and all our favorite people wouldn't be crammed in a safe house waiting to find out if their lives are in danger."

Jesse came over to me then, kneeling down on the carpet in front of me. "This isn't our town, Scar. We don't have our usual resources. What if we get killed? What happens to Annie?"

I took a breath, letting myself stroke his cheek. In his mid-thirties, Jesse's face only seemed to get more beautiful, especially when he was all scruffy like this. Like a Latino Henry Cavill in *The Witcher*. "You know what happens," I said softly. "We updated the wills after Annie trashed the house. If we die, Corry will take care of her."

I hated to put that level of responsibility on a young woman who was barely out of her teens, but at least there was a shit-load of life insurance money...assuming our bodies weren't hidden away by someone like me. I pushed the thought aside. "And when she's older, Corry will tell her that we died trying to make something that would help people."

He sighed. "Okay. I know, I can't tell you what to do. But I'm asking, Scarlett, please: will you wear the vest, and keep the Beretta on you?

"Yes to the vest," I said, even though it was a pain in the ass getting my knife holster on over the Kevlar. "But no to the gun. It wigs me out to always have it on me. But how about you and I don't split up again until this thing is over?"

Jesse's smile was resigned, but at least it was a smile. "Deal."

# 27

## LEX

The courtyard of the DeSoto was on the ground floor, but there were three additional stories forming a frame that went up around it: the hallways to the hotel rooms. Each painted white door had a brass plate with a number on it, and above that another, larger plate with the name of prominent figures who'd visited the DeSoto, like Abraham Lincoln and Mark Twain. We even walked past a door marked "Orvil Grant," which made Simon do a pretty funny double-take.

Dashiell's suite opened into a massive sitting room with blood-red carpet and Victorian wallpaper patterned with flower bouquets. Simon stood in the center of the room and turned in a circle, looking a little nervous. "Jeez. It looks like the walls should be lined with about a thousand Victorian dolls."

My clothes—or rather, Scarlett's clothes—were wet, and I suddenly longed more than anything to be fully dry. It felt like I hadn't been dry since I'd flown out of Denver. In the bathroom, I closed and locked the door and started unloading everything from my pockets and holsters onto the counter. All the muscles on the back half on my body ached with the movement. Being swung into a brick wall by your neck will do that. I avoided looking in the mirror as I pulled off my rain gear, the bulletproof vest, and the T-shirt and jeans I'd borrowed. When Jesse and I had stopped at my hotel on the way to the stakeout, I hadn't bothered changing out of the clothes Scarlett had lent me to replace my wet stuff. Now this outfit was wet, too.

Wait. I'd been wearing all my rain gear. How was I this wet?

Standing on the cold tile floor in my borrowed bra and panties, I held up my rain gear to the bathroom light. The pants had a bunch of very tiny tears—probably from brick shrapnel, since it was mostly my right side. When I held up the rain jacket, I found more tiny tears...and two different bullet holes.

One was in the extra fabric near my waist, and the other in the hood, at the back. I thought it through, remembering how I had dropped down. If I had been standing when these were fired, I thought these shots would have hit approximately my femoral artery and my forehead. If Sam hadn't warned me, I would definitely be dead now. Probably for good this time.

I stared at the bullet holes for a long time, thinking. Sam had once told me that she wasn't allowed to have direct influence on things. She was only supposed to guide and suggest, not interfere. There were a few times when she'd bent this rule before, but never so directly.

*Sammy?* I thought at her, wrapping a big bath towel around myself. *You there?*

My sister didn't answer. I wondered if she was in trouble for warning me. In the past, when she had hinted at something in my dreams, she'd been sort of...removed from talking to me for a while, like a little kid on a time out. Was that happening now?

This was a scarier idea that I would have expected. I'd gotten used to Sam being in my head, making wry comments and trying to cheer me up. Just knowing she was there, that she might chime in at any moment, was a comfort. I already missed her.

My burner phone buzzed on the counter. I picked it up. "Hello?"

"Hello, Lex." The witch sounded the way she usually did—friendly and capable, but a little brisk too. "I have John Wheaton on the other line, would you like me to connect you?"

"What? Yes, of course!"

There was a pause, and John's familiar voice was in my ear again. "Hey, Lex."

"Are you okay? Is Charlie okay?"

"We're fine," he assured me. "The safe house team has been checking in with Kirsten every twelve hours. It was my turn, so I asked if I could talk to you."

"Are you sure this is safe?"

"I drove two hours and bought a new disposable phone with cash to make this call. We're taking every precaution possible."

I reminded myself that the safe house group included smart, experienced people; they were going to be careful. And I shouldn't ask any more security questions in case someone had gotten to Kirsten's phone.

Still wrapped in the towel, I sat down on the closed toilet seat lid. "How is everyone holding up?"

"A little better now that we've got a timeline," he said, obviously choosing his words carefully. The LA team must have told them about the trial the following night. "But Charlie's having kind of a hard time," John added.

My chest constricted. "How so?"

"She's having nightmares. People shooting at us, you getting killed, that kind of thing." He paused, then added, "She's asking for you a lot. I know this kind of thing has always kind of rolled off her back in the past, but she's getting older. She remembers being scared now, you know?"

Tears burned my eyes. If it was bad enough for him to bring it up on this call, he was worried. And I couldn't think of a single thing to say that would help. "I'm sorry, John. Tell her I love her."

"I will. It's only a few more days, right?"

I could hear how hard he was trying to sound positive, and suddenly there was a lump in my throat, making it hard to speak. How could I tell him it might take longer now that I'd lost Adelaide and Orvil? They were our main link to Malcolm, our only bait. How could I guarantee Charlie's safety without confronting Malcolm? "I hope so," was all I could manage.

There was a tap on the bathroom door. "Lex? It's Scarlett. I brought another outfit for you."

"One second." I wiped my eyes and said into the phone, "John, I have to go. Say hi to everyone, okay?"

"I will. Be careful."

A few minutes later, the five of us were gathered in the small parlor of Dashiell's suite. Scarlett, Jesse, Simon, and Beau were all sitting on the couch and chairs, but I found that I couldn't keep still. Despite the ache in my back, I wandered around the room. I missed Quinn, but I couldn't justify the security risk in calling him just to hear his voice.

"Miss Lex?" Beau had taken an armchair near the door and was watching me like I was one-woman tennis match.

"We need to find them," I said, for about the fifth time. "I have no idea what's going to happen if we don't."

"What do you mean?" Jesse asked.

"The plan was for me to get here quickly. I press Orvil, Beau presses Adelaide, and we hang onto them at the other hotel until the trial," I said. "But not only did they get away, I didn't even have a chance to press him not to tell anyone about the trial. And Adelaide is a free agent."

Jesse glanced at Scarlett for a reaction to this, but the null was holding a bag of fresh ice to her head and looked distracted. "Scar?" he said, concerned. "Are you okay?"

"I—aw, shit." Scarlett stood abruptly, the hand with the icepack falling to her side. "I need to run downstairs to the lobby," she announced. Jesse started to stand, too, but she shook her head at him. "It's not—there's no threat, I swear," she said to him. She looked strained, like she was trying to hear a chord only discernible to dogs. "I've got my radius pushed out to cover most of the hotel, there are no other vampires. I just gotta run down to the front desk for lady things." She was already edging toward the door.

"I'll go with you," Jesse said. "Adelaide could be down there."

"She wouldn't leave Orvil when he's been pressed," Scarlett reasoned. She was backing toward the door, her eyes only on Jesse. "I'll be back in five minutes. You have my word." She turned and practically jogged out of the room, leaving Jesse to look at the rest of us with a bewildered expression.

I didn't say anything, but I had to wonder what she was up to. If it really was a "lady thing," the standard girl protocol would have been to ask me if I had whatever she needed.

After a moment, Jesse shrugged and turned back to me. "I don't know much about how pressing works, especially pressing vampires," he said calmly. "You pressed Orvil to come to the trial tomorrow night, didn't you?"

"Yes. But I've never tried to create a press that lasted more than a day," I said. "I don't know if it's even possible."

"It should be, if it works like a vampire pressing a human," Beau said. He was sipping from a very large glass of bourbon, and didn't seem particularly concerned about...well, anything, except downing his drink. It was like he'd gotten numb to the whole situation.

He was mourning, I realized, and immediately felt guilty. I'd barely talked to him since Maya died. Had she been more to him that a trusted assistant? I didn't know anything about her.

"But in the meantime, the two of them could be doing anything," Simon pointed out.

"Like what?" Jesse asked him. "What's our worst-case scenario here?"

I stopped pacing, blowing air through my cheeks as I thought about it. "Getting weapons. Rallying other vampires against us. Pressing the Galena police department to shoot all of us on sight."

Jesse muttered something in Spanish and rubbed the back of his neck. "So what do we do?" He looked at Simon. "Do you have any way to find them?"

I stopped short. "Blood. Adelaide left blood at the scene; you can find her with that, right?"

Simon looked regretful. "You said she was wearing a witch bag. Assuming she doesn't take it off—"

Shit. "She won't," I put in. "She's too smart."

Simon winced. "That's going to block me from locating her with magic."

My burner phone buzzed in my pocket. I wasn't sure why Kirsten would be calling back so soon, but I pulled it out and answered.

"Lex, I'm going to patch in Maven, Dashiell, and Quinn," came Kirsten's voice. She sounded...not frantic, exactly, but on the way there.

I was surprised, both at the tone and at Maven needing to speak to me herself. "Um, okay."

A second later, my boss's voice came on the line. "Lex, are you with the others?"

"Yes. Scarlett ran down to the lobby store, but she'll be back in a second."

"Put me on speaker, please."

I found the right button and set the phone down on the coffee table. "Okay, you're on. What happened?"

Maven cleared her throat. "We're aborting the mission," she said. "All of it. You'll all be returning home in the morning."

Everyone looked startled, but I was the one who blurted, "*What*?" It had been too loud. "Why?" I said more quietly.

Dashiell's voice came on the line. "Abbigail figured out how to get into Adelaide's cell phone, or at least one of them," he said. "We can't stop the calls or pinpoint her location, but we can listen in. Adelaide has spent the last hour and a half calling every skinner in the country we knew about, and a lot more that we didn't. She's summoning everyone to Galena."

It felt like my whole torso had turned to rock. I didn't even look at the others. "What does that mean?"

"It means," Maven said patiently. "Adelaide Preston is hiring as many skinners as she can find to go to Illinois. She's spreading the word that there's a vampire gathering in town and offering a hundred grand a head to kill any vampire other than Orvil."

"Blast and bollocks," Simon muttered. "That's pretty scorched earth."

Quinn finally spoke. My heart did a little leap at the sound of his voice, but he was all business. "She specifically mentioned Turner Hall in most of the calls," he said. "There's no way I can get Maven and Dashiell into town safely tomorrow night."

I had to sit down, perching on the coffee table in the center of the parlor. Scarlett had walked back into the room during this explanation, looking pale. She didn't have any kind of package or bag.

I glanced at Beau, whose face was completely unreadable. Funny, he was the only vampire I knew who seemed *less* emotional in Scarlett's presence.

"I don't get it, though." Simon's forehead was wrinkled in concentration. "If she wants the skinners to kill Maven and Dashiell, why didn't she just put a bounty on the two of them?"

"She knows that we have our own allies and spies," Maven said sensibly. "As does Beau. Revealing that the three of us are the true targets would create divided loyalty."

"Besides," Dashiell added, "she isn't really trying to kill us. She's just trying to keep us from putting Orvil on trial."

"It's smart," Jesse said reluctantly. "She can't break Lex's press without a null, so Orvil *will* go to Turner Hall tomorrow night. Adelaide found a way to make sure you can't be there waiting."

I had a feeling I knew the answer, but I had to ask the question. "If we find her, can Beau press her to cancel the hunt?"

"She thought of that as well," Dashiell said, his voice grim. "She's specifically telling each of them to go through with the plan even if she calls and tries to cancel it."

I put my head in my hands. If we didn't stop Orvil and Adelaide now, Charlie wouldn't be able to come home. She wouldn't be safe, not until they were dead. And it was all my fault.

"When?" I said woodenly. "When will they arrive?"

"That's the only good news, if you can call it that," Maven's voice said over the line. "No one she's spoken to will be able to get to Galena before late tomorrow morning. The closest skinners are her own people in Chicago, and most of them are still traveling back from Colorado and LA. You all have time to get out of town."

I checked my watch. It felt like the dead of night, but it was only ten forty-five.

"I'm afraid we've been outmaneuvered," Maven concluded. "I will be able to warn the other vampires in the area to cancel the Rendezvous; that should buy me a little goodwill with them. It's not the same as starting the parliament, but it's some small comfort."

"No." It was Scarlett's voice, but when I looked over at the couch where she sat next to Jesse, I almost didn't recognize her. Scarlett's hands were clenched into fists, her face red with anger. "No, that's not good enough. They have to answer for those attacks. Fuck, they tried to shoot Lex and Jesse tonight. We can't just let them run off."

Jesse put an arm around her, but his eyes were on me. He had something: an idea, the seed of a plan. I raised my eyebrows, and he nodded at me.

"I don't see how—" Simon started to say, but I interrupted.

"Maven," I said, my voice seeming to come from very far away, "how soon could you get here?"

"To Galena?" my boss sounded surprised. "You mean this evening?"

"Yes," I said. "Right now. How soon?"

There was a long pause. "If I take the jet from Denver, perhaps four hours."

"And Dashiell?"

"About the same," he said.

Beau was studying me. "What are you thinking, Miss Lex?"

"We have eight hours until sunrise," I said slowly. "And we have a null."

Of everyone in the room, it was Scarlett who looked at me, a slow grin spreading over her face. "You want to have the trial."

"Now?" Simon looked back and forth between us. "Tonight?"

"Yeah. I looked at Jesse. "You have an idea?"

"I think I know how to find them," he said. "Something I

did a long time ago with Runa to find Scarlett."

I waved a hand to cut him off. "Don't say anything else, just in case." I looked back at the speakerphone. Dashiell and Maven had been silent about the proposal. "If we start the trial at two-thirty am, we'll have plenty of time to get all our people out of town before sunrise…even if that just means driving away in a van with Scarlett keeping you all human."

Scarlett's face darkened. "What about Malcolm?"

I shook my head. "We were planning on Orvil calling him just before or after the trial; that won't work now. And he's not going to come here on his own when he thinks it's going to be open season on vampires tomorrow. But even if can't get Malcolm on this trip, we can make damn sure Orvil and Adelaide are taken off the board. It should at least buy us some time to come up with a new plan for Malcolm."

Beau snickered, a very un-Beau-like sound. "I like it."

I looked around the room. Jesse and Simon both looked worried but nodded firmly at me. Scarlett looked at the phone. "Dashiell? Maven?"

There was silence on the speakerphone, for so long that all five of us were glancing at each other, wondering if the call had disconnected. Finally, Maven's voice came over the line. "Lex? Are you sure?"

Part of me wanted to take it back. When I opened my mouth, though, what came out was, "I am not leaving Galena empty-handed. Let me try."

"I'm agreeable," Maven said. "Assuming the rest of you are still willing, of course. The risks have increased."

"Scarlett?" Dashiell asked.

The null met my eyes and nodded. "They need to answer for Rhys," she said flatly. "And for Louisa. And for the rest of us." I nodded back at her.

"Then I will get on my plane," Dashiell replied.

# PART III

# 28

## LEX

It wasn't quite that simple, though. "There's still a problem," Maven said. "The rest of the court."

"That's right," Quinn's voice again. He would have been working on logistics the whole time I'd been gone. "The other members of the parliament don't own private airplanes, and I don't think I can move up their timetables on short notice. It was a massive effort to get them there by tomorrow night, frankly."

There was another pause as we all took that in. They were right, of course. Maven had been carefully selecting good people from across the country for this job, but they weren't going to be able to get here in four hours.

"Does it have to be those specific people?" Jesse asked.

I looked at him. "What do you mean?"

"This is Maven's show, right? Whatever else, she's the leader, or head justice, or whatever. Dashiell's on the bench as well. That's two." He pointed at Beau, who looked strangely like a deer in headlights. "Three. We've already got three cardinal vampires from all across the country. Simon and Lex, that adds two powerful witches, and Scarlett can be the representative null,"he finished. "That's six, for a soft open."

The room erupted into noise. Simon, Beau, and I all began to protest at once, while Scarlett got up and moved toward the door like she might just walk out on the whole thing. Maven had to shout over the phone line so we would all shut up.

"You're absolutely right, Mr. Cruz; we don't have to use our final roster for this first trial—or to send a message about what happens when you come at our people," she said. "It wouldn't strictly be impartial, since Scarlett was one of the victims of the attacks, but then, it was never really going to be impartial after they attacked us.

"*But*," she added with a note of resignation, "I just don't think we can move forward without at least one werewolf on the bench, as you put it."

Scarlett, who had reached the door, now pulled it open. "I think we've got that covered," she said over her shoulder. Sticking two fingers in her mouth, she let out a short whistle. "Oi, dumbass! You're up!" she said to someone in the hallway. "Welcome to the majors, slugger."

A large, defensive-looking man slunk into the room. The last couple of days had been so crazy that it took me a moment to place Eli, the alpha werewolf of Los Angeles.

"Uh, Eli is here," Jesse said, either for the benefit of the speakerphone, or just generally out of surprise.

"I felt him in the lobby earlier," Scarlett explained, returning to her spot on the sofa. She was moving gingerly, but she was moving.

"You are supposed to be in Los Angeles," came Dashiell's extremely terse voice.

"And yet he's here!" Scarlett's voice had taken on a manic pitch. She pointed at Eli with both hands, like a master of ceremonies introducing a new act. "I was going to talk to him after the meeting, but instead he just *saved* the meeting! Yay, Eli! Consequences can wait 'til later!"

"Indeed," Dashiell said, ice-cold. "For now...I suppose I have a plane to catch."

My heart lifted. We were doing it. It wasn't too late to rectify my mistake, at least partially.

"As do I," added Maven. "We'll begin the trial at three o'clock, to give you a little extra time. Lex, this is your operation. See you soon."

And the line went dead.

Several people in the room began talking, but I tuned them out. I closed my eyes and gave myself a slow, deep breath, in and out. And then one more.

I opened my eyes. "Jesse," I called, and the room quieted. My friend looked at me inquiringly. "Tell me how we find them."

He shifted in his seat, a little nervous, but when he spoke his voice was clear. "Once, when I needed to find Scarlett, we used a spare key to find her car with a finding spell. Because it's a small part of a larger mechanism."

"Do we have Adelaide's spare key?" Simon asked.

"No. But if I were Adelaide, I'm not going anywhere without that HK," Jesse replied. "That was an expensive, customized weapon. After she shot at us from the street, she and Orvil ran off. No way she had time to pick up her brass."

"Or the spent bullets," I said, following his line of thought. I looked at Simon. "Do you think you could find the gun if you had casings and some spent bullets?"

"I've never tried using bullets," he said, almost apologetically. "But in theory...yeah, it could work."

"Excellent. We'll have to send someone over there and try to sneak past the cops. I'm assuming they were called about the shooting."

Eli, who had been leaning against a wall with his thick arms crossed over his chest like a bouncer, snorted. We all turned to look at him. "Have any of you turned on a television or radio in the last hour?"

The rest of us looked at each other. I shrugged. "Why?" I said to him.

"The city is evacuating. Right now it's voluntary, but it will become mandatory pretty fast if this rain keeps up."

"Which it will," Simon muttered.

"They're closing the floodgates at eleven," Eli continued. "I doubt local cops give a shit about someone shooting off a gun tonight, especially if no one was hurt and visibility was poor."

"Which it was," Jesse said under his breath.

"Even better," I said. "The Belvedere is only half a mile or so away, but it sounds like traffic will be a problem." I looked at Beau. "You'll be the fastest on foot. Can you go collect some bullets?"

The vampire set down his empty glass and rose to his feet—a little unsteadily. He still gave me a surprisingly polished salute. "Right away, Sergeant Luther. I shall retrieve the evidence post haste."

He sauntered toward the door, which would have looked very believable if he wasn't moving in a zigzag.

Scarlett waited until the door closed behind Beau to say, "And that's what happens when you have your first drink in two hundred years, kids."

"Hang on a second," I said, and ran out into the hallway after Beau. "Hey!" I called, and the vampire turned, looking blearily at me.

"Don't worry, Miss Lex. I shall be sober in but a moment," he said, giving a little bow.

"I know; I'm not worried about that. But I'm a little worried about you."

His eyebrows furrowed. "I shall carry on, Lex. I always do." He started to turn away, but I touched his shoulder.

"What is it?"

Beau sighed. "You have me at a disadvantage, lady. I am human and inebriated."

"I'll let you go as soon as you stop fucking around and tell me what's going on with you."

He threw back his head and laughed, but when he spoke, there was sorrow in his voice. "I suppose I have not recovered from what happened in my city four months ago. It feels as though it's all happening again." He leaned against the wall, staring off at nothing.

So I wasn't the only one who'd been rattled by Atlanta. I leaned on the wall next to him, trying not to worry about the time. "You don't have to stay here, Beau," I told him. "You're more than repaid any debt you might have owed. I understand if you need to go home and bury Maya."

"Maya." He shook his head. "No, you're wrong, Lex. I owe Maya a debt now, which I must see through. And I don't feel I've repaid my debt to you."

"Shouldn't I get a say in that?"

He smiled, but it faded quickly. "Lex...Odessa was like a daughter to me, my kin. I have had four months to look back at all the warning signs, the moments to which I should have paid attention. The times that I could have stopped her and did not. Because she was family, I refused to see what she was doing. The damage, the cruelty."

I understood, then, that we weren't just talking about Odessa. Beau had once told me he'd enlisted in the Confederate Army because he'd bought the propaganda the Southerners had been fed. He blamed himself for not paying enough attention.

"You came to my town to consult on the Unsettled, but you didn't just find the missing ghosts—you risked your life to save me, and to save Atlanta," Beau went on. "You nearly died helping me, and then you showed Odessa mercy because I asked you."

To my utter shock, he lifted my hand to his lips and kissed the back of it, a very courtly gesture that left me speechless. "My debt is repaid when I say it is."

"Beau—"

"It is also worth noting," he interrupted, "that Maven and Dashiell are trying to build a force for good. I wouldn't mind being part of a force for good for a change." He pushed off the wall. "Now I must be off, to attain both the evidence and my sobriety."

Shaking my head, I went back into the hotel room. Everyone had been talking loudly, but they quieted down as soon as they saw me.

Right. I was in charge.

"Jesse, can you take Simon and his spell stuff to your room and help him with preparations?" I asked. "We'll want to be ready the moment Beau gets back." And it would have to be done away from Scarlett.

The two men nodded and got up to go. "Scarlett, we're going to need an exit strategy," I said as they disappeared through the door. "Can you call our operator and have her turn your friend with the RV around?"

Scarlett pulled out her phone. "She will definitely not like that, since he's her baby daddy, but yes."

"Good."

While she made the call, I turned to study Eli, the only member of the group I'd never talked to. I didn't even know his last name, and now we were going to go into this thing together. If I gave him an order, would he do it?

The werewolf was still leaning against a wall with his arms crossed, giving me a challenging look. He'd defied Dashiell's specific instructions to stay in LA, and he clearly expected a reprimand. I wasn't going to give it to him.

Instead, I decided to gamble. "You and I have a mutual friend," I said. "I know him as Will Brighton, though I understand he had a different last name in LA. His wife is in my witch clan."

Eli's scowled lifted, and he actually looked pleased. "They got married?"

So I'd been right: Eli had been in on the conspiracy to fake Will's death and relocate him to be with Sashi. Which meant Will trusted him.

"Yes. And she's expecting their second child," I told him. "Twenty years after their first." It wasn't really my news to tell, but I couldn't see how it would hurt. Will and Eli wouldn't be allowed to have any communication with each other.

Eli grinned. "That's so awesome." For just that moment, I saw who he probably was with the people he cared about. It made me like him more.

On the sofa, Scarlett hung up her burner phone and looked at me. "Kirsten is going to have Hayne turn around," she reported. "He'll find somewhere close by to park and sleep, so he'll be ready for our call later."

"Good."

"Where are we going to do the trial?" Scarlett asked. "It seems like Turner Hall is compromised."

"Hell yes it is. I don't think the location is as important anymore, though, and a lot of places will be emptying out with the town evacuating. Maybe while Simon is getting Adelaide and Orvil's location, you and I can come up with a few possibilities."

Scarlett brightened a little. "I can work on that. I'll see if there's a pad of paper in the nightstand."

She went toward the suite's attached bedroom, but her radius didn't leave the room with her. I had to wonder if she was keeping it expanded on my behalf. Had Beau said something to her? Was the hotel lousy with ghosts, and he was trying to protect me? That sounded like him, but I decided not to make a thing about it. Priorities.

Speaking of which. I looked at Eli. "I'm not trying to downplay your ability to contribute later, but if this is going to be the war room for the next little bit, it would be really helpful if you could get everyone some coffee."

"Lots of coffee," Scarlett mumbled, coming back into the room with a notepad. "Eli's not above that, right Eli? Team player all the way?"

Eli rolled his eyes, but finally uncrossed his arms. Scarlett's jokes seemed to pull him out of his tough-alpha posturing, I noticed. Maybe her sense of humor wasn't as useless as I'd thought.

"As long as I get to do something that will deeply terrorize Malcolm later, I've got no problem being the coffee bitch," Eli replied. "I'll check downstairs and see what I can rustle up."

"And some snacks!" Scarlett called as he disappeared through the doorway and into the hall. "Don't worry," she told me. "As soon as he gets away from me, he's going to be starving. Werewolves have to eat a lot. He'll bring snacks."

On cue, my stomach rumbled. It had been a long time since early dinner with Laurel.

Laurel. Shit. "While we have a minute, I'm going to call and check in with Laurel and her sisters," I told Scarlett. "I can probably call them off if we're going to be out of here by dawn."

She just nodded, her eyes on her cell phone screen. She was already starting a list of places to hold the trial. I thought about reminding her she wasn't supposed to look at screens with a concussion, but decided against it. Scarlett was a grown woman. Besides, I sort of got the feeling if I told her not to help, she'd start running around in search of snacks or danger just to be belligerent. She was definitely like Sam that way.

I got out my phone and called Kirsten, who connected me with the water witch.

"Hello, Lex? I heard you had some developments?" Laurel sounded different than she had at the sandwich shop, her voice fast and tight with stress.

"Yeah. I won't go into the whole thing, but we're going to be out of here by dawn," I told her. "You've all done great work, but you can stop now." It would be a lot easier to operate quickly without the pounding rain.

"Yeah...about that." She sounded uneasy. Uh-oh.

"What happened?"

"Nothing happened, but, well, we've kind of...lost control of it," she admitted.

"Lost control of what?"

"The water. We called the rain, but, um, we got a little more than we bargained for. I did warn you that no one's done this kind of magic for generations," she added defensively.

Scarlett was watching me curiously. "I get it, it's fine, just tell me what this means practically." I steeled myself. "Are people going to die?"

"What—no! At least, I don't think so. We're checking the news; I know they're closing the floodgates and evacuating the town. There might be property damage if the floodwater breaches the levee, but that's it. We just have to let the rain tire itself out."

That made the flooding sound like an angry toddler having

a tantrum, which was a lot more scary than funny. "Okay, Laurel. Pack up and get out of town, okay? I'm not sure what's going to happen, but you've certainly held up your end of the deal."

"Okay." She sounded enormously relieved. "Good luck, Lex."

As I hung up the phone, a siren started up from outside the hotel, rising and falling. Scarlett, who had lived in Southern California all her life, looked at me with wide eyes. "What the shit is that?"

"An Emergency Warning System," I said grimly. "They're evacuating the city."

## 29

### LEX

I was *itching* to get out there and find Adelaide and Orvil, but I tried to distract myself with research. Scarlett and I sat on the floor and used the coffee table as a desk, creating a list of possible locations for a last-minute trial. I turned on my iPad so I could look at a map of Galena, checking distances and routes out of town. We'd avoided using the iPad, even though it only connected via wifi, in case the enemy could find our location that way. But now I was almost hoping they would.

Eli returned with the coffee, and then we met, and ignored, a very young bellhop who knocked on the suite door and told us we needed to evacuate. Thirty minutes dragged by, and I began to worry about how long it was taking Simon and Beau to come up with the location.

Even if he ran at human speed, Beau should be able to get to the Belvedere and back in less than fifteen minutes. I didn't know how long Simon's spell would take, but I'd been with Lily when she'd done a simple finding spell, and it had only take a few minutes.

Was it more complicated because they were trying to trace a gun? Had Beau gotten back and Simon had tried the spell, but it wasn't working? I hadn't expressly told them to update me either way, but surely one of them would call and let us know if the spell had failed?

Just as I decided to call their room myself, there was a knock at the suite door. I got up to get it. "Finally."

"Someone drunk Jesse's coffee," Scarlett called after me. "We maybe shouldn't tell him there was once a coffee."

I checked the peephole, in case it was another bellhop, but Jesse and Simon were clearly visible. And they didn't look happy.

I swung open the door. "The spell didn't work?" I asked immediately.

"We never got to try it." Jesse was already moving past me into the room, slowing down when he saw that Scarlett was fine. He gave Eli a cool nod and turned back to me.

"Beau didn't come back," Simon told me. "Kirsten tried calling him, but his burner phone didn't even ring."

"What?" I looked back and forth between them in disbelief. This possibility hadn't even occurred to me.

"I was going to run over and get the shells myself, but Simon thought we should come up here first," Jesse said. "Is it possible that Adelaide and Orvil are holed up in the Belvedere?"

As he spoke, Simon wandered over and looked down at the scribbled sheets of hotel stationery all over the coffee table. He opened his messenger bag and pulled out the massive Galena book, plopping down on the floor next to Scarlett.

"I guess it's *possible*," I said, trying to focus on Jesse's question. "But when I talked to Orvil I didn't get the impression that the Belvedere was their home base so much as their favorite meeting spot. Besides, going back there would be stupid. They're a lot of things, but they've proven that they're not stupid."

"Then what could have happened to Beau?" Scarlett asked. She had leaned back from the table so Simon could pick up the papers and shuffle them around. "Do you think maybe Adelaide came back to pick up her gun thingies and Beau ran into her?"

"Again, it's possible," I said, reluctantly this time. "It's hard to see Beau getting overwhelmed by the two of them, though. He's been a cardinal vampire for a long time. He should be at least as strong as Orvil; they were turned around the same time."

"Maybe Orvil and Adelaide have help," Jesse pointed out.

"Who, though? Kirsten said Adelaide's skinner team wasn't in town; she would have told us if that changed."

"The vampire who recognized me?" Scarlett volunteered.

"Maybe." Could two vampires and Adelaide overpower Beau? I suspected it was possible in a straight fight, but wouldn't Beau have just run? It's hard to get the drop on a cardinal vampire. "I don't like this."

"I can go over there and get the shells myself," Jesse offered. "Or we could all go. We can take Scarlett, or not take Scarlett."

"Oi! Don't talk about me like I'm not here," Scarlett said without heat.

Simon looked up, momentarily distracted from the lists. "Oi?" he asked her.

"I watched a lot of British TV on maternity leave," she explained.

"Sorry," Jesse said to her, "but you know what I mean—there are tactical advantages to having a null along, but there are disadvantages too." He turned back to me. "What do you want to do?"

I gazed at him without seeing anything, weighing my options. If Beau had walked into some kind of trap, it would be stupid to walk everyone else in after him. At the same time, though, I couldn't leave a man behind. Meanwhile, the clock was ticking—I had less than two and a half hours to produce Orvil and Adelaide before Maven and Dashiell arrived to put them on trial.

"Lex?" Simon's voice interrupted my thoughts. "Which way did you say they went after they shot at you?" He was kneeling on the floor by the coffee table, still staring at some of Scarlett's scribbled notes. The iPad screen was active, displaying a map of Galena.

I crossed the room and crouched down next to him, zooming in with the iPad. I had to turn it to the satellite view before I recognized where we'd been on Park Ave. "Here," I said, pointing. "There's trees in the way of the satellite image, but it's a cult-de-sac with a little path going this way." I tried switching between different views, but I couldn't get a sense of where the trail went—there was too much tree cover.

"Yeah, I was kind of afraid you'd say that. Look." Simon spun his fingers on the map and zoomed in, following the trail by satellite. The path went southeast, running parallel to the Galena River for a bit. Then Simon moved the screen to the east of the trail, zooming in on the roof of a building. From above, it was oddly symmetrical. "What is that?" I asked. There was no label on the screen, so it wasn't a public building. There also weren't any roads or even a driveway leading directly to it, which was unusual.

Simon picked up his Galena book and showed me a page. "Fuck," I whispered.

Scarlett, Eli, and Jesse all bent their heads to read the text. I took a step back to give them room. "Do you have any more photos?" I asked Simon. "Or a website or something?"

"Oh, there's a whole report just on that building, look." He tapped a few things on the iPad, pulling up a document from some kind of historical preservation society. I scrolled the photos.

"The Galena Marine Hospital," Jesse said, reading off the page. "It's a weird shape—almost symmetrical, but not quite." He zoomed the iPad in so we could see the shape from an aerial view. It was a little like the plus sign symbol of the Red Cross, if you held it in the middle and stretched it out.

Jesse looked up at me. "You think this could be the place where Orvil and Adelaide are hiding?"

I opened my mouth to answer, but something in the photograph caught my attention. I picked up the book, ignoring a grumble from Eli, who had still been reading. I pulled it close to my face until I was sure.

"This is the place," I told Jesse. "It explains why Orvil and Adelaide always met at the Belvedere, and why they disappeared from there earlier."

"How are you so sure?" Simon asked. He wasn't questioning me. He was just curious, in his usual Simon way. So I answered him.

"This whole time, I thought Maya was taken because Julien's people saw her scouting around town. I figured they were dialed into Galena, just like Adelaide and Orvil are." I shook my head. "But when she disappeared, she'd been looking at hotels for Beau. Her ghost said she stumbled into some men on the way out of one of them. This one was on her list." I pointed at a bed and breakfast at the corner of Third Street. It was less than a block away from the Belvedere. "They're practically across the street."

Simon looked a little skeptical, so I told him the rest. "Maya also said the men who killed her were talking about what to do with her. One wanted to bring her to Julien, in Dubuque, and the other wanted to…she said something like, 'put me well.'"

I turned the book to show him the Marine Hospital photo that had caught my eye. In the yard just in front of the brick building there was a rectangular shape—boards, covering a piece of concrete. "What does this look like to you?"

He studied it. "A well."

I nodded. "She didn't say 'put me well.' She said 'put me *in* the well.' It's the perfect spot to stash a prisoner…or a dead body."

His eyes widened. "But if Dubuque's men were the ones who killed Maya…"

"Yeah. Orvil and Adelaide are hiding out there, and they're working with Julien Dubuque."

"Oh good," Scarlett said darkly. "More bad guys. I was just thinking to myself, this is all too easy. We need more bad guys."

Eli harrumphed in agreement. Jesse put his arm around her.

"I fucked up," I told all of them. "It was right here in Simon's book the whole time, but I didn't slow down long enough to put it together. And now they've got Beau.We need to gear up and go."

Just like that, the room erupted into activity. Scarlett headed for the bathroom and Jesse went downstairs to get supplies from his room. I stood up to check my weapons again—but Simon's hand shot up and grabbed my right wrist.

He'd never touched me like that, and it was so surprising that I froze. He stood up then, too, looking down at me from inches away. "Stop," he said. "Stop right now."

My mouth dropped open. I pulled my wrist free, and Simon let me—but he reached down to touch my cheek. "Lex, I need you to hear me." His voice was so soft and pleading that I had to stand still and listen. "You're blaming yourself, and it's making you move too fast. Slow down. We don't have to run in blind."

I drew a shuddering breath. I knew I needed to step back, away from Simon. *Step back*, I told myself. Pull away.

A very different part of me wanted to lift my hands and run them through Simon's dark hair. Pull his face toward me. What the hell was wrong with me?

"Give me half an hour," Simon was saying now. "I can find you some maps or satellite images on this place, figure out what you're dealing with—"

"Weapons," I blurted.

Simon blinked, and the current between us finally let up. I was able to step back, away from his touch. "Guns are loud, and Scarlett has shorted out anything magical, like my shredders," I said unsteadily. I was already sidling toward the door. "I'll take Scarlett and Jesse to go get some more weapons, so you have time to get us a map."

His brow furrowed. "Where are you going to find weapons at this hour in the middle of a flood?"

I have to smile at the question. "Don't you remember? This is Galena."

# 30

## SCARLETT

At twelve thirty in the morning, Lex and I sat in a rented Subaru outside the De Soto, waiting for our partners.

Lex, Jesse, and I had just finished the world's most bizarre scavenger hunt, looting Galena's Main Street shops for weapons. Well, Jesse and Lex did all the looting. And I'm not sure it's technically called "looting" if the ex-cop member of the group is keeping a tally sheet of everything you stole or broke, to be repaid later. At any rate, the two of them got a shitload of rain gear and plenty of weapons.

I stayed in the car, because even I had to admit I needed to rest before the Marine Hospital. I kept my radius flexed out, though, so we wouldn't have to worry about surprise supernatural attack, and so Lex wouldn't have to deal with ghosts. I was also a little worried about being followed again—but the only person I felt in my radius, other than Lex, was Eli, who prowled up and down the block on foot, supposedly keeping an eye on things.

Now we were back to get Simon from his research deep-dive, but the hotel had completely emptied out. Even the lights in the lobby were off. Jesse had decided it would be fastest to just run up to the room to collect the witch. In the driver's seat, Lex had the windshield wipers going at full blast and a phone held up in front of her. She was going back and forth between reading about the Marine Hospital on the screen and watching for Jesse and Simon.

As we waited, I chewed on a cuticle, unnerved by the darkness of the town center. During the short time we'd been in Galena, downtown had seemed like a busy commercial area, with lots of shop windows and neon-signed bars. Even after the rain started, people had scurried around, shopping and getting food. Now, though, everything had been turned off. The whole scene had a very creepy "ten minutes after close at your retail job" vibe, only on a citywide level.

I decided to distract myself...by pestering the most dangerous person in our party. Classic me. "So. A marine hospital," I said to Lex. "The fuck is that?"

"You saw the entry in that book," she said without looking at me.

"Yeah, but I still don't get what this place actually *did.* And I'm not allowed to look at phones anymore on account of my head being a bastard." My headache had gotten a lot worse after helping Lex look for possible trial locations. Apparently the doctor's advice about not looking at screens hadn't actually been nonsense.

Lex did a dramatic sigh but started paraphrasing the screen she was reading. "In the 1800s there was a network of hospitals for sailors who got sick or hurt," she said, scrolling down the text. "It looks like the system wasn't very well organized, and it was controversial, because seamen had to pay a tax on their wages to fund the system. There was a lot of corruption and some scandals."

"Well, I do enjoy a seamen scandal..."

She ignored me. "The Marine Hospitals were mostly along the East Coast ports, but eventually they spread to the Mississippi."

"Including one in Galena," I surmised. "Because back then, the Galena River was wide enough to be a port."

"Exactly."

Take that, my concussion. "I thought this town's whole deal was historical tourism," I said. "And the building *is* cool-looking, in an Addams Family summer vacation kind of way. Why aren't the owners doing tours?" I'd seen signs for at least two separate ghost tour companies.

"I don't know." She stared ahead at the blur of water on the windshield for a second, then gave a little head shake. "I can't get used to it."

"I know. It's the rainpocalypse."

"Not that. There are no ghosts."

"Oh." I automatically looked out through my own windows, but of course there was nothing I would be able to see. One of the perks of being a null is that I never have to worry about the magical echoes of dead people following me around. "Um, should there be?"

"I guess I thought..." she gave a little head shake. "I figured you would cancel out the ghosts in your little sphere, but I would still see the ones outside it. And there's just... nothing."

"Because I'm not just cancelling out the ghost's magic," I said, trying not to take that "little sphere" remark personally. "I'm cancelling out *your* magic."

"Right. Yeah." She leaned back in the seat, looking surprisingly...relaxed?

I wondered, then, how difficult it must be for her to see

ghosts all the time. I'd never really thought about it, but if she saw them every single night after dark, in a town this old? It would be a lot.

"There they are." She pointed at the DeSoto's opening doors. Jesse and Simon walked slowly out, using their phones' flashlights to light the way. Both of them were wearing black rain gear, and Jesse was opening an umbrella to hold over Simon. The witch held a big piece of white cardboard to his chest to protect it from the rain.

When they reached the parked car, I thought they'd climb in, but instead Jesse pulled a white hotel towel out of his raincoat and used to dried off the hood of the car so Simon could lay down his cardboard.

"What does he have?" I asked Lex.

"A map, I hope." She was already halfway out of the Subaru, shutting the door behind her. Apparently we were going to look at the map outside.

"Great," I muttered, easing my way out of the vehicle. "More rain." I was wearing plenty of gear—I hadn't even known rain pants were a thing—but it still made me crabby.

Simon took what looked like a pack of markers out of his jacket. "I found a topographic map," he announced. "I know how to get there, and I've got this idea—well, it's not a sure thing, but it might help, and Jesse has a plan, too. But you can't take us straight there; we have to make a stop."

"Aw, he babbles," I said fondly. "Relatable content."

"Here, come look at this."

Lex and I both came around the hood to stand next to him. Even Eli stopped his lurking and stood at the back of the group.

I don't know what I was expecting, but it was just a piece of tagboard that Simon had scribbled on with markers. It looked like a few black squiggles to me, including one long thick line with a curl at the end like a candy cane. The only things I recognized were a ribbon of blue marker that probably represented the river, a big green circle, and a rough shape in the center of the circle that I knew was the Marine Hospital from the aerial photos.

Simon had drawn a circle in the center, representing the little tower thingie on top of the building.

Lex was looking at the drawing like it was the Rosetta Stone. "If there isn't a road to this place, how do we approach?" she asked.

"There's no *paved* road to the Marine Hospital, but there are theoretically two ways to get there. See this long line with the curve at the end like a backwards letter J?" Simon pointed to the candy cane line. "That's an escarpment, a line of cliff. It kind of curves around."

I tried to picture it. "Like a gigantic shepherd's hook that rises out of the earth?"

"Yes, exactly. The building is in this little clearing," he gestured at the green circle, which was nestled inside the curve of the hook, "but it's protected on almost all sides by that cliff. And I don't think we can climb it. I found a bunch of photos that visitors put on Instagram. The forest is incredibly dense, and there are barbed-wire fences. And that's on top of it being steep and pouring rain. But—" He drew a red line that ran along the long part of the candy cane. "Galena has a hiking/biking trail that runs right alongside the cliff. The Belvedere Mansion used to be the trailhead, but now Galena has put some tourism dollars into a nice, paved bike path that starts by Depot Park." He drew an X.

"Great," I muttered under my breath. "Another fucking bike path." Because I'd had so much fun on the last one.

"So we can take the bike path to the spot where the cliff curves?" Lex tapped on the spot.

"You could, yeah. I think there's an old trail that goes

around the curve to the Marine Hospital, but I don't know how well it's been maintained." He frowned.

Jesse was staring at the squiggly lines like they might move around and spell a plan to us directly. "You said there are two ways into the clearing?"

"Yes. The other option is to approach from the northeast." He pointed at to the top of the map, where several horizontal streets ended with an offshoot going south. It ended in a bunch of rectangles, a little northeast of the Marine Hospital.

"What are those squares?" Eli asked.

"Farm buildings. This road up here goes to a driveway that leads to the farm. It's privately owned, of course, but the farm is currently on the market, and the building is empty. There's still some land in between the farm and the Marine Hospital building, but it's on the same elevation, and I think it's just tall grass. Even in the rain it'd probably be walkable." He glanced up at me, then quickly away.

"Oh, I get it," I said, rolling my eyes. It made my headache flare, but it was worth it. "You think it's easy enough for even me to walk."

"Well...yeah."

"Okay." Lex checked her watch, an expensive-looking Rolex. It didn't really go with her clothing choices, but then, for all I knew she was in daily formalwear back in Boulder. She looked at Simon. "You said something about a plan."

"*Jesse* has part of a plan," he corrected. "I have an idea that goes with it."

"Tell us in the car?" she said to Jesse, straightening up.

"Yeah, but we have to make a stop before we go in."

"Then we should hurry. It's going to take a while to get anywhere, with the floodgates closed, and they've had Beau for over an hour already. Let's go."

She headed for the driver's side door of the Forester. It had been decided that Lex would be tonight's driver—partly because she had a lot more experience than Jesse with driving in rain, and partly because she had asked to. Apparently she couldn't usually drive at night because of the ghosts, so this was her equivalent of Maven getting to eat Oreos.

Jesse sat in the front, so he could help Lex navigate, and I climbed into the back seat. Simon got in on the other side to sit next to me. I expected him to scoot into the middle seat to make room for Eli, but he closed the door and reached for the seat belt.

"Wait — is Eli going to ride on the roof of the car?" I asked. "Because while that would definitely fulfill some of my *Teen Wolf* daydreams, I think it might be a little wet."

Ignoring me, Lex rolled down her window, letting rain spray in. I felt Eli hit my radius, and then he was looming over the driver's seat window. There was a big coil of rope looped around his neck, and I realized I'd missed something.

"You sure you know where you're going?" Lex asked him.

"I'll go up the levee, over the bridge to the bike trail by the Belvedere, and try the cliff," he recited. "I'll head for the southwest corner to check the well."

Lex nodded. "If he's in there, alive, get him the hell out before you do anything else. Promise me."

"I promise. If he's in the well, I'll make sure he's safe."

Lex gave him a curt nod and buzzed the window up.

"Okay, I have to tell you something about the building—" Simon started to say, but I interrupted him.

"Hang on a second, you said the cliff wasn't doable. So why is Eli approaching on foot?" And when did you decide this, I wanted to add, but didn't.

Lex glanced at me over her shoulder, probably reading my mind with her dark powers. "He had Kirsten call me while I was in one of the stores. He didn't think you'd approve."

"Of him going—oh. Crap."

"What?" Simon asked.

Jesse was looking at Lex too. "He's going to change?"

She nodded. "Eli suggested it. I don't like it either, for the record, but Simon is right about that cliff. As a wolf, Eli is the only one of the five of us who can make it up that hill in the rain, *and* the only one who can sneak around the woods unnoticed if the rain stops." She started the Forester and began creeping forward through the rain.

"And why don't we approve?" Simon asked me.

"Because as a wolf, he'll also be nearly impossible to communicate with, short-tempered, and easily distracted by prey," I said, not bothering to keep the bitterness and worry from my voice. "And if he bites a human or kills an innocent..." I shook my head. At best, he'd never forgive himself. At worst, we might have to put the alpha werewolf of Los Angeles on suicide watch.

"I get it," Lex said evenly.

I almost, *almost* snapped at her that she really didn't. She'd never seen Eli weeping and broken after he accidentally mauled someone to death.

But, just in time, I remembered that Lex's twin sister Sam had been killed by a rampaging werewolf. She understood what was at stake here, and I wasn't the only one who sometimes had to choose between two terrible options.

I took a deep breath and turned in my seat so I could look at Simon. The witch was focused on his phone again. "You were saying, Simon?"

"Right! It's about the building's history. It did start as a hospital for sailors, but it opened right before the Civil War, and then the Mississippi River was blockaded. Basically, there were no patients. By the time the war ended, it had been running at a loss for five years, and they closed down in 1866.

"The building was empty for a few years, and then it became a school for teachers," he continued. "After twelve years, the school closed because the location was too difficult to access every day. And then..." Simon sounded uneasy.

"What?" I asked.

He made a fuss about looking at his phone like he was checking details. "It was purchased by Frank Nash of F. A. Nash Medical Company. There's some evidence it became, um, a sanatorium."

Lex muttered a collection swear words that made my eyes widen.

"Wait, what does that mean?" Jesse peered around his seat to look at Simon. "Like it was an insane asylum?"

"Lots of ailments were treated at Nash's sanatoriums, including tuberculosis and yes, mental illness," Simon reported, still looking at the phone. "Anyway, Nash owned the building from 1912 to 1933, when he sold it...or maybe just abandoned it. It's not clear."

"So we're going to a literal abandoned mental hospital," Jesse muttered. "Because of course we are."

Lex had to swerve the car all the way to the left curb to avoid a downed tree in the road. This might have been terrifying, except we hadn't seen a single other car since we left the hotel. The people of Galena had taken the order to evacuate downtown very seriously. "How many owners since then?" she asked. Her tone suggested the question was important, but I didn't know what she was getting at.

"No one has ever owned the building for more than a couple of years," Simon reported. "It's like this albatross around the city's neck. That show *Ghost Hunters* even did an episode there."

"Great. Just fucking great." Lex stomped down on the gas, causing the SUV to jerk forward. "That complicates things."

"Okay, what am I missing?" I said. "You're saying this place is haunted, or whatever?"

I might not be able to see ghosts, but I could sure watch movies. The idea of a haunted insane asylum was creepy no matter how you sliced it.

But Lex was used to ghosts, right?

"Oh, it's definitely very haunted," Simon told me, though his eyes were on Lex. "Ghosts are created when people die with a great deal of trauma. A place like that must have hosted a lot of pain—physical and otherwise." But it was obvious from the way he was focused on Lex that there was more to the story.

I sighed. These guys were going to make me ask. "Okay, fine. What am I missing?"

Lex answered. "Simon thinks the ghost, or at least one of the ghosts, is a boundary witch."

# 31

LEX

Unlike the average ghost, the ghost of a boundary witch remains sentient, and could even affect her environment a little: drafts, bad smells, musty air, things being knocked over. This is the type of scary poltergeist activity you see in movies, and it's is *very* rare—boundary witches are rare in general, and we don't always leave ghosts behind.

In the years since I'd started to see ghosts every nightfall, I had only met one who was a former boundary witch: Nellie Evans, a nineteenth-century madam who still haunted her old brothel in Denver. Nellie was...well, not a friend, or even an ally, but she was someone who would trade information to me for small favors like television and music.

I understood why Simon thought the Galena Marine Hospital had its own Nellie. The building that housed Nellie's brothel had a very similar history: many different owners, all with big renovation plans that were mysteriously thwarted by the building itself. It wasn't something you could put it in a real estate condition report, but any prospective buyer who toured the building would notice a certain *vibe*. Sometimes one would kid themselves that it could be fixed with some paint and fresh flowers, and buy the property. Within a year or two, though, they would decide the place needed too much work and offload it to someone else.

Simon explained most of this to Scarlett and Jesse before he walked us through the rest of their plan. It was flexible, to account for Adelaide and Orvil's action, which was good, and especially dangerous for Simon and Jesse, which was not. "I don't like it," I said when he'd finished.

"I don't either," Scarlett said, though I could tell she was talking mostly to Jesse. "I thought we weren't going to split up anymore during this thing."

"I don't want to, but you'll be safe with Lex," he said, turning in his seat to look at her. "At least this plan has *me* taking the stupid risk and you hanging back where it's safe...for once."

That's kind of my point," I argued. "You and Simon will be too exposed."

"We'll have guns and Kevlar vests, and I've got shields for days," Simon pointed out. "Besides, if it starts to go to hell, Scarlett can go supernova and de-magic the shit out of everyone."

"Ooh, I *like* that description," Scarlett mused. "I think I'm going to put it on business cards."

The two of them started bantering about slogans in the back seat, sounding a lot like how Simon was with Lily. Since that was probably reassuring for Simon, I let them go on.

Next to me, Jesse reached over to touch my shoulder. "You okay with this?"

I cut my eyes sideways, but I couldn't read his expression in the dark. "He's terrible with guns," I told him in a low voice. "He's more of a diplomacy and research guy."

"I'll look after him," Jesse promised. "We'll be fine."

"I know you will." I sighed, wishing I had a better plan. "We're almost there."

When Simon and Jesse got out of the backseat and headed toward the building I found myself bolting from the driver's seat as well. "Simon," I called through the rain.

He turned back to me, and my heart wrenched at the look on his face. It was hope.

I couldn't speak.

He read something on my face, and in the dim light from the street lamps, his expression turned into resignation. "I know," he said, already turning away. "I'll be careful."

For a moment I just stood there in the rain, feeling like a jackass. What was I doing?

As I climbed back into the Forester, I worked very hard not to look at Scarlett. "You don't want to tell him you love him?" she asked, annoying as ever. "You get that we could all die tonight, right?"

Irritated, I reached forward to start the engine. "Yeah, well, I've died before."

THERE WAS heavy silence in the car after that. We still had to drive several miles west to another bridge, then double back to reach Blackjack Road, where we could get on the dirt path to the farmhouse. At that point, anyone at the Marine Hospital would be able to see our lights, but since it was still a road, I switched to fog lights only. This meant I had to slow down even further, but I was pretty sure even vampires wouldn't be able to make out the tiny amount of light in the rain.

Scarlett was silent beside me, which seemed out of character. I looked over and realized that despite the gallon of coffee she'd had at the De Soto, she was fast asleep.

My irritation with her vanished, and I felt a stab of fresh guilt. I didn't know what I'd been thinking, dragging someone with back-to-back concussions through flooded farmlands to a haunted asylum full of vampires. This whole night felt slapdash and thrown-together, and for a second I was tempted to call off the whole thing. Part of leading troops is knowing when to retreat, and I could admit that I'd underestimated Adelaide, and she'd made a smart move with the vampire bounty. The smartest response would be to pull back and regroup, then find another way to get at Orvil, Adelaide and Malcolm after our people had healed.

But now they'd taken Beau. I couldn't leave, couldn't *stop*, until I knew whether he was alive. And I knew Scarlett, Jesse, Simon, and even Eli were on board, because they'd do the same for their people.

I still wished we knew more about what we were walking into, though. In theory, the Marine Hospital could be swarming with a hundred vampires, in which case we were screwed. The more I thought about it, though, that scenario didn't feel right. Orvil and Adelaide had a particular nightly meeting place, the Belvedere, which suggested he went out to feed, rather than keeping humans on the premises. And when I pressed Julien he said Orvil always stayed in a different place when he was in Galena, and kept that location secret. That meant he was either concerned about his personal security, or he didn't like too much time with strangers.

*Julien also said he didn't know where Orvil was staying*, came a familiar voice in my head.

"Sam!" I said it out loud, then glanced at Scarlett, who was still asleep with her face tucked between the seat and the window. *You're back*, I thought at my sister.

*But I'm on thin ice. Today Sam will be playing the role of subconscious reminders only.*

It took me a second to understand: she was only allowed to remind me of things I had already learned, rather than guide me in new directions. *Copy that*, I thought back at her.

Then I considered what she'd said. Julien had been pressed when I questioned him about Orvil's location; he literally couldn't lie to me. Which meant when I talked to him, he truly hadn't known where Orvil was.

"He got in touch after our visit," I muttered under my breath. But wait: if Julien and his people didn't know Orvil was at the Marine Hospital, why had one his men suggested putting Maya's body in the well? Or was I wrong about that? Could I be wrong about the Marine Hospital entirely?

I wasn't sure if it was allowed, but it was worth asking. *Sam*, I thought. *Can you remind me of Maya's exact words?*

*You asked her what the two bad guys were worried about,* came Sam's answer. *She said, "About what to do with me. One wants to bring me to Julien, while the other wants to put me in the well."*

Sam had smoothed out Maya's quiet voice, added the swallowed words from my memory. I relaxed a little. I was sure the Marine Hospital was the right place. There was more than one well in Galena, of course, but it seemed like too much of a coincidence for them to mean a different spot. One of the two men had suggested taking Maya's body to the well at the Marine Hospital, but the other had wanted to bring it to Julien, and he'd obviously won out.

Did that mean Orvil had a human spy working for Julien? Or was the Marine Hospital well just an easy place for dumping bodies? That wasn't as far-fetched as it sounded: On the rare occasions when we had to dispose of a body in Boulder, Maven used the same abandoned mine shaft. Happily I'd only had to be involved with that one time.

Still, I suddenly felt like an idiot: I'd dismissed the two men who'd killed Maya as being just a couple of human subordinates, but that didn't mean they weren't decision-makers. Hell, *I* was a frickin' subordinate. I should have tracked them down and figured out what they knew, but I'd gotten wrapped up in my little vendetta with Adelaide. Now it was too late.

There was nothing to do but keep this information in mind and remember that no matter what, Julien was involved in this now. He'd said Orvil wasn't a friend, but I'd also embarrassed a vampire in front of other vampires. Julien must have called Orvil afterwards.

I had no idea if that meant the two of them were actually working together, but I would have to act as though they were. "So up to three vampires," I mumbled, counting to myself. "Orvil, Beau, and possibly Julien. Adelaide. Possibly those two humans." Orvil and Adelaide were loners, by all accounts, so even if there were a few extra hostiles, this didn't seem too bad. I checked my watch. We had nearly two hours to deal with, say five to ten enemies—and Scarlett could make them all human. In terms of threats, Simon and I had faced a lot worse, alone.

But my gut still churned with acid. There was too much I didn't know. And now my thoughts were just back to the beginning.

At that point the road went from pavement to waterlogged gravel, and I had switch on just the fog lights and pay close attention to driving. I let Scarlett sleep through until we reached the farmhouse, but she woke up, yawning, when I turned the engine off. After checking to make sure the interior lights were disabled, I hit the button for the Forester's tailgate and went to stand underneath it and get my gear together, giving Scarlett a moment to collect herself.

She joined me a few minutes later, moving stiffly. "Hey. How do you feel?" I asked as she stepped under the overhanging tailgate beside me. I'd already set out a tiny camp lantern so I could see what I was doing.

"How do I feel, hmm...." Scarlett squinted forward into the darkness for a second, like it might provide the answer. "Well, physically, I feel like I barely survived a cluster bomb attack two days ago, but hey, that part makes sense. I feel like I really miss my kid, and also like I may never see her again. I miss my bargest. I wish she could be in this fight with us."

She shucked her raincoat and T-shirt, revealing a Kevlar vest and some kind of leather belt that rode high on her waist. The belt glinted in the lantern glow, and I realized it was full of throwing knives. "And I feel like we're walking into a trap, but I can't figure out how it could be a trap," she continued. "Which kind of makes me want to walk in even more. I sure hate trap mysteries."

I grinned at her. "God, you're weird."

"*Me*?" She checked the straps on her belt and vest, then put one foot on the bumper and rolled up her the leg of her rain pants. "You know what your problem is?" she said to me, strapping an ankle holster around her leg, "You've met too many people like you."

I handed her the small Beretta that fit with that holster. "Is that a line from a movie?"

"Sure is. And if you can tell me the name of the movie, I'll eat these ugly new hiking boots Jesse stole for me."

"No deal."

With the sidearm secured, she rolled down the leg of her rain pants and put the raincoat back on, leaving it unzipped. "Are you ready?"she asked.

I looked down at myself. I wasn't wearing my forearm sheaths, since Scarlett had shorted out my shredder stakes. Simon had theorized that Scarlett couldn't undo my mother's bloodstone, since the gravitational magic of crystals operated on its own frequency, but I'd left it back at the hotel anyway. I wouldn't be able to do much magic with Scarlett nearby, and it didn't seem worth the risk.

But I had the Kevlar vest and my Glock in a left-handed hip holster. The waterproof pockets of my raincoat and cargo pants were full of more magazines, along with a few other goodies, including a Gerber Mark II fighting knife I'd found in the sporting goods store. It was similar to the Gerber model I had at home. "One second," I said. I put my own raincoat back on, also unzipped, and strapped an AR-15 rifle to my chest, slinging it around to my back for easy transport.

"You're right, that look was totally missing something," Scarlett said, deadpan.

I looked down at myself. In a weird way, I felt like I was back in the army again: no magic, lots of firearms and sharp edges. The AR was even the civilian equivalent of the M4 rifle I'd had in the Army. I voted for stricter gun laws in every election I could, but Adelaide was going to be armed to the teeth. I had to be ready. "Let's go."

THE MARINE HOSPITAL wasn't far, and it was on the same elevation as the farmhouse. As soon as we stepped off the farm's gravel driveway and into the tall grass, though, Scarlett struggled to keep her balance, her arms shooting out like a surfer. I had my own experience with concussions and vertigo, but eventually I got annoyed and grabbed her arm, putting my mouth close to her ear.

"Listen," I whispered, as matter-of-factly as I could. "You and I are going to hold hands until we get within sight of the building. I'm going to help you balance, and you're not going to joke about it, because we need to stay quiet. No arguments."

It was a sign of how shitty she must have been feeling that Scarlett simply nodded and offered me her left hand, which I took with my right. At least we both still had our dominant hands free. Her fingers were cool and slippery with rain, but her grip was strong, and we trudged ahead.

The Marine Hospital building seemed to appear out of nowhere.

I'd seen plenty of photos, of course, but it still took me by surprise: a massive brick structure, rising out of the tall grass like a monument. A number of the windows were illuminated, including the windows in the cupola, but the main source of light outside was one of those freestanding work lights. It had been set up at the southeast corner of the building, on top of the concrete block that formed the service door, just as Simon had described. What he hadn't known about, however, was that there was a dark crawlspace right below those stairs. Actually, "crawlspace" probably wasn't accurate. It was like a miniature manmade cave, a rectangular hole that had probably been left when the concrete steps were added.

We'd talked about the Marine Hospital being inside a clearing of grass, but now with light coming out of several windows I could see that the trees around the clearing didn't quite form a full circle. There was an opening in the grass on the south side of the building—that was the makeshift driveway that led to the bike trail. I couldn't see it, but the well was just past that.

Scarlett squeezed my hand suddenly, hard, and I thought I heard a tiny squeak over the rain. I turned to see what she was looking at—and discovered the tree we'd almost run into. It was maybe the biggest white oak tree I'd ever seen, with nearly symmetrical branches coming out of the trunk on the same plane, like the arms of a saguaro cactus, only traveling outward instead of bending up. Each one of those arms was bigger around than my waist. It was more than large enough to hide both of us.

I tugged Scarlett's hand toward the tree, and she resisted for a moment, making a face of exaggerated terror. She mouthed the word, "Too creepy."

I rolled my eyes just as big, and she allowed me to pull us to the trunk, so we were hidden from the building. It wasn't until we were already crouched there that I realized the grass around us was shorter than the wild grass we'd trekked through to get here. Someone had mowed around this tree, like a small second clearing. Odd.

I made a *stay here* motion with my hand, and then lowered myself to the ground so I could belly-crawl toward the Marine Hospital building. I soon wormed my way through the wet, tall grass, and tried to brace myself for any creepy-crawlies that might appear. I wasn't afraid of bugs, but I didn't want to get startled and make a noise, either.

I stopped at the edge of the big clearing and watched for movement. There were some figures moving around inside the building, but the outside seemed clear. I looked over my shoulder and found Scarlett. With her jacket hood up and the rain still pouring down, she was nearly invisible. I nodded at her.

I couldn't feel her pulling in her radius, but I closed my eyes and concentrated on my boundary mindset. Then I took a deep breath, bracing myself, and opened my eyes toward the Marine Hospital.

# 32

## SCARLETT

Lex, being both fearless and apparently unfamiliar with all horror movies, made me wait by the scariest tree I'd ever seen. It was huge and spidery, with branches that seemed to hang in space like they might dangle marionettes...or dangle *other* people-shaped things from ropes. It was the best cover from the Marine Hospital building, but I decided I still would not touch this tree.

While I pulled in my radius, Lex crawled away to count the number of life forms, or whatever, inside the building. I worried a little about how ghost-infested the building was, and how much it might affect her.

When she belly-crawled back to me, though, she seemed calm...but a little puzzled. "Four humans and three vampires," she whispered. "The humans are probably Adelaide and some of Julien's day people, and they're all in the basement, except one on the first floor. Two of the vampires are on the first floor, too, and one is outside. I'm assuming it's Orvil, Julien, and

Beau. Unless Eli already got Beau out, in which case a vampire we don't know yet."

Those numbers were within the acceptable ranges we'd talked about, so why did Lex look confused? "What's wrong?" I whispered. "Too many ghosts?"

She shook her head. "Not enough ghosts," she corrected. "I was expecting dozens, inside and out. But I only saw a handful." She checked over her shoulder again, like one might have followed us over from the building.

"Any sign of the boundary—" I began, but Lex jerked her a hand in a *wait, be quiet* gesture. She edged closer to me behind the tree, getting really low to the ground and peering around it. Curious, I copied her on my side of the trunk.

Someone was strolling along the outside of the clearing. We were looking at the east face of the building, which meant this person was coming around the southern lawn. This must have been the vampire Lex had seen outside—she was patrolling.

She hadn't bothered with the hood of her black rain coat, and as she got closer to the work light I saw the buzz cut. It was the vampire who'd been following me earlier, the one I'd chased up the stairs until I puked.

Lex and I stayed silent and still, waiting for her to make her way around this arm of the building. As she passed in front of the window closest to us, though, we got a brief glimpse of her profile in the rain.

And something clicked in my brain.

Without thinking I grabbed Lex's arm urgently, but she just glanced at me and held a finger to her lips. Even in the rain, we were risking vampire hearing now. I managed to wait until the vampire was all the way around this arm of the building and had disappeared from sight before whispering, "I know her!"

"She's the one who was following you by the steps?" Lex guessed.

"Yeah—but I *know* her! Her name is Kendra; she works for Malcolm!" In my defense, she'd been a human with hair to her waist when I knew her, but obviously things had changed. "Lex, this is bad. We have to call off the guys. We need to wait for Dashiell and Maven."

I couldn't make out Lex's face in the darkness, but I could practically feel the confusion coming off her. "Why? You met her years ago. She must have started working for Orvil, either before or after she was turned."

I shook my head, struggling to keep my voice in a whisper as the words tumbled out. "That's not it! Listen, Kendra barely spoke and she couldn't fight. I asked Jameson once what her job was, and he said she loves making people bleed. She knew how to make it last for ages, right up to the point of death. Malcolm called her his personal chef. If she's here, Malcolm is here!"

"She could still have—" Lex started to say, but I sort of flapped my hands until she went quiet. I *really* wanted to yell and scream right now.

"Listen to me," I hissed. "I don't care if Orvil is his son; Malcolm does *not* share his people. He wouldn't let her go work for Orvil. Malcolm is *here*."

"By my count—"

I couldn't help myself. "*Fuck your count!* Does your magic eye work through brick walls that are two feet thick? Can it make it to the opposite side of the clearing? How about through a ghost-infested building? I am telling you; *Malcolm is here!* Call the guys!" We still had cell phones, although of course they'd all been turned off.

I was expecting Lex to yell at me or get mad and put a hand over my mouth. Something. Instead, though, she reached up with both hands to push loose strands of wet hair behind both her ears. "Scarlett," she said very softly. "I need you to stay calm. If you freak out and expand your radius into that building, they will know we're here. Breathe."

That brought me up short. She was right; my radius had been expanding a bit. I reigned it in, taking deep breaths. Giving me a moment, Lex looked speculatively at the building, then back at me. I'd calmed down enough to realize what I was asking of her: that she disregard her instincts and her own magic to believe what most people would see as a hunch.

But I knew I was right. Malcolm jealously guarded his people; he collected them like little treasures. He would never let someone in his inner circle go work somewhere else. That was the main reason he'd come after Jameson in Las Vegas, at least at first. You had to trust your employee in order to let them go out in the world with your secrets, even temporarily. Malcolm wasn't capable of trust, including the people in his entourage, like Jameson and Kendra. He made them dependent on him emotionally and financially. If someone got past all his manipulations and really did leave, he had them killed.

I was as sure of that as I was of anything. But how could I make Lex believe me? She was a super soldier, and I was a mouthy null with two concussions, a patchwork life and like three party tricks. So I just looked at her, my eyes pleading.

Whatever she saw on my face in that moment, she abruptly leaned to one side and dug into the pocket of her pants, though I didn't know if she was going for her phone or something else.

In the end, it didn't matter. Because right at that second, we heard the sirens. Then the red and blue lights were bouncing off the rain over the tall grass like a moving glow, coming from the direction of the bike path. Seconds later a Galena Police car came screaming up the slippery path to the south side of the building, bouncing and skidding through the mud.

It parked in the "driveway," the area of matted grass leading up to the service door, and both front car doors opened as two men stepped out. They were wearing police hats with those fun shower cap protectors, and "Galena Police Department" jackets zipped up to their noses.

Lex had grabbed my hand and was already pulling me up to circle around the north side of the building. We stayed on the outside of the grass clearing, well away from the light, and I had to pay attention to my footing and keeping my radius in, since the ground sloped downward back here.

I did glance over in time to see two people practically explode out of the service door, all their attention on the police car. They slowed down on the stairs, probably remembering that they were supposed to be humans. I recognized Julien and Orvil from the photos. There was a lit window next to the service door, and I caught a brief glimpse of Adelaide Preston before she ducked back out of sight.

"Hello?" The officer who'd exited on the passenger side clicked on one of those heavy-duty police flashlights, shining it through the rain toward the building. "This building is private property; you are trespassing," he called, his voice booming with simultaneous authority and boredom. Classic Cop Voice. "More importantly, there's an emergency evacuation order in place for the city of Galena. I'm going to need everyone out of there right now. We'll need to do a sweep of the building."

We had circled the clearing almost to the north face, so I sneaked a quick look before I lost sight.

Orvil had gotten down the stairs first, and now he sauntered over to the police officers like he had all the time in the world, while Julien Dubuque waited at the bottom of the stairs. Both vampires were wearing dark clothes under trench coat-style raincoats left open.

"Why, Officer, of *course* we have permission from the development company who owns this building," he said, his voice a purr of charm. He was still walking toward them.

The cops had police-issued rain jackets zipped up to the bottom of their noses, and hats pulled very low over their eyes, which would make it really difficult to press them. Orvil would have to get close.

Then again, one of them was a witch, and the other was wearing a witch bag that Simon had whipped up with supplies from the witch shop.

Jesse waited until Orvil was six feet away before he held up his hand. "Hold right there please, sir," he ordered, still using his Cop Voice. "Even with the owner's permission to be here, we're going to need you to evacuate immediately. City safety orders are *not* optional." He looked at Simon. "Radio the station and report it."

Simon, who probably had no idea how to use the police-issue handheld radio clipped to his belt, gamely pulled it out and turned slightly away to speak into the device. I relaxed a little—if the vampires thought the whole police station knew where these two officers were, they'd be less likely to just kill them.

Lex tugged at my hand again, marching us determinedly around the outside of the clearing We were nearly to the north side of the building now, and I lost sight of the "police."

Even with Lex holding my hand, I had to concentrate to keep my feet in the area outside the clearing. We were on the edge of the thicker part of the forest, but tiny, thorny branches still tore at my clothes and exposed skin. I was really starting to hate Midwestern forests. As we moved away I could just barely hear Jesse and Orvil calling back and forth over the rain, though I couldn't make out the words.

Then a new, louder voice joined the conversation. "I'm afraid that won't be possible, Officer...?" Julien Dubuque sounded less genteel, more savage, than Orvil had. He sounded like he was just about out of patience.

I froze, thinking of what he'd done to Maya. This wasn't a vampire that respected humans. And Jesse was ten feet away from him.

Lex felt my resistance and turned to glare me. One of the illuminated windows was creating just enough of a glow through the rain that I could see the silhouette of her face, looking impatient. She pointed in the direction we'd been heading: the hospital's old entrance door, on the opposite side of the building from Jesse and Simon's diversion.

I stepped up close beside her to whisper, although vampires would have to be within human earshot to overhear us. No super-hearing around nulls. "I saw Adelaide in the window, watching out of sight," I told Lex. "That's my guy back there."

Lex glanced past me, at the way we had come, and her face softened. "Go for that little cave under the stairs," she whispered. "Count to a hundred, then go nuclear."

I nodded, and Lex turned to go. But it was my turn to tug at her hand, so she turned to face me again. "Malcolm. Is. In there." I told her firmly. "Be careful."

Then I turned and ran across the lawn in a straight line, toward the eastern face of building.

# 33

## LEX

The original plan had actually been pretty simple: Simon and Jesse would create a diversion that draws Adelaide and Orvil out front. While they kept the couple busy, Scarlett would sneak me into the building—apparently her "radius" was also a safe space from supernatural hearing or scenting—and then pull back so find the resident boundary witch, assuming there was one. If she would talk to me, I could hopefully get intel on Orvil and Adelaide's plans, as well as anyone else inside the Marine Hospital. Most importantly, she could hopefully tell me what had happened to Beau in case he wasn't in the well.

Then Scarlett would expand her radius to cover the whole building and Jesse and Simon could "arrest" Orvil and Adelaide. Simple.

Until Scarlett decided to turn back.

When she said she wanted to split up, I knew I should protest. I would be vulnerable to supernatural detection and attack, not to mention she and I would have no way to communicate without alerting the hostiles.

But I stopped caring about any of that when she said she'd spotted Adelaide watching Jesse and Simon from the window. Adelaide knew her way around a long-range firearm, and I wasn't sure if Simon would have his shield up already. I wanted Scarlett keeping an eye on them more than I was worried about getting into the Marine Hospital by myself.

*She also said Malcolm is in the building*, came Sam's voice in my head. I ignored this. I still wasn't sure I believed Scarlett's theory. Besides, a boundary witch would be able to tell me for sure. Best to stick to at least that part of the plan.

Scarlett and I had needed to go slowly, picking our way along the inside of the tree line. Now, though, I decided I'd had enough of stealth. I sprinted the rest of the way along the tree line, then pivoted to run across the sodden grass on the east side of the building. I balanced gingerly in the center of each step, like I was moving on ice. There were two ghosts wandering around the yard on this side, but neither of them were close enough to bother me. Again, I had to wonder at the lack of remnants on the property. Were they all inside?

I made it to the brick face of the building and turned to jog along the side, moving north toward the old entrance. It was all well and good until I was slowing down before the corner and damn near fell into a brick pit of some kind.

Throwing my weight backward, I managed not to fall in, but I lost my footing on the wet grass and collapsed onto my stomach, landing with my head dangling down into the dark pit. There was so little light on this side of the building that I couldn't see the bottom. The words *mass grave* popped into my head, and a wave of fear and memory washed over me.

I forced myself to reach out and feel the edge. The hole was rectangular and lined with stone, and I could just make out what looked like two windows that had been bricked over. Okay—this had probably once been a basement egress that they'd closed up. Still, the thought of falling in there unnerved me enough that I rolled onto my back, the AR digging painfully into my spine, to get up...which is why I was in time to see the dark shape lunging for me from four feet away, fingers already extended and grasping. They must have been watching from the tree line and charged when they saw me go down.

There was no time to get up, so I threw myself into another turn, same direction, hoping they might trip and go down into the pit. I used the momentum to roll up to my feet, whirling around to see the figure push off the edge of the pit and jump toward the Marine Hospital building. They took a couple steps up the vertical face and flipped in mid-air, landing gracefully on the lawn on the other side of me. When I spun to look at them the pit was at my back again.

Goddamn vampires.

The figure spoke, her voice surprisingly bright. "Wanna see something cool?"

Before I could answer, there was a sharp noise: *clap clap.*

On a window far above our heads, a dim light flicked on, illuminating the buzz-cut female vampire who'd patrolled earlier. She was grinning, her calf-length raincoat still swinging from her movement. "Fun, right? Some former owner installed them above the second story windows, back in the 80s when the Clapper was a huge deal. I think he used to host ghost tours for his friends out here."

She tilted her head back to look speculatively at the higher stories. With no shredders, I brought up the rifle—but there was a rush of movement, and she jerked it away from me, yanking hard enough to snap the little metal pieces that held the strap in place. She stepped back with the rifle held out in both hands, looking at like it was a dead animal. "I never liked guns," she said distastefully. Turning, she pitched the rifle like a spear, throwing it into the woods. Fuck.

But at least I had enough light to press her now, if I could get her gaze anywhere near me.

"You must be Kendall," I said casually, hoping for a glare. No one likes it when you mess up their name.

Her head was swinging all around now, her nostrils flaring. "Ken*dra*," she corrected. Her eyes dropped.

I automatically followed her gaze and found a little tear in the palm of my right hand. The AK had cut me when Kendra yanked it away. The wound was oozing a few drops of blood, though they kept washing away in the rain. "What on earth is that heavenly smell?" she asked.

I sighed. "Death, I guess?"

"Oh. You're the black witch."

She did the strangest thing then: she *blurred* toward me and dropped on her knees, gently taking my hand in both of hers like she might propose. Then she sort of nuzzled against my palm, right next to the wound. I couldn't even see her eyes; only her buzzed skull.

"Don't let the rain get it," she cautioned me, holding her other hand above the cut like she was keeping a precious candle lit. "I heard about you, but I've never smelled blood like that. God, I'm actually *salivating*, can you believe it? I haven't done that since I was alive. Mmm." I felt the tip of her tongue on my palm then, and had to fight not to squirm away in disgust. She *licked* my *hand*.

I've been around vampires for years; it shouldn't have unnerved me as much as it did. But I'd been expecting a fight, not...this.

She squeezed my palm painfully, drawing more oozing blood for her to lick. I felt something sharp trace up my wrist—a small blade? A sharpened fingernail?—and realized she was drawing the line of my vein. The urge to jerk my hand back was overpowering, but would that push her into a frenzy? Even now, she had to be smelling my rising panic.

*Remember what you did the first time Quinn smelled your blood?* said Sam's voice in my head.

The memory came back then: the empty septic tank, scraping my head as I fell, Quinn's eyes dilating as he started to lose it.

I'd talked to him. I'd made him see me.

"Yeah, I've heard vampires can smell the death magic in my blood, but of course I can't tell any difference," I said conversationally. I didn't want the pit at my back, so I took a single step sideways, as though I was just shifting my weight. But she moved with me, blocking me up against the edge of the pit. She was still lapping at my scrape. "You're from New York, right? It's a big place; you must have met some boundary witches there." Another step.

Kendra stopped licking my blood long enough to say, "None that I know of. Certainly none that would bleed for me."

If I got the Glock out of my hip holster and held it to her head, I was pretty sure that would at least paralyze her for a while while she healed. But after the rifle, was there *any* chance I could get it out and aimed before she stopped me?

And I was running out of time. I'd only told Scarlett to count to a hundred.

Letting her suck on the tiny wound, I slowly reached beneath my open raincoat and slid my thumb over the snap of the holster's safety strap. I didn't hear it unsnap, but the vampire tensed. "Oh no, I wouldn't do *that,*" she cautioned, still not looking up. "Then I won't be so friendly."

Think, Lex, think. She'd smell an outright lie, but there were ways around this. "Would you be open to a deal?" I offered. "I've heard you enjoy a good, um, vintage, more than killing. Maybe you and I could move inside, out of the rain, and you could make a cut. I could let you feed properly, someplace nice and dry."

"Mmm." She stopped licking long enough to nuzzle my hand again. "I'm so tempted. But I think you'll try to press me."

Well, she had me there.

I felt a sharp slice along my wrist, and realized she'd cut me. An animal part of me was desperate to back away, but I could feel the edge of the pit through my boots. There was nowhere to go.

I took a breath, trying to make my voice as casual as possible. I even leaned sideways, cocking one hip and put my free hand in my raincoat pocket. "Shouldn't you save some of that for your boss? I heard Malcolm's not big on sharing."

"In most ways he isn't," Kendra agreed, head still bent over my wound. "But he's used to me being his tester—"

I didn't bother taking the Gerber knife out of the jacket pocket; I just rammed it forward, aiming for her eye socket. But Kendra's vampire reflexes were too fast, and the knife buried itself in her cheek until I felt the click of the point hitting the bone. She leapt backward, screaming, but it only took her a second to pull the knife out of her cheek and throw it over her shoulder, where it disappeared into the woods. Another weapon lost. Blood was spurting from her cheek and her eyes were wild as she advanced on me. I reached for boundary magic, but she was bent low, intending to attack me at the waist and knock me down.

Then a blur hit her from the side, both of them flying across the grass. The form was huge and dark and four-legged, and for just a second I thought it might be Scarlett's bargest—but no, this was a werewolf. A big one. He was black and silver and absolutely gorgeous, in the deadly way they all are in this form. Eli.

He and Kendra grappled for a second, but he'd chosen his moment perfectly. It took Eli about three seconds to get his teeth around her neck and clamp down. Even through the rain, I could hear the crackling snap as her upper spine shattered. The body went limp.

I looked down and realized the Glock was in my hand. I didn't remember pulling it.

I had enough experience with werewolves not to approach him with his prey. I waited while Eli hunched over the body for a moment, his shoulders moving. Finally, he licked his chops and trotted over to me, the rain already washing the blood off his muzzle.

I looked past him. He had gnawed at her until the vampire's head was completely detached from the body. It lay with its eyes open, staring up into the rain.

My gorge rose for a moment, but I managed not to vomit. Vampires could die by destroying the heart or detaching the head; Eli had just gone for the fastest route. I forced my gaze away and looked at the wolf, reminding myself not to be afraid. Like that was possible.

"Are you...you?" I asked, feeling stupid. Other than Tobias, I didn't have much experience talking to werewolves in this form.

At the words, Eli stopped and sat down, his big tail curling around his legs. He yawned.

I decided to take that as a probably.

My wrist was still bleeding—it wasn't a serious cut, but if I didn't get it covered it was going to attract attention from vampires. I holstered the Glock and reached for the bottom of my T-shirt, but it was a strong fabric from an outdoors store, and I was having a hard time tearing through the seam. I looked at Eli. Awkwardly, I held out the tail of the T-shirt between both hands. "Can you..."

He extended a paw and swiped down once, his claws

cutting through the fabric like it was frosting. I swallowed hard and ripped the skirt in a circle around myself so I had a long strip of fabric and a bare midriff. Quickly, I wrapped the makeshift bandage around the wound, talking to Eli at the same time. "Scarlett is going to push out her radius in a few seconds, but I need to find someone first. Can you paw the ground if you understand that?"

He blinked at me, then lifted his huge right paw and slid it across the grass.

"Okay," I said, relieved. Eli was in there. "Please paw again if you found Beau." I made myself add, "Or his remains."

He sat unmoving.

"Paw if you smelled Beau inside the well?"

He didn't paw, but his body gave a tiny shudder. Okay, he'd smelled something, or someone, in the well, but I wasn't going to play twenty questions to figure it out.

"What about around the grounds? I know it's raining, but could you smell that Beau has been here?"

He raked the paw across the grass again.

"So he was here, but you don't know where. And I'm guessing the rain makes it hard to be precise with tracking."

Eli pawed the ground.

I pushed wet hair away from my face. "Okay. I'm going for the front entrance. If you're ready to be human, go around that way." I pointed south, toward where Scarlett was hiding. "If not, back out of the clearing for now. Paw if you understand."

He did. I turned and ran for the north side of the building, though not before saying, "Thanks, Eli," over my shoulder.

I gave the pit a very wide berth and found myself on the deserted north side of the building. The old entrance was just as Simon had described: a massive door about four feet off the ground, with a big metal plate over it that read simply "US Marine Hospital." The door and its frame were made of an aged gray wood, bleached from the sun and scarred by time. There must have once been stairs leading up to the door, but now it was just the brick ledge in which the doorframe was set.

Holstering the Glock, I used both hands to hoist myself onto the ledge, pressing my arms against the door frame to keep my balance. Holding onto the door frame with my left hand, I used my right to feel around for a knob—but I couldn't find anything. It was too dark to tell for sure, but I didn't think the door had knob at all. I planted my feet on either side of the doorframe so I could lift both hands to clap, just in case the former owner had rigged the whole house.

I was, then, completely unbalanced when the ghostly head bloomed out of the wood right in front of my face.

"Finally!" she cried, and I toppled backwards out of the entrance.

# 34

## SCARLETT

I had intended to run across the lawn toward the building, but the debrided road rash on my leg screamed at me, so it turned into more of a limping half-jog. Anyone watching from a window on this side would probably see me, but I hoped they were all distracted by the "cops" on the northeast side.

"One," I panted. Lex had wanted me to count to a hundred before I pushed out my radius. "Two."

Vertigo suddenly appeared at the edges of my skull, threatening my balance. I couldn't concentrate on staying upright and keeping my radius in at the same time, so I put my arms out like a tightrope walker, my eyes fixed on the red brick in front of me, which was starting to swim a little. "Three," I mumbled.

I almost cried out with relief when my fingers touched the brick wall of the eastern side of the building. "Four."

I tried walking with my right hand on the brick, then gave up and put my left hand on there too, stepping sideways back toward the service door and Jesse, counting in my head now. The voices got louder again as I neared the southeast corner, where the work light was set up. Jesse was shouting about civil disobedience and calling for backup, while Julien's voice sounded more placating now.

Turning around, I pressed my back against the brick and closed my eyes so the vertigo wouldn't affect me so much. I slid my right hand along the slippery brick until it found the edge, and focused hard on keeping my radius in as tightly as possible. Then I did a sort of duck-and-twirl sideways, into the cave.

*Sixteen*, I thought. *Seventeen*. The space was pitch black, but I raised my hand above my head and found that the ceiling was high enough for me to stand. I had gotten as high as twenty when I reached the far end of the little cavern and found a crack in the masonry large enough to peer out.

I could see Julien and Orvil's backs, and Jesse standing in front of the police car as he shouted at them. He had his gun out and pointed at Orvil, who had advanced to a few feet away, quite possibly close enough to smell that Jesse was lying. Any second now Orvil was going to attack and presumably hit Simon's shield. They would know this was a diversion.

I couldn't go nuclear, as Simon had put it, until I got to the count, but there might be another way to defuse the situation with giving away my exact location. Concentrating hard, I pushed my radius out slowly as I could, so it reached the closest vampire, Julien, first.

Julien Dubuque started doing the elaborate gasping/choking/flailing hands thing that all vampires experience when their body's systems come back online without magic. Molly once described this as waking up from a coma only to find that you'd been beaten nearly to death, and I imagine it's pretty jarring. Julien was particularly dramatic about it, looking more than anything like he was having a seizure.

As I'd hoped, Orvil broke off his argument with Jesse and turned to check on his backup. I waited until his whole body was turned in my direction before I eased my radius out even farther to encompass him as well.

Jesse was already reacting, darting forward with the package of zip ties we'd found in a small sporting goods store. He took out half and tossed the package to Simon, who was on his way to Julien.

Their movements seemed a little too casual, and I desperately wanted to yell out a warning about Adelaide watching from the window. But it was taking a lot of concentration to fight off vertigo, hold my radius at this exact distance, and still try to count. As it was, I was braced against the mortar with both hands so I wouldn't sway, and I felt like I had missed something. *Thirty-one*, I thought dizzily. *Thirty-two*. What was I forgetting.

The Cardinal vampire of the upper Mississippi was just starting to breathe regularly as Simon began attaching one zip tie after another around his wrist. I couldn't see either their faces, but I heard the rage in Julian's voice as he growled, "I knew I recognized you."

“Aw, you should've said something," Simon said gaily.

“She's here with you somewhere,” Orvil said to Jesse. “The little null girl with the big mouth.”

“She really prefers that female-identifying adults be referred to as women,” Jesse said mildly.

"Oh, I think most women do now," Simon put in.

Jesse had turned his prisoner around to bind his hands, so both of them were facing the building.

Both vampires were now zip-tied human rage machines, but Orvil had an eye on the building. Waiting for Adelaide.

Maybe sensing this, Jesse glanced up, seeming to look right at me—but he was probably eyeing the service entrance and its window. "His girlfriend's a little trigger-happy," he said to Simon. "Get behind him, then pat him down."

Simon glanced up at the building and quickly did so, moving so Julien's body was between him and the door. He and Jesse both pulled a few things out of the vampires' pockets, though I couldn't see what.

*Sixty-six…sixty-seven…*

"Adelaide," Jesse yelled at the entrance. "I know you're there. Come on out! Show me your hands!"

A few long seconds ticked by with no response, and I got to seventy, sweat dripping down my face and into my clothes. Then Jesse casually pulled out his handgun and held it to Orvil's head.

I winced. Jesse hated this kind of gangster shit—but he still made it look like he threatened people's lives every day. "Last chance, Adelaide," he said in a bored voice.

There was a creaking scrape above my head, and then the shuffle of sneakers on concrete.

"What do you want?" came a guarded female voice.

"You and Orvil need to answer for Scarlett," he said gruffly. "And Louisa, the vampire you killed, and your attempts on the other nulls."

I couldn't see her face, but her voice was full of derision, and I imagined a very snotty expression. "And this is you bringing justice, is it?"

"No," Jesse lowered the gun, but kept it right at his leg. Adelaide must have had her hands up. "This is me making an arrest. You'll stand trial for what you did. Let's go." He motioned for her to come down the stairs.

I don't know how Adelaide responded, but Julien broke into a snotty eye roll, and Orvil outright chuckled. "That is so precious, I could almost cry," Orvil drawled. "But I'm afraid we have other plans tonight. We're in our own negotiations, you see."

Even with sweat pooling in my shirt, my insides went cold. Malcolm. I'd been right. He really was here.

Only then did I realize I'd lost count. *Um...a hundred,* I thought.

Closing my eyes for focus, I pushed my radius out as far as I could go. If I concentrated really hard I could sort of take attendance, even at that distance. In addition to Simon and the two vampires in front of me, I felt a werewolf, Eli, off in the woods to the north, plus Lex, and an extra vampire, and something higher—

*Oh no.*

My eyes popped open, and I wobbled in my little hiding spot, though I was able to keep my radius pushed out, for whatever that was worth. "Jesse!" I shouted, no longer caring if I gave away my position. "They've got a—"

At that second, all the lights in the building, including the freestanding work light, went dark.

## 35

LEX

The entrance doorframe wasn't high enough for me to break anything when I fell, but it wasn't fun landing right on my ass. I scrambled to my feet, cursing. Above me, the ghost's whole body had emerged to pause in the doorframe—though the back third of her was inside the door.

"Oh my," she breathed. "And I thought I heard colorful language from all those sailors."

She appeared to be in her mid-twenties, fair and light-haired and fragile-looking. She wore button-up boots and an ankle-length skirt underneath a striped blouse. There were accessories, too: a waistcoat, a little bow tie, a pair of rounded wire spectacles. "Hello," I said. "I'm Lex. Were you, um, expecting me?"

She waved a slim hand. "Not you precisely, of course, but I've been waiting *ever* so long for another evocator." This was an old-fashioned term for boundary witch, although I'd only heard Nellie use it. "I simply didn't expect you to arrive on such a busy night. My name is Katherine Eddows Sutcliff, but do call me Kate."

Why did that name ring a bell? Right. The sexist tour guide. "Weren't you a nurse in the Navy?" I ventured.

Her face lit up. "You've heard of me! Oh, I'm blushing! Well, I would blush, except of course I'm quite dead." She beamed at me to show this was a joke.

"It's good to meet you, Kate," I said cautiously. I tried to remember what else the guide had said about this woman. Some kind of scandal with her female boss, but that could mean anything in 1920. "But I feel a little exposed here in the yard. Is there somewhere inside we could speak?"

Kate glanced at the door around her. "Oh, not this entrance, no. They've boarded it up from the inside." She made a dainty little hop and sort of floated to the ground in front of me. Up close, she seemed tiny—maybe 5'2" in her heeled boots.

"If you'd like to get inside, you'll want the basement door," she announced, floating to my right, toward the western face of the building. "It's this way here. Shall I tell you about myself while we go? The others won't hear me, and I *have* been waiting ages."

"Um, sure." Feeling ridiculous, I followed the ghost around the side of the building. A tangle of vines and bushes blocked this corner of the building, and the western face had a depression along the brick exterior, kind of like the pit I'd seen before, though this one looked shallower. There was no one in sight, but I hated the lack of cover. I kept as close to the bricks as possible.

While I did my best to be furtive, Kate floated along confidently, speaking with the clear, enunciated tones of, I suspected, a finishing school. "I was born in in 1895, and grew up mainly in Chicago," she said. "My mother used her evocation abilities to encourage my father's business, until we were quite well-off. She made sure each of her children got a chance to use our magic."

I nearly stumbled at the phrasing. In order to activate our magic, boundary witches have to die in adolescence. I drowned in an accident, but Kate was saying her mother had killed her and her siblings.

The ghost paused. "Well, the eldest three," she amended, turning to look at me. "My brother Elliot didn't survive his first death, and Father forbade Mother to try with my two youngest brothers—oh, good evening, Mr. Hiddell," Kate called suddenly, looking up to wave at someone ahead. I tensed, but she was talking to one of the remnants in the yard: a sixty-something man wearing a white straitjacket. Remnants aren't sentient, so he didn't look up—or pause in the action of running as fast as he could at the brick wall, head-first. I looked away.

"Anyway, here are the stairs," Kate said to me, gesturing in front of us. I stopped abruptly. We were at the corner of the long in-ground area, and I realized there was indeed a railing sticking up. I had to stare into the darkness for a few seconds to see a quarter-circle staircase, partially covered in vines. It led down into the depression, ending twelve feet away at a door. "Do you still want to go inside?" Kate asked. "They've left this entrance unlocked tonight."

I had to be nearly out of time by now. "I do need to talk to you, but I don't want us to be overheard," I said. "Can you tell if anyone is close enough to listen?"

Kate cocked her head sideways, and for a moment she looked so much like Sam does in my dreams, when she's listening to instructions, that goosebumps broke out on my arms.

Then the ghost smiled at me. "No one will hear you," Kate said cheerfully. "What shall we discuss?"

"I'm looking for my friend," I began. "I think he might have been brought here across his will. He's a vampire named Beau." I quickly described the Southern vampire. When I got to the boots, Kate's face brightened.

"Oh yes, he was here with the others, earlier tonight," she said, pleased to be of service. "They had bled him quite a bit to subdue him. He looked quite ill."

I winced. There weren't many ways to restrain a vampire—silver only made them a little itchy—but removing most of their blood very quickly and not letting them feed would definitely weaken them. "Is he still here?" I asked urgently.

Kate's pleasant smile disappeared. "I couldn't say."

"What do you mean? I thought this was your domain."

"They dragged him to up the Emptiness," Kate explained, a little haughty. "I cannot follow there."

I had no idea what that meant. "*Who* dragged him? Do you know the names of the people staying here?"

"A couple, Adelaide and Orvil," Kate replied promptly, then wrinkled her nose. "I do not care for them. They don't respect my building. And they bring the Emptiness, which upsets me."

"Anyone else?"

"I don't *know* how many are in the Emptiness," she said, annoyed. "I cannot keep my consciousness on all places at all times, and people go in and out. There are several men who come and go. Recently the dark vampire with the glittering eyes arrived as well." She lowered her voice conspiratorially. "I don't care for him either, if I can be frank."

"I think that's a vampire named Julien," I told her. "I stabbed him in the leg the other night." Was that just *last* night? It didn't seem possible.

Kate grinned broadly, pushing up her ghostly spectacles. "Oh, good on you!"

"But I'm really trying to find my friend," I said carefully. "Can you tell me where you last saw him?"

"On the second story staircase, of course, on his way to the Emptiness," she said, impatient.

"The Emptiness is upstairs?"

"It was then," Kate replied, "and I believe it still is now. But the Emptiness goes where it wants." She pouted. "These questions are so dull, and I've been waiting forever to meet you. Don't you want more of my story?"

I rubbed my forehead. "Of course I do. I just have a hard time concentrating when I'm so worried about my friend." Her face softened, turning thoughtful. "Are you aware of everything that goes on in the building?" I asked.

She beamed. "Oh, more than that. My authority includes the entire clearing. And my tree, of course."

"So you were aware when my friends and I arrived," I concluded. "What happened right *before* we arrived?"

"The dark vampire and the couple arrived with your Beau, and took him to the Emptiness," Kate said promptly. "The human men and the woman vampire circled the grounds, watching for threats. When the woman vampire was at the far side of my building, the werewolf stole one man away into the forest. The second man saw and fled down the road. He's been working for two vampires at once and losing his nerve for days now. I don't think he'll be back."

I'd been right: Orvil had a spy in Julien's camp. And Eli had taken out some of the guards. The humans were off the board. "Then what happened?" I urged.

"The werewolf peered in my well, but did not like its smell. The woman vampire kept circling. She does not like the human men, and so did not notice their absence. Then the automobile with the color lights arrived, and the second Emptiness."

Wait, what. "A *second* emptiness?" I asked cautiously.

The look Kate gave me now was completely baffled. "Yes," she said very slowly, as though I were thick. "From which you emerged."

I finally thought I understood. Scarlett was the second Emptiness, a place of non magic. Which meant...

"A null," I said to myself. "There's another null here."

At that moment, every light inside the building went out.

# 36

## SCARLETT

"Jesse, they've got a—"

But before I could get the word "null" out of my mouth, every light in and out of the building abruptly went out, plunging the whole area into complete darkness.

In a normal blackout, the first thing that happens is shouting—people verbalizing their needs for answer, reassurance—but the area around me fell silent as everyone tried to figure out what to do.

Personally, I decided getting the fuck out of a dead-end cave was a good first step.

The vertigo had subsided, so I felt my way along the wall to the opening, following the sound of the rain. I could sense, rather than see, the change in space when I reached the lawn. Then I saw Jesse's flashlight go on, followed instantly by the muzzle flash and *pop* as he shot at Orvil and clicked the light off again. There was a cry of pain, and then all hell broke lose.

Adelaide must have had guns on her, because simultaneous

pops were going off above my head, and then Jesse and Simon returned fire, aiming high to avoid hitting me. In the quick bursts of light I saw one of the bound vampires running away, while the other ran toward Adelaide. I had a feeling she was going to hand off one of those guns.

I needed to get somewhere safer.

The pistol was still secure in my ankle holster, but I left it there, reaching for a throwing knife instead. I was an okay shot, thanks to Jesse's insistence on practicing, but I wasn't a soldier or a cop, and vertigo could strike at any second. If I started shooting in the dark, I was just as likely to hit one of my own people as the bad guys.

I circled around the building to my left, the way I'd come from, and pressed myself against the building so I was turned toward the gunfight—but not in the line of fire. I did *not* call out for Jesse, because he would feel compelled to answer me, and that might give away his location.

There had been a few cries of pain now, but I was almost certain none of them was my fiancé. I just had to stay alive and keep my radius expanded, and he would find me when it was safe to do so.

Then I was going to find that null.

As soon as I'd expanded my radius all the way I'd felt it: that light-bending-through-water feeling of a second null nearby. That was what I'd missed: when I pushed out my radius to reach Orvil, being so careful and deliberate about it, I hadn't felt any kind of spell fizzle out. I didn't break Lex's press, because *someone else had.*

The sensation of another null wasn't distinctive enough for me to tell if they were someone I'd met before or not, but I was praying it wasn't Corry or Charlie. The bad guys might have gotten to our safe house...or they might have a null I didn't even know about yet. Either scenario would be complicated.

I was so distracted by these thoughts that I never heard Adelaide Preston come up behind me. The first thing I felt was the weight of her slamming into my back as she wrapped her arms around my neck. Something wet and chemical-smelling was suddenly covering my mouth and nose. A drug.

I inhaled reflexively from the shock of it, but then I held my breath and forced myself to think. Instead of trying to throw her off my neck, I remembered the goddamned knife in my right hand. I reached up with my left and found her arm, and then I speared her with the short knife, clutching the handle hard so it wouldn't slip out of my fingers in the rain. I yanked the knife out and did it again, over and over, feeling the blade tearing at muscle and chipping at bone each time.

I don't know how many times I stabbed her before Adelaide cried out and released me. The wet chemical cloth fell away from my face, and I flailed out with both arms, my left thumb tangling in something as Adelaide tried to push me away. It was a strap, something attached to her. I automatically hooked it and held on, holding her in place.

Then I brought my right arm around with the knife it what promised to be an absolutely gorgeous stabbing roundhouse punch—only she screamed and detached herself from whatever I'd hooked, pulling away. I stumbled, thrown off-balance, and the throwing knife finally slipped out of my wet fingers. Swaying, I felt at the thing in my hand until I recognized the shape of some kind of fancy binoculars. No, wait. It was a binoculars...hat. A binoculars hat. Was that a thing?

Oh.

The drugs. I had breathed some of the drugs. Too much drugs. I was falling.

My knees broke the fall. Somewhere very far away, pain screamed at me.

In the last seconds before I passed out, I threw the binocu-

# 37

## LEX

I was still standing at the southwest door of the building, having a whispered conversation with the boundary witch ghost, Kate, when the lights went out. I saw the inside of the building go dark, but it took me a second to realize that a set of lights remained on: the ones that the now-deceased Kendra had turned on by clapping. Adelaide and company must have been using a generator to power the outdoor work lamp and the few lights inside the building. She'd cut the generator, but the clappers must be on a different system.

Then the sound of gunfire begin, from the southeast corner near the service door.

I dropped into a crouch, drawing the Glock, and looked at Kate for advice—but the boundary witch ghost had vanished.

Of course—Scarlett had expanded her radius.

I knew better than to sprint into the middle of gunfire. I went slowly, staying low to the ground as best I could without slipping on the wet grass.

I turned the corner just in time for someone to barrel past

me, his shoulder hitting me right in the chest as our raincoats smacked against each other. He kept running, and the whole thing happened so fast that he was past me before I recognized the cedar-and-bergamot cologne. Orvil.

I slowed down, torn, but then there was another *pop* of small caliber gunfire ahead and I kept going into the darkness.

By the time I felt my way to the concrete steps leading to the service door, the gunfire had ended, and I couldn't hear anything in the rain. I had a flashlight, but turning it on would make me a target.

Fuck it—worth a try. I clapped my hands twice.

I was still pretty surprised when three spotlights flicked on above the windows on this side of the building.

The area where Jesse had argued with Orvil and Julien as a fake cop was empty now. I turned in a circle, the Glock up, looking for my friends.

"Lex! Over here!" It was Simon's voice, in a stage whisper.

With the Marine Hospital, and therefore the lights, at my back, I squinted into the darkness. There was a man sitting with his back against the dark police car, and more figures beyond him, near the edge of the clearing. I lowered the Glock and ran forward.

When I was nearly on top of them, Simon clicked on one of the miniature lanterns we'd stolen so I could see what was happening. He was sitting against the police car in a puddle of sodden grass with both hands clutching his thigh. About ten feet away, Julien Dubuque, human now, was lying on his stomach at the edge of the clearing, his hands still zip-tied behind his back. His mud-streaked face was bright red with rage—but then, I would probably be mad too, if I was being held down by a completely nude man. Eli, who'd returned to human form when Scarlett expanded her radius, was now kneeling on the vampire's back with a look of grim satisfaction...and apparently no body shyness.

I decided not to comment on any of that.

"Hey," Simon smiled at me as I approached, though it looked pained. "Don't worry; I've got an illusion over this little area. They can't see us from the house."

"You're hurt?" I asked Simon, dropping to my knees beside him. I picked up the little camp lantern so I could get a better look at the leg. It seemed like way too much blood. Sweat was beading on his face before the rain swept it away.

"It's a through-and-through, but the bullet missed the artery." It was Jesse's voice. I leaned away from the car and looked around, finding him by the back bumper, rummaging through the trunk. He pulled out a big first aid kit and an umbrella and came around the side of the car to us. "We both took a couple of shots in our vests, but Simon's leg is the worst of it."

"Can we drive him out of here?"

Jesse shook his head. "They shot out the tires. We'll clean the wound and get it bandaged, but I think he'll be okay for now."

I tried not to let the relief show on my face. "Okay." I glanced over my shoulder at Eli. "Um, everything all right over there?"

"Oh yeah," the werewolf said smugly. "I got to kick this guy's ass."

"And with so little protective cover," Jesse said dryly. He unzipped the heavy-duty first aid kit and pulled out a set of surgical gloves. He handed me the umbrella, and I understood he wanted me to hold it open so he could do the bandaging. The rain had let up a little bit, but you still wouldn't want it in an open wound. "Where's Scarlett?" I asked as he began cutting through Simon's rain pants.

Jesse looked up just long enough to nod at the building. "Under the stairs, hidden in that little cave. I yelled for her to stay where she was and stay quiet. I'll go get her as soon as we've got you mobile, Simon."

My friend was propped on his elbows to watch the proceedings. He gave Jesse a thumbs up but looked at me with a weak smile. "Why am I always the one to get hurt at these things?" he joked.

I didn't smile, because it wasn't funny. This was the third time Simon had been seriously injured helping me. I took his hand and squeezed.

"Because, dude," Jesse told him, "you're the Xander." He splashed a little alcohol on the wound.

Simon hissed with pain, then glowered at Jesse. "You take that back. I'm obviously the Willow."

"Nah, I think that's your sister. But you can be the Amy if you want."

I had no idea what they were talking about. "You guys want to save this bromance for later?" Eli called, looking annoyed. Well, as annoyed as you can look while completely naked, sitting on an enemy. "Stop flirting and keep an eye out, for God's sake. They could be in that tower with a rifle."

I didn't think even Adrienne would try using a sniper rifle in the dark rain, but I didn't blame Eli for the paranoia. Rolling his eyes, Jesse pressed down on Simon's wound to apply the bandage.

"What's...that guy's problem?" Simon asked him through gritted teeth.

"I took his girl and nobody likes him," Jesse replied under his breath.

"I heard that," Eli snapped.

I looked up sharply. I'd barely heard the comment

crouching right next to Jesse, and Eli was ten feet away, in the rain. "You did?"

At that moment, Julien Dubuque struggled to his feet, bucking Eli off him. He was vampire again.

Eli leaped at him with a balletic disregard for physics—he was no longer human, either. So fast I could hardly follow it, the vampire's leg swept up and forward, stomping Eli in the chest. Eli went down on his ass, but still between Julien and the forest, already reaching for the vampire's ankle.

"Shit!" I had already dropped the umbrella and started toward them, but Julien saw me coming and kicked Eli viciously in the knee, causing a sharp, sickening *crunch* that seemed to echo around the clearing. Eli went down, and Julien turned toward the woods.

I had no chance of catching a running vampire, I knew, but I sprinted after him anyway. Which is why I had a front row view when Julien took three more steps and ran full-force into Simon's invisible barrier.

My friend had projected his shield to the edge of the clearing. Vampire or not, Julien hit the barrier so hard that he bounced a full six feet backward, toward me. I was ready, though, and sidestepped so Julien would land flat on his back on the grass, looking, slightly stunned. I was a little surprised he hadn't broken his neck.

"Eli, if you can move, lean on him," I ordered.

With a groan that was more growl than human, the naked werewolf crawled over to Julien on his hands and good leg, leaning all his weight against the stunned vampire.

"What the hell is going on?" Jesse said, but didn't wait for any of us to answer. "*Scarlett*!" he shouted toward the building. There was no answer.

Jesse looked at me, wild-eyed. "Why would she stop

expanding her radius?" he demanded. "She knew what we were doing."

"Jesse, go look under the stairs and come straight back," I ordered. "I'll cover you."

He was already running for the little cavity under the steps. I got my Glock up and swept the building for movement, blinking rain away from my eyes. But there was no movement, no other lights that I could see.

Jesse came running back with fear on his face and something in his hand. "Is this what I think it is?" He tossed it toward me.

I caught it one-handed, recognizing it immediately. "These are military-issue night-vision goggles. Adrienne cut the light so she could free Orvil and take Scarlett. I don't know why she'd leave them behind, though." In a situation like this, these would be invaluable.

"The strap is broken," Jesse pointed out. "I think maybe Scar ripped them off her." He had started toward the trunk of the police car, where more weapons were stashed. "If they took her, they want her alive for now. I'm going in there."

"Jesse, slow down!" I took a step toward him, but in my peripheral vision I saw that Julien had started to buck Eli off, kicking at his dislocated knee. The injured werewolf was struggling to hold him down. Running over, I pushed Eli aside and dropped onto Julien's chest. I jerked his chin sideways, reaching for boundary magic.

It had been a long time since I pressed a vampire without my mother's bloodstone. But the first time I pressed a vampire, I'd hadn't had even had the bloodstone, or my tattoos. I didn't even know what I was doing.

I'd come a long way since then.

With my palms on either side of his face so my griffin tattoos touched his skin, I looked into Julien's eyes. Vampires saw pressing humans as being able to shove their will down a one-way street, but I was proof that traffic can be reversed sometimes. I thought of a tunnel and pressed myself, my magic, into it. "Tell me everyone who is inside that building," I demanded.

Julien's face twitched as he fought me, but he couldn't stop himself. "Malcolm and his two people, Kendra and Mikey. Beau. Yazhu. The null."

"Yazhu?" Simon said behind me. Injured or not, of course he still wanted to understand. "Who is that?"

Eli answered first, his voice gritty with pain. "The cardinal vampire of San Francisco. She was keeping an eye on Corry for Dashiell. Supposed to be an ally."

*Another* cardinal vampire? It was too dark and rainy for any kind of sniper, but I suddenly felt like there was a target on my back. Of course, at that exact second a voice spoke right next to my ear.

"Oh *my*! That man is *completely nude*!"

"Shit." I jumped so hard I nearly broke the press. As it was, I had to lean in closer, so my eyes were inches away from Julien's.

"I can't talk right now, Kate," I said through gritted teeth.

"Oh, please may I observe?" the ghost begged. "I met so few vampires in my living days; I never got to try this!"

"Tell me if *anyone* is coming this way, and you can observe. Deal?"

"Yes! Ooh, I'm the lookout!" She was positively thrilled.

"Lex, are you okay?" Simon said weakly.

I nodded for him, but couldn't look away from Julien. "Tell me Beau's status," I ordered. "Is he alive?"

"Yes. Malcolm is trying to turn him. That's why I'm not in there with them. Malcolm didn't think my presence would help, after my man killed his assistant."

Jesse appeared at my side. "Lex, I need to go find Scarlett *right now*."

"Count to two hundred in a whisper," I told Julien, who immediately began to chant numbers under his breath. I kept my gaze on him, feeding boundary magic into his eyes, but I spoke to the others out of the side of my mouth.

"Jesse, there are at least five vampires in that building, including two cardinals, and you don't know where she is," I snapped, feeling an odd sense of deja vu. This was more or less the same conversation I'd had with Eli hours ago, but now I was the one pushing for caution. "Hang on a second."

I could still feel the presence of the boundary witch ghost on my left. "Kate, you know who Adelaide is, right? Where is she?"

"I don't know," came the ghost's impatient voice. "She disappeared in the Emptiness."

"And you said that was up, right?"

"Not the *first* Emptiness," Kate said slowly, like I was an idiot child. "The new one. The one that flexes."

Okay. "You were right, Jesse, Adelaide took Scarlett," I told him. "And there's a second null in the building."

"*What*?!" both Eli and Jesse said, at the same time Kate asked, "What is annul?"

Oh, for God's sake. I was starting to feel like a telephone operator here, but there was no time. "Kate, give me a moment. Jesse, if you don't give me three more minutes I will shoot you in the leg to keep you from going in there half-cocked. I swear it on the soul of my sister."

There was a pause and then a sullen, "Fine."

"Good." Ignoring everything else, I pressed my will into Julien Dubuque. "Stop counting," I snapped. His mouth closed in a thin line. "Tell me why Malcolm is here," I ordered.

"I called him," Julien said tonelessly. "After you humiliated me in front of my people. He knows you are after Orvil. He has hidden himself from magic to lay a trap."

"What trap?"

"This." Julien gestured to indicate the whole clearing, including the building. "Maven and Dashiell will come, tonight, and forces will be in place to ambush them."

I clenched my teeth, too furious to speak. God, I'd been so stupid. Adelaide hadn't summoned all those skinners to Galena to keep Maven and Dashiell away while Orvil was under my press. If there was another null here, Orvil would have broken it almost immediately. No, she'd summoned the skinners to force us to move rashly—before we were ready and before Maven and Dashiell, the real heavy hitters, could get to town. Hell, she probably had some kind of safe word or passcode in place to call the skinners off again in the morning. But I'd been off-balance and unprepared, and I'd let her play me. Again.

To Julien, I demanded "Tell me Malcom's plan for this trap."

"I cannot," he said. "Malcolm has hidden the details from me. He doesn't trust me yet. I only know we were not supposed to kill the girl until he can talk to her. Malcolm has a personal issue with her."

Jesse said a few very intense swear words, but I couldn't lose focus. "Tell me what you *think* he's going to do," I said to Julien.

"I believe he has more vampires in the woods, or on their way," Julien said mechanically. "He'll try to kill Maven by force."

Of course he would. Shit. "Eli, what time is it?" I said loudly.

A pause. "Two-thirty."

"Turn on the phone and call Kirsten. Tell her to make sure they don't come here."

Kate, who had been doing that head tilt thing, suddenly brightened. "I found Adelaide and her vampire," she said.

"They are circling the main story, looking out the windows. They do not see you."

Good. I put extra power into the press, my eyes boring into Julien's. "Close your eyes and count off a thousand seconds in your head," I told him. "Do not move until you reach that number."

Immediately, Julien's eyelid dropped, his body completely still.

I finally looked up. "Jesse?" But he was gone. Of course.

Spinning around, I saw Eli and Simon, both men listing to one side to keep weight off an injured leg. Eli had retrieved a pair of cutoff sweatpants when he'd gotten his phone from the trunk, and he stood there looking completely unbothered by the rain. "Which way did he go?" I demanded.

Both men pointed west, around the way I had come, and I relaxed a tiny bit. Jesse was headed for the original front entrance—he didn't know it was boarded up. "Okay. Eli, did you get through to Kirsten?"

"Yes," he said, not sounding happy. "I passed on the message, but she said Maven and Dashiell are probably still going to come here. I agree."

I rubbed my forehead, slicking back a tangle of wet hair. "Yeah. I was afraid of that."

When we had made our original plan, we'd counted on Malcolm needing to stop Orvil's trial so he wouldn't look weak. Now Malcolm had found a way to flip it. If Dashiell and Maven let Scarlett and the rest of us die, no one would ever believe they could run a government.

But if they came to save us and failed, we would all die, and Maven's parliament would die with us.

"I was able to warn them about the other null, at least," Eli pointed out. "They're going to bring body armor and weapons.

Hayne will join them. We still need to get them out of town before morning, too."

"Gods above and below, it's going to be a war zone," Simon sounded awed.

"I won't have that," Kate, who had been remarkably quiet through most of this, now had her hands on her hips, looking furious. "I can't allow that in my home, Lex, I simply cannot."

There was a certain tone in her voice that concerned me, but I had too much else to worry about at the moment. I looked up at the Marine Hospital building, looming imposingly over us. Scarlett was somewhere inside, and now Jesse had gone in after her. Malcolm would keep Scarlett alive as a hostage, but there was no reason not to kill Jesse. My stupid friend had rushed in without thinking...much like I had when I'd decided to come here.

I sighed and looked at Eli. "I'm going in there to get my people," I told him. "You still want to take a run at Malcolm?"

He grinned, a flash of white teeth. "Fuck yes."

"Gear up," I said, turning to address Simon, too. "Both of you."

## 38

### SCARLETT

Before I even opened my eyes, I had time to register two things. First, I was sitting indoors, blindfolded, with my wrists tied behind my back and my legs tied together at the ankle. Second: *everything* hurt. All the road rash burns hurt, especially the bad one on my leg, but also my shoulders, knees, and, in a *big* way, my head. I sneezed.

My head had been sore for days, of course, but that had been at the site of the concussions. Now it ached on the inside, from the...wait, was that chloroform? Had I actually been chloroformed, like a damsel in a gothic horror novel? God, that was embarrassing. I would definitely feel super humiliated if I wasn't also dealing with a *screaming fucking headache.*

Wait. There was something else. I tried to tune into my radius, but it was strangely slippery, like in old movies when someone sees in doubles, only for my...magic sensors, or whatever you call it, instead of my eyes. I felt drunk. Or maybe high. A little bit of both? I felt like I could more or less hold a conversation, but I would sound like someone in a stoner movie.

Squirming around, I tried to feel for my weapons. I was pretty sure Adelaide had taken off both my knife belt and the ankle gun, but I thought they might have missed the extra knife I'd tucked into my right ankle boot. Most people will stop checking a certain spot when they find a weapon.

"I think she's waking up," said a female voice.

Shit, the squirming. I really should have thought about faking sleep for a while so I could figure out what to do.

Oh well—they were just going to have to deal with me like this.

"Good evening, obnoxious fuckers," I announced. "I would dearly appreciate if someone could remove this blindfold so I can insult you individually and by name."

Strong opening remarks, I thought with satisfaction. Good job, Scarlett.

"I think you gave her a little too much diazepam," said the woman's voice, very dry now.

"Is *that* what that was?" I turned my head in the direction of her voice. "I was scared it was chloroform. I hate being a gothic horror cliche, you know?"

"It was both." This was a quiet male voice, only a few feet away, and it made me go still. I *knew* that voice. How did I know that voice?

No.

*No.*

I listed sideways, kind of a lot, and would have fallen all the way over if a pair of strong hands hadn't caught me. They pushed me back upright, and then felt at my neck, checking my pulse. "Rhys," I whispered. "Tell me it isn't you."

"Aye, lass, I'm sorry." His voice was husky and filled with regret.

I had to swallow down a sob. "You're alive, and you're working for *Malcolm*?'"

"That's enough," said a new voice. Male, possibly someone I'd met before. Was he a vampire? I tried to check my radius, found it just a kaleidoscope of spinning impressions.

Right, yes, drugs.

The blindfold was tugged roughly off my head. "Ow!" I complained, blinking against the sudden light. The generator, or whatever power source, had been turned back on, and this room had a standing lamp in one corner. "I have like twelve concussions, you dickweed."

Gradually, the scene swam into focus, although my attention was immediately captured by the surroundings: a large, rectangular room with brick walls and a high ceiling that was somehow also brick. Ragged, faded yellow wallpaper was peeling off the walls, and the only pieces of furniture were a couple of loveseats covered by sheets that looked to be more dust than fabric. I sneezed violently, which made my head ache. It was dusty as hell in here. It was like I'd walked onto the set for the next *Conjuring* movie, complete with a brick fireplace filled with spiderwebs and wood floors that had turned gray with age.

Yup. This for sure felt like an abandoned mental hospital.

More importantly, there was only one door in or out. I was sitting against the wall right across the room from it, but there were three figures in between me and the exit. There was a boarded-up window on the wall near me, and a second window farther on that had been broken.

Rhys, the Scottish null, was kneeling on the floor in front of me. He was in his mid-forties, balding and craggy, with muscular hands and forearms from working with wood. The other male stood over us: a massive, sullen-looking white man with a shaved head and biceps that seemed to be eroding the sleeves of his designer T-shirt. "Mikey the vampire!" I exclaimed. "How you doing, man?"

Malcolm's bodyguard gave me the same reaction I'd always gotten from him in New York: a surly, we-are-not-amused glower. It always made me more...well, me. "Aw, you haven't aged a day!" I batted my eyes at him. "What is it, keto diet? Botox?"

"I see you haven't changed yourself," Rhys said, his voice sad and somehow fond. "A smart arse when you're scared."

My eyes fell on him, but despite the something-pam I'd been given, I wasn't ready to banter with the traitor. "I talked to Maura," I said, my voice as cold as I could make it. "She's devastated. And furious."

Rhys didn't answer, but his body sort of curled inward like I'd punched him in the stomach. Good.

"Can we move this along?" said the female voice.

She was the farthest away of the three figures, so it took me a second to locate her in the gloom: a petite Asian woman about twelve feet away, just inside the room, with her arms crossed tightly over her chest like she was trying not to touch anything. She wore a short, designer dress that would have made Olivia salivate with envy, about a hundred grand worth of jewelry, and her hair in a sleek knot. She also appeared to be wearing Ugg boots. I thought she was a vampire, but my radius was so blurry, I might have been picking up someone in another room, or Mikey. "I like your slippers," I told her.

The woman actually looked down at her feet before catching herself. "He wants to see her," she said to Rhys.

Mikey took a step toward me. "I'll carry her down there."

Rhys held up a hand placatingly. "It would be better for him to come in here," he advised. "I know how she comes off, but she's more dangerous than she looks."

"Fuck you; I look *so* dangerous," I muttered.

"I'll ask him," Mikey said, and turned to stalk out of the

room. He must have left my radius, but I couldn't feel it. That was a concern, but even the concern felt slippery in my brain.

When he was gone, Rhys turned away from me to pack up some kind of medical kit that had been laid out on the floor. I watched him in silence for a few minutes. It wasn't first aid, I realized; it was hypodermic needles. He really had injected me with that drug after Adelaide made me inhale something.

"What the hell happened to you?" I asked him in disbelief. "I thought you were a good person. My brother and his family send you Christmas cards, for fuck's sake. You sent me a gift basket when my kid was born."

He avoided my eyes, but I caught him sneaking a quick look over his shoulder see if the lady with the Ugg boots was watching us. She was.

"I can't help you, Scarlett. I work for Malcolm now," he said, loud enough for anyone in the room to hear. In a much lower voice, he added, "Or he kills my family."

"Why didn't you—" I began, but Mikey was coming back into the room. I hadn't noticed any kind of change to my radius, which currently felt shifty and slick, like a puddle of oil under a car.

Then, right behind Mikey, the cardinal vampire of New York strutted into the room.

Maybe I'd just spent too many years fearing him, building him up in my head, but in person Malcolm was kind of underwhelming. Within my radius (or maybe Rhys's, or both), he was just a short, burly man with wild eyes and an air of being just barely civilized. Which was probably giving him too much credit.

"Say, have we met?" I said as he strode over to me. I made a show of blinking up at his face. "I'm sorry, you look so familiar. Maybe you just have one of those faces."

Annoyance flashed in Malcolm's eyes, but he turned to look

at Rhys. "You're sure the dosage is correct? I don't want any more surprises."

"Aye, I'm sure. I used to experiment with drugs in the bad old days." Rhys stared down into his lap. "I can't suppress her aura without killing her, but with the drugs she's not in control of it. She can't change its size or take magic away from anyone."

"Good." Malcolm finally turned to me, squatting down on his heels in front of me, like Wyatt does when he addresses Annie.

"So," I said, because it was genuinely bugging me, "when did you get to town? I thought you *never* left New York."

He smiled. "Oh, I just arrived in this shithole. See, I got a call last night from the local cardinal, something about an attack on some friends of mine."

"Oh, you mean Orvil Grant, your son and heir?" I said brightly. "And the woman you hired to kill me? Those friends?"

Over his shoulder, the Asian woman reacted to this a little. So it really *wasn't* common knowledge that Malcolm had turned Orvil.

"And then I heard *you* were involved," he went on, through gritted teeth, "and I thought, what the hell, maybe I'd move some things around, come say hello in person."

I snorted. "Sure, sure, you decided to come to yourself on like, a cool vacation whim. Nothing to do with not letting word get out about various murders you've committed."

For a second his facade slipped, and he glared at me with so much loathing that my stomach flipped over.

"You know, you didn't bother me much when you were in my city," he mused. "But since then, you've been nothing but a thorn in my shoe."

"It's thorn in my *side*," I corrected, "or rock in my shoe. You gotta pick an idiom and just commit, my dude."

I thought I saw the woman suppressing a smile behind him, but Malcolm only frowned at me.

"See, you're making my point exactly. You used to be respectful. I could tolerate you. Now." He shook his head. "You get my boy killed, you're knocked up with his bastard, and five minutes later you're swanning around with some Hollywood popinjay."

"*Popinjay*? Is that like—"

"Close your fucking mouth," he said casually, "or I will take that dusty sheet right there and start pushing it through your teeth until I feel calm."

My mouth snapped shut.

"Where was I?" Malcolm looked thoughtful. "Right. So you're a harlot, that's obvious, but I got nothin' against harlots. They serve their purpose. The whole time, though, you're also running around depriving people of magic, fucking around with our entire ecosystem." He shook his head. "I figured you'd burn yourself out or get yourself killed. I was willing to wait for Dashiell to wise up and stop you. But it turns out the cardinal of Los Angeles is too *progressive* to do shit. And just look at you."

He reached toward me then—I couldn't help but flinch—but instead of hitting me, he picked up the bedraggled shoelaces on one of my hiking boots, which had come undone. He tied my shoe with a sad clucking noise, looking into my eyes as he pulled the knot tight. "I was always gonna have to stop Maven and Dashiell from their silly world domination plan. But after what Kendra found out about you in Colorado?" He sighed. "I had to move up my whole timetable and put you out of your misery myself. And now look where we are."

"Out of my misery?" I whispered. I looked at Rhys, who'd stood and taken a few steps back from us. The other null wouldn't meet my eyes.

"Yeah, honey, you heard me." Malcolm looked at me with great pity. "It's not your fault, really. But hurricanes and sluts, they just destroy everything. And you're both."

"Wow. Just...wow. This must be what speechless feels like," I said, but of course, I couldn't actually close my mouth. "I literally don't know where to—the sex-shaming, the misogyny, the archaic possessive New York assholery—"

Okay, I was starting to sputter. Get it together, Scarlett. I shook my head until it screamed with pain.

"Actually, you know what? Fuck all that. I don't care what you think of my character, because you're going to be dead soon. But what I do care about, you sanctimonious knockoff of a knockoff of a bad Marlon Brando impression, is this: *you* sent skinners to kill Jameson. *You* killed him. He was my friend, I cared about him, and you made him dead. So *fuck* you." And I spat in his face.

Malcolm did hit me then, a casual backhand that sent me toppling sideways, just as I'd expected. I curled into a defensive ball, but no other blows followed.

He must have signaled to Mikey, because the thug vampire stepped forward and yanked my body upright again. I'd bitten my lip when Malcolm hit me, and now a line of bloody drool was going down my chin. Awesome.

Again, I looked at Rhys, but he had his face studiously pointed at the floor. Malcolm followed my line of sight.

"Rhys, go to the basement and have another visit with other guest," he ordered. "He's healing too quickly."

Rhys turned and scurried out of the room without another word. Now it was just me and three vampires.

Awesome.

# 39

## LEX

It didn't take Simon and I long to reload weapons and gather spell supplies, tucking as much as we could beneath our rain jackets. It took even less time for Eli to put on sneakers and a Kevlar vest over his bare chest. He also carried a massive sidearm—a Desert Eagle, I thought, which would have been uncomfortably large for my hands. He didn't bother with any rain gear, other than a plain baseball cap that kept it out of his eyes.

Meanwhile, Kate was still keeping an eye out for anyone coming our way, but she reported that everyone was currently inside, including both nulls.

It made me nervous that the vampires hadn't sent anyone out here to find us. I worried they were preoccupied with killing Jesse and the others. Or they *wanted* us to come in, as part of the trap to lure Maven and Dashiell into the building. Or both. Ultimately, though, we had to go in no matter what.

"How's the knee?" I asked Eli, strapping on my backpack. Jesse had brought it along in the police car.

"It will be fully healed in a few minutes."

Kate had been following this conversation closely, the only one of us not soaking wet in the rain. "So he definitely won't die?" Kate sounded a little crestfallen.

"Uh. No."

Eli said, "Lex?"

"I think she's listening to the ghost," Simon told him. "Lex, what's her name?"

This got Kate's attention, and she clapped her hands soundlessly. "Oh, are you going to introduce us?"

"That's a good idea. Let's see if we can do this properly." I unhooked one backpack strap so I could pull a couple of cotton drawstring bags out of the front pocket, handing one each to Eli and Simon. They each upended the bag, revealing a chunk of cassiterite.

Simon looked up and grinned at me. "Ghost FM. Cool."

"If it works," I said wryly. "Time to test your theory about nulls not permanently affecting crystals. Show Eli what do to."

While Simon briefly walked Eli through activating his chakra, I looked at Kate and explained as succinctly as I could. "These are communication stones; they override our usual type of magic. I've used them to talk to ghosts during the day, and once Simon was able to talk to a boundary witch ghost... although I've never tried it with a werewolf. Anyway, if they work, these two will be able to hear you as long as they've got the stone touching a chakra point."

Kate clapped her hands again in joy. "Oh my goodness, I never imagined! You clever girl, you!"

"Um, thanks." I paused. I could feel the clock ticking—it had already been several minutes since Jesse had ran toward the Marine Hospital, and longer than that since they'd taken Scarlett. But if we were going to use Kate for comms, I needed to know if I can trust her. "Kate...I have to put saving my people first, but I don't want those vampires to destroy your home. And when my friends are safe, I'd like to hear the rest of your story, and help you if I can. But I need to know if you're willing to assist us tonight."

She gave me a measured look, an expression I hadn't seen before from her. "When you say you want to save your friends," she said pensively, "you mean you want them to live?"

Okay, that was terrifying. "Yes."

"But then you'll all go away again, and I'll have no one new to play with." She pouted.

Goosebumps broke out on my arms, but I kept my voice level. "I'm pretty sure we're going to kill a lot of people to get them out, if that's any consolation."

She waved her hand dismissively. "Only *vampires*. They don't even leave ghosts."

Right. "That's true," I acknowledged, trying not to sound frightened. "And I can see how it might sound more fun to let us all die than to help us. But if vampires die in a null's radius, they die as humans who can leave ghosts." This seemed likely, but I had never actually tested it. "And if any of my friends die here tonight, I will lay their ghosts immediately."

"Hmm." She fussed with her spectacles again, noncommittal.

I thought about threatening her, and almost opened my mouth to say something along those lines. But I didn't think Kate was quite sane, and I didn't know enough about her—or boundary magic itself—to be certain I could win that fight.

So instead, I said, "You joined the Navy nurses to help, right? You wanted to use your magic to help soldiers."

Something flickered on her face. "I was an idealist then."

"Be an idealist for me now," I stepped back, gesturing to Eli and Simon. "I am a soldier, and we are on a rescue mission. I could use your help, Ensign Sutcliff."

She frowned. "Navy nurses don't have ranks. We're women; it's not allowed."

"It is now."

"Really?"

"Yes."

"Lex?" Simon was at my shoulder. "We're ready. I can hear her." He tucked the crystal carefully under his bulletproof vest so it would touch his heart chakra.

"Okay." I looked at the boundary witch ghost again. "Will you help us?"

She straightened her shoulders, sticking out her hand. "Shake on it?" She gave my wrist a pointed look.

"I won't be able to...oh." I quickly unwound the makeshift bandage from my wrist. The wound was still bleeding sluggishly, and I smeared a few drops onto my palm. Then I reached out and shook Kate's hand, which felt firm and real. Kate's eyes widened, and her skin seemed to flush. "Oh, my! You *are* strong."

"Thanks, I guess." I angled my body to include Eli and Simon. "Kate, this is Eli, alpha werewolf of Los Angeles, and Simon, a powerful witch from Colorado. Guys, this is Kate... uh..." I glanced at Kate, who smiled prettily, pushing up her spectacles.

"Katherine Eddows Sutcliff," she supplied.

"Right. Katherine Eddows Sutcliff, Kate to her friends."

Kate straightened up, puffing out her chest. "Good evening, gentlemen. I'm so pleased to make your acquaintance."

"It's good to meet you too," Simon said, not in any particular direction.

I looked at Eli, who was holding the cassiterite in a clenched fist. "Can you hear her?"

"I don't know..."

"Try the heart chakra," Simon advised, and came over to

take the stone out of the werewolf's hand, stuffing it down his vest to rest over his heart. Eli looked momentarily surprised, but werewolves don't have a lot of body shyness.

"Kate, can you say something else?" I asked when Simon stepped back.

"Hello, Eli," Kate purred.

Eli jumped. "Jesus...hi." He looked at me with round eyes. "I...how is this possible? This is witch stuff."

"No, it's not. Different frequencies. Simon can explain it later. The important thing to remember is that it won't work in Scarlett's presence. She won't short out the crystals, but if you go in and out of her radius you'll probably have to activate your chakras again."

I turned toward the Marine Hospital, about to ask Kate where everyone was, but Simon touched my arm. "What do you want to do with this guy?"

My eyes dropped to Julien Dubuque, whose eyes were still closed as he counted. I'd nearly forgotten about him. I wasn't actively pressing him at the moment, but he still had to finish my command.

"Kill him," Eli advised. "He's with Malcolm now. He's just going to keep trying to kill us unless we kill him."

I toed Julien's prone form. Eli had a point: this vampire would kill me in an instant if he could. He had orchestrated this entire trap, and our lives were in danger because of it. If Quinn were here, I thought, he'd kill Julien just to make sure he couldn't follow us into the building. And I wasn't sure I disagreed.

Kate said excitedly, "Oh, you should *absolutely* kill him. Please, Eli, I haven't had a proper death in *so* long. It will strengthen me."

"Um..." Eli raised his eyebrows at me in alarm. Kate's eyes

were lit up with interest, and she almost seemed to be glowing a little brighter than before.

"That's not how we do things," Simon told her, with a little bit of the lecturer tone creeping into his voice. "We don't just murder people, even if they cross us. That's kind of the whole point of why we're here."

He was right, and I needed to act like it. To Eli, I said, "Break his neck, and put him in that well. If we survive the night, we'll take him out and put him on trial."

Simon nodded approvingly. I stepped back, making room for Eli to bend over Julien. There was another sickening *crack*, louder and denser. Kate let out a blissful sound that was unsettling on several levels. She seemed to be inhaling something, though I couldn't imagine ghosts needed to breathe.

I glanced down at Julien, and saw that his clothes were collapsing. No, that wasn't it—the vampire's body was reverting to the state it would have been in after death...two hundred-some years ago.

"He's dead!" Simon sounded alarmed.

"Whoops," Eli said, a little too cheerfully. "Must have twisted too hard. The spinal column completely separated. My bad." He started toward the building, leaving us to follow.

"Oh, I *like* him!" Kate said happily. "What a wonderful night!"

Simon shot me a look, but I spread my hands helplessly. There wasn't much I could do, and I certainly wasn't going to shed any tears over Julien Dubuque. I motioned to Simon, who began limping toward the building.

When we were still fifteen feet away, the rain simply... stopped. All four of us, even Kate, paused.

"Is it...*not* raining?" Simon whispered in astonishment. "I forgot what this feels like."

"Yeah." I started transferring things out of my outer rain

gear and into my other pockets so I wouldn't drip water in the building and give myself away. It was a good moment to make our plan.

I looked at the boundary witch ghost. "Okay, Kate, this is where I need you. Where is the second Emptiness?

The boundary witch blinked at me for a moment, and I guessed she must be sensing her way around the property. "Oh. I see." She found my eyes. "They *were* together, on the southeast side of the second story, in what used to be a ward. Now one of them is heading toward...she paused, then finished, "the tower."

How were we going to figure out which was which? "There was another man with us, Jesse. Can you tell me where he went?"

"He went in a window, but made it to the main story undetected," she reported. "He is still there, hiding under the stairs that go up to the second story. He is listening to the voices coming down from that floor. Voices carry in my building."

"If that's Jesse's focus, then Scarlett is there," I decided. "Second story, southeast corner. Okay. Are Adelaide and Orvil still on the main story?"

"Orvil is. Adelaide goes back and forth between first and second floors. Neither has spotted Mr. Jesse yet. He's really quite sneaky." She sounded impressed.

"Okay." I looked at the others. "I'll go around the building, take the basement door, and make a lot of noise so Adelaide and Orvil come running. You two—"

"No!" Kate said it so loudly that Simon flinched and I stopped in my tracks. "You can't go in the basement door, Lex."

"You mean the same basement door you tried to convince me to walk into earlier?" I started west, in that direction.

"Lex! Wait!" Kate floated quickly in front of me, and put her hands up so I would have to walk through her or stop moving. I skidded to a stop.

"Kate, I'm getting my friend."

"Not you," she blurted. "Send the werewolf. He's the least sensitive."

Nerves churned in my stomach. "Kate..."

"Trust me," she pleaded.

"Why should it?"

"Because you and I have an understanding now. We shook hands. Send the werewolf through the basement, while you and the witch take the service door. "

"Isn't it being guarded?"

"By Orvil, yes. I can move something around in another room so they go investigate."

Both men had heard all of this and were looking at me for a decision. I nodded at Eli, who turned and loped around the side of the building toward the basement door. Simon and I started east, toward the service door, with Kate alongside us.

Suddenly, the boundary witch stiffened. "Adelaide changed course—she's going toward Mr. Jesse!" she exclaimed.

I looked around wildly. "Go, Kate, help him *now*. We'll find another way."

Kate disappeared.

# 40

## SCARLETT

"I can see that this conversation is pointless," Malcolm said, tucking away a cloth handkerchief. "I was probably just being sentimental, letting you stay alive this long. You can't understand why you have to be put down. You're just not capable of seeing it."

"That's funny." I spat blood onto the floor of the creepy room, which at least gave it some color, and grinned at him. "I was about to say the same thing to you."

Malcolm stood up, turning his back on me like I wasn't worth another second of his eternal time. "Well, Yazhu?" he said to the Asian woman. "Shall we continue our conversation upstairs? Mikey can deal with...this."

Yazhu. I knew that name...somehow. Come on, Scarlett's brain, sober up.

"What's the point?" She gave him a bored look. "The Mad Cavalier will never agree. And I understand he's very popular in the Southeast. Even New Orleans respects him, and you know how elite that crowd can be."

I snorted. "Says the woman in the twelve thousand dollar dress."

The Asian woman, Yazhu, gave me a single eyebrow raise, like I had mildly interested her.

Malcolm ignored me, his attention on Yazhu. "Popular or not, our world is still our world. One cardinal can be replaced by someone more amenable."

Yazhu shook her head. "You persuaded me that Maven and Dashiell's totalitarian regime is a threat to us all, but Abner Calhoun is another matter. I have no grievance with him, and he claims to be here repaying a debt. I did not agree to destroy him just because he won't stand with us in opposition."

Stand in opposition?

Yazhu. That was the name of the cardinal vampire of San Francisco. I'd never met her, but she'd been supposedly looking after Corry. She was Dashiell's ally.

Wait. New York, San Francisco, the Upper Mississippi... Atlanta. This was a lot of cardinal vampires in one building.

Standing in opposition to Maven's parliament.

I started laughing. "Wait, *seriously*?" Both Malcolm and Yazhu turned to glare at me. "You and your Dark Side buddies are starting your own Evil League of Evil?" Tears of laughter rolled down my cheeks, my whole body shaking with it. "You were so scared of having any kind of oversight that you started the vampire Injustice League? Oh my God, I think I might pee." I knew, even as I giggled, that this whole idea was going to seem really scary when the drugs wore off. It just wasn't scary *yet*.

"Can we kill her now?" Mikey said to Malcolm.

"Yes." Malcolm looked at me with disgust. "She has no further value." He started toward me.

I was too woozy to scrape together much of a plan...except, of course, the throwing knife I had pulled out of my boot when I'd curled up in a ball earlier. It was behind my back now, hidden in one fist. It had taken me a few minutes to cut through the zip ties on my wrists—it turns out that's *really* difficult when you're dealing with vertigo and a shitload of drugs, plus trying to chat to cover the sound of your fumbling.

I'd done it, though. Now that my hands were loose behind my back, I just had to wait for Malcolm to get a little closer. If I could cut his throat, or any major artery, I hoped it would create enough chaos for me to—

"That's not entirely accurate, though, is it?" Yazhu said casually.

Malcolm had just started to reach for me, but now he straightened up and turned to look at her. "What do you mean?"

"She *has* value." Yazhu said. "We could use her as bait for the LA people. We could turn her to our side. Or we could simply hold her as a threat to our enemies, just as she was used to threaten us."

Malcolm threw up his hands. "You're missing the whole point! An ability like this shouldn't exist in the world. Nulls need to be taken off the board. I thought you understood that."

"I understand you have a vendetta against this child because of what happened with your pet," Yazhu said stiffly. She was still standing just inside the door, but now she took a single step toward it, edging farther from Malcolm. "But in trying to kill her and the others, you started a war with Maven before we had enough forces in place. I'm not sure I'm willing to–"

A gunshot suddenly echoed around the empty brick space, and Yazhu crumpled to the dirty floor. For one quick second I thought Malcolm had shot her, but no, he looked as shocked as I felt. It had been someone in the hallway. Someone with an assault rifle.

Then a lot of things happened very quickly.

Without a word, Malcolm raced to the other end of the big room, as far away from me as he could get. I still couldn't feel my radius, but I could tell from his body language when he became vampire again.

Meanwhile, Mikey had produced an ugly-looking handgun, and he crept over to the doorway, stepping over Yazhu's body. And I used the throwing knife to cut through the zip ties around my legs.

Mikey was focused on not letting anyone get through that doorway, but Malcolm saw me free myself. He hissed at Mikey, "Shoot her!"

Mikey looked my way, but it was too late: I had the knife up and threw it at his right eye from ten feet away, an easy shot.

The blade hit him in the throat. Stupid drugs.

Still, it had the desired effect. The vampire bodyguard grabbed his throat with both hands, which meant his gun clattered down to the floor eight feet away from me. Rivulets of blood still spilled from between Mikey's fingers, and he looked at me with bulging eyes. Then he took a step backward, into the dark hallway—where there was another *crack* of gunfire and Mikey's head more or less exploded. He was dead before he hit the ground.

Malcolm and I looked at each other for one long, hateful second. Then we both leapt for the gun.

I was closer, by a lot, but I was also only just getting the feeling back in my legs and arms, and I'd spent all week having the shit kicked out of me *before* I'd been drugged. I had only crawled halfway when Malcolm made it back across the room and picked up the gun.

There was a scuffle and some shouting from the door, people fighting, and I recognized Jesse's voice. I couldn't help but look that way, though the hallway was too dark to see anything.

During those precious seconds, Malcolm pointed the gun at me and pulled the trigger quickly. The bullet hit my Kevlar vest.

It hurt, like the time in fourth grade when Tommy Bitare had punched me in the chest. But the new pain just kind of blended it with all the other pain, and I struggled to my feet.

Looking annoyed, Malcolm raised the gun toward my forehead this time. We were maybe six feet away from each other, and based on the sudden silence, Jesse wasn't coming to help me.

"Hurricanes and sluts," Malcolm said, like he was pronouncing his sentence. I could actually see his fingers tighten as he started toward the trigger.

"Title of your sex tape?" I suggested. It might have been the drugs, but as last words went, I felt pretty satisfied.

Malcolm paused, not understanding the joke. "What?"

Then the window imploded.

# 41

## LEX

After Kate went inside to help Jesse, I stared up at the building for a moment, thinking through my options. Adelaide and Orvil had been on the first floor, so if we just raced in the service door, we'd be running straight into their fire. Could I press Orvil fast enough to keep Adelaide from shooting me? It seemed unlikely.

Then we heard a gunshot coming from inside the building, up high.

"The door!" Simon started toward the east side of the building, the service entrance, but I grabbed his wrist and dragged him the opposite way. "This side," I called over my shoulder.

"Lex, what are we doing?"

Dropping his hand, I clapped twice, hard enough to hurt my injured hand, and damn if those little Clapper spotlights didn't pop on, illuminating the west side of the building. "How did you—" Simon began, but I was dragging him by his elbow again.

I glanced up at the building, back at the ground, until I thought I had it lined up. "Simon, you trust me, right?"

"*What*?"

Grabbing his shoulders, I spun us around so he was farthest from the building. "Throw me," I ordered.

Simon's brow furrowed in confusion. "What do you—"

"The catapult spell! The one your mom used on me the first time we met." I stabbed a finger toward the boarded-up second story window, where I was pretty sure the gunshot had originated. "Throw me there!"

"You can't ask me to throw you into a brick wall—" Simon argued.

"I'm not." Without a thought, without the slightest moment of second-guessing, I grabbed a fistful of his shirt, leaned forward, and kissed him.

It was nothing, really, a fast brush of lips. But it was also everything.

"I trust you," I told him firmly. "Throw me." I turned toward the building and crossed my arms in front of my face to protect it.

I heard Simon mutter the words, and then I was flying.

The boards themselves weren't a problem—after who knows how many years, and a full day of hard rain, it was like crashing through cardboard. But Simon had used a little too much power, probably worried about getting me high enough, and I went farther than expected. I tensed myself to roll—but I didn't land on a wood or brick floor, as I'd expected. Instead, I landed on a living person. A man.

"Lex!" Scarlett's voice yelled.

There were a few seconds of pure confusion, as the man and I both tried to untangle ourselves and figure out what the hell had just happened at the same time. By the time I realized

I'd just slammed into fucking *Malcolm*, Scarlett was yelling at me to get down. And I realized she had picked up a gun.

I dropped to the floor.

Scarlett shot at Malcolm once, twice—then the cardinal vampire of New York was out of the room and running down the hall, screaming orders to someone I couldn't see. Instinctively, I started to follow him, but my foot slipped on a chunk of plywood, and I only just managed to catch myself in a plank before I face-planted into the old floor.

"Jesus, be more of an athlete," Scarlett muttered. Then: "You okay?"

I checked myself. "Yes."

"Did you just fly through a boarded-up window to save me?"

"Nah, I just really hated that window." I raised my voice. "Jesse! You alive?"

"Under the stairs! The HK is out of ammo; I could use some help!" There was more gunfire in the hallway.

Scarlett started toward the door, but I grabbed her elbow with my right hand while I pulled the Glock with my left. "Stay behind me," I ordered, and for some reason, she actually listened.

Keeping most of my body in the room, I peered around the door—and saw only darkness. There was a light in this room, but my eyes didn't have enough time to adjust before someone shot at me from the room opposite ours, across the long hallway. I only just managed to yank my head back before I got shot.

I looked at Scarlett, who was pressing herself against the brick wall next to me. "What can you feel in your aura?" I demanded. "How many vampires?"

She shook her head. "They gave me drugs…it's all confused."

Shit. "Can you pull it in so I can get some intel?"

Instead of answering, Scarlett turned and limped her way to the farthest side of the big room, maybe twenty feet away, where she lowered herself awkwardly to the floor.

It worked. Right on cue, Kate popped into the room next to me, her face lit up with excitement. She was perfectly visible to me, glowing in a way that didn't reflect light around her. It seemed strange that she was the only ghost here, but there was no time to worry about it. "Ooh, look at these beautiful deaths!" she crooned, looking at the bodies on the floor between us. She was standing inside the male body. "No ghosts, which is a shame, but I'll still treasure them." She frowned at the mess from where I'd burst through the window. "Oh, Lex, look what you did."

"*Kate*! Who's shooting at Jesse?" I heard two more shots *ping* off the metal staircase.

"Adelaide," Kate said darkly. Apparently she wasn't a fan either. "I helped Jesse find her fancy gun, which seemed to upset her. Now she's in the ward across the hall, trying to shoot at him through the stairs."

I put a new magazine in the Glock. "And everyone else?"

"Malcolm is on the main floor with Orvil. They are making plans for Malcolm to escape back to his city. Eli is standing at the top of the basement stairs, listening to them."

"Where is the other Emptiness?"

Kate pointed upward with a single finger, and I understood: the tower. They had Beau up there with the other null. "There's a shortcut in the ward across the hall," she whispered, even though I was the only one who could currently hear her. "A second set of stairs that goes to the roof. You can break through another exterior board and climb into the belvedere from there. It was only built fifty years ago; I don't care if you damage the tower."

I nodded. But first things first—I had to get Jesse out of there. "Kate, can you stand right in front of Adelaide for a moment?"

Her whole face lit up. "Of course! Now?"

"Count to ten first. Go."

I dropped down to my belly, just inside the room, and listened intently. There was another shot from beneath the stairs—Jesse returning fire—and two more from the ward. I leaned into the doorway with only my head and left arm exposed, just as Kate appeared in the darkness. I shot at her twice, fast, and pulled back into the room, listening intently.

There was a series of thumps, and a deep, rattling gurgle. "Kate!" I yelled.

"Oh! This is a *good* one!" Her voice had that barbaric tone that made me nervous.

"Scarlett, stay here." I dug in my pocket, pulling out a small high-powered flashlight. I shone the light into the hall.

Adelaide's body was visible, lying on the floor in the next doorway. She was moving a little, but her gun was in the hall. I started into the hall as farther down, Jesse peered out from behind the impressive iron staircase. I hadn't really gotten a good look at it, but every step was made of metal, with intricate metal vines forming the riser. That's why Adelaide had kept shooting at him—she'd hoped to get a shot through the latticework.

"Lex?" he said, holding up a hand to shield from the flashlight beam. I lowered it.

"It's me. Are you hit?"

"A couple of grazes, through the damned stairs. Is Scarlett with you?"

"She's in that room." I pointed. "Go. I'll cover you."

I kept the Glock trained on Adelaide's prone form while Jesse raced past me to get to his fiancé. Adelaide didn't seem capable of going for the gun, but I had to wonder why Orvil hadn't come up the stairs to help her. Had Malcolm already escaped? Did Orvil go with him?

Where was Simon?

I used my foot to slide the gun farther away from Adelaide, then stepped across the threshold to the ward where she had collapsed with her hands underneath her body. Kate was already kneeling next to Adelaide, her hands hovering over the woman's body like she was warming them at a fire. "Can you feel it?" she whispered, her voice full of reverence.

Without answering, I dug my toe under Adelaide's body to roll her over, keeping the flashlight beam on her. For just a moment I imagined her clutching an IED or maybe a hand grenade, but she had both hands pressed against her lower abdomen, and they were stained red. Kate squealed with delight and repositioned herself over Adelaide's wound.

"You bitch," Adelaide gasped, glaring at me.

"Where are you hit?" I asked Adelaide. I couldn't really tell anything besides "lower abdomen," and I wasn't going to get close enough to check. She almost certainly had other weapons hidden on her.

She glowered at me. "Spine."

"Oof. That sucks. Want me to call an ambulance?"

I caught Kate's crestfallen look, but Adelaide just let out a gurgling laugh. Emergency services were going to be awfully busy tonight, with all the flooding. "Get...Orvil," she said through pain-clenched teeth. "He...promised."

"Yeah, I'm not going to help you become a vampire, Adelaide," I clicked off the flashlight, glancing around. This room was pitch-black, but I could see a little bit of light coming up from the stairwell, and more from the room where Scarlett and Jesse were.

I turned the flashlight on again and shined it around the

room we were in, where Adelaide had been hiding. The windows in here weren't just boarded up; they were covered in blackout curtains and what looked like vinyl sheeting. Probably where Orvil had spent the daytime hours.

In one corner, there was a jagged gash in the brick wall that was mostly covered by a rough wooden board. The word "door" was probably too sophisticated. "That's the shortcut?" I asked Kate.

She followed my gaze, nodded, and instantly turned her attention back to Adelaide. "She's dying," Kate said rapturously.

I lowered the light back to Adelaide. She was dressed all in black, with camouflage face paint smeared over her exposed skin.

"You're an ambush predator," I said, mostly to myself. Adelaide had chosen this spot to wait while Scarlett was being questioned, thinking one of us would rush up to save her. It would have been a perfect location for a trap, if Jesse hadn't found her rifle first.

Adelaide was clearly starting to fade, but she still glared at me accusingly. "How...did you...see..."

"I had help from a ghost, Kate. She was like me when she was alive."

I don't know what I expected Adelaide to do—curse at me, probably, or gloat that I'd had to cheat in order to beat her. But instead she started to giggle, like a great joke had been made at my expense.

"Katherine...Eddows...Sutcliff," she gasped, swallowing half the syllables. She was starting to fade, her voice dropping to a whisper. "You really...don't do...homework..."

"What does that mean? *What do you mean*, Adelaide?"

"Someone...lied..." Adelaide went still.

I reached for her neck, felt the thready pulse slow and then stop. I looked up and around. The hallway was still dim, crumbling, and completely empty.

Why hadn't Orvil come to save her? Who had lied?

I glanced at Kate. She still knelt next to Adelaide with her hands held above the woman's stomach, unmoving except for tendrils of her hair, which seemed to crackle with energy, snapping around like she was in a high wind. I opened my mouth to say her name, but the word caught in my throat. There was something *wrong* with her face. Her eyes had gone black from lid to lid, and her face...I couldn't even describe it, but the words that popped into my head were "black hole."

"Kate?"

The boundary witch ghost didn't respond. Did I have time to go into my boundary mindset and check on her?

"*Lex*!"

I jumped, but it was Jesse's voice, and he sounded panicked.

After a quick scan of the hall I hurried back to the room I'd burst into earlier. "I'm coming in!" I called at the doorway.

The work lamp was still on in here, and I could make out Scarlett and Jesse at the farthest end of the room. Jesse was sitting on the floor now, with Scarlett slumped over, her head resting in Jesse's lap. My friend was sitting with his back against the wall and a gun in the hand that wasn't cradling his fiancé.

"She won't wake up," he said, his voice pleading with me.

I ran over to them. "What happened?"

"When I first got in here she was mumbling a little, but now—"

I held a hand against her neck. "Her pulse is strong," I told him, and lifted one of Scarlett's eyelids. "Pupil response looks good. I think maybe she passed out from the drugs."

"Drugs?"

"She said they gave her something to prevent her from expanding her radius or doing the cure thing. I think she'll be okay, Jesse." I put a hand on his shoulder. "I gotta go up to the tower for Beau, and then we'll get her to the car. Just stay right here, okay?"

But before I could even stand up, I heard cries coming through the open window. *Simon*, I thought.

I went to look out the window I had burst through. The plywood was shattered, but the actual brick was too sturdy to be affected by one flying witch. This view faced west, but at the south end of the building, I could see car headlights bouncing toward the Marine Hospital. Someone was here. I leaned way out of the opening to get a better look, but even with the Clapper lights, it was too dark for me to make out much that far away.

Then, on the southwest lawn, a flash of light went up into the air and exploded, and I recognized Simon's homemade fireworks. I'd seen them before, when he and Lily decided to DIY the Fourth of July. Now he was using them like a flare.

As the bits of light trailed down, they finally illuminated what I hadn't been able to see down in the clearing: a brawl. Simon was standing in the center of a circle of vampires, his hands held up to lock in a spell. The bits of firework stopped several feet above his head, landing on the invisible dome of his shield. Orvil was standing about six feet away, his body so tense I could see it from here. There were four more vampires with him, several of them circling the shield, trying to find a way past. I didn't know them, but they had to be working for Malcolm, part of the trap Julien had mentioned.

Judging by the tears and bloodstains on Simon's vest and clothes, this fight had been going on for a while...which explained why Orvil hadn't been on hand to help Adelaide. And why Simon looked so exhausted. How much longer could he hold a shield like that?

I had shifted my weight to run down there when I remembered the headlights. I lingered for another second, long enough to see Quinn's face suddenly appear as he lit a road flare, and then another, tossing them at the vampires around Simon. They hissed and jumped back, distracted, and there was more light in the clearing now. Maven, Quinn, and Dashiell seemed to appear next to Simon's dome, protecting it. And the fight started in earnest.

I needed to get down there, but they would be okay without me for a few more minutes. I turned and ran back through the room. "The cavalry has arrived," I yelled to Jesse as I ran past. "Stay here with her!"

I ran across the hall, to the secret not-quite-a-door in Malcolm's daytime room.

I was going after Beau.

Turning on the flashlight, I dragged back the wood panel serving as a door and found a set of rickety-looking wooden stairs going up, just as Kate had said.

I started up the first stair—but it disintegrated under my weight. I reached out, trying to catch myself on the higher steps, but I couldn't get any purchase; only handfuls of splinters that crumbled away and fell, with the smell of rotted wood filling my nose. My hiking shoes scraped uselessly against flat, crumbling brick, and then I was falling, sliding down into the darkness.

# 42

## SCARLETT

Don't get me wrong, it's *always* nice to open my eyes and see Jesse. And resting my head on the leg of his jeans while he plays with my hair...Man, that shit never gets old.

Seeing his complex expression of terror, exasperation, and panic, though? That had been getting old all week.

"I'm okay," I said in a very calm and rational voice. "They gave me some drugs, that's all."

Okay, fine. What I really said came out more like, "S'okay. Gamme dregs."

He stroked my hair, not looking reassured. And then I remember *who* had given me the drugs, and I felt my face crumple. "Scarlett?" Jesse sounded alarmed. I didn't usually cry at life-threatening events.

"Rhys." There, my mouth was working again. Well, as much as it ever did.

My fiancé, the detective, only needed about four seconds to process this news. I knew him so well that I could watch it happen on his face. "Of course," he muttered. "I should have known. He was attacked *days* before the rest of you. And if they pressed Maura and the kids..."

I was too tired and hurt to play the "I should have seen it" game. I wanted to go home and hug my baby. "Where's Lex?"

"She went up to the tower to get Beau. And Maven and Dashiell are here fighting Orvil. It's over."

"The tower?" felt my face crease. Hadn't Malcolm told Rhys to go *down* to Beau?I sat myself up so I could look into Jesse's face. "Are you sure?"

"Yeah. Well, Simon told me it's actually called a belvedere, with a lower-case b." Weakly, I lifted one hand and made a blah-blah-blah gesture. "But yes, Lex said Beau's in the tower."

I had started to sink back down to lay on Jesse again, but I stopped, shaking my head painfully. "See, I don't like that."

"What, Beau in the tower?"

"Mmm." I started to stand up.

"Scarlett, lay down. I've got some water here; we need to flush out your system."

I had to use the brick wall for support, but I made it all the way to my feet without help. Go, me. "What are you doing?" Jesse's voice was full of tension now.

I did my best Arnold voice, which was not unlike my Scarlett-on-drugs voice anyway. "Got to catch the red-eye."

He got to his feet, reaching for my arms. "No, no movie references," he insisted. "Scar, you're hurt; you can't control your radius. Maven and Dashiell are going to subdue Orvil, and Malcolm probably ran off. You can rest."

"Malcolm didn't run off," I pulled away from him. "Lex is going after Beau, but someone tricked her about his location. And right now everyone's distracted with the fight outside."

Jesse's brow furrowed. "What are you saying?"

"Lex is walking into a trap. And I'm going after her."

"No." Jesse pivoted to stand between me and the door. "I believe you. But you don't have control of your radius, and you need rest. *I'll* go find Lex."

"It has to be me," I said wearily. "Malcolm is probably there too. I don't know what his plan is, but there's a reason he wants nulls off the board. I ruin his plans. I was *made* to ruin his plans."

That thought perked me up a little. I started to step around Jesse, but he closed the distance between us, cupping my face in his hands. "Scarlett," he whispered. "You're hurt. I can't lose you."

"Don't you get it? *This is it!*" I cried, pulling away from him. I managed to find some strength to put into my voice. "This is the moment, the chance that we risked everything to take, to stop Malcolm. Are you going to help me or not?"

I stood there glaring at him, breathing hard, but I also felt myself start to sway, and had to reach out for the wall to steady myself. Dammit, drugs and concussion. I was trying to make a point here.

Jesse reached for my waist, and I let him support me with both hands. He bent his head down, so our foreheads were touching. I could feel the deep, shuddering breath he took, and it reminded me that I needed to keep breathing too.

"You're right," Jesse said quietly.

"Of course I am." I had to lean back and wipe my face on my sleeve. "About what?"

"This is why we came, and we have to make sure Lex is okay."

"Oh, uh-huh, yes, I'm definitely right about that. Come on." I took his hand. "We'll go together."

"Always."

. . .

Getting down to the basement was a little harder than I'd expected, though. I'd been unconscious when someone had carried me up here, and it was immediately clear that I was still wobbly from the drugs/concussion/vertigo combo. And I kept getting distracted trying to figure out what was in my radius and then I bumped into things.

After a few minutes of this, Jesse knotted the belt of his raincoat and I held onto the back of it. Jesse and his gun led the way out of the room and down a wide, dark hallway to an extraordinary metal staircase carved with waves and dolphins. I didn't know much about architecture, but even I could see that the design was unique, despite the dust and spiderwebs. It made me a little sad to see something so artistic in this building, which was really just a creepy monument to good intentions and bad money management.

Focus, Scarlett.

We made our way down the first set of stairs, across a landing, and down more stairs to the main floor, where I had to pause to catch my breath. Faint shouting was audible through the broken windows on this story, but both of us ignored it. Jesse was a good fighter, but he was human, and I couldn't control my radius. There wasn't a lot we could do to help Maven and Dashiell right now, but maybe we could help Lex.

On the main floor, we went around to the back of the staircase, expecting another set of stairs going down...but there was nothing.

"Where are the basement stairs?" I asked, looking around. "Maybe there's just regular stairs somewhere, not the fancy thing?"

"Here, you sit. I'll look." Jesse sort of handed me off underneath the metal staircase, where I leaned against the wall and caught my breath. He hurried around nearby, poking his head in all the closest doorways. I didn't want to sit down on the floor, but my body didn't give me much of a choice. I flopped down onto my butt, propping myself on my hands to keep from falling over. I didn't even want to think about the bandage on my leg, which had gotten soaked through hours ago. How did gangrene work, exactly? It seemed like something I should be worried about.

Jesse came back shaking his head, looking generally disgusted. "Well, I've seen what a two-hundred-year-old toilet looks like, but no basement stairs."

There must have been open windows on this end of the building, because we heard the shouting again, and then more glass breaking. Jesse tensed, both of us listening intently, but whatever had broken the glass stayed outside.

"I don't know what you—" Jesse began, but I held up a hand. "Shh!"

"What?"

"Voices. Shush." I listened again. Where was that coming from?

Below.

Gritting my teeth in distaste, I lay my head all the way down onto the floor, pressing my ear against the wooden boards.

Voices.

I knocked on the floor, listening to the hard thunk, and then knocked again a foot to my left. The sound was different. Jesse and I looked at each other, and Jesse reached into his pocket at came out with…a very intense-looking pen. "It's a tactical pen," he explained sheepishly. "Simon gave it to me." He clicked a button, and a surprisingly bright flashlight beam appeared.

"This floor is probably the only wood I'd seen in the building, other than the top of the railing," Jesse said, running the light along the floor.

"Look, there's a seam!" I traced it with my fingers. "It's a trap door. Well, maybe not a trap door, but a hatch. Someone must have blocked off the basement steps."

"But how do we get it open?" Jesse handed me the pen and pried at the seam with his fingers.

"It must be locked from below."

Just then there was a sudden scream from the basement, loud enough to carry through the floorboards. I couldn't be positive, but I thought it was Lex's voice.

"Jesse, go!" I pushed at him. "Go outside, circle around the fighting. Find another way into the basement!"

"I can't leave you—"

"Yes you can! I've got a gun, and look, a tactical pen!" I waved the flashlight. "I'll hide right here until you open the hatch from below. Go!"

Jesse kissed me quickly and scrambled to his feet. He gave me a last look, but I waved impatiently. "Go, *go*! Help her!"

He turned and ran off, toward the opposite side of the building—east? I'd gotten all turned around.

It wasn't until his footsteps disappeared in the distance that I realized I was now alone, in the dark, in a haunted insane asylum. The fact that ghosts couldn't appear near me suddenly didn't seem so impressive.

"Great," I said out loud. "I get to hang out in Vincent Price's wet dream all by myself. If there's a vat of acid in that basement I'm out of here."

There was no response from the house.

After listening to the heavy silence for a few more seconds, I picked up the fancy pen thing, turning it around in my hands. "What makes you *tactical*?" I mused, fiddling with the buttons. The main feature seemed to be a very hard pointy end. It wasn't sharp enough to cut anything—I was very used to knives—but maybe it would break glass or old boards if you were trapped? Was that a tactic?

Just for fun, I tried driving it into the seam of the hatch. I was able to gouge out some splinters of dry wood. This was entertaining for a few minutes, until my hand started to hurt and I got a jagged splinter in my thumb, under the nail. "Ouch," I grumbled, pulling at the hard pointy end of the pen. It came off in my hand, like a cap.

"Oh. Cool." I examined the part underneath. "Hey, I know you." My father had liked camping. He'd even made Jack do Boy Scouts, although my parents had decided Girl Scouts really wasn't for Scarlett when I started marking up all the cookies and spent the profits on a Game Boy.

"*No*!" It had come from the basement, and was so loud that I dropped the pen. "No, *please*!"

This time, I was sure it was Lex. And Jesse wasn't moving fast enough. Or had he made it down there, and Malcolm had him too?

I looked at the gouged wood of the hatch, and the fire rod in my hand.

"Fuck it," I said aloud.

# 43

## LEX

I didn't lose consciousness when I fell down the laundry chute. That was something, I guess.

The chute itself was about four feet wide and two deep, and it obviously hadn't been touched in many, many years, quite possibly since the building had patients. I know because I fell through spiderwebs so thick they felt like gauze. I put my hands out, trying to stop or even slow my fall, but my palms and boots tore against hard brick. It happened so fast that I couldn't get a grip on anything. I didn't even have time to feel claustrophobic or figure out how to land without hurting myself. The best I could do was try to slow it.

When the fall finally ended, it was on a stack of mildewed linen that had been folded so long ago that they seemed to dissolve beneath me. My left ankle rolled painfully and I screamed, catching myself on my hands on the brick floor.

And I began dying.

First I drowned, twice at least. When I rolled away from that, I was shot in the chest, slowly bleeding out while my children watched and screamed. Then it was consumption, my lungs full of blood that I coughed and coughed, my body wracked with spasms.

I sobbed through my next death, a stabbing, but I managed to get just enough of myself back to find a source of my blood—a scrape on the meaty base of my thumb—and began to laboriously drag it along the floor in a rough circle, crying and choking through the next two deaths. After I hung myself and drowned again, I tucked myself into a ball and tried to reach for boundary magic—but for the first time since I'd found out what I was, I couldn't find it. Couldn't get a hold of my self, the Lex of me, much less pull in something else. All I could do was die. Again and again.

I was lost.

*Allison Alexandra Luther,* came my twin sister's voice. She sounded terrified. That, more than anything else, made me listen. *You will* not *fall into this bullshit.*

I sobbed. I was run down by a horse, then, and held down underwater by two men. *ALLIE!* My sister shouted at me now, the loudest I'd ever heard her. *CHARLIE. NEEDS. YOU.*

It was so loud that it was the only thing in my head, just for a moment. I pressed my tattoos into the edge of the blood circle, pulled at my magic, and whispered the word.

"Wall."

My circle sprang to life, and suddenly I was alone in my head again.

Panting, I got to my feet, forgetting the rolled ankle. I cried out and almost fell out of the circle, but I caught my balance and stayed upright, looking around. I was in a medium-sized room made entirely of red brick—walls, floors, and ceilings. A single bare bulb on one wall provided light, so there was electricity down here. There was a rounded stain at my feet, like maybe this room had once held at least one large tub. Right.

Laundry room. There was an opening in one wall, but no door. At least, I didn't think there was a door. Personally, I couldn't see anything at all past the ghosts. Hundreds of them.

The main layer, as I would come to think of it, seemed to be Unsettled: sailors who had drowned at sea. I could tell because their ghostly uniforms and boots were soaked through, and they stared at me with wet, bulging eyes. When they opened their mouths to speak to me, nothing came out but Mississippi River water that slopped down their chests and vanished.

It was creepy, but it was nothing compared to the others.

Dozens—probably hundreds—of ghosts had been compressed into the basement, squashed between and on top of each other and the Unsettled. They pressed against the misshapen circle I'd made, as though I was standing inside a glass tub. There were remnants, I thought, judging by the vacant eyes and restless bodies that twitched and jerked, too jammed in place to reenact their deaths. But there were wraiths, too, eyes blazing with rage and bloodlust, their mouths opening and closing as they looked at my wounds on my hands. Some drops of my blood must have landed on the floor when I fell, because there were several locations where ghosts wriggled tightly against each other, jockeying to get their mouths toward a spot I couldn't see. They were too tightly packed to even lash out at each other.

I don't know how long I stood there staring with my mouth open, while the hundred ghosts packed into the room stared right back at me. At some point, though, I started to cry.

"I'm so sorry," I whispered to them. "I'm so sorry this happened to you."

"Oh, don't be," said a voice. There was a current of magic in the air that was almost visible, and suddenly the ghosts pulled back on either side, creating an aisle of space. Kate's ghost stood in the middle of it, her arms held up like Moses parting the Red Sea. She smiled at me, pushing her spectacles higher on her nose with one hand while the other held the ghosts in position. "Come this way, please."

I looked down at my circle of safety, then the aisle she'd created, and the condensed ghosts on either side.

"I'm good, thanks." I could wait out the dawn right here in my tiny lopsided circle.

"I told him you'd say that." Kate said cheerfully. "By the way, I do so appreciate that chunk of magic rock you sent; it's been wonderful being able to communicate directly." She turned her head to call over her shoulder, "She said no!"

There was a meaty smacking sound, and then a familiar voice cried out in pain. "Beau!" I yelled.

"Do not do anything he says!" Beau hollered, but then he screamed again, and the sounds of violence continued.

"That won't stop until you come talk to the vampire," Kate said, crooking her finger at me. The other hand was still controlling the ghosts. "Don't worry, I'll hold them back for you. Can't have you going insane, not yet."

Cautiously, I scuffed at the circle of blood and stepped onto the little aisle Kate had created. My ankle ached, but I thought it was sprained, rather than broken, and I was able to limp along slowly. Several ghosts nearby opened their mouths like they were moaning, but it was soundless.

I followed Kate into the basement hallway. I couldn't see what was beyond her; there were too many ghosts in the way. "How are you doing this?" I asked.

"While I was a guest here, I spent months and months scattering my blood around the soil, harnessing the spirits already on the property. And of course, creating more."

Kate had been here as a patient, not a nurse. I'd suspected as much. "You killed the other patients?"

"Some of them." She shrugged. "And nurses, realtors, the

unhoused...anyone I could, really. You see, Lex, the more I used my magic, the more powerful I got—and the less anyone seemed to listen to me." She pouted. "I could have helped *so* much more during the Great War, but apparently acts of mercy aren't considered *patriotic*."

"You used too much boundary magic," I said, dazed. When Sam had warned me about damaging my psyche, I'd thought I was only hurting myself. But if this was what happened...if *Kate* was what happened...my God.

"There's no such thing as too much," Kate sniffed. "I grew tired of being underused, undervalued in this world. So I decided to make my own world. No one *appreciates* necromancy, haven't you found that to be true?"

With the hand that wasn't holding back the ghosts, she gestured around the basement. I still couldn't see much of anything except walls of ghosts, and lots of brick. "It took years of planning and preparation, but I managed to create my own little paradise, where I can control things for eternity."

"Then what are they?" I nodded at the ghosts.

Kate frowned. "Even paradise requires a battery, Lex."

I shuddered with revulsion, but Kate gave me a wide, satisfied smile. "I must say, it is nice to finally have someone else here who can appreciate my masterpiece. In here."

We'd reached a doorway. Kate did something with her hands, controlling the ghosts, took a step to the side, and inclined her head, indicating that I should go in.

I looked through the doorway, expecting another chamber of horrors. Instead, though, I found myself in a kitchen. It was still brick, but the cupboards and counters were probably from the 1970's or so, likely the result of one of the many attempted renovations on this building. There was even a Formica table, where Malcolm sat with his hands folded. There was a sidearm on the table in front of him, pointed in my direction.

"You must be Lex Luther," he said, chuckling. "God, that name kills me. Come on in, say hi to your friend. Hands up, please."

I raised my hands and limped into the room. As I came around the doorframe, I found that my chamber of horrors idea hadn't been far off.

They'd tied Beau's hands together with thick chains and attached them to a hook that had been cemented into the brick. His legs were bound with more chains, which had been hooked to an old-fashioned anvil so he couldn't kick. He didn't look like a Southern dandy anymore. He was clearly human, his chest bare and covered in bruises and cuts. One of his eyes was swollen shut, and he was so emaciated and weak that he couldn't lift his head to look at me.

"Beau!" I started forward, but Malcolm put his hand on the gun and made a clucking noise. I froze, swallowing tears.

A man with ropey forearms stood next to him, clothes soaked with sweat, and his hands taped like a boxer's. He wouldn't meet my eyes. "You're the other null," I said. It wasn't a hard guess: there was a clear space around him, no ghosts.

Lifting my chin, I forced my eyes back to Malcolm. The more upset I appeared, the more leverage he would have. "What is the point of this?" I said coldly.

"We've been having a disagreement about loyalty," Malcolm said. "I want him to swear an oath, he's being a stubborn bastard, we're going around and around. You know how it goes."

"Oh, sure," I said sarcastically. "Normal negotiations stuff."

Anger flashed in his eyes. "I don't know what's wrong with you people," he snapped. "We had a perfectly good system, and you're determined to fuck everything up for some ridiculous notion of *justice*." He said "justice" like anyone else might say "genital herpes."

Until that moment I'd still been reeling from the fall and going through so many ghosts, but suddenly I felt perfectly clear. And furious. "A perfectly good system?" I repeated. "Is that what you call it? You squat in your city like a fat spider, spinning webs all over the country that get people in our world killed. That's not a system. That's an autocracy."

"I don't know what you mean," Malcolm said with great dignity. "Humans are one thing, but I've never killed anyone in our world."

"What about Hazel Pellar?"

He shrugged, as though he had no idea who that was.

"You should remember her," I said, with as much venom as I could muster. "Her son is outside right now, kicking your son's ass. While you hide in here like a little bitch."

He glowered. "I'm not hiding. I'm waiting for dawn, or for Maven and Dashiell to come down here and meet my new null."

That explained the gun, and the location. He was playing two possibilities: get Beau to swear an oath of loyalty and cement a conspiracy against Maven, or wait for Maven and Dashiell and the others to come down here and pick them off one by one with a null and a gun.

Either way, he'd wait out the dawn down here, and then he could waltz out with the null to protect him during the day. Given how he clearly felt about nulls, though, I didn't this guy had much of a life expectancy after that.

Maven had talked before about how Malcolm's greatest strength was his flexibility, his ability to think outside the box. I could see now what a threat he was.

"I gotta thank you, by the way," Malcolm went on, "for those rocks you were handing out. We got one away from the werewolf, made it a million times easier to talk to my new eyes and ears. Before I was having to use this guy to translate." He gestured at Beau. "You can imagine how reliable that was."

I suppressed another shudder. Beau could see ghosts too. And he'd been down here all night, in and out of humanity, in and out of the press of those ghosts.

"So why am I here?" I asked Malcolm.

"Oh, you're here to die. I just need you to do it next to Rhys here. I made a deal with Miss Kate."

"*After* you bleed her," Kate reminded him. "I want her blood. I have instructions for where it should go on the grounds."

"Miss Kate, huh?" I said to Malcolm. "How long have you two been working together?"

"Oh, it's a new relationship." Malcolm smiled. "Mutually beneficial. All I gotta do is kill a bunch of people on her land, and frankly, I was gonna do that anyway."

In the doorway, Kate preened. "You see, Lex? I'm the head witch in charge. I can't have you running around disturbing my afterlife."

"You and I had a deal," I pointed out. "We shook hands."

"Yes, and I felt your power." She shook her head. "And when you said you'd put your dead friends to rest, rather than using them?" She scoffed. "I honored my word as long as I could, but then I got a better offer. I'm on the side of death, Lex. Always. Go on, over by your friend."

"There's too many of them." I pressed myself against the brick wall next to the door, not moving, eyeing the ghosts. A number of them saw what I was doing and writhed, staring hungrily at the cuts on my arms.

Malcolm started to raise his gun, but Kate said sharply, "No, don't." To me, she added, "Come on, now. I can hold them back. Or I can lower my hands, and these spirits will overtake you again. And with all those cuts on you? They're going to suckle you like piglets."

I couldn't move yet, but just in time, there was a rattling noise somewhere else in the basement, like a bucket being knocked over.

"What was that?" Malcolm asked Kate. He stood up from the table, taking a step toward the doorway.

She tilted her head to the side. "That *man* is down here," she said angrily. "He broke one of my windows."

"Which man? Is he alone? Dammit, the whole point of this is to keep them from finding out I'm down here!"

I kept my hands out to the side, but now that Kate and Malcolm's attention was elsewhere, I slowly moved them up and down against the brick like I was making a snow angel.

"It's the Spanish man," Kate said impatiently. "The handsome one. He broke through a window and he's coming this way."

"Jesse, run!" I shouted, turning toward the doorway. While I did, I smeared blood up in a curve against the wall, where my head had been. It blended well with the red bricks.

Malcolm turned the gun back to me. "Don't say another fucking word," he hissed at me. "Miss Kate, where is he now?"

She listened for a moment, then smiled broadly. "Oh, it's quite all right. He's fallen in the cistern. I did wonder if that lid was rotted through." She squeezed her fist, shaking it a little with excitement. "There's no ladder; he's sure to drown in there. Oh, what a wonderful night indeed!"

"Glad you're happy," Malcolm said dryly.

Then Kate gave me a sharp look. "Why do I smell so much of your blood? I though those wounds were superficial."

"Feeling faint," I mumbled, and then pretended to sink down against the wall.

Kate saw what I'd been doing, and her glowing face filled with sudden alarm. "No, don't—"

I finished drawing the circle of blood on the wall and shouted, "*Door!*" Then I dove across the room toward Rhys and Beau, with Kate screaming curses at me.

Malcolm squeezed the trigger, shouting at me, but his first shot missed, and I made it behind Beau, with Rhys between us and the gun. I was inside Rhys's aura—but the gate to the other side I'd drawn on the wall was still open.

The air seemed to tremble for one moment, like something holding its breath. Then a thousand furious ghosts rushed the gate all at once.

I couldn't see them anymore, thankfully, but that much trapped energy being released created actual, physical gale-force winds, which erupted through the basement, opening and closing cupboard doors and rattling chairs. I ducked against Beau as my hair and clothes rippled and the air itself roared. It was like being underneath a train station while a locomotive went by.

At one point Malcolm, red-faced and unsettled, had to put his gun down so he could cover his ears. I was very grateful not to know what he was hearing. I did try to tug Beau free while Malcolm was distracted, but the heavy chain was padlocked, to subdue him as a human or a vampire. I had no chance of picking it. All I could do was whisper, "Hang on, Beau," and wait.

Finally, it all stopped. Everything in the kitchen went still, with chairs knocked over and cupboard doors hanging off their hinges. "Miss Kate?" Malcolm yelled, like someone trying to talk on the phone in a loud room. "Miss Kate?" He waited, listening. "Aw, fuck. She got caught in the stampede."

The vampire pulled the cassiterite out of his shirt and threw it across the room, then turned to glare at me. The null edged closer to the wall, trying to be invisible. “Now you’ve cost me my eyes and ears,” Malcolm said to me, seething.

“It had to be done. That was sick, what she was doing to them,” I said matter-of-factly. “No one deserves that afterlife. Not even you, and I think you’re a piece of shit.”

“Whatever.” Malcolm bared his teeth and raised the gun at me. “You gonna step out of there, or do I get to shoot your friend, too?”

With a last regretful look, I limped away from Beau, raising my bloodied hands. “Stop right there,” Malcolm said, when I was only a couple of feet from both Beau and the other null. “I know what you are. You still need to die close to Rhys.”

The little spark of hope I’d held onto was extinguished then. Boundary witches can survive just about anything, but Malcolm was making sure I wouldn’t have my magic when I died. Which meant I couldn’t talk to Sam. And I wouldn’t go where she was.

Tears fell down my cheeks, infuriating me. I hated that this clown was going to see me cry. But at least I’d freed those ghosts. That was a note to go out on. Malcolm got up from the table saying something smarmy, but I didn’t have to listen.

I closed my eyes, and he shot me four times.

The first bullet was probably aimed at my head, but like a lot of vampires, Malcolm was a terrible shot. It hit me in the neck, and then the next one in my thigh. One in the vest, and then the last one, the worst one, in my lower stomach, near where I’d shot Adelaide. Maybe it was fair.

The brick floor rushed up to meet me. There was so much blood. Had I fallen into a pool of it? It couldn’t possibly all be mine.

Then I was lying on my side beneath Beau, close enough to touch the anvil attached to his feet. And I couldn’t move. Malcolm was walking toward me, gun lifted at my head.

"Do you smell that?" the null said suddenly.

Malcolm stopped. "Rhys," he said in a warning tone.

"I'm serious. It smells like smoke." He took one step toward the door to the hall.

Malcolm jumped backwards, snapping, "Don't come any closer to me, you moron!" Then: "I smell it too."

"In my defense," called a familiar voice from the hall, "I did *not* know there was insulation under the hatch. Did you guys know some insulation is *flammable*? Boy, do I feel stupid. In retrospect, I really don't have the maturity to handle this tactical pen."

Malcolm looked like his head was about to explode. He motioned for Rhys to stay still and skulked toward the doorway. I couldn't be certain, but I thought he was human, which meant Scarlett was probably just outside the door.

"Scarlett, run!" I yelled, but of course, it came out as a mumble.

I wanted to tell her so many things. That she needed to go help Jesse. That I was sorry for misjudging her. That she reminded me of Sam, and that was about the highest compliment I had to offer. But I was too weak to make any of those words come out.

Something small skittered into the room, low and black and flashing lights. Malcolm jumped toward it, firing the gun wildly, until it clicked empty.

Scarlett Bernard burst into the room into the room with her own gun raised. "Tactical pen!" she cried, and shot Malcolm in the head.

I passed out.

# 44

## LEX

Rochester, MN

B*eep. Beep. Beep.*

The sound of the heart monitor annoyed me at first, but then I found it sort of comforting. And then annoying again. Every time I surfaced, always with my eyes still closed, I went back and forth on it.

Then, one of the times I registered the beeping, I felt strong enough to crack my eyelids.

"Oooh, hello, sleepyhead!" sang a way-too-cheerful voice. "Oh my god, I can't believe I was the one here when you woke up. Simon's gonna be *so* jealous. Everyone who's in town has been taking turns coming to visit you, 'cause you had to have like three surgeries and it was a whole thing."

Begrudgingly, I dragged my eyelids the rest of the way up and saw Scarlett Bernard sitting next to my hospital bed, waving a spoon at me. She had new bandages on both her hands—but the bruising around her eyes was nearly gone, and overall she looked better than she had since this all began. She was also eating my Jell-O.

"What day is it?"

"Monday."

"Where are we?"

Her eyes sparked with excitement. "Oh, get this: we're at the Mayo Clinic. You got airlifted here from the teeny clinic in Galena. And guess who pulled the strings to get you here?"

My eyelids were already starting to droop again. Scarlett was a little exhausting. "Who?"

"Sashi's mom!"

That woke me right up. "Really? They haven't spoken in years."

"I know, right? But I met her years ago—did I not tell you that? Anyway, I made the first phone call, and Dr. Noring was ecstatic to treat 'a member of Sashi's witch clan'"—Scarlett did air quotes around this—"And then Sashi called her to thank her, and now Grace and Sashi and Will are all flying out in a couple of days for a reunion. The tactical pen also puts families back together." She dug a new bite of Jell-O out of the container. "It's one of its many tactics."

"God, you're weird."

"Says the lady who took three bullets and died twice on the operating table because her blood's full of death, or whatever."

There wasn't a lot I could move easily, but I did lift one finger to point at the bandages on her hands. "Did you climb through a burning hatch to save me?"

She looked at the bandages. "Nah. I just really hated that hatch."

For just a moment, we smiled at each other. Then Scarlett popped the bite of Jell-O in her mouth. "I gotta tell you, dude, you missed the world's most anticlimactic trial."

"Yeah?"

"Uh-huh. They did it right away on the fucking lawn at the haunted insane asylum, *classy* touch, right, and the whole thing probably took fifteen minutes, because we pretty much all just wanted to go home by then. Even Orvil was like, 'yeah, I'm guilty, kill me so this fucking night can end.'" Her face darkened. "They put Rhys on trial, too."

"Really? What did he get?"

"Fifteen years of service to Maven. So that's a fun thing you get to deal with later."

"Great. Is Jesse okay?"

She bobbed her head. "He was super embarrassed about falling in the cistern, but he's fine. He went back to Cali to liberate the safe house. Hmm, what else? Simon is fine, Eli is fine—although he got stuffed in the well by one of Malcolm's vampires, which I found a *little bit* funny." She held her fingers half an inch apart.

"Beau?"

"Ah, yes." She leaned forward to pull something out of the back pocket of her jeans. With a flourish, she brought out a small, sealed envelope. "He sent this for you. Want me to read it to you?"

I would have preferred to read it in private, but I could barely keep my eyes open, let alone hold something up. "Sadly, yes."

A little gleefully, Scarlett ripped open the envelope and pulled out a simple black-and-white card with Beau's initials on it. She made a show of clearing her throat, and put on a terrible Southern accent. "Ah-hem. Dear Lex, I must return to Atlanta to lay Maya to rest. Thank you for giving me a cause worthy of a fight, and a fight worthy of the cause. My debt is repaid when I say it is. Warmest regards, Beau." Scarlett looked up. "What does all that mean?" she asked in her normal voice.

"It's…soldier stuff," I told her. I felt my eyes closing again. "I think I'm gonna sleep now."

"Cool. Can I have your sandwich?"

But I was already asleep.

THE NEXT TIME I woke up, Quinn was in the room.

I watched him without saying anything for a few minutes. He was frowning at a laptop screen, looking for all the world like James Bond having to fill out expense forms. I thought of all the times he'd bailed me out, the times I'd bailed him out. Our first kiss. The first time he'd come to play board games with my family. It all felt like so long ago.

"Quinn."

He looked up, snapping the laptop closed and setting it aside to take my hand. "How do you feel?"

"Fuzzy. Is Maven okay?"

He nodded. "After your surgeries, when we were sure you would live, she had to go back to Colorado. She and Dashiell have a lot to do to promote the new parliament."

I nodded. That was all pretty much what I expected. "She wants to thank you for stopping Malcolm," Quinn continued. "That night, we were all so caught up in the fight in front of us. We all thought he'd left."

"It was mostly Scarlett."

Quinn smiled. "That's funny; she said it was mostly you."

I looked at him, feeling like I was seeing a stranger. Why hadn't we had this conversation before Galena? Why had it seemed so important not to push him on it? "Are you going to ask her to turn you human?"

He seemed to go from still to somehow even stiller. "Not anytime soon," he said carefully. "She's still healing."

"But that's what you want, isn't it? You want to go be Holly's dad."

Quinn's eyes dropped to his lap. "If I go soon, I might still be able to get away with the age difference."

"I get it," I said, sighing. "If I wasn't allowed to live in the same state as Charlie, I'd go mad."

He looked at me then, his eyes as soft as they ever got. "I do love you," he said, "as much as vampires are capable of it, anyway. But the same..." he opened and closed his fist near his stomach, looking for words.

"I know," I told him. "The same quality that lets you love me also makes you want to be with your daughter. You're a good man, Quinn. That's the quality." It was a lot of words, considering how crappy I felt, but they needed to be said.

His lips quirked up. "Thank you for that," he said quietly. "Listen...if Maven and Scarlett agree, and I turn human and move to Georgia...well. I know in another dozen years you'll need to leave Colorado." Quinn gave me an expectant look.

I felt ancient all of a sudden, and so tired. "No. It wouldn't feel right. It *hasn't* felt right, not for a little while now."

"We've hardly seen each other," he reminded me.

"Yeah, but that's been...okay. Hasn't it?"

"I suppose it has," he said. "I understand." He traced my hand with one finger. "We'll still see each other at work, you know. For a while."

"I know. We'll figure out how to make that okay, too." I turned my hand over to grab his, as fiercely as I could. "I hope they let you do it. I hope you get to go be with Holly."

Quinn smiled at me then, a wide, sad smile that seemed to project love in my direction. "I hope good things for you too, Lex. Even if it'll be awkward at first."

"What?" Then I got what he meant and felt my cheeks turning pink. "That's not— we haven't—"

“I know.” He bent to kiss my cheek. “I’m going to go back to Colorado tonight, get my things out of the house. Goodbye, Lex.”

“Goodbye.”

I HAD a lot of doctor visits that day, discussing the various bullet wounds and what they’d done to my body. There wouldn’t be long term damage from the shots to my neck and thigh, but the abdomen was another matter.

The visitor I’d been waiting for arrived the next morning. Simon came in carrying an absurdly large vase of purple—you guessed it—lilies. “You’re here,” I said stupidly. I looked him over carefully. He had some bruises and still looked exhausted, but he smiled at me like I’d just told the funniest joke of my life.

“I am. I was here before, but I’m glad you’re awake now.” He thrust the flowers at me. “These are from Lily and me. She wanted to come, but she’s putting out some fires with the clan this week. She said she’ll fly out tomorrow unless you’re ready to be released.”

“Can you put those on the table?”

“Oh, right, duh.” Simon set the vase on my bedside table and pulled the chair up to the bed. Then, for an eternal few minutes, we just looked at each other awkwardly.

“Are you okay?” I finally asked him.

“Me?” He looked surprised. “I’m fine.”

“You got shot,” I reminded him.

Simon grinned at me. “Just a flesh wound. Honestly. Dr. Noring said if you’re going to get shot I picked an excellent location.”

“That sounds like her.” I’d had several days now to get used to Sashi’s mother and her brusque bedside manner.

There was another awkward silence. "Quinn said he's moving his stuff out of your house," Simon said carefully.

I rubbed my face. "Yeah. About that." I took a breath. "Simon, I've thought about it a lot. You can't be in love with me."

He raised his eyebrows. "Oh?"

"I think it's because of that time when I put Billy Atwood's life force into you to save you. It made some kind of magic connection or something. It's not real."

"Oh, I see. My feelings aren't real. Thank you, Lex, that really explains everything. Goodbye then." He rested his chin in his hand, smiling at me.

"You know what I mean. I shouldn't have kissed you at the Marine Hospital. I'm really sorry about that."

Simon shook his head. "Don't tell me what I feel, Lex. I know you don't feel the same way, and that's fine. But don't tell me it's not real."

"It's not."

"Lex." He took a breath. "I'm in love with you."

"*Why*?" I demanded, my voice raised. I was hurting and frustrated, and this conversation wasn't at all going the way I'd planned. "Why would you love me? *I broke you!*"

Simon looked shocked. "What are you talking about?"

"Before you met me, you were with Tracy, and you had this full life with your work and the witch clan. You had a happy, peaceful future. And then you started helping me, and you *died*. You died because of me, Simon, and after I brought you back you were never the same." I finally got control of my volume, lowering my voice. "I ruined your whole life, Si. You should hate me."

He just regarded me in silence for a few minutes. It was excruciating. "Alexandra Allison Luther," he said formally. "Before I met you, I was sleepwalking through a life that other people had planned out for me—my mother, Tracy, even Lily. You didn't bring me back; you *woke me up*. And sometimes that's hard, and sometimes it's thrilling and dangerous. But I will love you every day of the rest of my life, because you made it possible for me to really live it."

"I can't have kids," I blurted.

He blinked. "What?"

"The fourth bullet, the last one. It went into my uterus. They couldn't save it." Looking stricken, Simon reached for my hand, but I pulled it away. "It's fine, really, I didn't want to have kids anyway."

*Oh, babe. Don't do this.*

I took a shuddering breath, ignoring Sam, as well as the tears falling from my eyes. "It's okay," I said to Simon. "I've got Charlie, and the world doesn't need any more boundary witches running around. But *you* want kids, and you'll be a great dad someday, and I want...I want Lily, I think." My voice had gotten very small. "Could you get Lily to come?"

He opened his mouth, closed it, nodded. "Thank you," I said weakly. "I'd like you to go now."

"Lex—"

"*Please* go." It came out as a sob, and I realized I was begging.

"We'll talk another time," Simon said softly.

He got up and left, and despite what Sam said in my head, I knew that was best. I squeezed my eyes shut. I would be alone now, and that was okay. I had my busy, messy, wonderful family, and Charlie, and my rescue animals. I had a challenging, risky job that I loved. I was lucky. Besides, I'd never wanted kids, and now I wouldn't have to worry about it.

I was going to be fine.

# EPILOGUE

SCARLETT

Los Angeles, CA
Six Months Later

The flower girl missed her nap.

Jesse and I had suspected this could happen, of course, with all the commotion and excitement, but we still tried to convince Annie to take even a short afternoon nap. It was a wasted exercise. By late afternoon, our daughter had gone from tired to manic to just generally inconsolable.

Which is how she ended up weeping theatrically into my fancy silk bridal robe because her flowers were white instead of her current favorite color: black.

"Here, let me take her," said Corry, holding her arms out for the baby. Well, at almost fifteen months, not so much a baby anymore. But it was hard for me to think of her as anything else. "We'll go stand in the ocean and count seagulls."

"Thank you." I handed Annie off to my maid-of-honor and looked at the lapels of the pretty silk robe with some regret.

Molly had insisted on buying it for me as a bridal gift, even though she should have known better. I looked down at Shadow, who was panting happily up at me. "Between you and Annie," I told her, "there's a reason why I don't do nice things."

Shadow licked her chops. I reached down and scratched at the downy fur on one side of her head, until her clubbed tail wagged with happiness. But I caught her eyeing the door. "You want to go stand in the ocean with them and look for sharks, don't you?"

The bargest went on alert, sitting up straight with her ears perked up as she looked at me hopefully. I laughed. This was a good sign. When I'd first come home from Galena, she'd refused to be more than two feet away from me...which got really awkward in the bathroom. I waved her away. "Go on. If you see Jaws, fuck him up for me."

She raced off, her claws struggling to get traction on the fancy stone floor, and I was smiling as I turned back to the mirror to check my hair and makeup.

The Winding Way beach house we were using for the wedding belonged to one of the richest vampires in LA, who was currently on a five-year trip to Europe to restart his identity. Dashiell had secured use of the house and the beach for the day, though he hadn't said how. Jesse and I had decided we didn't really want to know.

After I had arrived and was getting ready in the master suite, Simon and Kirsten had put together a massive ward around the entire property, complete with an illusion effect. Anyone who saw it would think the whole area was closed off for a film shoot. "I'm so jealous of that excuse," Simon told me later. "My life would be so much easier if I could just yell 'film shoot' every time we have to hide something suspicious."

He and Jesse had become tight since we'd returned from Illinois, talking on FaceTime a couple of times a week. He'd even come out for a few days in December for Jesse's bachelor party, and I'd encouraged Jesse to make him a groomsman. It was nice seeing my husband-to-be make a new friend.

"Scarlett?" Lex poked her head in the door. All the bridesmaids were in shades of green, but I particularly liked Lex's dress choice, which had a halter top and a kicky skirt that meant she could move around freely. It was a surprisingly feminine, vintage look, but somehow also very Lex. "The vampires just arrived. We're ready."

I smiled at her ruefully. "Who ever heard of a beachfront wedding at night?"

"Oh, I think you'll like what we've done." She grinned back at me.

Molly was waiting for me at the door to go outside. Her green dress was Alexander McQueen, and if she hadn't picked out my wedding dress, I might have worried that I was being upstaged.

"Omigod," she said when she saw me. She fanned herself with her hand, tears in her eyes. "Oh my God, you look–"

"Molly," I warned. "We talked about this."

She nodded vigorously. "Yes, yes, I promised. Okay." She took a breath. "You ready?"

"Walk me to my brother, please." I held out my arm, and she linked hers inside.

When we walked out, I took a second to take in the scene before anyone noticed *the bride* had arrived. The bridal party had teamed up to string lanterns along the beach. Lex had been right: it was amazing. The aisle was made up of parallel lines of seashells, along with more strung lanterns, and chairs set out on either side for people to sit. There were fire pits set out, too, where the guests could warm up or make s'mores if they got peckish before the pizzas and cake later. January in LA wasn't exactly frigid, but it was cool enough that the warmth from the fire felt great.

And there at the front: Jesse.

He always looked handsome, but the tuxedo...if I'm being honest, it kind of took my breath away. He'd been looking for me, and when he saw Molly and I step out he winked and smiled at me, and I think my heart actually skipped a couple of beats. How gross.

The guests were already seated, and I took a moment to appreciate the mixed group. Jesse's studio friends were here, looking obnoxiously trendy, and some of his cop friends as well. Half the Colorado Old World had come. No one had noticed Molly and me yet, mostly because they were all playing with the favors that had been set out on each chair: individual tactical pens, engraved with the date. "Tactical pen," I whispered to myself.

Molly brought me over to Jack and Shadow, who were walking me down the aisle together. She kissed my cheek and signaled to the DJ at her booth by the house. Then Molly went to join the group of bridesmaids and groomsmen waiting by the back of the aisle.

The music cued up, and everyone stood up and turned to look at me, my least favorite part. There were some oohs and ahhs, but I mostly appreciated the cheers and clapping from my niece and nephews in the front row of chair. Jack and Juliet both tried to shush them from the back of the aisle, but it didn't have much effect. I grinned and waved at the kids, because I gave no fucks about good behavior at my wedding. I certainly didn't intend to have any.

I can't say the next part went off without a hitch, no pun intended. No wedding goes perfectly. In my case, there was a delay while the exhausted flower girl cried because Shadow hadn't gotten to eat a shark like she wanted. In the end, Corry had to walk a sniffling Annie down the aisle with Annie's little fists wrapped around her index fingers, like a tiny, fussy marionette.

That made the groomsmen/bridesmaid pairings uneven, but I was still able to line up Lex and Simon together.

They were the last pairing, right before me, so I was able to watch their body language the whole way down the aisle. It started stiff and formal, but then Lex nearly slipped in the sand, and Simon reached out and caught her hand. They went hand-in-hand the rest of the way, and when they reached the front, Simon held on for a few extra seconds, until Lex turned to look at him. A current passed between them, and Lex looked at him with something like wonder before they let go. Jesse met my eyes, and we grinned at each other.

Then it was my turn. I walked down the aisle with Jack on one side and Shadow on the other. Way too many people took pictures of me for my liking, but at least I got to be barefoot. Four-inch wedding stilettos were for suckers.

Jack and I reached the front of the aisle, where a grave Dashiell stood holding a copy of the Bible, waiting to perform the ceremony. I'd mostly asked him to officiate for the comedy value, but he was taking the job *very* seriously.

First, though, Jack turned to me and gave me a light hug. "I wish Dad were here to do this," he whispered, tears in his eyes. "Mom too. Sorry, that was probably the wrong thing to say. You look beautiful."

He turned to go join the groomsmen, but I squeezed his hand. "*You're* here, Jack," I said quietly. "That's everything."

My gangly, awkward brother bent to kiss my cheek. "Love you, Scarbo," he whispered, and went to take his spot with the groomsmen.

Most of the ceremony was a blur, like moving through a dream I'd gotten to design with Jesse. But then it was time for me to read my vows, and suddenly everything went into very sharp focus. I'd tried to write it down so many times over the last few months, but in the end I just looked into Jesse's eyes and told the truth. It's a stupid cliche, but all of a sudden we really did feel like the only people there.

"The thing to know is, I never saw you coming," I began. "I wasn't looking for you, and maybe that's why when I found you, it terrified me. We terrified each other."

He smiled at me, because this was true. "We spent so much time trying to avoid falling in love with each other, and I often thought we were too different. That we'd never be able to bend." I smiled. "But some things are just made to go together, I guess. And I don't regret a second of any moment I have spent with you, because it got us to here. Not just this moment, but this day, and this week, and every second of this weird life we made together. I wouldn't want any other."

I took a breath, wrapping one hand in Shadow's fur. "Right. Vow stuff. I promise to let you win an argument every now and then, so your self-esteem doesn't suffer too much. I promise to fight your battles and let you help me fight mine, and I promise to see you, really *see* you, every day of my life, for as long as you'll have me." I was crying. He was crying. It was all just a lot of crying. So gross.

"I love you," I told Jesse. And at that moment, the flower girls squirmed her way out of Corry's arms, ran over on wobbly toddler legs, and threw herself at our legs. "We love you," I amended.

"Oh my God, this is so awkward," Jesse said gravely. "I was about to say the exact same thing."

I laughed. I picked up our daughter and held her in my arms for the rest of the ceremony, even though she wrinkled my dress and fell asleep with her fingers tangled in my nice hair.

Actually, now that I think about it, the whole thing was perfect after all.

The End
(for now)

## ACKNOWLEDGMENTS

Thank you so much for reading *Old World War.* This was the hardest book in the series for me to write, and it would never have reached its final form without a lot of help.

My endless gratitude goes out to my supporters on Patreon, who helped keep the lights on and the dogs fed these last two years, including while I was writing this book. Thank you so much to Brouge Ramos, my editor, who was patient with my endless delays, freakouts, and geekouts. Thank you to Arwen Duckwitz for all your enthusiasm and help with research, and Clarissa Yeo, who put together a cover that honored all the ones that came before. Elizabeth Kraft took the beautiful photo of Lex for the cover, and Gene Mollica was kind enough to grant me access to a Scarlett photo to complete the series.

My daughters, Molly and Mattie, put up with endless history lessons about Galena at the dinner table, and I'm grateful to them for humoring me...and for being mine.

A very special, very heartfelt thank you to Brian Duckwitz, my very patient Galena tour buddy. I started writing this book as we started dating, and I'm finishing it as we're moving in together. As it says in the dedication, you made this possible in every way.

With this particular book, I also need to say a few words about Galena, which is a real place that I fell in love with while writing. Here's what happened:

I had been wanting to write a Scarlett/Lex crossover novel for years, something to wrap up the ongoing story of Malcolm and Maven's parliament, but I was thwarted by two huge factors: first, how to write a New York story, when so many great New York stories already exist (and, thanks to the pandemic, I couldn't travel there to do research). The second factor was life events: the pandemic, a divorce, financial problems, moving to a new town, and so on. It seemed like this book might never happen.

Then, in June of 2021, Brian and I took a weekend trip to Galena, which included a tour of the Belvedere Mansion. The tour guide told us that the Belvedere, like many buildings in Galena, has walls made out of two layers of brick. Being me, the first thought that popped into my head was, "What a great place for a vampire fight."

And an obsession was born.

Over the last year I've lost count of how many research trips I made to Galena. I fell in love with the history, the architecture, the stories, and especially, the Marine Hospital.

I think of this book as my love letter to the city (despite how badly I treat it with the flooding and chaos and whatnot), and I encourage you to visit if you can. Most of the locations in this book are real, although all the Galena residents you meet in *Old World War* are my creations, and not based on real folks. There are several great museums and foundations where you can learn more about this remarkable town. Please bear in mind that any deviations or mistakes in *Old World War* are mine alone.

Simon's much-referenced reference book about Galena is real: it's called *Galena Illinois, A Timeless Treasure* by Philip A. Aleo, and it's great. The in-depth report about the Marine Hospital is also real, and can be found at https://www.galenafoundation.org/marinehospital. The Marine Hospital has recently been purchased by a developer, and there's a lot of controversy flying around right now about the future of this remarkable building. My fondest wish would be for someone to offer tours of the building exactly as it is, but there are a lot of reasons why that's unlikely to happen. If you're curious to see the inside as it is now, though, I recommend the *Ghost Hunters* season 13, episode 6 episode, called "Haunted Hospital."

Finally I want to apologize to the DeSoto House for calling its decor ugly. While I admit that it is not to my personal taste, I respect the commitment to historical accuracy. You do you, DeSoto House.

# ABOUT THE AUTHOR

Melissa F. Olson is the author of sixteen books in the Old World universe, the PI mystery *The Big Keep*, and numerous short stories and novellas, including the *Nightshades* trilogy for Tor.com. Her journalism and academic work has been published in The International Journal of Comic Art, the compilation Images of the Modern Vampire, Litreactor.com, and Tor.com, among other places.

Melissa has been a writing teacher, English professor, and TEDx presenter, but she now divides her time between writing, editing and attending the occasional convention, where she speaks about issues related to genre, feminism, disability, and parenting. Read more about her work and life at Melissa-FOlson.com.

Manufactured by Amazon.ca
Bolton, ON